Charles Gibson

Two Gentlemen in Touraine

Charles Gibson

Two Gentlemen in Touraine

ISBN/EAN: 9783337190989

Printed in Europe, USA, Canada, Australia, Japan

Cover: Foto ©Andreas Hilbeck / pixelio.de

More available books at **www.hansebooks.com**

TWO GENTLEMEN IN TOURAINE

BY

RICHARD SUDBURY

HERBERT S. STONE AND COMPANY
CHICAGO AND NEW YORK
MDCCCXCIX

CONTENTS

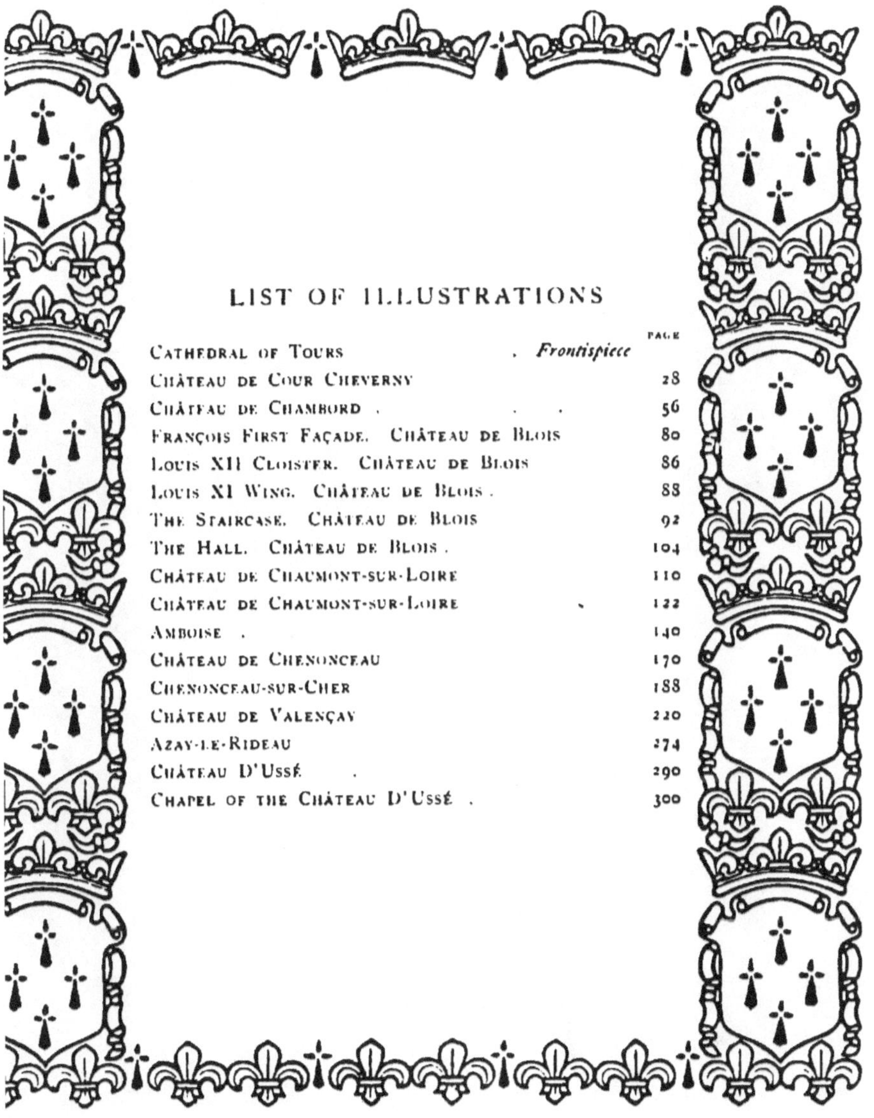

LIST OF ILLUSTRATIONS

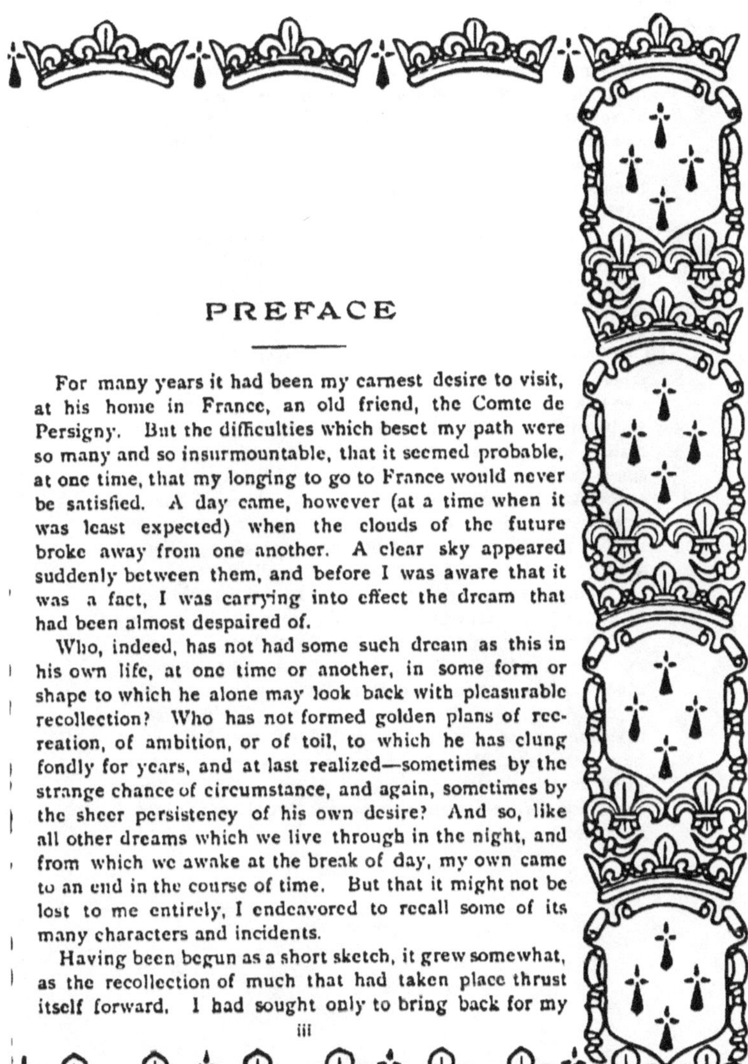

PREFACE

For many years it had been my earnest desire to visit, at his home in France, an old friend, the Comte de Persigny. But the difficulties which beset my path were so many and so insurmountable, that it seemed probable, at one time, that my longing to go to France would never be satisfied. A day came, however (at a time when it was least expected) when the clouds of the future broke away from one another. A clear sky appeared suddenly between them, and before I was aware that it was a fact, I was carrying into effect the dream that had been almost despaired of.

Who, indeed, has not had some such dream as this in his own life, at one time or another, in some form or shape to which he alone may look back with pleasurable recollection? Who has not formed golden plans of recreation, of ambition, or of toil, to which he has clung fondly for years, and at last realized—sometimes by the strange chance of circumstance, and again, sometimes by the sheer persistency of his own desire? And so, like all other dreams which we live through in the night, and from which we awake at the break of day, my own came to an end in the course of time. But that it might not be lost to me entirely, I endeavored to recall some of its many characters and incidents.

Having been begun as a short sketch, it grew somewhat, as the recollection of much that had taken place thrust itself forward. I had sought only to bring back for my

PREFACE

own gratification an itinerary which had afforded me
many happy hours and much recreation. But so full
of romance are the Historical Monuments of Touraine
and so ideal is the beauty of their surroundings, that
imagination has often overstepped fact and reality. And
I must crave forgiveness, if the mists that overhang the
banks of the river Loire have, at times, found their way
between the leaves of this volume. For though it lays
claim to a certain correctness of description, in regard to
things which actually exist in France to-day, it must also
acknowledge a degree of fancy and some fictitious characters.

Where two minds of different nationality meet, in
friendly intercourse, there is better opportunity to hear
two sides to any argument which may occur. Where two
such minds wander through the rendezvous of art and
history and power, swayed by the inclination to gather
some knowledge from the whole mass, there is time for
speculative thought. One of them may be engrossed in
new sights and scenes and in obtaining his own impression of the whole, while the other may obtain as different
a view from his very familiarity with it all.

Having been induced to publish the papers, resulting
from these wanderings through Touraine, I am, in offering them to the public, inclined to shrink from a possible
misunderstanding. For in many cases, the words of
others have been put down as the representative opinions
of certain classes of people in France, merely to show
that they exist, and not as individual convictions. I
beg, therefore, that this may be generously borne in
mind by those who may chance to accompany us upon
these idle peregrinations through the "garden of France."

Boston, 1899.

Two Gentlemen in Touraine

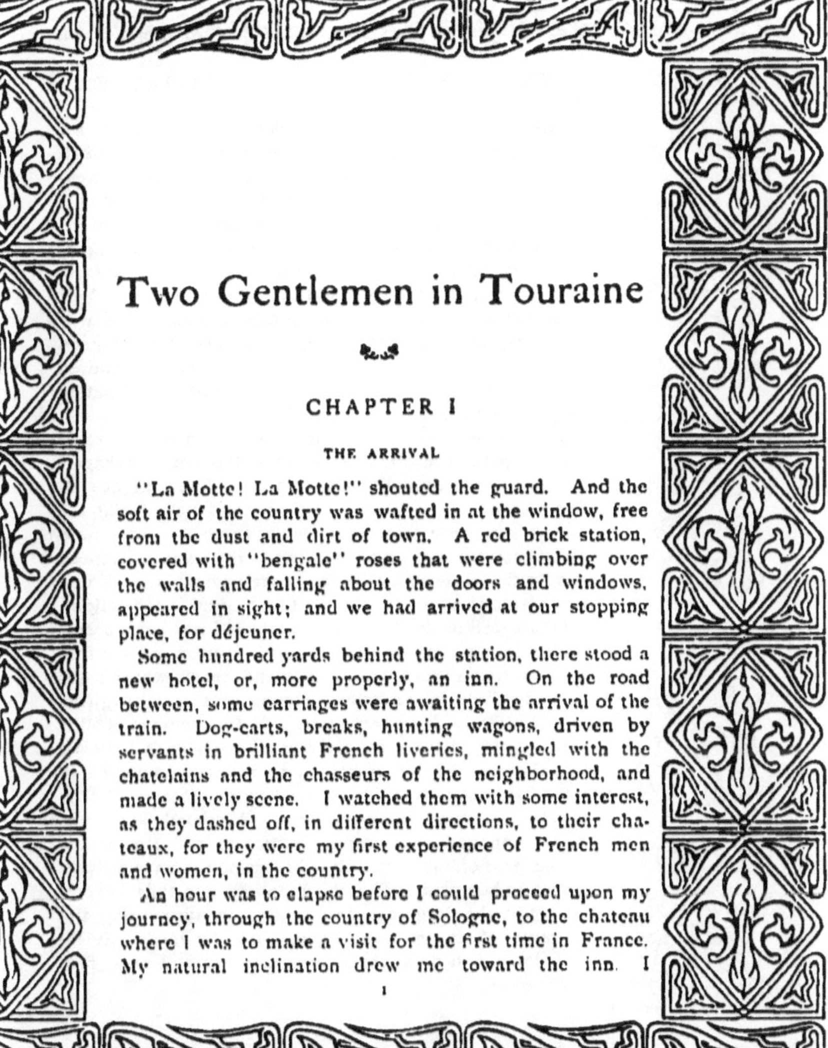

CHAPTER I

THE ARRIVAL

"La Motte! La Motte!" shouted the guard. And the soft air of the country was wafted in at the window, free from the dust and dirt of town. A red brick station, covered with "bengale" roses that were climbing over the walls and falling about the doors and windows, appeared in sight; and we had arrived at our stopping place, for déjeuner.

Some hundred yards behind the station, there stood a new hotel, or, more properly, an inn. On the road between, some carriages were awaiting the arrival of the train. Dog-carts, breaks, hunting wagons, driven by servants in brilliant French liveries, mingled with the chatelains and the chasseurs of the neighborhood, and made a lively scene. I watched them with some interest, as they dashed off, in different directions, to their chateaux, for they were my first experience of French men and women, in the country.

An hour was to elapse before I could proceed upon my journey, through the country of Sologne, to the chateau where I was to make a visit for the first time in France. My natural inclination drew me toward the inn. I

1

entered it, and was about to order my déjeuner when I found that my host had already prepared for my arrival, and that I was to be served with more than usual attention. I learnt afterwards, that this was an honor which I had but scarcely appreciated, at the time, for this inn is well known to have the most superior cuisine of Sologne. It is presided over by three maiden sisters, who are facetiously known by their clientele as "the three graces." If their name contains a little French sarcasm in its wit, they are, at all events, living exponents of their good cooking, for they are each possessed of several hundred pounds, which the visitor is told, shows little inclination to depart from them.

My eye wandered down the long table of the table d'hôte, and out into the neat-looking kitchen. Perhaps I had some vain thought that some one I knew might suddenly appear from among the pots and pans. But the guests who were coming in, two or three at a time, were all unknown to me, and I was left to my own meditations and to the observation of the scene around me. There was an air of negligence about this country inn, a delightful disregard of the formality to which I had been accustomed in more public restaurants. It gave out the first spirit of that French spontaneity and charm which I was later to find so prevalent among this socially gifted people. One of "the three graces"—the smallest of all, I subsequently discovered, although I confidently believed that she must be the largest, as my eye rested upon her— was sitting at a small table, peeling potatoes and other vegetables, all at the same time. A second Grace was busily engaged in swinging lettuce to and fro, at the farther end of the room, and she seemed to have a lively action to her arm. The third, and by this time beyond all doubt the largest, was occupied in tormenting the contents of an unhappy frying pan, by tossing it up and down, and up again, over a very hot and noisy fire.

Dieu! what a flavor there was escaping everywhere; what a crackling of wooden branches, and what a hopping and popping of the contents of the pan! It seemed to me that I had never experienced so delicate an odor as that which was given out from the culinary mysteries of "the three graces."

I might well have remained all day, in contemplation of the scene, and in speculating over the possibility of such an ensemble existing in any other than a Latin country. But I was brought to myself, before many moments, by one of the Graces, who reminded me that the "tramway" would leave before I was aware of it, and that I had yet to do justice to her arts in the creation of a particularly tasteful déjeuner. The pleasures of feasting were soon engrossing my thoughts. The poulet and the salade were already old friends; and the fromage-à-la-crème had made my acquaintance, before I had time to make even a formal bow to so accomplished a production. The verre de vin rouge was being drunk to the health of the Graces. The courtesies of the compensation were interchanged. A whistle sounded from the further side of the station; and it was time to be off. I waved a grateful farewell to my three hostesses, and crossed the narrow track. Awaiting me was a miniature train, known in France as "le tramway," with a private wagon attached to it, and a porter in attendance. I stepped inside, amid the bustle of the guards and laborers, and we started almost immediately, toward our destination.

I felt not unlike some "fairie prince," as we proceeded through woods and forests, bearing an enchanted air which seemed to grow in its enchantment every minute. The whole atmosphere breathed a suggestion of dreams and fancies; and it was not difficult for one's thoughts to roam off into one's surroundings. As we travelled leisurely along, through the lines of imaginative foliage, I began to feel that my travels of many thousand miles were almost

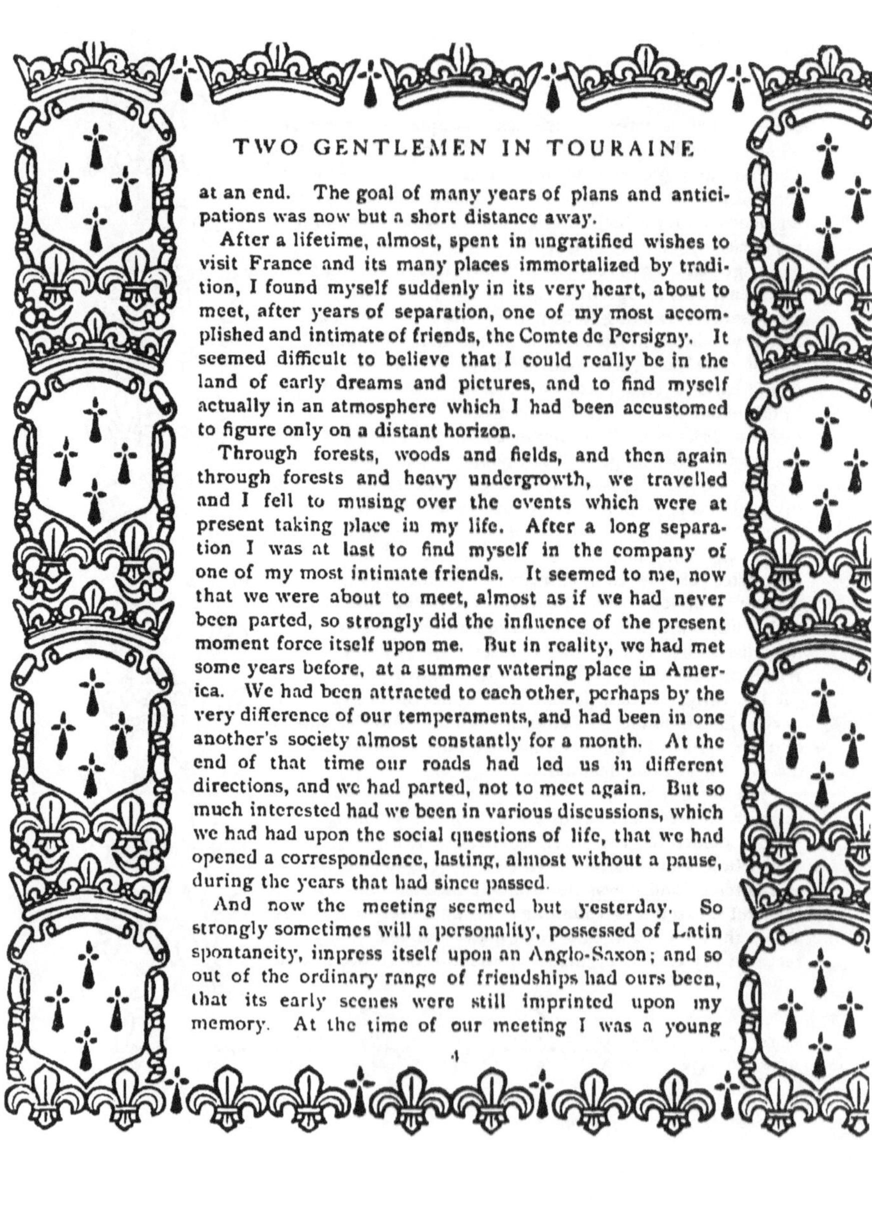

at an end. The goal of many years of plans and antici-
pations was now but a short distance away.

After a lifetime, almost, spent in ungratified wishes to
visit France and its many places immortalized by tradi-
tion, I found myself suddenly in its very heart, about to
meet, after years of separation, one of my most accomplished and intimate of friends, the Comte de Persigny. It
seemed difficult to believe that I could really be in the
land of early dreams and pictures, and to find myself
actually in an atmosphere which I had been accustomed
to figure only on a distant horizon.

Through forests, woods and fields, and then again
through forests and heavy undergrowth, we travelled
and I fell to musing over the events which were at
present taking place in my life. After a long separation I was at last to find myself in the company of
one of my most intimate friends. It seemed to me, now
that we were about to meet, almost as if we had never
been parted, so strongly did the influence of the present
moment force itself upon me. But in reality, we had met
some years before, at a summer watering place in America. We had been attracted to each other, perhaps by the
very difference of our temperaments, and had been in one
another's society almost constantly for a month. At the
end of that time our roads had led us in different
directions, and we had parted, not to meet again. But so
much interested had we been in various discussions, which
we had had upon the social questions of life, that we had
opened a correspondence, lasting, almost without a pause,
during the years that had since passed.

And now the meeting seemed but yesterday. So
strongly sometimes will a personality, possessed of Latin
spontaneity, impress itself upon an Anglo-Saxon; and so
out of the ordinary range of friendships had ours been,
that its early scenes were still imprinted upon my
memory. At the time of our meeting I was a young

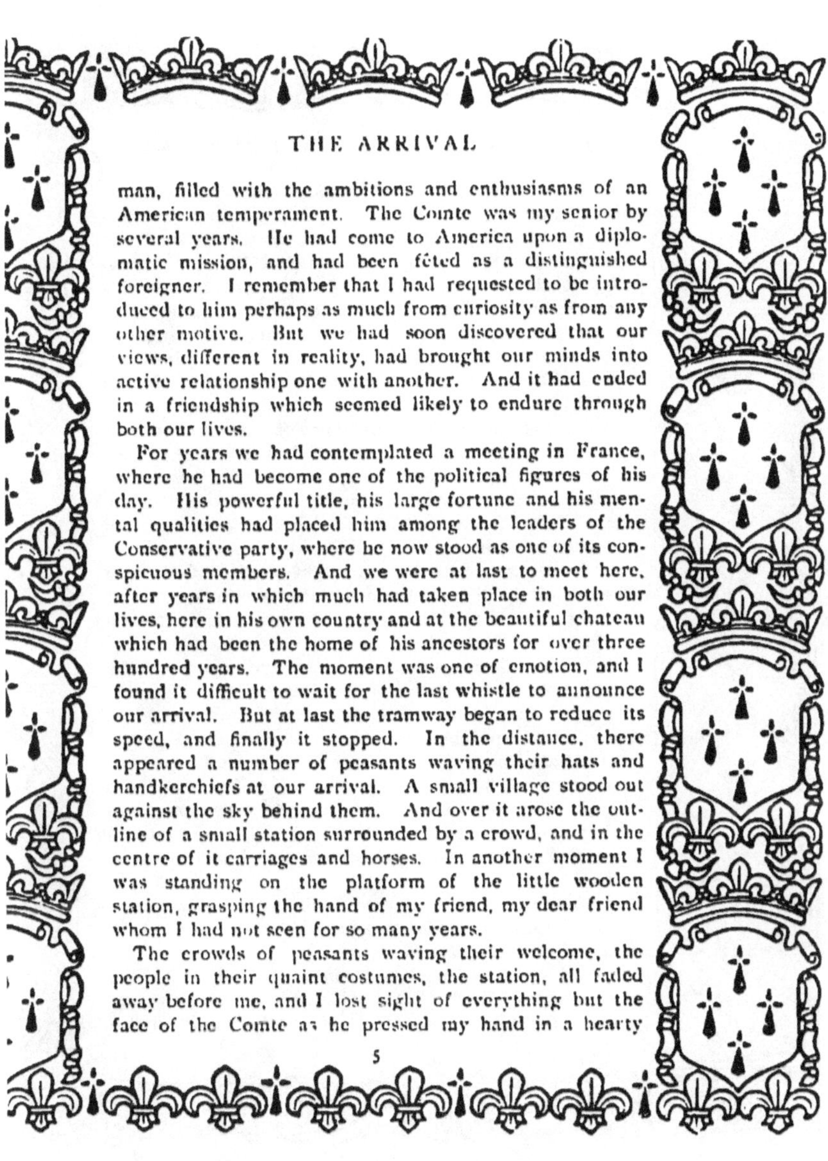

man, filled with the ambitions and enthusiasms of an American temperament. The Comte was my senior by several years. He had come to America upon a diplomatic mission, and had been fêted as a distinguished foreigner. I remember that I had requested to be introduced to him perhaps as much from curiosity as from any other motive. But we had soon discovered that our views, different in reality, had brought our minds into active relationship one with another. And it had ended in a friendship which seemed likely to endure through both our lives.

For years we had contemplated a meeting in France, where he had become one of the political figures of his day. His powerful title, his large fortune and his mental qualities had placed him among the leaders of the Conservative party, where he now stood as one of its conspicuous members. And we were at last to meet here, after years in which much had taken place in both our lives, here in his own country and at the beautiful chateau which had been the home of his ancestors for over three hundred years. The moment was one of emotion, and I found it difficult to wait for the last whistle to announce our arrival. But at last the tramway began to reduce its speed, and finally it stopped. In the distance, there appeared a number of peasants waving their hats and handkerchiefs at our arrival. A small village stood out against the sky behind them. And over it arose the outline of a small station surrounded by a crowd, and in the centre of it carriages and horses. In another moment I was standing on the platform of the little wooden station, grasping the hand of my friend, my dear friend whom I had not seen for so many years.

The crowds of peasants waving their welcome, the people in their quaint costumes, the station, all faded away before me, and I lost sight of everything but the face of the Comte as he pressed my hand in a hearty welcome. His tall figure stood before me, straight and distinctive in outline. I thought him wonderfully little changed since we had last met, though he spoke often of the gray hairs which I found it impossible to discover in his locks. He was a noble type of a Frenchman, the Comte. His light brown hair fell back in a slight wave, from his broad forehead, showing two large temples that were neither high nor low, but that spoke of a wonderful intelligence behind them. No one could look upon the Comte de Persigny and not be sensible that he was in the presence of a man of unusual qualities. The eyebrows, a little darker than the hair above, were smooth and even, though they seemed to protrude almost unnaturally, owing to the strong development of the forehead. Beneath them shone a pair of deep-set eyes, bearing that indescribable look which we find in all men who have thought much and thought deeply. It is difficult to convey the impression of this look in a man's eyes to any one who has not observed it for himself. There is in it an air of concentrated energy, shown by a development about the eye, one which by description might apply to a far different physiognomy, but which seen in the actual man is unmistakable. It is there, an indisputable proof of mind and intellect, a sign that speaks more eloquently for the bearer's qualities than any speech or language could describe. Such was the chief characteristic of the Comte's appearance, as I looked upon him in the full glare of the morning sunlight, and tried to think how to begin all that I had to say to him.

At last we spoke, a thousand things of no importance in one breath, and then a thousand others, before the first had been disposed of.

"Well, my dear friend, welcome to Persigny," said the Comte, as I alighted. "It is indeed a longed-for pleasure come true, to have you here. In fact, I thought at one

time that you would never come to us; but then your letter came, telling me of your sudden departure, and here you are in truth. You have changed so little that I am almost inclined to believe that we are not in France at all, but back again where we first met. Do you remember it? What a pleasant month that was! I have amused myself in recalling its circumstances as I was driving over to meet you.'

Remember it! Had it not been in my mind, imprinted there in an unchangeable die, the years past, and had it not again formed the picture of the hour that had just ended? I told my friend as much, and we turned to pass through the little station and to enter his carriage amid the cheers of the peasants and the barking of a pair of huge mastiffs. The Comte jumped in, and seated himself at my side. The postilion, clothed in a red and green livery, cracked his whip; the great Percherons bounded forward, and we started. I was indeed at my journey's end. And we were upon our way to the chateau. I was soon conversing as of old with my friend the Comte, who was asking of my arrival at Paris, of the journey there, of a number of friends and acquaintances, and all the time adding information as to himself and his mother.

I had no words at my command, nor chance of expressing them if I had wished to, so I contented myself with listening to the Comte and with taking in the surroundings. The brilliant livery of the postilion shone in the sun, and mingled with that of the footmen. The round bells about the necks of the postières jingled a merry chime. The postilion emphasized his "Yuck hue!" with the crack of his short-handled whip, as we dashed through the long street of the village. The slate steeple of the church, with its gilded cross and its ever-turning weather-cock, was already behind us. The old bell, having rung the "Angelus,"—as it had done at noon for no one knows how many years—had now ceased and was

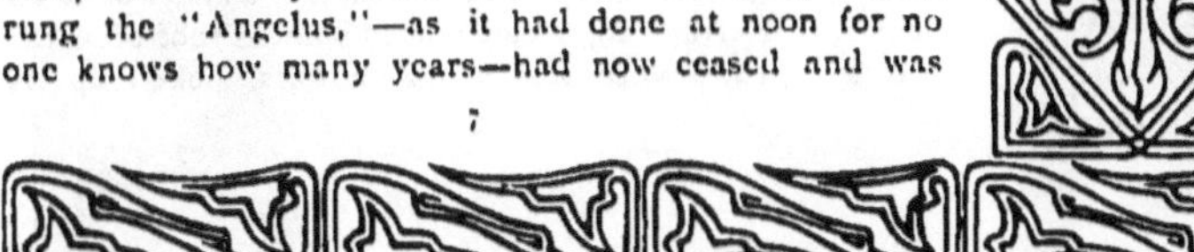

waiting in silence for the ending of the day that it might begin again. Young women and old were leaning against the doors, or lower windows, of the houses, which were bright with pots of flowers in full bloom. Some of them, still blushing roses of spring, peered at us with wide-open eyes and dropped a curtsey with some grace, while others, more like the leaves of autumn, bowed discreetly, and some even smiled. All bowed, all curtsied; all cried a welcome and cheered us on our way.

Before long, the village had become a thing of the past, and we were rolling swiftly over a sandy road, as smooth as the alley of some private park. It seemed to me, on beholding, for the first time, one of these beautiful roads of France, like a long golden riband, bordered by emerald green. Some unknown being had unrolled it, in a straight line, toward the horizon. And we seemed to be driving straight into the sun, or rather to where the sun would be some hours later. To the right and left all was green, an extraordinary green such as it was a delight to look upon. At times some darkened pines would break the fields, and then a wood of heavy oaks, with here and there the silver leaves of a birch tree coquetting with the rays of the sun, would appear in sight. Often an indefinite carpet of heath would be spread beneath the trees, its pink and violet shades giving a delicacy of coloring that drew forth many an expression of delight.

Still we rolled on, over the golden road. Here the thatched roof of a small house, on which the dark moss had grown so thick that it had covered it with a velvet mantle, was nestled in among many trees and flower-covered bushes. A little pond with ducks, or geese, or even a brood of young turkeys on the bank, would be near by. Further on, a hut, whose pointed roof of earth was overgrown with weeds and flowers, poked up its head. It had been built by the woodcutter, and stood little more than ten feet from the ground. There he lived, year in, year out. It was his nest, the oak above his head, the pine needle as a couch. A canvas bag was hung as a curtain to the door and a cloud of thick black smoke, making its way through the leaves, told of the fire which was to cook his mid-day meal.

Close to the side of the road there appeared a lake, some kilometers in extent. Its waters were unruffled, save by the ever-growing circles of a carp jumping from the water. Some lapwings were hovering above the reeds that lined the edges. From time to time they dove among them, to feed their little ones within the nest. High above, a large and cruel hawk struck terror into their gentle hearts by his wide and sweeping circles.

At length there appeared some fields of wheat surrounded by woods and clumps of trees. Above them and far in the distance, some high slate roofs and chimneys rose against the sky. They were those of the chateau toward which we were directing our steps. Between us was another little village, nestling into a valley which seemed but the suspicion of a valley without its reality. The road turned to the left, and joined another at a slight incline. A cross of stone stood at the corner, and as our cavalcade passed by, I saw the Comte lift reverentially his hat. I realized that the strong sentiment of the Roman Catholic Church predominated here. In another moment we were passing through the single street of the village, and the Comte was saying: "My dear friend, welcome to Persigny; we are here at last, and has it not a picturesque surrounding?"

It had indeed. I had never seen so rustic or so artistic an effect. The whole place seemed almost in miniature, —an ideal set in true reality. The street itself was so narrow that one could cover it in a single stride. The

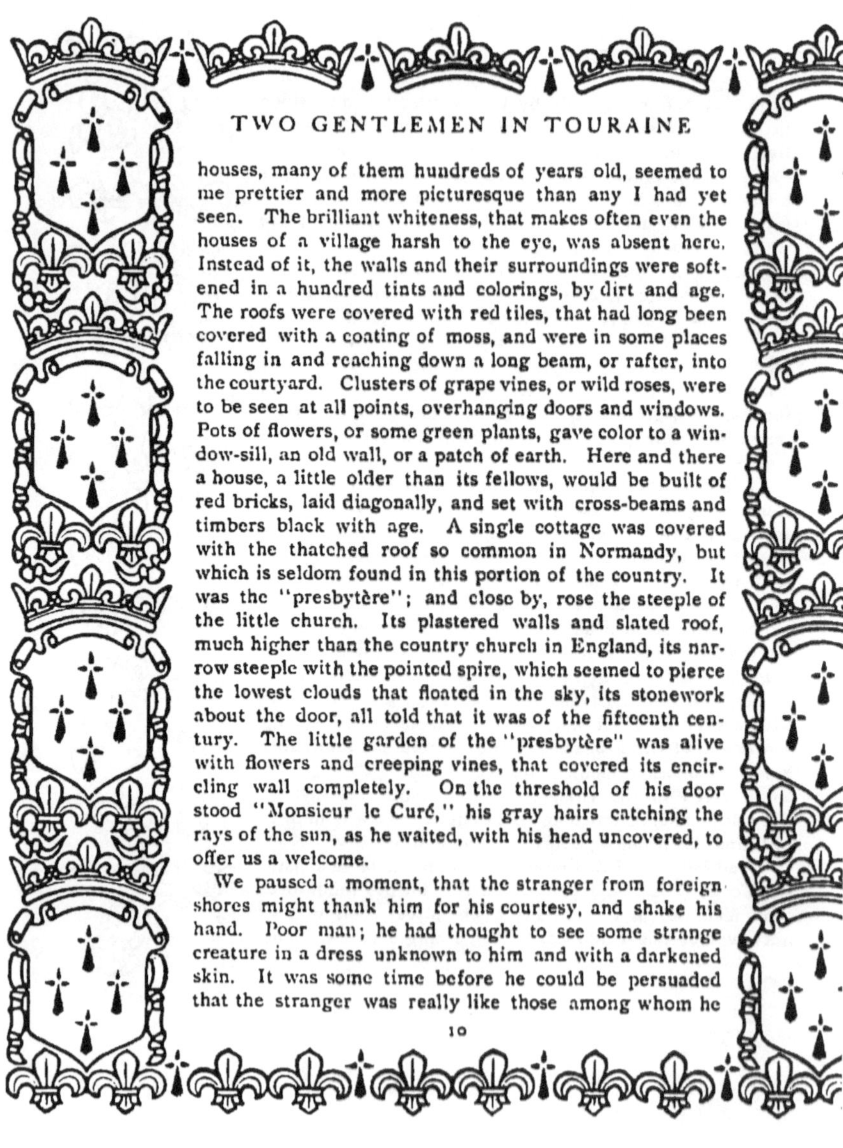

houses, many of them hundreds of years old, seemed to me prettier and more picturesque than any I had yet seen. The brilliant whiteness, that makes often even the houses of a village harsh to the eye, was absent here. Instead of it, the walls and their surroundings were softened in a hundred tints and colorings, by dirt and age. The roofs were covered with red tiles, that had long been covered with a coating of moss, and were in some places falling in and reaching down a long beam, or rafter, into the courtyard. Clusters of grape vines, or wild roses, were to be seen at all points, overhanging doors and windows. Pots of flowers, or some green plants, gave color to a window-sill, an old wall, or a patch of earth. Here and there a house, a little older than its fellows, would be built of red bricks, laid diagonally, and set with cross-beams and timbers black with age. A single cottage was covered with the thatched roof so common in Normandy, but which is seldom found in this portion of the country. It was the "presbytère"; and close by, rose the steeple of the little church. Its plastered walls and slated roof, much higher than the country church in England, its narrow steeple with the pointed spire, which seemed to pierce the lowest clouds that floated in the sky, its stonework about the door, all told that it was of the fifteenth century. The little garden of the "presbytère" was alive with flowers and creeping vines, that covered its encircling wall completely. On the threshold of his door stood "Monsieur le Curé," his gray hairs catching the rays of the sun, as he waited, with his head uncovered, to offer us a welcome.

We paused a moment, that the stranger from foreign shores might thank him for his courtesy, and shake his hand. Poor man; he had thought to see some strange creature in a dress unknown to him and with a darkened skin. It was some time before he could be persuaded that the stranger was really like those among whom he

had lived for sixty years, so different had he expected him to be!

As we passed on, once more, I noticed that every door was filled with some rustic figure and that every window had some head within it. Many clapped their hands and shouted as we passed, while others were waving hats and handkerchiefs. The little public square was crowded with a score or two of peasants, who had assembled to give us a rustic welcome. And as we passed by we bowed our acknowledgments to the cries which came to us from all sides, and "Vive Monsieur le Comte! Vive Monsieur le Comte!" sounded in our ears as we drove on.

Soon we had passed the village and were at the gates of the park. In another moment I gave a cry of sudden delight. As we entered the long avenue leading to the chateau a scene of rare and unexpected beauty appeared before us. We had just entered a large hollow rectangle at least a kilometre in length, and hemmed in upon the right and left by walls of drooping oak trees. The centre of this rectangle was occupied by a sheet of water, —a canal, as my friend called it. Its waters were dotted, here and there, by the white wings of swans. And at its farthest boundary the high roofs of a chateau of the period of Louis XIII were reflected in the water. So still was everything, and so like a mirror was the lake, that it seemed as if another chateau had been placed symmetrically underneath the one that rose from the beautiful lawn leading to its rush-covered bank. And yet it was but a reflection of the pure architecture above, a photograph of the reality. We were traversing one of the great avenues which ran on either side of the canal, and met in front of the "marquise" of the chateau. Tall trees lined the way, and shaded us from the heat of the mid-day sun, while giant palms in massive wooden tubs, waved above the head.

"My dear friend, what a beautiful spot is this that you live in!" I exclaimed. "Why did you never tell me that it was like this?"

The Comte looked at me with a pleased expression on his countenance. "I thought," said he, "that some day you would come and see it for yourself, and so I would not spoil your first impression of it by description. You see that I was right," he added, with a smile.

As we approached nearer to the chateau, I could scarcely find time to absorb the beauty of the scene around me, nor could I find words with which to express my feelings. An arch, formed by overhanging trees, enveloped us for a moment, and as we emerged from it we drew up before the door of the chateau. Several persons were standing about it to receive us, and as we alighted, the Comte turned to a lady, a little taller than the others, saying: "This is my mother; once more, my dear friend, welcome to Persigny."

The Comtesse de Persigny smiled a welcome to me and extended her hand with the utmost cordiality. I seemed at once to become one of her own family. For the stiffness of which the representatives of the older noblesse of France are sometimes accused, melts away, with their grace of manner, when they wish to admit any one to a more intimate relationship. And the most formal members of a secluded aristocracy become the most congenial of companions, to those whom they receive among them. I was soon introduced to the ladies and gentlemen standing near us, and I afterwards discovered that they formed part of the company that were staying at the chateau. They at once besieged me with many questions about myself, my country and my journey to France. So many were they, however, and so indifferent was my command of the French language, that I fear many of them remained unanswered. But my interlocutors passed over my unsuccessful attempts at conversation with a laugh, or with some witty remark, and we soon passed into the chateau.

Here I was at last, and I was to take up for a time the life and customs of a Frenchman. The atmosphere around me had indeed changed, and I began to realize that I was truly in a strange land, led by standards and ideas far different from my own. The fascination of it grew upon me, as the life into which I had thus suddenly fallen impressed itself upon the mind; and as I wound my way to my room, through many ancient corridors and passages, I felt almost that it was some strange dream, rather than reality.

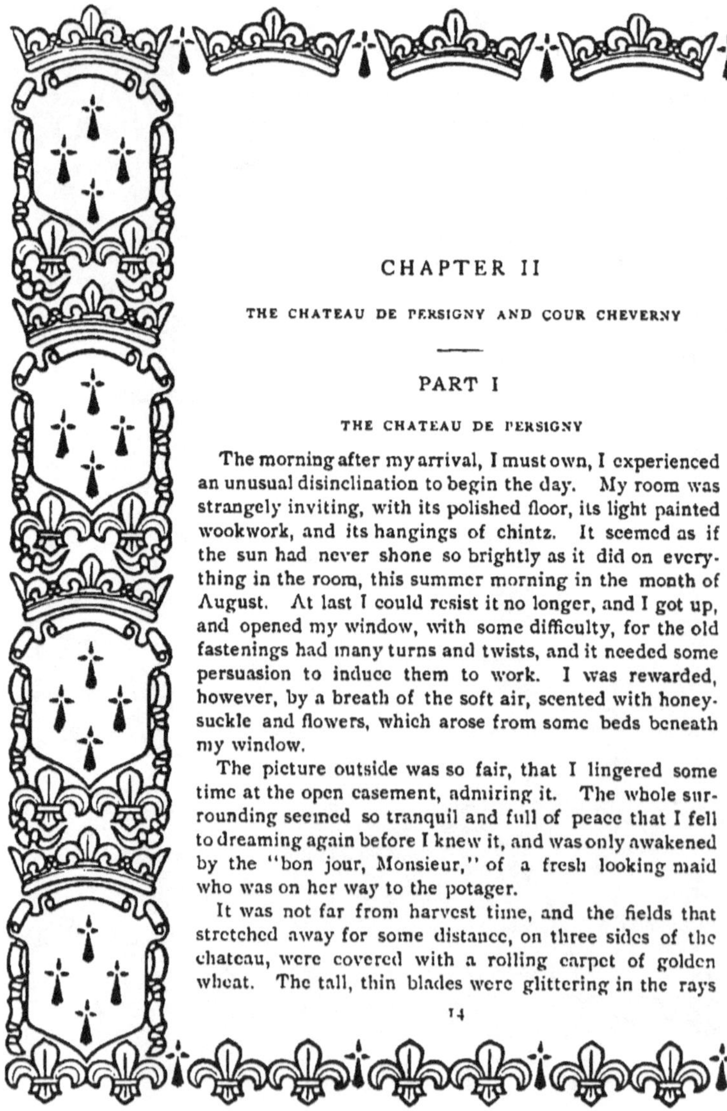

CHAPTER II

THE CHATEAU DE PERSIGNY AND COUR CHEVERNY

PART I

THE CHATEAU DE PERSIGNY

The morning after my arrival, I must own, I experienced an unusual disinclination to begin the day. My room was strangely inviting, with its polished floor, its light painted wookwork, and its hangings of chintz. It seemed as if the sun had never shone so brightly as it did on everything in the room, this summer morning in the month of August. At last I could resist it no longer, and I got up, and opened my window, with some difficulty, for the old fastenings had many turns and twists, and it needed some persuasion to induce them to work. I was rewarded, however, by a breath of the soft air, scented with honeysuckle and flowers, which arose from some beds beneath my window.

The picture outside was so fair, that I lingered some time at the open casement, admiring it. The whole surrounding seemed so tranquil and full of peace that I fell to dreaming again before I knew it, and was only awakened by the "bon jour, Monsieur," of a fresh looking maid who was on her way to the potager.

It was not far from harvest time, and the fields that stretched away for some distance, on three sides of the chateau, were covered with a rolling carpet of golden wheat. The tall, thin blades were glittering in the rays

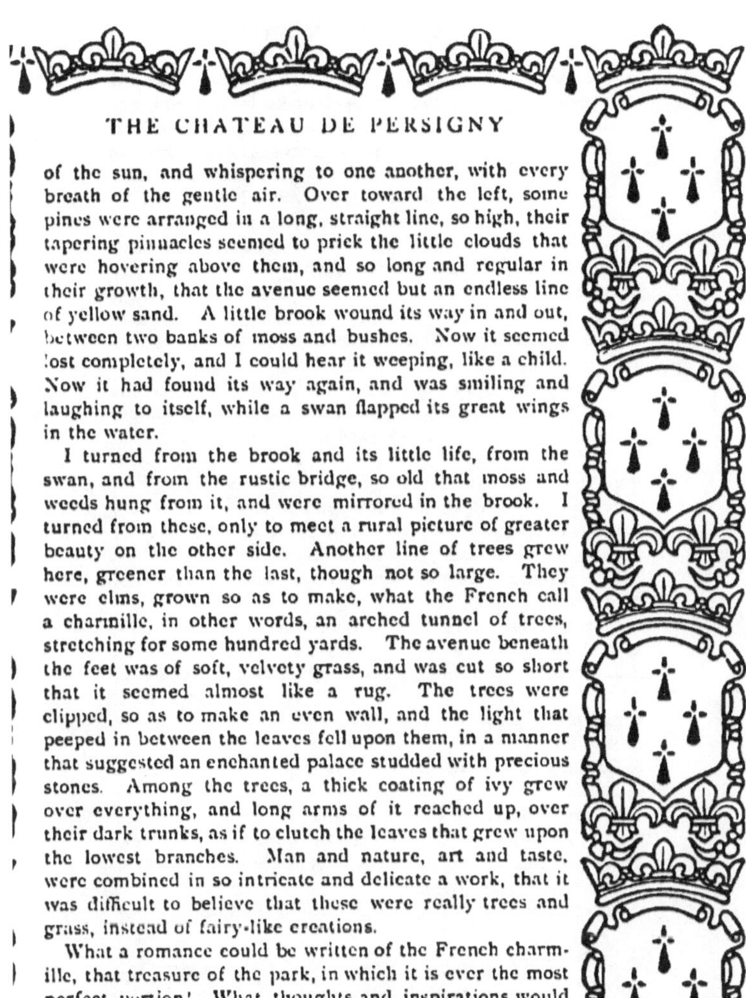

of the sun, and whispering to one another, with every breath of the gentle air. Over toward the left, some pines were arranged in a long, straight line, so high, their tapering pinnacles seemed to prick the little clouds that were hovering above them, and so long and regular in their growth, that the avenue seemed but an endless line of yellow sand. A little brook wound its way in and out, between two banks of moss and bushes. Now it seemed lost completely, and I could hear it weeping, like a child. Now it had found its way again, and was smiling and laughing to itself, while a swan flapped its great wings in the water.

I turned from the brook and its little life, from the swan, and from the rustic bridge, so old that moss and weeds hung from it, and were mirrored in the brook. I turned from these, only to meet a rural picture of greater beauty on the other side. Another line of trees grew here, greener than the last, though not so large. They were elms, grown so as to make, what the French call a charmille, in other words, an arched tunnel of trees, stretching for some hundred yards. The avenue beneath the feet was of soft, velvety grass, and was cut so short that it seemed almost like a rug. The trees were clipped, so as to make an even wall, and the light that peeped in between the leaves fell upon them, in a manner that suggested an enchanted palace studded with precious stones. Among the trees, a thick coating of ivy grew over everything, and long arms of it reached up, over their dark trunks, as if to clutch the leaves that grew upon the lowest branches. Man and nature, art and taste, were combined in so intricate and delicate a work, that it was difficult to believe that these were really trees and grass, instead of fairy-like creations.

What a romance could be written of the French charmille, that treasure of the park, in which it is ever the most perfect portion! What thoughts and inspirations would

it not raise in the minds of those who wander over the
soft green carpet to the tiny nook at its farther end, and
then sit against the marble statue, brought from Italy
perhaps, and dream away more than one happy hour in
the cool and shade! How many of us have done just such a
thing! And how many more of us would long to do likewise! Was there ever a more romantic spot for lovers to
meet, and there to forget all, save peace and happiness?
Was there ever a more perfect setting for a poet's fancy
than the charmille of some chateau's park? Surely, there
could never be. And so I thought, as I gazed down at
the one beneath me, which had been engrossing my attention so particularly.

A sharp "rap, rap, rap," at my door announced that the
Comte was up and about. And I turned from the beauty
of the scene without, to say good morning to him.

"I have been enjoying the beauties of the garden about
your chateau," said I. "Why have you never told me how
much there was here—so artistic and so fairy-like? Why,
I almost imagined myself in a land of dreams and
fancies, as I was airing myself at the window."

The Comte answered my remark with a smile of
pleasure.

"Yes; it is a lovely spot, and it seems to become more
and more attractive to me every day. I have made a
great many improvements since I inherited the chateau.
And if you will come out with me, we will take a walk
through the stables and gardens and view a part of the
park. But I fear that you will be tired if we attempt
to do the whole of the park in one day, for it is over ten
miles."

"I am afraid that I shall have to work up my way to
that," I replied. "But I will be with you in a few
moments, and we will then see everything that you care
to show me, before déjeuner."

I dressed myself, and hastened to join the Comte. But

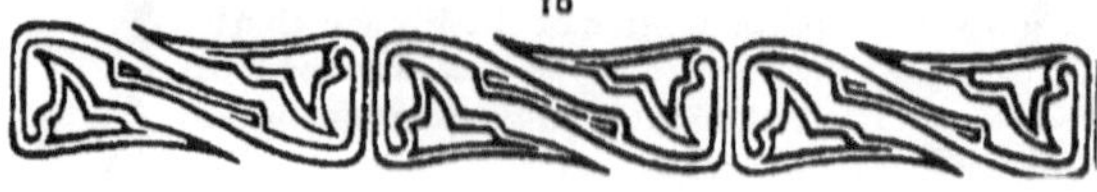

on my way down, I met some of the guests of the
chateau. The Marquise de la Signe, an elderly dowager,
with a wonderful complexion, and a color to her hair that
was surprising considering her age, accosted me at the
second landing of the staircase. I bowed politely, and
she held out her hand for me to kiss. I performed my
duty to her evident satisfaction, for she tapped me on the
shoulder with her fan, and added:

"Monsieur est tout-à-fait Français. Vraiment, tout ce
qu'il y-ade plus Français. J'espère que Monsieur a très
bien dormi?" And this last inquiry she accompanied
with the slightest inclination of her head.

"Oh, very well, thank you. And now I am going out
to view the park, with our host. May we not have the
pleasure of your company?"

"Oh, Monsieur is too kind. But I never go out before
the afternoon," replied the Marquise with a shake of her
head. "I haven't been out in the morning for two years.
It is so bad for the complexion, you know," she added,
with a merry twinkle in her eye. "But if you are not too
tired, with your exertions this morning, we will walk for
a quarter of an hour in the charmille, after tea—when the
sun has set. Life is so much pleasanter when the sun
has set." And my interlocutor waved her hand in a
graceful farewell.

I thought, as I wound my way down to the gallery
below, that the Marquise de la Signe must indeed be a
philosopher to have decided, at her age, that the sunset
was the pleasantest portion of life. And I could not help
thinking what a pity it was that more people were not of
her turn of mind. In the gallery, I encountered the beau
of the party, le Prince de Gourmet—an old friend of the
Comte's mother, a perfect type of the French nobleman,
of high position, but of low purse, who loves the best of
everything and, somehow or other, always obtains it, an
indispensable addition to every respectable chateau, to

every salon and to every hotel in the Faubourg Saint Germain. Perhaps the Comtesse de Persigny had once entertained the idea of becoming a princess. Perhaps even the Prince had had serious thoughts of making a permanent residence at the chateau. There was no telling. But somehow or other, the Comtesse never changed her name, and the Prince had never made the contemplated stay. He still came for his three weeks in August and his fortnight in December,—for Christmas,—and was always the life of the party, the ever welcome guest, and nothing more.

If Madame de la Signe's maid had unknown ways of making her mistress's head seem twenty years the younger, certainly the Prince's valet had discovered an "elixir of life" by which his master should never grow old. The Prince's age no one had ever known. In fact, he was even known to have said that no gentleman— or lady either—ever had an age. If any did have an age, why, all he could say, was, that they could not be ladies, or gentlemen. As for him, he had never been born at all. He had found himself in Paris one day, and had found it so pleasant there that he had stayed ever since, and should do so always. He had never been out of France, and never would go under any consideration, never—never. Thus the matter was settled, and the Prince's friends had begun to believe that, after all, he probably never had been born, and never would die. He had remained the same for so many years, there was every reason to believe that he would continue to do so. Thus the Prince had become a permanent fixture in French society, a pillar of the Faubourg and an indispensable addition to all country parties.

Before saying good morning to so unique a character as le Prince de Gourmet it was impossible to refrain from an admiring glance at his appearance. Yes, there could be no question, his valet understood the art of—what shall

we call it?—the art of wigging—yes, and the art of dyeing
and painting and powdering and dressing,—in fact, all
the arts which could possibly enter into the toilet of a
gentleman, a perfect gentleman of the old school. The
Prince's hair was of a beautiful greyish brown—a little
powder, that was all, and electrified, so as to stand up or
lie down, so as to bristle like the spikes of a porcupine,
or curl like a baby's ringlets. It was a wonderful head
of hair. There was no doubt as to its superiority.
There was no rival to it. It was the first of its kind in
France. A certain barber in the Rue Castiglione had
made his fortune by it. And this I heard later from the
Comte himself. All the world knew it, and all the world
went there, now, he affirmed, if they wished to look
comme il faut. I must go when I returned to Paris. I
would go.

The Prince had been out for an early airing this morning, and was attired in a short jacket of buff-colored stuff,
fitted in at the waist to a marvelous degree. Knicker-
bockers, of a different shade, encased the Prince's limbs,
and the buckles at the knees were hidden by the tops of
the long stockings, knit by no less a personage than the
Comtesse de Persigny herself. Ah, Cupid, Cupid! where
would you not lead us? Where would you not show your
face and strike your persistent arrow? Not many years
ago you may have pointed your bow and arrow at a lady's
cheek. And now it is upon the victim's calves! There
they were, the light brown stockings with their great
squares of different colored worsted; there they were,
resplendent, upon a pair of padded calves. A faint
suspicion of dust upon his boots told that Monsieur
le Prince had been to walk around the garden, up the
avenue, and home through the potager, where he had
picked his daily bunch of bleuettes (pink bachelor's but-
tons grown especially for him), which he had picked
for years on his daily walk that never varied. He was

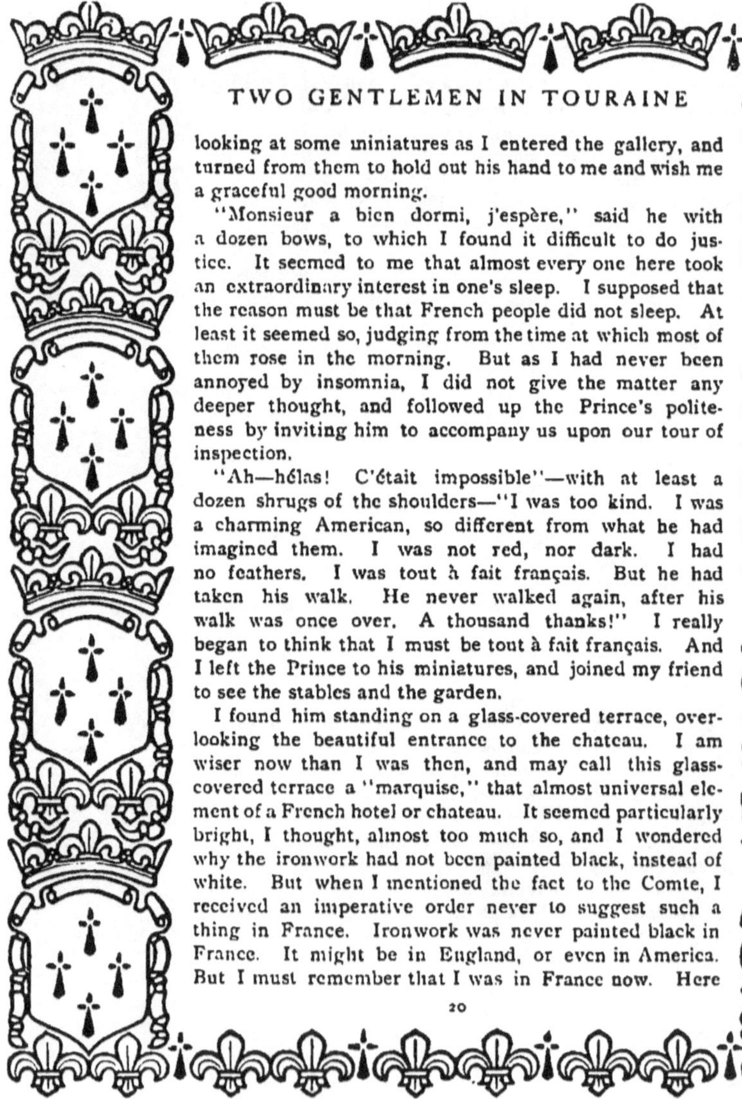

looking at some miniatures as I entered the gallery, and turned from them to hold out his hand to me and wish me a graceful good morning.

"Monsieur a bien dormi, j'espère," said he with a dozen bows, to which I found it difficult to do justice. It seemed to me that almost every one here took an extraordinary interest in one's sleep. I supposed that the reason must be that French people did not sleep. At least it seemed so, judging from the time at which most of them rose in the morning. But as I had never been annoyed by insomnia, I did not give the matter any deeper thought, and followed up the Prince's politeness by inviting him to accompany us upon our tour of inspection.

"Ah—hélas! C'était impossible"—with at least a dozen shrugs of the shoulders—"I was too kind. I was a charming American, so different from what he had imagined them. I was not red, nor dark. I had no feathers. I was tout à fait français. But he had taken his walk. He never walked again, after his walk was once over. A thousand thanks!" I really began to think that I must be tout à fait français. And I left the Prince to his miniatures, and joined my friend to see the stables and the garden.

I found him standing on a glass-covered terrace, overlooking the beautiful entrance to the chateau. I am wiser now than I was then, and may call this glass-covered terrace a "marquise," that almost universal element of a French hotel or chateau. It seemed particularly bright, I thought, almost too much so, and I wondered why the ironwork had not been painted black, instead of white. But when I mentioned the fact to the Comte, I received an imperative order never to suggest such a thing in France. Ironwork was never painted black in France. It might be in England, or even in America. But I must remember that I was in France now. Here

it was always white or gray or sometimes silver. We
stood a moment, taking in the beautiful scenes opening before us, and then the Comte broke the silence.

"I did not have time yesterday to tell you why I
dragged you away from Paris so soon," said he. "We
had not been together for so long that the pleasure of
seeing you once again and under such different circumstances, of picking up the threads that had been dropped
or lost altogether, occupied all my thoughts at our meeting and every moment of yesterday. I am looking
forward to the next few months—for you are not to think
of going before the late autumn—with more pleasurable
anticipation than I can well express. In fact, to tell the
truth, my English is not up to the undertaking. I fear
it has become rather neglected of late, for it is over a
year since I have been in England, and nearly ten months
since I have spoken a word that was not French.

"But I must tell you why I wished you to come—apart
from our 'fête de famille' of to-day. I am anxious to
start to-morrow on a tour of the beautiful chateaux of
Touraine, of which you have so often written me, and to
which we have so often contemplated a visit. One of
them, the Chateau de Cour Cheverny, is in this neighborhood, and we will start for it early to-morrow morning,
if you are not too tired of this continual movement. We
would wait another week, but the season is late, and I
am anxious for you, who are so fond of flowers, to see
the parterres and gardens of some of these chateaux
while they are at their best. I know so many of their
owners that we shall see them in an interesting way.
What say you? Shall we go to-morrow?"

Of course I agreed, with an exclamation of pleasure
at the thought of seeing the wonders of Chambord
and Blois, of Chenonceau and Azay-le-Rideau, remembering the romance and history lurking among their
beautifully ornamented towers and walls. Visions of

TWO GENTLEMEN IN TOURAINE

Catherine de Medici, of François I, of Henry II, and Henry III, of the beautiful Diane de Poitiers, and last but not least, of the unhappy Marie Stuart, arose before me in an enchanted picture that carried me back into the history of the Middle Ages and the happier Renaissance.

Go? Of course I would go. In spite of the beauties of the park and the gardens of the Chateau de Persigny, I could scarcely wait for the morrow, that we might start on this long-projected trip. How happy I was at the thought! It seemed to me I had not been so happy since the day I had left school and realized that it was a thing of the past. I believe that I was more interested than the Comte, though he was in very good spirits and almost as enthusiastic as I over the intended tour.

"This, indeed, is what I have always wished to do," said he, "but I have never found just the person to do it with me. It is necessary to be rather more than simply genial to travel alone in this way. One must be truly fond of the subject, and willing to put up with some inconveniences. For the auberges are not always of the best, and the weather is sometimes very hot. But in spite of this, I am sure that we shall enjoy it. We will go a little out of the beaten track and visit the beautiful chateaux of Valençay and of le Lude. For in the gardens of this last there is one of the most beautiful terraces in France."

"I agree to everything in advance," I replied. "And would it not be a good plan to go on foot some of the way? If it is possible, I should like very much to do so. I have always wished to take a walking tour. I have always longed to travel in a perfectly "laissez aller" fashion, studying the country and the rural life as I wandered along, stopping here and there, to speak to a peasant, or some other members of a lower class, and if possible, to form some idea of their condition of mind and of the motives which actuate their ways of thinking."

"Admirable, mon ami, admirable," exclaimed the Comte, as we walked off in the direction of a large iron grille on our left. "Admirable. I join you in your mood completely. And to make the whole idea a perfectly rural one, we will ask Monsieur le Curé to take us to the station at Mur, in his old, rustic pony-carriage. We will have nothing to do with victorias or postières. The placid 'Bichette,' the old pony of the Curé, who has eaten so many extra rations of oats, and nibbled at so many of the neighboring lawns, that she can scarcely waddle along the even roads, shall be our rustic steed. And Monsieur le Curé himself shall be our guide, as far as the station at all events."

So it was decided; and as we passed through the iron grille toward which we had been directing our steps, we proceeded to give ourselves up to the enjoyment of the stables of Persigny, though I fear that our hearts were far too full of the anticipation of the morrow.

I could not refrain from uttering a word of admiration as we entered one of the great courts of the stables. It covered an area of at least an hectare, enclosed by long, low buildings. In the center, a large stone basin rose, high above the head, as did the soft spray of a fountain springing from it. At the further end of this court a second gate, whose ironwork, though less elaborate, was as effective as the one which was now behind us, opened into another court. The buildings and arrangements there were not unlike those of the first, save that they were used for the farms and their various appendages, instead of for the horses and carriages of the chateau.

"As you see, all our horses are on this side of the court, and the carriages upon the left," said the Comte, as we stood by the fountain. And as I looked, I could see carriages, of all kinds, ranged in a long row against the

wall. They looked wonderfully inviting, with their shining red wheels and green bodies, while here and there was one painted to imitate basket work. I felt almost sorry that we had decided to be so rustic upon our trip; but the Comte "pooh-poohed" my nonsense. I was altogether too fond of luxury, but we would have none of it here. We were to be all for art and architecture and the study of those marvels of the French Renaissance, with the history connected with them—"at least, with as much of it as possible," I put in, for I had no idea of attempting to absorb all the history that was lurking about Touraine. We would devote a little energy to each subject, and end, in all probability, by knowing nothing valuable about any one of them. But then, that was so natural, and so like most of the world, that we might as well content ourselves with this principle of being "a Jack at all trades and a master of none." The Comte was inclined to object to this, as being too much the tendency—and the evil tendency, moreover—of our age. He said that this was the great trouble to-day and that he, for one, and I, for two, must not follow in such mediocre footsteps.

The old wooden gate of the potager had closed behind us, by this time, and we were sauntering down a long box-lined alley, between rows of tiny, distorted apple trees. They could not have been more than a foot high, and seemed to be so crippled and deformed that their limbs had to be supported upon sticks and wires. The old plaster-covered wall on our right was covered with creeping vines of pears and apples, while a few last bunches of wall-roses hung in clusters here and there. Long lines of mignonette and heliotrope followed one another in an untrained mass. Dahlias and sunflowers, at the back, lent their effective lights and shades to beautify the picture which we were now enjoying. Soon, the potager with its hot-beds, its flowers, its vegetables, its gardeners and all its quiet rural life faded away behind us, and we were wandering through long alleys, lined with underbrush and covered with grass. For nearly twenty miles, the Comte told me, the whole park was covered by this network of avenues, stretching, it seemed, for endless distances in a straight line, and cut at intervals by other avenues leading no one knew where. Many of these my friend himself had never explored, nor could one do so, even if one would, so many were they, and so confusing were they in their likeness one to another.

After walking some time in the honey-scented air, we came to a small open space, where nine of these avenues met one another and, as if angry at having been discovered, dashed away again in all directions. We sat a moment in the shade of a tall post, which held up a number of signs bearing the names of the various avenues. These were named after members of his family, the Comte explained to me, as we made our way to a little farm not far away, where the tenants, overjoyed at Monsieur le Comte's visit, pressed their best wine upon us. We were obliged to drink it, to the last drop, lest they should be offended, and I doubt if it was much effort to me, for it was far better than many of our own wines.

At last, it was time to return, and we thanked the kindly peasants, complimenting them upon the condition of their cottages, upon their farm and upon everything, in fact, that it was possible to praise. The whole family followed us, as we departed, bowing and curtseying, till we were at some distance from their humble dwelling. And we returned to the chateau by grass-grown lanes, and by the "charmille," to find the Prince de Gourmet impatiently awaiting his déjeuner. "It was after midi; what could be the matter? En effet, there could be no doubt about it, the déjeuner was at least five

minutes late," and the maitre d' hôtel was severely repri-
manded (because the gentlemen had been out walking
and he had waited for them).

A pleasant surprise took place that evening. It was
the fête day of Madame la Comtesse, and such bustling
among the maitre d'hôtel, the footmen and the entire
culinary department, such preparations and running
hither and thither, could not easily be imagined. As we
entered the dining-room for dinner, after having formed
a procession in the furthest drawing-room and made a
tour of all the others, we saw the result of these elaborate preparations. The great dining-room of the
chateau had been transformed into a bower of plants
and flowers. Orchids hung from the walls and covered
the centre of the dinner table. Upon the sideboard
at the further end of the dining-room was displayed the
great service of gold plate, which made its appearance
only twice a year, or upon some special occasion. As we
sat down to dinner pistol shots were heard outside the
window and some fireworks threw their variegated
lights into the room. The effect was emphasized by the
cheers of the tenantry, who had formed in a circle before
the chateau to pay their tribute to Madame la Comtesse
on her fête day.

The cheers were so persistent that the Comte was
forced to go to the window and to make a graceful speech
in thanks, which elicited only more enthusiasm from the
loyal tenantry. At last the dinner was served, much to
the satisfaction of the Prince de Gourmet, who was seated
at the right of the hostess and who received a rose from
her bouquet after all was over, a little attention which
had taken place for no one knows how many years.

As we parted later in the evening, I felt a sincere
regret that the first day at the chateau had come to an
end, and that we were again to travel on the morrow.
But sorry as I was to leave a place to which I had so long

looked forward, it was difficult to complain, with such an interesting journey before us. So we bade affection-ate au revoirs to all before retiring, and prepared to start early the next morning. The Marquise pressed my hand, and begged me to come and see her at her hotel in the Faubourg. The Prince wished us good luck on our journey, and Monsieur le Curé, who had been invited to the chateau for dinner, left us to prepare the pony and cart for the drive to the station.

PART II

COUR CHEVERNY

At an early hour we were up and out, to be in time for Monsieur le Curé and to meet him at the village. It would save at least half an hour if Bichette did not come to the chateau. So we decided that it was both shorter and simpler to go to her.

The mail had just arrived as we reached the little plaster-covered cottage that served as the postoffice, and the postmaster, who untied the bags in a tiny room opening upon the highway, handed us our letters as we paused. A grand collection of many-colored envelopes they were, bearing in their right-hand corners bright stamps of many nationalities. And many hopes and fears, such as only mails may inspire, were raised within us, only to remain hopes and fears for the present, as Monsieur le Curé had just drawn up with Mlle. Bichette and the antiquated pony cart. We were forced to start at once that we might not lose the train. To be sure, it did not leave for two hours; but then we had eight miles to go, and this was a good deal for so portly a dowager as Bichette. But never mind, we resolved to burn a candle to Notre Dame if the temptations of the road were not too much for her, so we arrived in time.

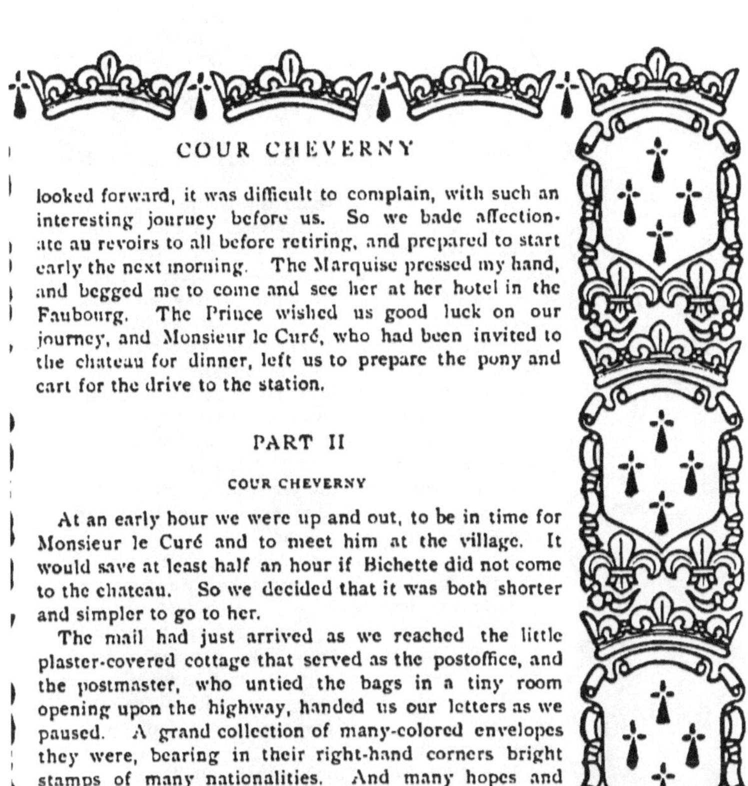

Allow me to introduce to the company this dignified lady, upon whose kindly mercies we had thrown ourselves. We have made a mistake. It is Madame Bichette, and not Mademoiselle—Madame Bichette, the only possible companion for a worthy curé de campagne, Madame Bichette, a most respectable and deliberate pony who renders many valuable services to her dear master. With her he goes from one steeple to another, from a fellow curé to a neighboring chateau, and returns home by rain, sunshine, or moonlight.

At last we were seated and ready. "Will you be kind enough to start, Bichette?" says Monsieur le Cure. And after tossing into the air an intruding fly which had just settled upon the end of her nose, Bichette began to move—carefully, "piano, sano."

Drops of rain from an almost cloudless sky showed signs of a dampness in the atmosphere which is discouraging to any one who rejoices in bright and sunny expeditions. However, we kept our anxiety to ourselves lest we should disturb Bichette, who had just reached the climax of her powers, a gentle trot, or more properly a waddle, that shook the pony cart with every step. We kept our anxiety to ourselves, I say, and opened our letters, in spite of the rain.

"Hue, Bichette! Allons, gentiment!"

And as we were tossed up and down, until our teeth were nearly rattled out of our heads, the news from home and from abroad danced up and down, down and up, before our eyes, like an ignis fatuus.

Dear me! So and so is married, and scarcely realizes it. Another one is dead, and others still see the day. But never mind. Our business this morning is to catch the train, and Monsieur le Curé whispers unknown inducements to Bichette, unknown things that cause her to trot along as fast as possible, mindful only of the flies.

Two little villages, with miniature streets and almost

miniature houses, were passed through, and left behind. The old walls of a deserted monastery appeared on our right, great hanging branches of ivy, vines and roses clinging to them in a confused mass. And they fade away again behind us. Bichette is surprised, even at herself, and is well-nigh overcome, by the time we reach the little station of soft white stone, which is our destination. After a time, the engine and its long line of carriages come rattling and shambling along. And we make no end of "au revoirs" to Madame Bichette and to Monsieur le Curé. The latter is very sorry that he cannot accompany us further; but he has promised to breakfast with a friend near by. Bichette pokes out her head, and neighs, a long, contented, lazy neigh. Her master bares his venerable head with only a few silvery locks left, and as the train whistles, and puffs off, we can see his black form standing by the side of his companion. A pretty, rural picture that leaves a kindly impression upon those who have been looking at it!

We had intended to go straight to Blois when we set out from the beautiful surroundings of the Chateau de Persigny; but like most intentions, made in all good faith, this did not long remain unbroken. In spite of showers, the day was beautiful in its coloring, and little clouds were dotted over the clear blue sky, like tiny bits of snow-white fleece, just severed from the coat of some young lamb. Now and again some darker clouds appeared, and these were sometimes followed by a large, black mass that hid a thunderstorm. We ran into one of these, en route for Blois; and as the train flew through it, the verdant vineyards, the brilliant fields of wheat, the undulating country, changed at every moment, in a variety of shapes and colors that were rendered even more wonderful by the storm.

It was impossible to gaze at these ever-moving pictures of nature without a feeling of joy. The dark green

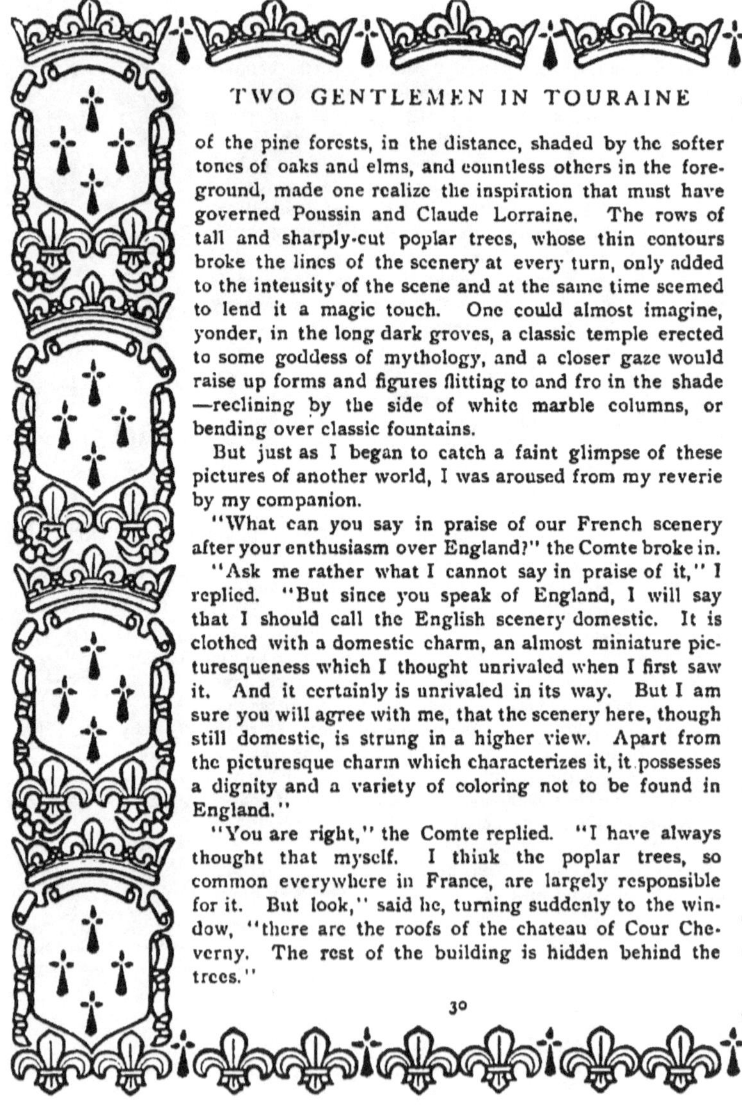

of the pine forests, in the distance, shaded by the softer tones of oaks and elms, and countless others in the foreground, made one realize the inspiration that must have governed Poussin and Claude Lorraine. The rows of tall and sharply-cut poplar trees, whose thin contours broke the lines of the scenery at every turn, only added to the intensity of the scene and at the same time seemed to lend it a magic touch. One could almost imagine, yonder, in the long dark groves, a classic temple erected to some goddess of mythology, and a closer gaze would raise up forms and figures flitting to and fro in the shade —reclining by the side of white marble columns, or bending over classic fountains.

But just as I began to catch a faint glimpse of these pictures of another world, I was aroused from my reverie by my companion.

"What can you say in praise of our French scenery after your enthusiasm over England?" the Comte broke in.

"Ask me rather what I cannot say in praise of it," I replied. "But since you speak of England, I will say that I should call the English scenery domestic. It is clothed with a domestic charm, an almost miniature picturesqueness which I thought unrivaled when I first saw it. And it certainly is unrivaled in its way. But I am sure you will agree with me, that the scenery here, though still domestic, is strung in a higher view. Apart from the picturesque charm which characterizes it, it possesses a dignity and a variety of coloring not to be found in England."

"You are right," the Comte replied. "I have always thought that myself. I think the poplar trees, so common everywhere in France, are largely responsible for it. But look," said he, turning suddenly to the window, "there are the roofs of the chateau of Cour Cheverny. The rest of the building is hidden behind the trees."

COUR CHEVERNY

"We should have stopped here on our way to Blois,"
said I.

"It is perfectly possible to do so now, and we will,"
exclaimed the Comte, seizing our bags and umbrellas in
true French excitement. But alas, just as we were about
to get out of the carriage the train started, so that we
decided to stop at the little station of Mont and walk back
to Cour Cheverny, a few miles this side of it.

"Here we are at last," said my companion, as we
alighted finally in the midst of a second thunderstorm.
"Now we shall have a walk through pretty country, and
I will tell you all I know about the chateau which we
are about to visit."

We were soon walking along a wood-lined road, somewhat muddy after the shower, and on which the trees,
above and at the side, continued to drop shining particles of water, that looked like pearls or diamonds in the
afternoon sunlight. They were chiefly pines, the trees
about us now; but as if unwilling to be excluded from
any gathering, stray clumps of poplars could be seen
rearing up their tall thin heads above the others. Here
and there, a little stream might be discovered, winding
its way along through a bit of wood, and sometimes
diving down beneath the road as we passed above.
Some old and trembling boards served as a bridge, as
they had these twenty years, and doubtless would for
twenty years to come. Out came the moving bit of
water again, only to jump down a tiny bank and lose
itself at last in some muddy pool. Now an open space
would appear, and a little farm house, almost covered
with vines (almost hidden beneath the moss and lichen
that grew upon it), would nestle itself in against a background of dark trees. Only patches of its red tiled roof
would appear, and these almost black with age, while
the soft green of the moss harmonized with the rest.
Amid such picturesque and peaceful surroundings we

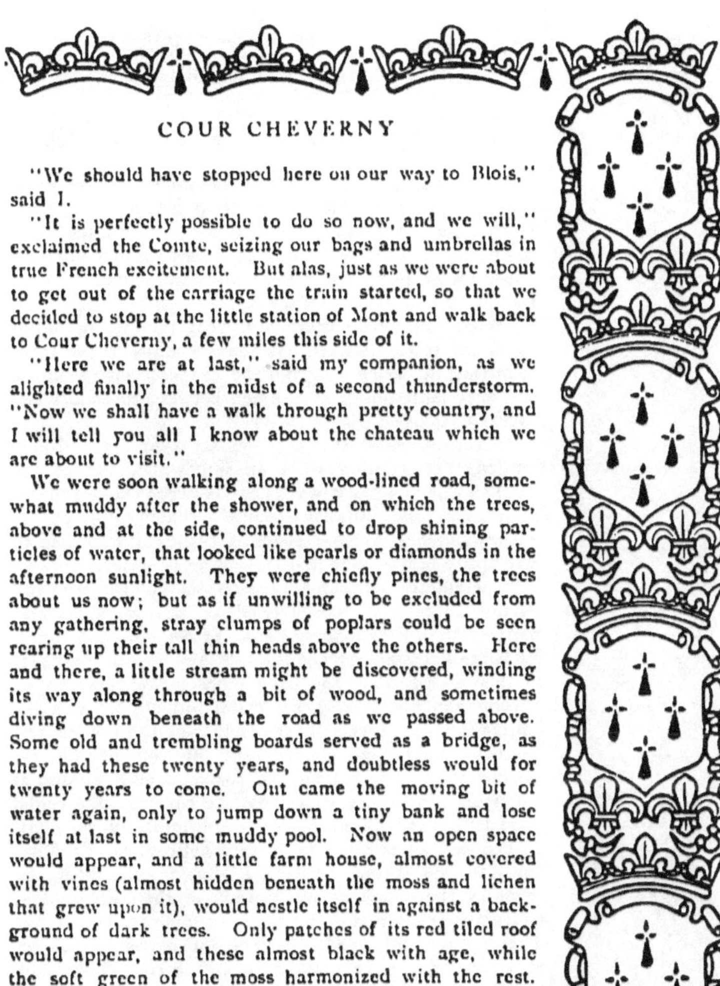

fell to speaking of the chateau before us and of other things until at last the conversation took a deeper tone. I remember that I returned to my favorite theme of comparing France with England, perhaps a dangerous one considering my companion. But at all events before I knew it, I found myself saying:

"What differences there are, what interesting differences there are, between the lower classes of the three countries: America, England and France! One seems to find even more points in common between these last two countries than between the first."

"I am surprised to hear you say that," the Comte replied, "considering what an impassable barrier the English Channel has always been between the characters of French and English people. Their attempts to understand one another seem as futile, at times, as an attempt to bridge over that stormy bit of water."

"The affinity between the lower classes of England and France," I replied, "is the result of Europe, while that between the corresponding classes of England and America is the outcome of blood relationship. And I fear that in this case Europe has been more far-reaching in its effects than blood. What I mean is just this, that the cultivation, and especially the civility of the French and English country people, peasants if you like, is far greater than it is among the corresponding classes of America. In France especially, the courtesy, the genial good will, until offended, and the interest in the most refined and artistic things, is very noticeable. In England, the peasantry—perhaps I should call them the tenantry there—are as picturesque in their life, and as civil in their address. But they are less communicative. They are well informed only upon the particular subject to which they have been born and bred. This they know, with that thoroughness which is, perhaps, one of the greatest characteristics of the English race. And the interest which they take in their subject and in their own special phase of life, is most attractive and inviting to study. Here, on the contrary, the peasants seem to show a much more varied knowledge of what is going on around them. And they display a more general fondness for the things of beauty that surround many of their lives. Very naturally their knowledge is less thorough; and probably if one investigated it, one would find very little actual intelligence. But the love of art for which the French people are so renowned seems to have come out in every class, even in the lowest, although it may be oddly mixed with the utmost simplicity and ignorance.

"In America, as well as in many parts of England, the effect of a rapid and popular legislation for the lower classes—ofter far too popular—has been to raise their ideas and ambitions far above their means or their powers of perception. By this legislation they are given powers and privileges to which they are incapable of doing justice, as well by their education as their place in society. As we see, the results are discontent and in many cases a chaotic overthrow of classes, as well as of an entire social order."

The Comte was silent for some minutes after I had finished speaking. He was evidently thinking over the various questions that presented themselves in so large a subject as this comparison and discussion of classes. At last he said:

"I have always thought that the proper solution of this great, this almost universal problem of to-day, is not the assimilation and eventual destruction of classes—for this would be obviously impossible while men live—but on the contrary, a proper ordering and division of these classes, and more than anything of their relative behavior one to another. The present troubles all over the world, in Europe as well as in America, have come, almost invariably, from the fact that various members of society abuse

the responsibilities of their positions. They come, more than anything, from the master maltreating his servant and from the servant turning against his master. One of these is as culpable as the other, and has almost always been so. The one class has been as much at fault as the other, and I do not know but that the master is most to blame, for in nine cases out of ten he has begun the abuse. Whatever their behavior may be, however, neither of these classes can live without the other. Therefore, the most philosophical way of living would be for each class to work for the other's interest, each in its own particular position, instead of continually endeavoring to change places one with another. However much they try, classes will never succeed in changing places. By so doing, they not only fail in their object, but they do much to destroy cultivation and order. Until men open their eyes wide enough to see this, all the radical legislation in the world will not effect its boasted object of bettering the condition of the lower classes. As far as I can see, from the results that we have around us, it seems only to embitter them."

The Comte had been speaking earnestly, in answering the questions which the conversation had called up to both our minds. Perhaps he had some flagrant example of this very subject before his mind to give more vehemence to his words. It was difficult for me to tell, so short had been my actual experience among his surroundings. But at all events, I learned from what he said that we were both of the same opinion in regard to this subject, however divergent we might discover ourselves to be upon others. I was glad that we had touched upon this topic, as of late it had been much impressed upon my own mind. And I looked forward to some future discussions of the same great problem with an almost youthful enthusiasm, so eager are we all in this world to dip deeply, perhaps often too deeply, into those social questions with which we are incapable of battling. But besides this, there was something deeper and more full of meaning to me in this short conversation upon a serious subject. For it told me that many fears which I had had upon my travels, fears which all of us have felt and which I had forced back, almost before they had had time to form themselves and to appear before my mind, had been unfounded. The Comte and I had not met for so long, we had lived such different lives during that time, among such different people and in such different surroundings, that there seemed every reason for us to have developed different ideas, tastes, and sympathies. And while I had been traveling through the north of France three days before, I had been unable to hide from myself the possibility of the existence of just this thing. The thought was almost a sad one; for it had cast a shadow over an otherwise cloudless sky. What if, after the correspondence which had taken place between us, and the desire on both our parts that the philosophical subjects discussed in it should be of permanent benefit to ourselves—what if, when we met again, our views had changed and we should find only disappointment and delusion? What if after our decision to spend a month together in France, devoted largely to conversations upon our favorite topics, we should find that we had ceased to be congenial? The thought and the fears which it brought with it, were not unnatural after all. How many of us have found just this delusion in our lives, more than once, and each time found it to be more painfully real! How many of us have built a beautiful ideal upon that fair-sounding name of Friendship, and found to our regret, too late, that we had failed, and that the wall fell in one moment, after it had taken years to build! How many of us there are! We dare not even stop to think how many.

So I found in my particular case, with my Comte, my

35

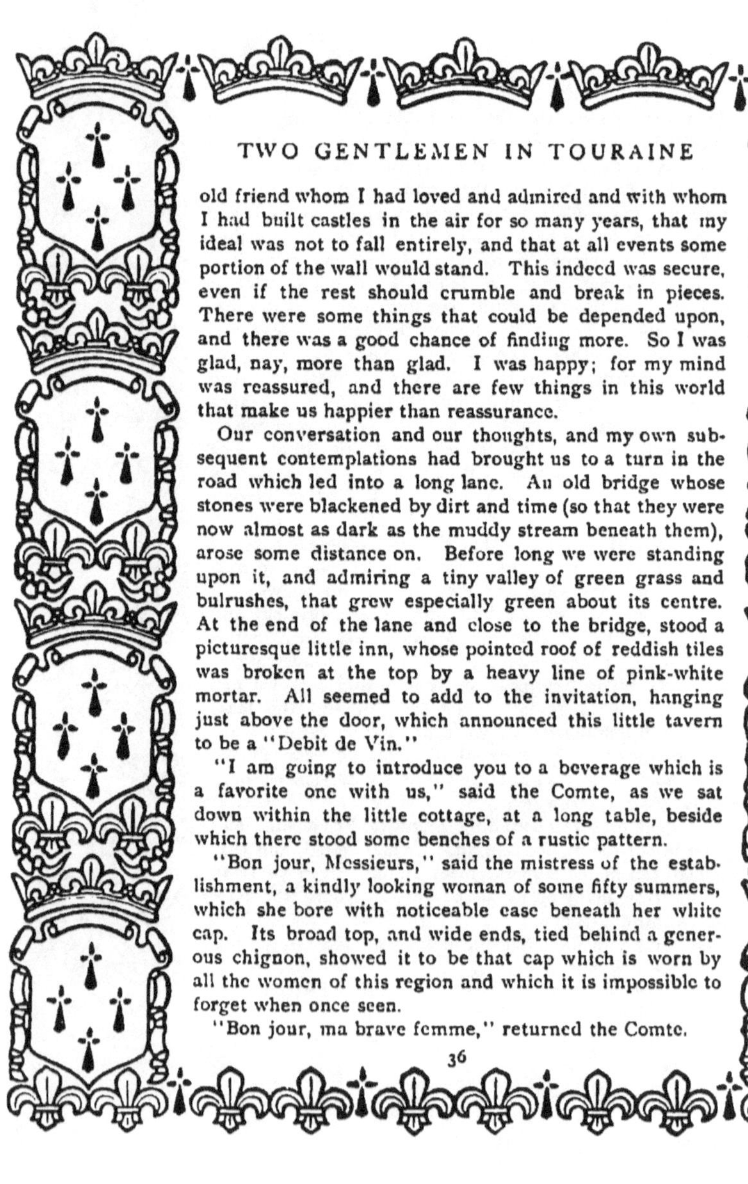

old friend whom I had loved and admired and with whom I had built castles in the air for so many years, that my ideal was not to fall entirely, and that at all events some portion of the wall would stand. This indeed was secure, even if the rest should crumble and break in pieces. There were some things that could be depended upon, and there was a good chance of finding more. So I was glad, nay, more than glad. I was happy; for my mind was reassured, and there are few things in this world that make us happier than reassurance.

Our conversation and our thoughts, and my own subsequent contemplations had brought us to a turn in the road which led into a long lane. An old bridge whose stones were blackened by dirt and time (so that they were now almost as dark as the muddy stream beneath them), arose some distance on. Before long we were standing upon it, and admiring a tiny valley of green grass and bulrushes, that grew especially green about its centre. At the end of the lane and close to the bridge, stood a picturesque little inn, whose pointed roof of reddish tiles was broken at the top by a heavy line of pink-white mortar. All seemed to add to the invitation, hanging just above the door, which announced this little tavern to be a "Debit de Vin."

"I am going to introduce you to a beverage which is a favorite one with us," said the Comte, as we sat down within the little cottage, at a long table, beside which there stood some benches of a rustic pattern.

"Bon jour, Messieurs," said the mistress of the establishment, a kindly looking woman of some fifty summers, which she bore with noticeable ease beneath her white cap. Its broad top, and wide ends, tied behind a generous chignon, showed it to be that cap which is worn by all the women of this region and which it is impossible to forget when once seen.

"Bon jour, ma brave femme," returned the Comte.

"Hélas! Messieurs, que mauvais temps nous avons pour les récolettes!" added the woman, with a very strong accent. "And what will ces messieurs take to refresh themselves?"

"Ces messieurs" would take a little curacoa and water, if she pleased. Of course she pleased, and off she went to get it.

"La—— c'est bien," said the Comte, with a contented sign, as she placed the glasses and a jug of water before us.

"Click" went the glasses in a hearty health to madame; and down went the curacoa in a surprising manner. And then we sat a moment taking in our quaint surroundings and thinking that perhaps another glass of curacoa and water might help us upon our way. Indeed, I took to curacoa and water like a true Frenchman, and the Comte was delighted at the success of his receipt.

I shall not easily forget the picturesque and mellowed scene in that little "Debit de Vin." If I had been an artist, a painter, I might perhaps have caught the inspiration of some olden days and kept it upon a bit of canvas. But I was not, alas, and it was to-day and not yesterday in which we were living, however much I might wish it to be otherwise. So I contented myself with taking in all that my eyes could grasp, and I have the scene yet before me, as clearly as it was when I was there.

The old walls were darkened with age and tobacco smoke, and the simple woodwork was so mellowed and so softened in its coloring by the misty haze of time that it might have been the most artistic carving. A great cupboard, of the time of Louis XV, stood in the corner, scarcely visible among the shadows and the little clouds of smoke about it, yet seeming to say: "Ah, if you only knew one-half the things that have taken place

before my old and worm-eaten doors! If you had only witnessed one quarter of the scenes that I have witnessed, how happy would you be! I have a past that no one knows, and that no one will ever know. I have the secrets of many a noble family 'locked into my depths, and I could tell you stories that would open your youthful eyes if I chose—stories of centuries ago that no one knows, and that no one will ever know." And the old face, carved in the pane, just above the doors of the cupboard, seemed almost to wink its eyes and move its lips, talking to itself. I was becoming strangely infatuated with the old cupboard, I found, as well as with its surroundings. The room was growing hazy with smoke, and its mistress had betaken herself to a corner, and was now darning stockings. I thought once more that the picture was worthy of a master hand, and then I was awakened from my dreams.

The crack of a whip was heard outside, and as we peered through the rather dirty window-pane, we could see an old, private omnibus draw up at the door. It was drawn by a very portly pair of French horses. A still more portly French coachman was seated upon the box, swathed in a black French livery. He was seated, I say, but it would be more correct to describe him as balancing himself upon the topmost pinnacle of a very high cushion. It was built up in the middle, so as to form a species of tower, from which he looked down upon the rest of the world. His face had a wistful expression, as though he would say: "How shall I ever get down?" At all events, it had the desired effect of looking eminently respectable, eminently old, and above all, eminently comfortable.

In some unaccountable way, while we were not looking, the coachman had managed to roll down from his dignified position, and to roll himself into the one and only room of the "Debit de Vin." His octogenarian livery seemed to breathe forth age and respectability at every wrinkle. His great black hat was ruffled up the wrong way, not unlike a turkey gobbler when it has been displeased. And the heavy whip which he dragged at his side nodded condescendingly to right and left as he entered. In another moment he was drinking his glass of white wine with an old soldier, who had a number of war stories to tell in a patois that was difficult to understand. We arose to go, and once outside, stood for some moments looking at this little rural tavern with its air of quaintness, thinking of the scene and of the characters within. The coachman came out, to mount once more upon his precarious perch, and seeing that we were on foot, he took the liberty of offering us a lift, with a great deal of bowing and scraping and a good deal of embarrassment at making advances to the "messieurs."

"If the messieurs are going as far as Cour Cheverny, perhaps I could give them a lift. It is several kilometres from here. I am going there for Madame la Baronne de M——, who is returning from Paris." And with this, the coachman took off his hat with a tremendous flourish, bowed lower than most of those who rejoice in so generous a figure are able to do, and opened the door of the omnibus. It was evident that he did not intend us to see his ascent to the box. Perhaps, we thought, he might be sensitive upon this point, so the Comte contented himself by looking through a corner of the front window, just to satisfy his curiosity. At last we were ready, and the horses were wound up and set in motion, like so many automatons. And the wheels began to move, and we realized that, somehow or other, the old coachman of Madame la Baronne was more limber than he had looked.

"Pauvre Madame de M——!" sighed the Comte, as we jogged along the even road, with a fourth thunder-storm lowering over our heads. "Pauvre Madame la Baronne!

Little does she realize, as she sleeps away the last hour of her journey from Paris, the good uses to which her omnibus is being placed. My dear friend, have you a two franc piece? I have used up all my change."

I had, and the Comte could breathe more easily, now that his sudden fear was allayed. Before many minutes we were in the little town of Cour Cheverny, and leaving our kindly friend the coachman, with many thanks and with the two franc piece, we proceeded at once to the gates of the chateau.

And what was the first impression which we received? What effect upon us was produced by the approach to the first of this wonderful group of historical monuments, which we were about to visit? Alas, I fear it was a little of a disappointment, for although the estates of Cheverny are very large, the cultivated portion of the park is only fifty acres. The entrance is therefore a little unsatisfactory, although it is impossible to be indifferent to its picturesque surroundings.

An old arch, built of pinkish brick and cream-white stone, in the period of Louis XIII, appeared at the opening of a high wall which we had been following. As we passed beneath it, I could not refrain from remarking that it bore a certain resemblance to the old Temple Bar of London. It was Temple Bar in pink and white, Temple Bar looking newer and brighter than the original. As we emerged from beneath it, the children of the gate-keeper presented themselves for a salutation, and there being no one else to ask, the Comte accosted them.

"Is Monsieur le Marquis at home?"

"Non, messieurs!" answered the whole flock at once. "He will not return for a month. But there is no one at the chateau, and the messieurs may see everything, if they care to."

"Ah, as I thought," said the Comte, not heeding the children's last remark. "Monsieur de V—— is generally here in the autumn and winter only, when, however, he is always surrounded by plenty of company, for his family alone numbers twenty."

As he spoke we emerged from a large group of trees and shrubs and reached the open space before the chateau. A long, symmetrical building stood before us, built of the most brilliant white stone, whose yellowish tint reminded one of milk that has been left over night for the cream to form upon it. The unbroken façade stretched away for nearly three hundred feet, and as we stood at one end of it, the whole chateau seemed a long, narrow elevation. On the other side, the effect had been somewhat changed by two wings, projecting into a moat. This moat had been filled with ivy, greens and flowers, that almost covered its stone sides, and grew about the arches of an old bridge, leading from the rear of the chateau. The stone used here is different from that in front, and the effect is softer, being of a grayish hue. As we retraced our steps, and came back to the first façade, the contrast made the brilliant coloring of its stone even more noticeable. The facings here were such as to produce the appearance of clapboards of wood, instead of stone, and as might be supposed, this effect lessened the beauty of the architecture, which was that of the famous Philibert Delorme.

As in so many of the greater French chateaux, so in Cheverny we miss instinctively that natural and softer finish, always such a feature in the English country house. The ivy, that is there allowed to climb over the walls and to soften a façade perhaps otherwise too harsh, is absent here. No shrubs or growth of any kind are allowed to break the formal symmetry of the façade. The grass and lawns even are at a distance, and the only relief from the glare of the unsympathetic gravel, covering the open space before the chateau, is a row of orange trees. And even these seem stunted in their growth, as

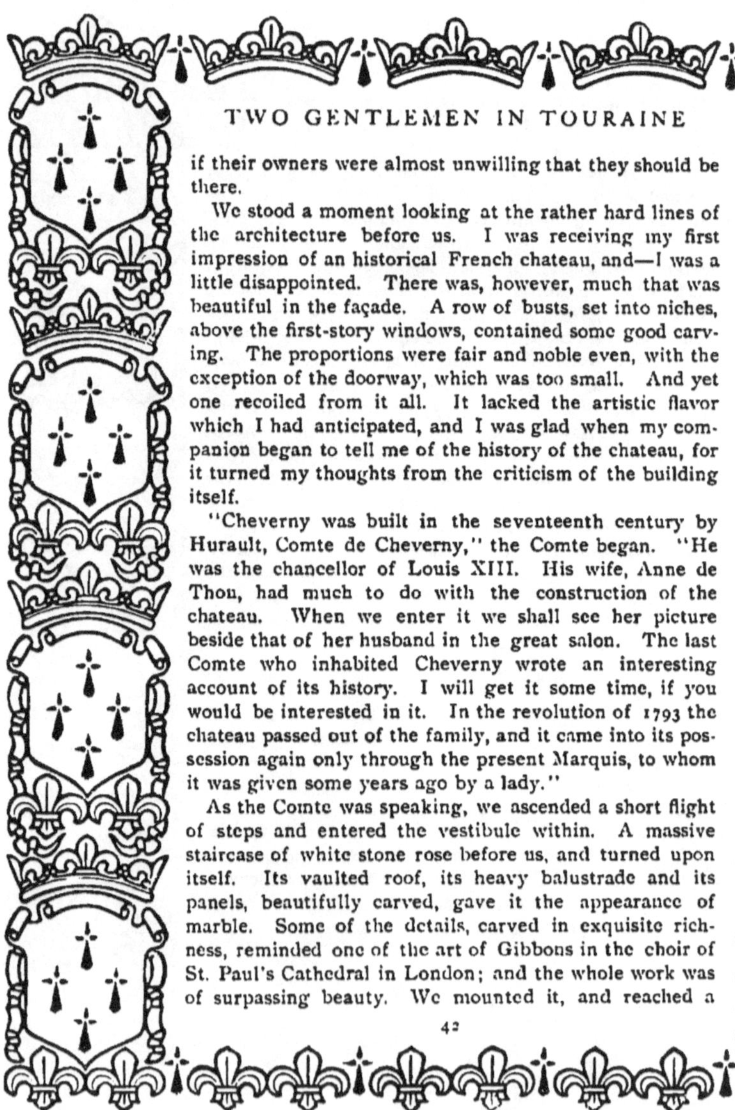

if their owners were almost unwilling that they should be there.

We stood a moment looking at the rather hard lines of the architecture before us. I was receiving my first impression of an historical French chateau, and—I was a little disappointed. There was, however, much that was beautiful in the façade. A row of busts, set into niches, above the first-story windows, contained some good carving. The proportions were fair and noble even, with the exception of the doorway, which was too small. And yet one recoiled from it all. It lacked the artistic flavor which I had anticipated, and I was glad when my companion began to tell me of the history of the chateau, for it turned my thoughts from the criticism of the building itself.

"Cheverny was built in the seventeenth century by Hurault, Comte de Cheverny," the Comte began. "He was the chancellor of Louis XIII. His wife, Anne de Thou, had much to do with the construction of the chateau. When we enter it we shall see her picture beside that of her husband in the great salon. The last Comte who inhabited Cheverny wrote an interesting account of its history. I will get it some time, if you would be interested in it. In the revolution of 1793 the chateau passed out of the family, and it came into its possession again only through the present Marquis, to whom it was given some years ago by a lady."

As the Comte was speaking, we ascended a short flight of steps and entered the vestibule within. A massive staircase of white stone rose before us, and turned upon itself. Its vaulted roof, its heavy balustrade and its panels, beautifully carved, gave it the appearance of marble. Some of the details, carved in exquisite richness, reminded one of the art of Gibbons in the choir of St. Paul's Cathedral in London; and the whole work was of surpassing beauty. We mounted it, and reached a gallery above, which led to the guard chamber, the principal room of the chateau and one which was worthy of a royal residence. From this beautiful room, which it would take too long to describe in detail, we passed into the "King's room," built for Henry IV of France. It was filled with Flemish tapestries of a high order, the bed being draped also with them. Perhaps the most interesting thing in this room is the King's trunk, a massive chest studded with nails, which stands in one of the deep recesses of the windows.

The gallery and dining-room beneath these apartments are wonderfully rich in ornament, the furniture being carved in the most elaborate manner. On the other side of the vestibule is a boudoir, hung with a series of pastelles in oval frames. They looked as if they might have been by Greuze, so delicate was their coloring and so soft their effect. On the top of a high cabinet rested the helmet and cuirasse of Henry V, Comte de Chambord, when a child. The miniature bits of armor, beautifully fashioned and perfect in every detail, spoke eloquently of their dead master. We left this boudoir somewhat subdued and impressed. It seemed almost an inner atrium, a sacred spot, where that which was most personal to the chateau had been collected.

Passing through a billiard room, where the most noticeable object was a collection of minerals gathered together by the father of the present owner, we came to the grand salon. This room, like most of the interior of the chateau, is entirely decorated in the elaborate style of the Renaissance. The beams of the ceiling are left unplastered, and like portions of the Chateau of Blois, are painted in an intricate detail. The walls are decorated in a similar manner, and a beautiful collection of pictures has been let into the panels. Nothing can exceed the startling effect which this form of decoration

produces upon the observer to whom it is new. It seems almost fantastic, so unaccustomed to it are we. But after a comparison of the variety of its details with the decora-tions of the rest of the chateau, we are forced to the con-clusion that this portion of it is almost simple. The more temperate shades which have here been employed, lose somewhat in their startling effect when contrasted with the brilliancy of reds and yellows, and at length we are induced almost to accept this strange mélange of orna-ment as beautiful. A large and very artistic looking portrait caught my eye.

"That is Philipe de Vibraye," explained the Comte, who had not spoken for some time. "Here is his wife; a fine picture, is it not? That picture beyond, of Mlle. de Saumery, is by Mignard. And here we have Mlle. de Montpensier, Louise, 'la grande Mademoiselle,' the cousin of Louis XIII. There are Hurault de Vibrage and his wife, Anne de Thou. You remember I spoke of these pictures before we came in."

We paused a moment in front of the portraits of these two personages who had built Cheverny, and then passed on to a beautiful Van Dyke, a portrait of the Comte de Midicis. This, with a beautiful picture of Anne of Austria, and a copy of Raphael, concluded the collection. Before leaving this room, however, in which were gath-ered together so many works of art and so much that was beautiful, we looked for a few moments at the view out of the back windows. It was worth looking at and remembering. Directly opposite, and at the further end of a great lawn, surrounded by shrubs and flowers, stood a beautiful little building, one story in height. The brilliant whiteness of its stone set off the details of a pure bit of Louis XV architecture, and its slate roof rose so high above the round windows of the upper portion of the wall, that in any other country than France it would have seemed out of proportion.

"That was used as an 'ambulance' in the war of 1870," my companion explained, as we once more emerged from the chateau. "The great lawn in front, ending in one of those long vistas, only to be found in French parks, was originally laid out in 'jardins à la française,' but it is now allowed to produce, in undisturbed tranquillity, an indifferent crop of grass."

Walks and avenues on our right led into bowers of unknown depth and beauty, and clumps of trees, which looked like the opening of a forest, overhung the path. We had no time to test their true extent, however, for the afternoon had worn away before we knew it, and our visit was coming to an end all too soon. As we wound our way homeward, through a garden (enclosing within its high, old-fashioned walls, flowers and fruit and all that goes to make a garden alluring to the heart), and through the stable courts, showing here and there a bit of ancient carving, high against a tower, I looked back upon my first experience of an historical chateau, with mingled feelings of pleasure and of disappointment. Like all things which we picture to our minds, it had been different from what I had expected. But like some others also, it had proved more beautiful in many ways than I could have imagined. The first of this group of chateaux, which we had so wished to see, the first of that wonderful galaxy of architectural beauty, the first of that historic group of royal and noble residences, which are famous the world over as the Chateaux of the Loire, had passed before us and was left behind. Even now it had faded away into the shades of the night.

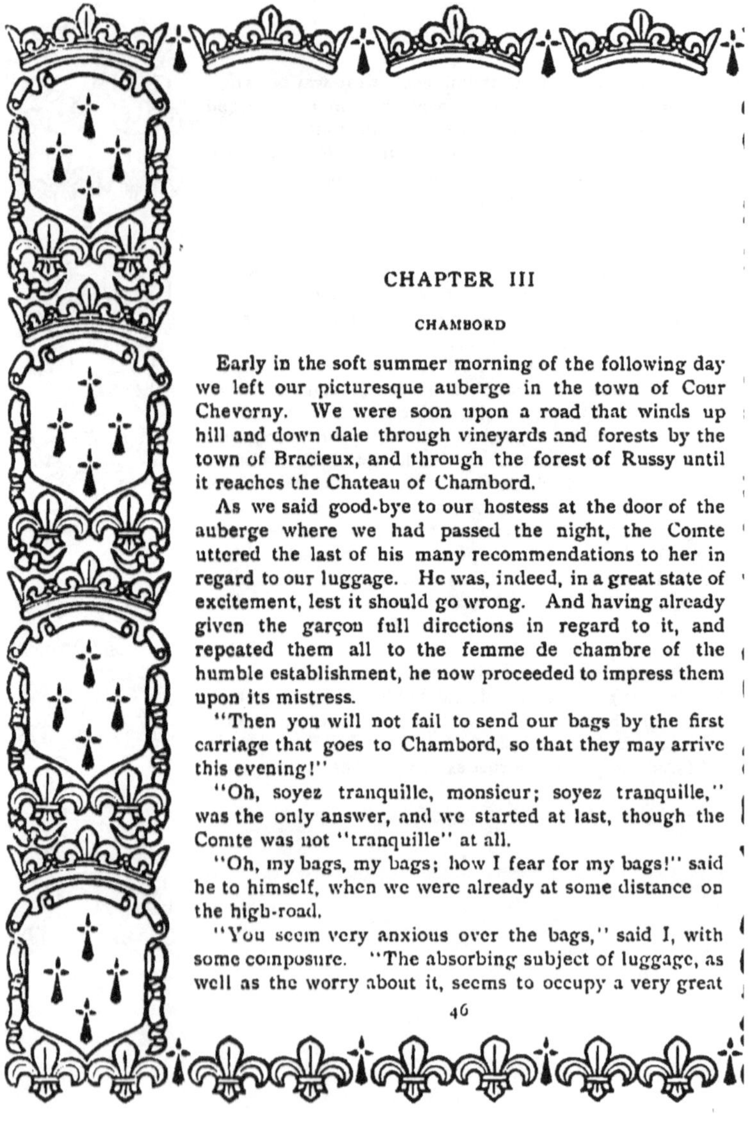

CHAPTER III

Early in the soft summer morning of the following day we left our picturesque auberge in the town of Cour Cheverny. We were soon upon a road that winds up hill and down dale through vineyards and forests by the town of Bracieux, and through the forest of Russy until it reaches the Chateau of Chambord.

As we said good-bye to our hostess at the door of the auberge where we had passed the night, the Comte uttered the last of his many recommendations to her in regard to our luggage. He was, indeed, in a great state of excitement, lest it should go wrong. And having already given the garçon full directions in regard to it, and repeated them all to the femme de chambre of the humble establishment, he now proceeded to impress them upon its mistress.

"Then you will not fail to send our bags by the first carriage that goes to Chambord, so that they may arrive this evening!"

"Oh, soyez tranquille, monsieur; soyez tranquille," was the only answer, and we started at last, though the Comte was not "tranquille" at all.

"Oh, my bags, my bags; how I fear for my bags!" said he to himself, when we were already at some distance on the high-road.

"You seem very anxious over the bags," said I, with some composure. "The absorbing subject of luggage, as well as the worry about it, seems to occupy a very great

46

place in French minds. In our country we check our
luggage, and do not bother ourselves about it until it
reaches its destination. It is very simple."

"Have you not been in France long enough to learn
that nothing is simple here?" replied my companion.
"All is more or less complicated, and nothing more so
than explanations. We have always to start from the
beginning, to stop and consider each point, then to
repeat it all over once so as to impress it upon the mind.
Then it has to be repeated a second time, to keep it
impressed, and still a third time for the impression to
sink deeply into the intelligence and to have its desired
effect. Do you suppose, for instance, if I had said to our
landlady this morning, 'Ma brave femme, you must send
our luggage to Chambord,' do you suppose there would
have been the least chance of its getting there? Certainly not. I was obliged first, to tell her the number of
pieces, then where she could find them in the room
(without looking for them), then the simplest means of
getting them to Chambord, which I found was by the
'diligence' to Bracieux and by a private cart from there.
Then I was forced to extract, with some difficulty, the
price, and finally to state that I would pay exactly one
half of what was asked and that only when the luggage
was delivered. All this had to be repeated, over and
over again, at least three times. So you see," the
Comte concluded triumphantly, "luggage is not such a
simple matter, after all."

I could not repress a smile, as I asked: "And are you
satisfied, even now, of the safety of our bags?'

"Certainly not," was the decided answer, "nor shall I
be, until I see them, safe and sound, this evening."

By this time we had walked some distance, and our
road was now crossing a plateau covered with vineyards
and with, here and there, the trees of a park, broken by
the pointed roofs of some small chateau. Two young

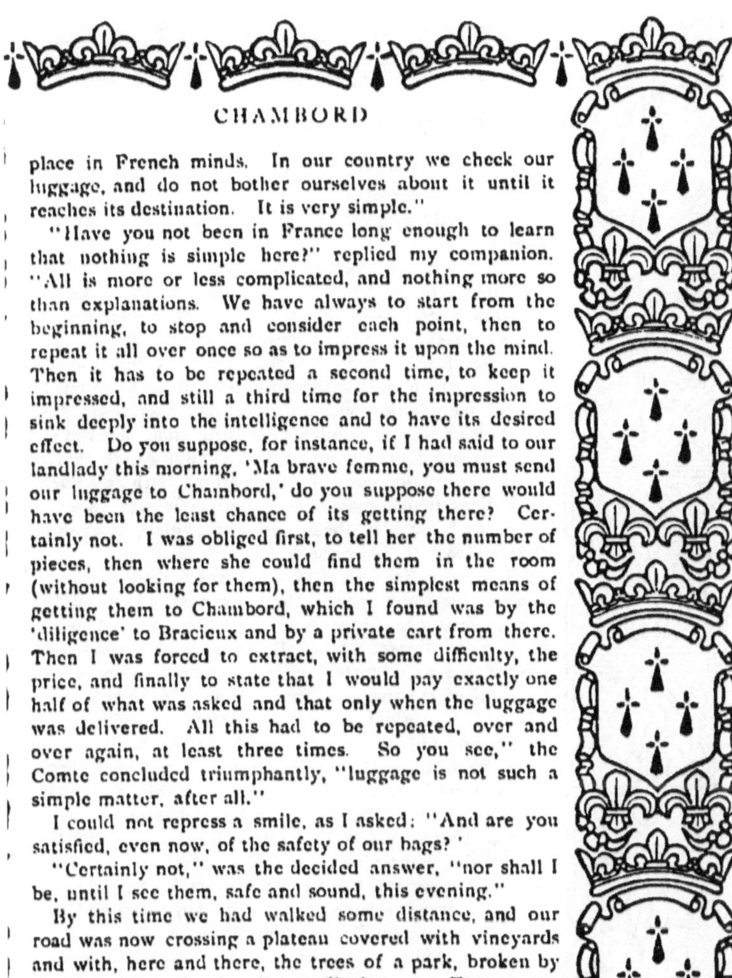

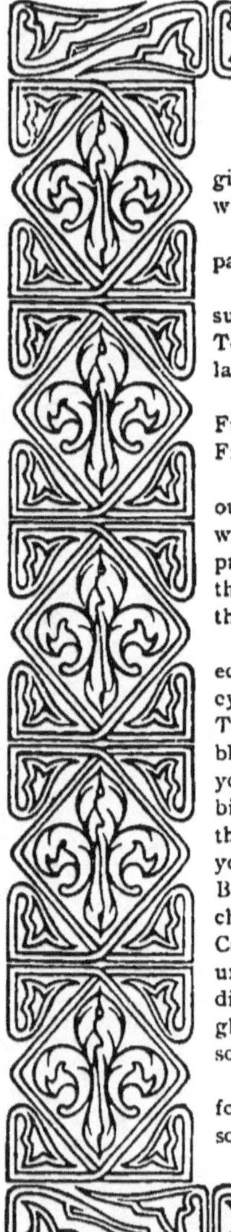

girls appeared upon the road, with flannel dresses and with white sailor hats.

"Evidently English girls," I remarked to my companion.

"And why not French?" asked the Comte. "Do you suppose," he added, "that in our damp climate of Touraine there are no French girls with golden hair and large blue eyes and fair complexions?"

"I am afraid," said I, "that I have too often associated French golden hair with some form of preparation, and French complexion with a good deal of making-up."

"At this rate you leave very little that is genuine to our fair sex," the Comte replied. "But I wish that you would place aside your old associations, with any Puritan prejudices which may have found their way in among them, and consider these two young girls, as examples that are easy to find here."

They were French, after all; I was forced to acknowledge it, for their speech, their manners, and even their eyes, were peculiarly Latin, as they passed us by. They were dressed identically alike, and a strong resemblance told us that they were undoubtedly sisters. The younger of the two was teaching the elder to ride upon a bicycle. The Comte did not approve of this exercise, I think, nor did he find it entirely fitting for these two young girls to be alone upon the high-road to Bracieux. But the roofs of a pretty chateau, half hidden by large chestnut trees, appeared near by and seemed, to the Comte at all events, to be a sort of silent sponsor for these unattended young ladies. He looked ahead in the most dignified manner; but I must confess I allowed a stray glance to wander back to those golden locks, and I had some little difficulty in recalling it again.

"Don't, don't," said the Comte. "We shall be taken for tourists of the worst sort." But the temptation was so great that, in spite of my friend's disapproving remark,

I looked again—and they looked and "our eyes kissed," as a Frenchman would say.

This meeting with the two young ladies riding their bicycles upon the high-road did not seem to put the Comte in as pleasant a mood as it did me. Poor Comte, ever so afraid that his foreign companion might not receive the most favorable impression of France and of the French people!

Before long, we passed a little village of no importance but very pretty—Tour-en-Sologne. Beyond this, the valley of the river Beuvron runs, for a hundred and twenty-five kilometres, through the country of Sologne. We crossed the road from Blois to Bracieux at right angles, and stopped for a few moments to rest at a little auberge, over whose doorway there hung a sign bearing the familiar inscription, "Loge à pied et à cheval." A small wooden table and two straw-covered chairs were placed at our disposal, in front of this diminutive public-house, and before many moments we were contentedly sipping our proverbial curacoa and water. A young woman was washing and scrubbing the small panes of glass in the windows, for it was Saturday—a washing day the world over. We endeavored to draw her into conversation, but for all our efforts we could but extract the rather laconic answers of "yes" and "no."

"So this is the road to Bracieux?" we enquired.

"Yes," answered the woman.

"Is it a pleasant bourg?"

"I don't know. I've never been there."

"And the little chateau on our right—to whom does it belong?" I asked.

"I don't know."

"What is the name of it?" put in the Comte.

"I don't know. I've never been there."

"Probably you have just arrived in this part of the country?" suggested the Comte, in some amusement.

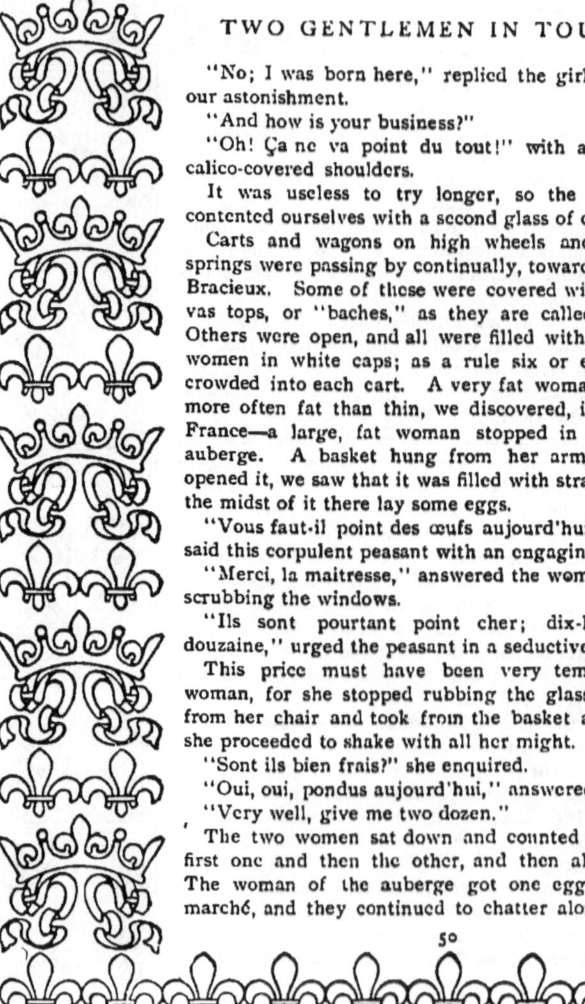

"No; I was born here," replied the girl, somewhat to our astonishment.

"And how is your business?"

"Oh! Ça ne va point du tout!" with a shrug of her calico-covered shoulders.

It was useless to try longer, so the Comte and I contented ourselves with a second glass of curacoa.

Carts and wagons on high wheels and innocent of springs were passing by continually, toward the village of Bracieux. Some of these were covered with green canvas tops, or "baches," as they are called in Sologne. Others were open, and all were filled with peasants and women in white caps; as a rule six or eight of them crowded into each cart. A very fat woman—people are more often fat than thin, we discovered, in this part of France—a large, fat woman stopped in front of the auberge. A basket hung from her arm, and as she opened it, we saw that it was filled with straw and that in the midst of it there lay some eggs.

"Vous faut-il point des œufs aujourd'hui, messieurs?" said this corpulent peasant with an engaging smile.

"Merci, la maitresse," answered the woman for us, still scrubbing the windows.

"Ils sont pourtant point cher; dix-huit sous la douzaine," urged the peasant in a seductive tone.

This price must have been very tempting to the woman, for she stopped rubbing the glass, came down from her chair and took from the basket an egg, which she proceeded to shake with all her might.

"Sont ils bien frais?" she enquired.

"Oui, oui, pondus aujourd'hui," answered the peasant.

"Very well, give me two dozen."

The two women sat down and counted out the eggs, first one and then the other, and then all over again. The woman of the auberge got one egg pardessus le marché, and they continued to chatter along at a great rate, and we left them still chattering, while the carts were still passing toward Bracieux in an unbroken stream.

"Bracieux, Bracieux? The name sounds familiar to me," said I, as we started once more.

"Of course it does," said the Comte. "Who does not know Dumas' "Trois Mousquetaires"? and that le sire de Bracieux plays a conspicuous part in that famous history. The village yonder, with its white steeple, half hidden behind the silver leaves of the willows, bears the same name though hardly the same fame. It is very well known for its market, however, which brings many people to the place every week. It is one of the best in Sologne, and indeed Bracieux is better known for its butcher (who is no mean celebrity) than it is for itself. His meat is greatly sought after by all the neighboring chateaux, and their owners come to Bracieux once a week for supplies. I might even tell you—although you have neglected to ask me—that this butcher sells his meat, at present, for eighteen cents a pound. I say at present, because the price of meat is one of the most conservative things that there are in France. It hardly ever changes more than a sou or two, in a lifetime."

"You seem to be a perfect rural encyclopedia, my dear friend," I replied, amused. "One may go to you, and not in vain, even for the price of meat. Really this is most instructive."

"Well, well, all things have their importance, and if you had ever directed a chateau in France you would have learned how useful it is to know all these little details. If one entertains a large number of people, not only the guests but the servants, who in any house amount to fourteen or fifteen, have to be looked after and fed. And, pray, who is to see to all this, if not the master?" And here the Comte gave a frantic wave of his hand in the air, as if to emphasize more distinctly his remark. "Nothing in France," he continued, "makes us

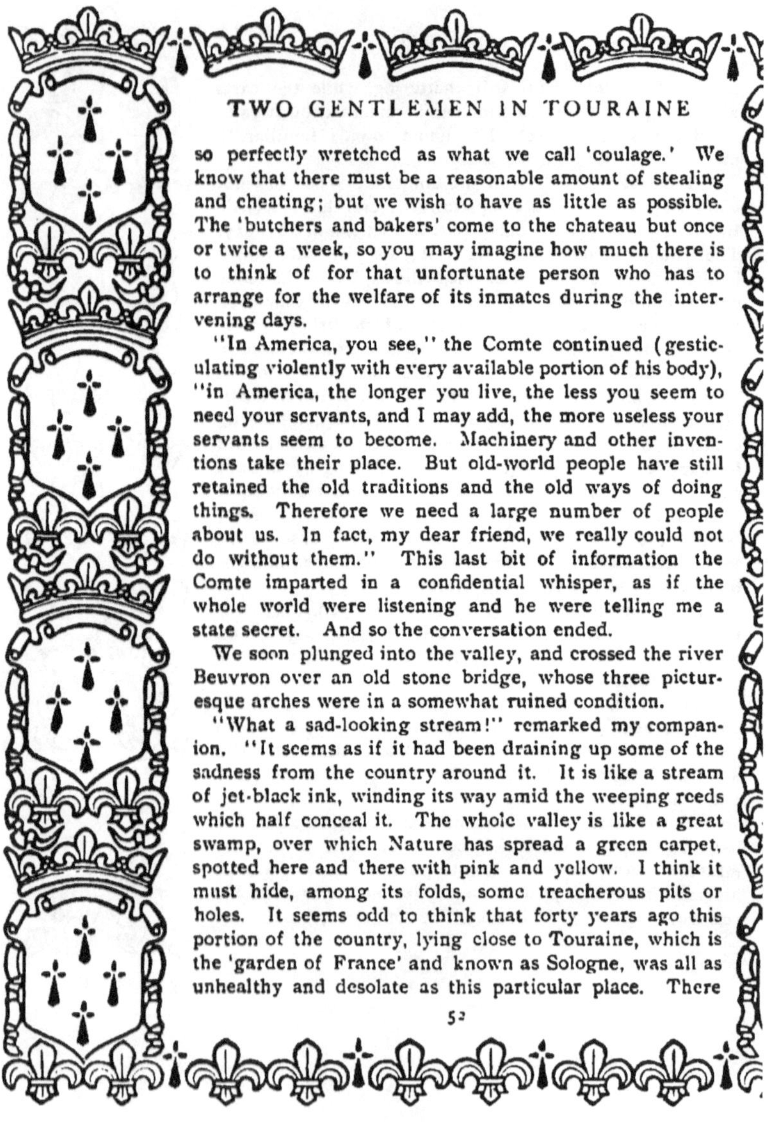

so perfectly wretched as what we call 'coulage.' We know that there must be a reasonable amount of stealing and cheating; but we wish to have as little as possible. The 'butchers and bakers' come to the chateau but once or twice a week, so you may imagine how much there is to think of for that unfortunate person who has to arrange for the welfare of its inmates during the intervening days.

"In America, you see," the Comte continued (gesticulating violently with every available portion of his body), "in America, the longer you live, the less you seem to need your servants, and I may add, the more useless your servants seem to become. Machinery and other inventions take their place. But old-world people have still retained the old traditions and the old ways of doing things. Therefore we need a large number of people about us. In fact, my dear friend, we really could not do without them." This last bit of information the Comte imparted in a confidential whisper, as if the whole world were listening and he were telling me a state secret. And so the conversation ended.

We soon plunged into the valley, and crossed the river Beuvron over an old stone bridge, whose three picturesque arches were in a somewhat ruined condition.

"What a sad-looking stream!" remarked my companion. "It seems as if it had been draining up some of the sadness from the country around it. It is like a stream of jet-black ink, winding its way amid the weeping reeds which half conceal it. The whole valley is like a great swamp, over which Nature has spread a green carpet, spotted here and there with pink and yellow. I think it must hide, among its folds, some treacherous pits or holes. It seems odd to think that forty years ago this portion of the country, lying close to Touraine, which is the 'garden of France' and known as Sologne, was all as unhealthy and desolate as this particular place. There

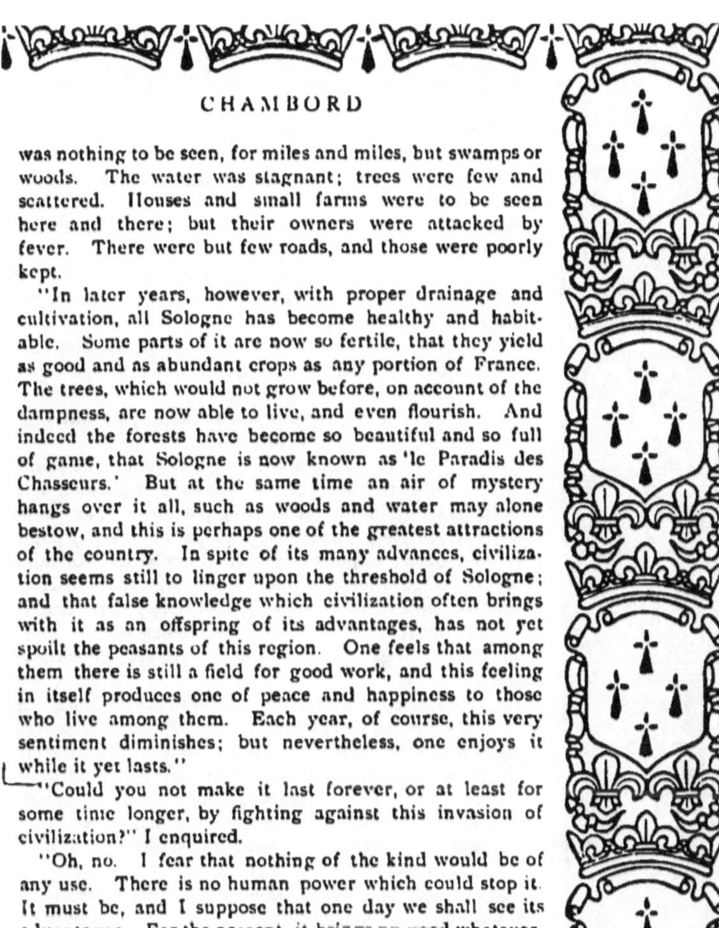

was nothing to be seen, for miles and miles, but swamps or woods. The water was stagnant; trees were few and scattered. Houses and small farms were to be seen here and there; but their owners were attacked by fever. There were but few roads, and those were poorly kept.

"In later years, however, with proper drainage and cultivation, all Sologne has become healthy and habitable. Some parts of it are now so fertile, that they yield as good and as abundant crops as any portion of France. The trees, which would not grow before, on account of the dampness, are now able to live, and even flourish. And indeed the forests have become so beautiful and so full of game, that Sologne is now known as 'le Paradis des Chasseurs.' But at the same time an air of mystery hangs over it all, such as woods and water may alone bestow, and this is perhaps one of the greatest attractions of the country. In spite of its many advances, civilization seems still to linger upon the threshold of Sologne; and that false knowledge which civilization often brings with it as an offspring of its advantages, has not yet spoilt the peasants of this region. One feels that among them there is still a field for good work, and this feeling in itself produces one of peace and happiness to those who live among them. Each year, of course, this very sentiment diminishes; but nevertheless, one enjoys it while it yet lasts."

"Could you not make it last forever, or at least for some time longer, by fighting against this invasion of civilization?" I enquired.

"Oh, no. I fear that nothing of the kind would be of any use. There is no human power which could stop it. It must be, and I suppose that one day we shall see its advantages. For the present, it brings no good whatever, nothing but rebellion against that which has always been and which is only replaced, in these days, by something

undesirable. Periods of social transition, my friend," the Comte continued, shaking his head, "beware of them; beware of them. The reaction will come one day, however; and may it be a sound one when it does."

"I fear that Providence alone will have to create this reaction, for you do not seem to help her much in the matter," I ventured to remark.

"Well, yes, perhaps, perhaps. But let us drop the subject. I suppose we must endure those things which we cannot avoid."

"And that through your own fault, you old fogy conservatives," I added, with a smile.

"Ah, I know it. But, my friend, I cannot fight alone, so let us drop the subject, as I already suggested, and live for a while in this crumbling past which has for us conservatives such a saddened fascination. What could give us a better opportunity than Chambord? Remains of great things and great men, both have their fascination. Remains of rank, royalty, and riches must and do have this, more than anything else, indescribably more than those things which claim to interest us without them."

We pursued our way for some time in deep silence. A little in front of us, and close to the stream, there appeared in sight a pretty "gentilhommiere," of the fifteenth century, whose high-pointed roofs were just visible through the poplar trees which mounted guard upon the banks. Its name was Villesavin. The yellow walls, pierced here and there by ornamented windows, showed in a mild relief against the green about them.

"Let us stop and ask if we may visit this place," said the Comte. "It makes me think of some nest containing birds, built upon a reed bending over the river. It should be half concealed, like this, by wide, pointed leaves and should show only when the wind moved them aside. The bird is called Loriot, I believe. His plumage

is beautiful and bright. Do let us take one look at the
bird that inhabits this nest."

"You might liken it to a cage as well as to a nest," I
answered, "for see how small is the park which surrounds
it."

"Yes, that is true; but cage or nest, let us try and get
into it." And we walked along, beside the gray walls of
the inclosure, until we came to a modern gateway, placed
between two round towers that seemed, on the contrary, to be fairly overwhelmed with age. We pulled at
the iron bell-rope, and an answer came back to us, in the
deep, bass note of the bell. Soon after, the key turned in
the door and an old woman, who looked as if she might
be an elder sister to the two towers, poked out her head
just far enough for us to see a pointed nose and a
still more pointed chin. She looked not unlike the
wicked fairy, who used always to be present at the
christening of bygone princesses, and to throw upon
them her enchantment.

"May we visit the park and the chateau?" enquired the
Comte.

"I will go and see," muttered the old woman, between
her toothless jaws, and so saying, she closed the postern
once more upon us, and we could see only the tops of the
trees sweeping over the high walls. They were so thick
that their branches seemed to intermingle, as if centuries
had passed since they were first planted, and as if all had
fallen asleep since then and still slept, thus leaving the
trees to grow unmolested and in all directions. They
were so thick that their branches, covered with ever-
greens and ivy, seemed almost impenetrable. We waited
outside for some time, sitting upon a large stone. The
footsteps of the old fairy sounded, in a strange staccato,
upon the graveled path. Soon they grew indistinct.
A murmur of voices, brought by a gust of wind, came
toward us, and died away; all was silent again.

55

"How strangely unreal, how sad, and yet how alluring is this place!" said the Comte. "I feel as if we were
upon the threshold of some haunted or secret palace
which we were about to enter, and from which we were
never to return. They are discussing whether or not
we are worthy to be received into these sacred precincts;
and we are awaiting their decision with beating hearts."

"They take certainly time enough to make up their
minds," said I.

"Perhaps it is a chance, a last chance, which Heaven
gives us, to escape from that fate which overhangs
all who go therein. Let us wait no longer. I am
afraid; yes, I feel afraid to cross the threshold of
this crumbling door. Let us hasten away from this
haunted place, and as we flee, let us not cast our eyes
behind us, lest they meet those of the old fairy who
seems to have already thrown a strange and mysterious
charm over me and over my thoughts. For pity's sake, I
entreat you to leave. The gray towers, the trees, the
walls with their clusters of leaves so dark that they seem
almost black, how they all stare at us, as if somehow we
were a prey to them. But hark! There are the steps
upon the gravel. They grow more distinct. They are
louder. It is too late to run—too late." And the postern
opened, only ajar, showing a deep wall of green and a
path winding its way through it and lost in a further
one, greener, deeper, thicker yet. The pointed nose and
the still more pointed chin of the wicked fairy made their
way through a crack of the door, and at last, a husky,
hollow voice cried, in a dissonant key:

"Young men, this is an abode of love. Behind these
bowers and walls of stone, a god, my master, conceals
the goddess of his dreams. Woe to that man who shall
lose himself in this veil of mystery; and woe to him
who, wandering through these paths, shall cross the
winged god. His arrow, poisoned, never misses its

mark. Go, young men, and retrace your steps. Beware,
lest you ring this bell again, for Love might escape from
the door, ajar, and the master would pursue you. Woe,
woe to you, if you should cross his path!" And the
door banged to, so hard that the towers of stone seemed
to shake, and the trees seemed to whisper "beware!"

"Well, my dear fellow, if this is what you called French
hospitality, many thanks for it."

"Do not joke about such serious matters," returned
the Comte, in the most concerned manner. "This
woman will bring to us some ill luck; I feel sure of it.
Why did we stop? Why did we ever ring this cursed
bell?"

"So you believe in the evil eye, then?" I asked.

"Oh, no. But there is, however, in all of those who
belong to the Latin races, a latent germ of superstition
which cannot be killed, and against which we fight in
vain. Therefore, let us drop a heavy curtain over
Villesavin and its impressions; let us blot it out from
our lives and never mention it or think of it again."

"Very well," said I, and turning toward the object of
our aversion I added: "Farewell, wicked fairy; good-bye
forever, and welcome the beautiful forest of Russy!"

"Here we are, at the very entrance of the forest,"
broke in my friend, "on the avenue called 'l'allée du
Roi.' It is so long and straight, that it is lost in the horizon, without making a single curve. The trees, which
join over our heads like the vaults of a flamboyant
cathedral, grow nearer together in the distance, and
the vaults grow smaller, until they seem finally to join,
far away before us. I wonder if you see all this as I do,
and if you feel the same enchanted air hanging over
everything?" and the Comte turned to me with an
enquiring look, as he added, "I wish that I could make
you understand the fears and expectations which are
passing through my mind just now. You know that I

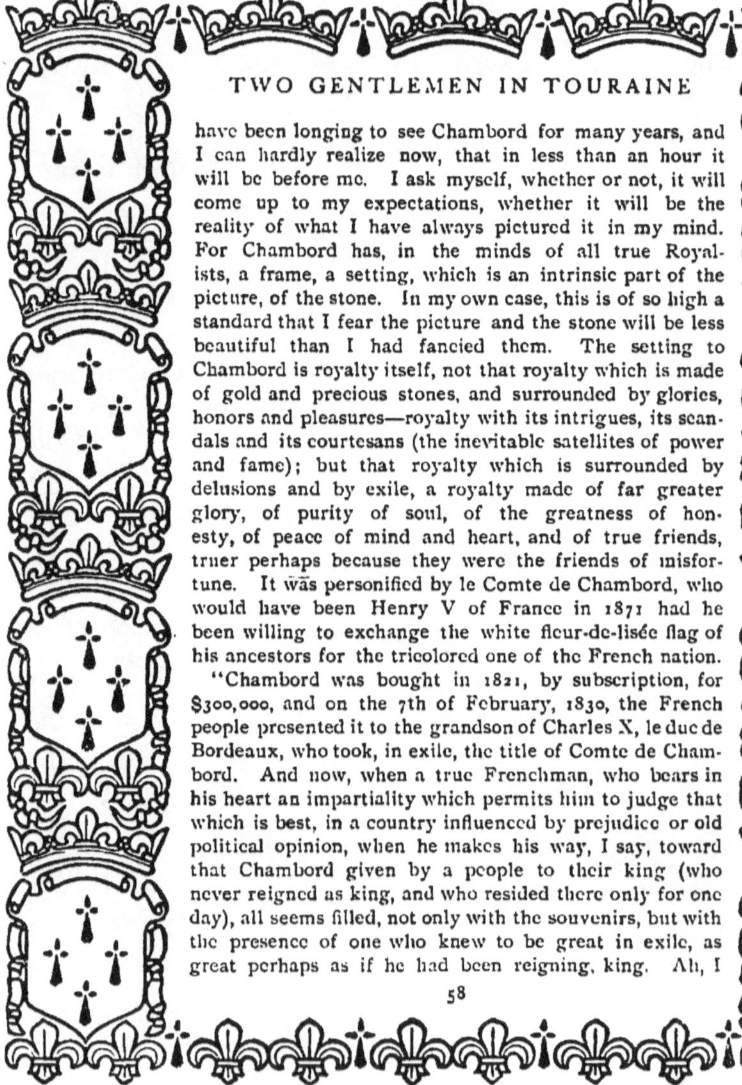

have been longing to see Chambord for many years, and I can hardly realize now, that in less than an hour it will be before me. I ask myself, whether or not, it will come up to my expectations, whether it will be the reality of what I have always pictured it in my mind. For Chambord has, in the minds of all true Royalists, a frame, a setting, which is an intrinsic part of the picture, of the stone. In my own case, this is of so high a standard that I fear the picture and the stone will be less beautiful than I had fancied them. The setting to Chambord is royalty itself, not that royalty which is made of gold and precious stones, and surrounded by glories, honors and pleasures—royalty with its intrigues, its scandals and its courtesans (the inevitable satellites of power and fame); but that royalty which is surrounded by delusions and by exile, a royalty made of far greater glory, of purity of soul, of the greatness of honesty, of peace of mind and heart, and of true friends, truer perhaps because they were the friends of misfortune. It was personified by le Comte de Chambord, who would have been Henry V of France in 1871 had he been willing to exchange the white fleur-de-lisée flag of his ancestors for the tricolored one of the French nation.

"Chambord was bought in 1821, by subscription, for $300,000, and on the 7th of February, 1830, the French people presented it to the grandson of Charles X, le duc de Bordeaux, who took, in exile, the title of Comte de Chambord. And now, when a true Frenchman, who bears in his heart an impartiality which permits him to judge that which is best, in a country influenced by prejudice or old political opinion, when he makes his way, I say, toward that Chambord given by a people to their king (who never reigned as king, and who resided there only for one day), all seems filled, not only with the souvenirs, but with the presence of one who knew to be great in exile, as great perhaps as if he had been reigning, king. Ah, I

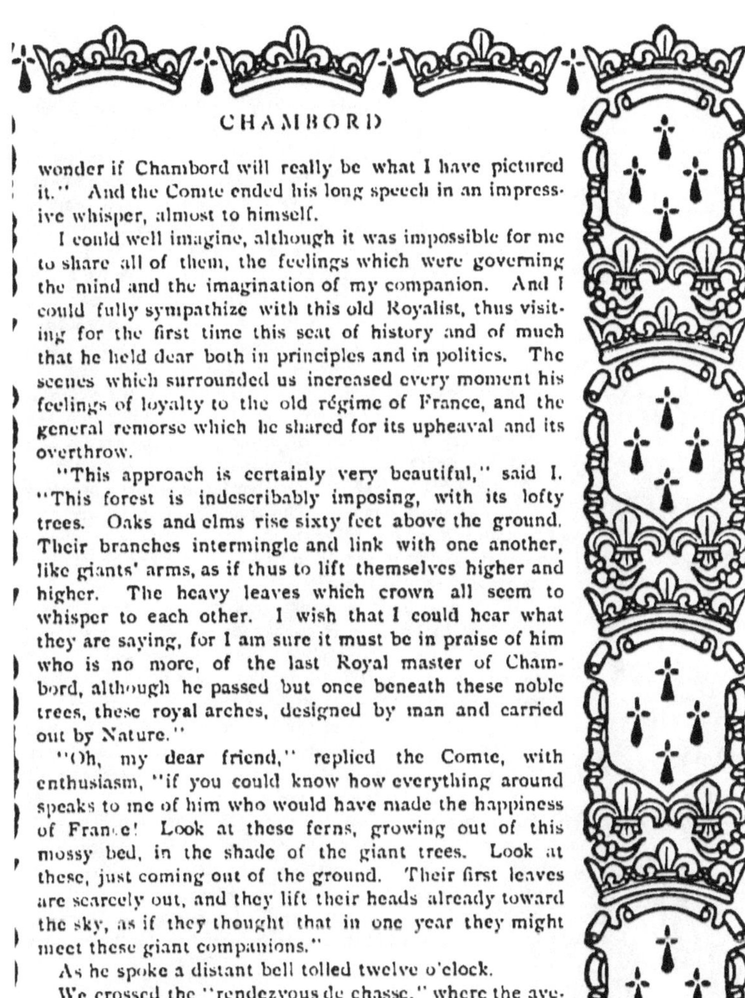

wonder if Chambord will really be what I have pictured it." And the Comte ended his long speech in an impressive whisper, almost to himself.

I could well imagine, although it was impossible for me to share all of them, the feelings which were governing the mind and the imagination of my companion. And I could fully sympathize with this old Royalist, thus visiting for the first time this seat of history and of much that he held dear both in principles and in politics. The scenes which surrounded us increased every moment his feelings of loyalty to the old régime of France, and the general remorse which he shared for its upheaval and its overthrow.

"This approach is certainly very beautiful," said I. "This forest is indescribably imposing, with its lofty trees. Oaks and elms rise sixty feet above the ground. Their branches intermingle and link with one another, like giants' arms, as if thus to lift themselves higher and higher. The heavy leaves which crown all seem to whisper to each other. I wish that I could hear what they are saying, for I am sure it must be in praise of him who is no more, of the last Royal master of Chambord, although he passed but once beneath these noble trees, these royal arches, designed by man and carried out by Nature."

"Oh, my dear friend," replied the Comte, with enthusiasm, "if you could know how everything around speaks to me of him who would have made the happiness of France! Look at these ferns, growing out of this mossy bed, in the shade of the giant trees. Look at these, just coming out of the ground. Their first leaves are scarcely out, and they lift their heads already toward the sky, as if they thought that in one year they might meet these giant companions."

As he spoke a distant bell tolled twelve o'clock.

We crossed the "rendezvous de chasse," where the ave-

nues of "Pologne" and "du Roy," with five others, meet and depart again in all directions from the pointed fingers of a white sign-post. Here, the forest is composed entirely of pine trees, and the air is scented, far and near, by their fragrant odor. We sit down to rest, leaning against a young tree swayed to and fro by the wind as it passes by. And we dream and muse on all around, on the beauty of Nature and on the chateau which we are so soon to see. We listen to the wind and the trees, and we seem to hear the waves of an eastern sea as they break over the sandy beach—loud and louder, then soft again, but always with a wonderful depth and an indefiniteness which holds us in an increasing expectation. Another wave breaks, prouder and louder than the last—breaks with the roar of thunder—on the sand. Can you not hear it? It is the wind playing with the pines.

As we come nearer to Chambord the scenery becomes sadder and more barren. The trees of the forest are now small and far apart. Vegetation seems to fade away and to die almost, as if unable to live longer in the heart of so much glory passed away.

"What a strange contrast this is," said the Comte, "and how in keeping is such sadness with one's inner feelings! Passed monarchy! What is there sadder than its crumbled glory, if it be not the death of old and honored institutions? And what is there more barren or more shallow, if it be not the barrenness and shallowness of modern ones? See, even the trees partake of my feelings. They are shrivelled up, for they need the air of royalty to make them grow."

"But, my dear friend," I broke in, "why are you, with all your loyalty to the old régime and its royalty, with much of which I sympathize, why are you, with it all, so full of prejudice and narrow-mindedness?"

"That I do not know," replied the Comte, "perhaps you may account for that better than I. But how could we part with the only thing left to us of our past ideal, the souvenir of bygone greatness? They have tried to take everything from us; but one thing, however, is left to us—at least I suppose it is—the liberty of thought."

We continued upon our road, in silence, for some time after this; and at last there arose, out of the heath and the stunted underbrush around us, a long line of a greenish hue broken here and there by whiter places. This line of green trees (for so it proved to be) is unbroken for many miles, on the right as well as on the left; but directly in front of us, and on the road, is an open space of several metres.

"The park!" exclaimed the Comte, taking hold of my arm. "Excuse me, my dear friend, my limbs give way beneath me. May I lean upon your arm? Imagine—the park of Chambord! We are treading upon sacred soil. We are about to traverse that avenue so often rutted by the royal equipages of Francois I and his court, of Henry II and a hundred others, coming in a long, illustrious line, down to the present master, the Duc de Parme, Comte de Bardi."

And as we passed through the modern gateway, with its house also modern with its roof of red tiles and its walls of gray, I saw the Comte lift his hat in respect, as if he were passing a cross at the corner of two roads, and I should not wonder if he had tears in his eyes.

"Five thousand hectares of park—twenty-four kilometres of walls, at least—five farms, a church, a village— five hundred inhabitants—an income of thirty thousand dollars a year—how great this park is!" I heard the Comte mumbling to himself, as we were walking over the avenue leading through the park. "There is a small roof," he continued. "It must be one of the farms. I wonder if it could be the one called 'Liña,' after one of the children of Berthier, Prince de Wagram, who owned

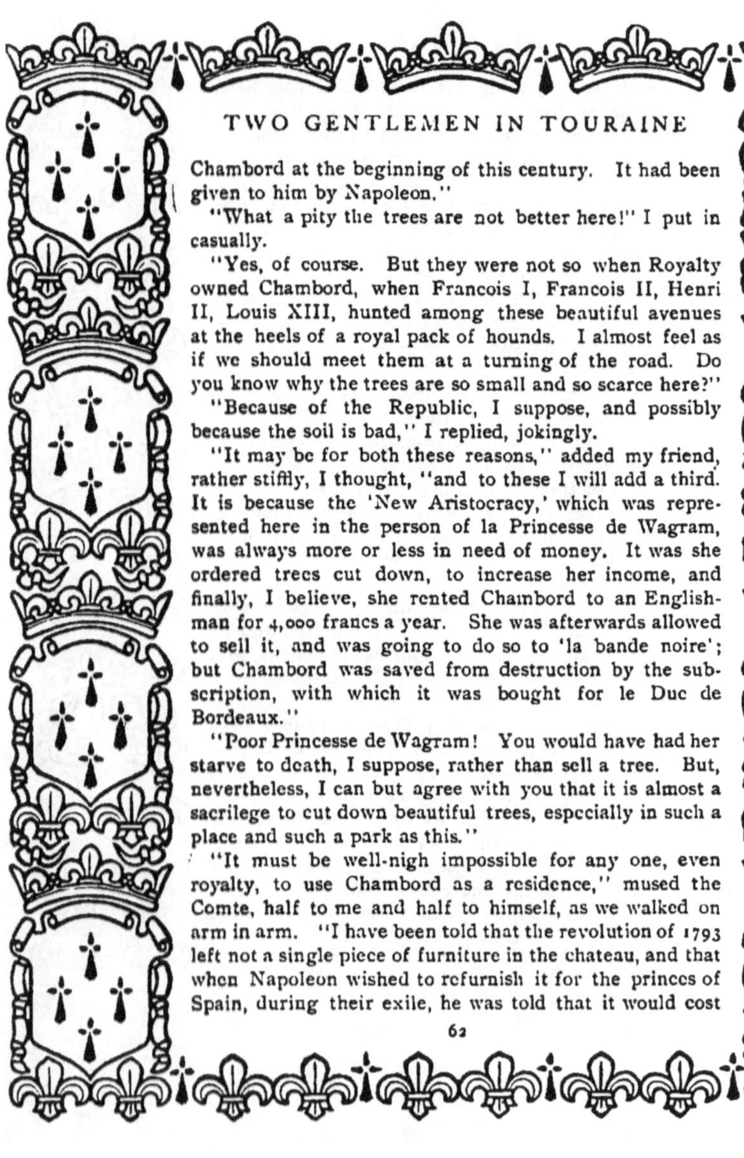

Chambord at the beginning of this century. It had been given to him by Napoleon."

"What a pity the trees are not better here!" I put in casually.

"Yes, of course. But they were not so when Royalty owned Chambord, when Francois I, Francois II, Henri II, Louis XIII, hunted among these beautiful avenues at the heels of a royal pack of hounds. I almost feel as if we should meet them at a turning of the road. Do you know why the trees are so small and so scarce here?"

"Because of the Republic, I suppose, and possibly because the soil is bad," I replied, jokingly.

"It may be for both these reasons," added my friend, rather stiffly, I thought, "and to these I will add a third. It is because the 'New Aristocracy,' which was represented here in the person of la Princesse de Wagram, was always more or less in need of money. It was she ordered trees cut down, to increase her income, and finally, I believe, she rented Chambord to an Englishman for 4,000 francs a year. She was afterwards allowed to sell it, and was going to do so to 'la bande noire'; but Chambord was saved from destruction by the subscription, with which it was bought for le Duc de Bordeaux."

"Poor Princesse de Wagram! You would have had her starve to death, I suppose, rather than sell a tree. But, nevertheless, I can but agree with you that it is almost a sacrilege to cut down beautiful trees, especially in such a place and such a park as this."

"It must be well-nigh impossible for any one, even royalty, to use Chambord as a residence," mused the Comte, half to me and half to himself, as we walked on arm in arm. "I have been told that the revolution of 1793 left not a single piece of furniture in the chateau, and that when Napoleon wished to refurnish it for the princes of Spain, during their exile, he was told that it would cost

9,000,000 francs. Four hundred and forty rooms are not easy to furnish. Oh, there is the castle now!" And, in fact, there appeared, just over the hill which we were climbing, and some miles away, a mass of spires, campaniles, high stone chimneys and carved stone windows, the whole showing in relief against the dark slate of the roofs. It was not unlike a confused mass of stone openwork, in different shades. In a few minutes all disappeared once more behind a bit of shrubbery. We crossed another "rendezvous de chasse," surrounded by well trimmed fir trees. Alleys and paths, now in good order, now altogether wild, crossed and recrossed each other, and we were forever upon the long, straight road with the "campanile" of Chambord showing, from time to time, in the centre of the open space before us. As we drew nearer, the roofs and pinarets grew more and more distinct, though still far from us. The great, gray mass seemed to grow up slowly out of the ground, suggesting the effect of a mirage, in a wilderness.

"Are you not overwhelmed with a sense of almost overpowering sadness?" said the Comte.

"Yes, indeed, I am," was my reply. "It gives an impression of solitude, of silence, of fear lest anything might come to disturb the fascination of this wilderness, —a wilderness which has not, perhaps, the grandiose effect of a true wilderness, but which has the depth of a past without a present. Life seems to have shrunk from this place, and one fears that it may come back to disturb the stillness of death."

"Yes, yes," the Comte rejoined, "it is a monument, born of Royalty, which needed Royalty, to live, and which will sleep in death-like quiet until its Royalty returns."

"And therefore has a good chance to sleep forever," I put in.

"Who can tell? The wheel of fortune, you know, is a capricious one and may turn once more, so that it points

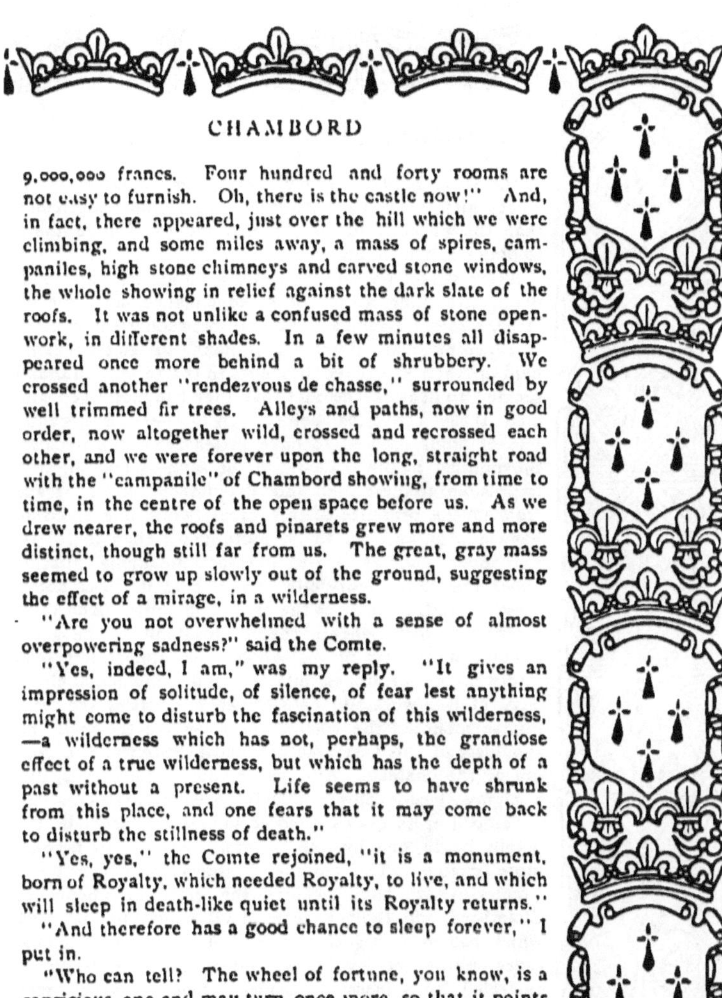

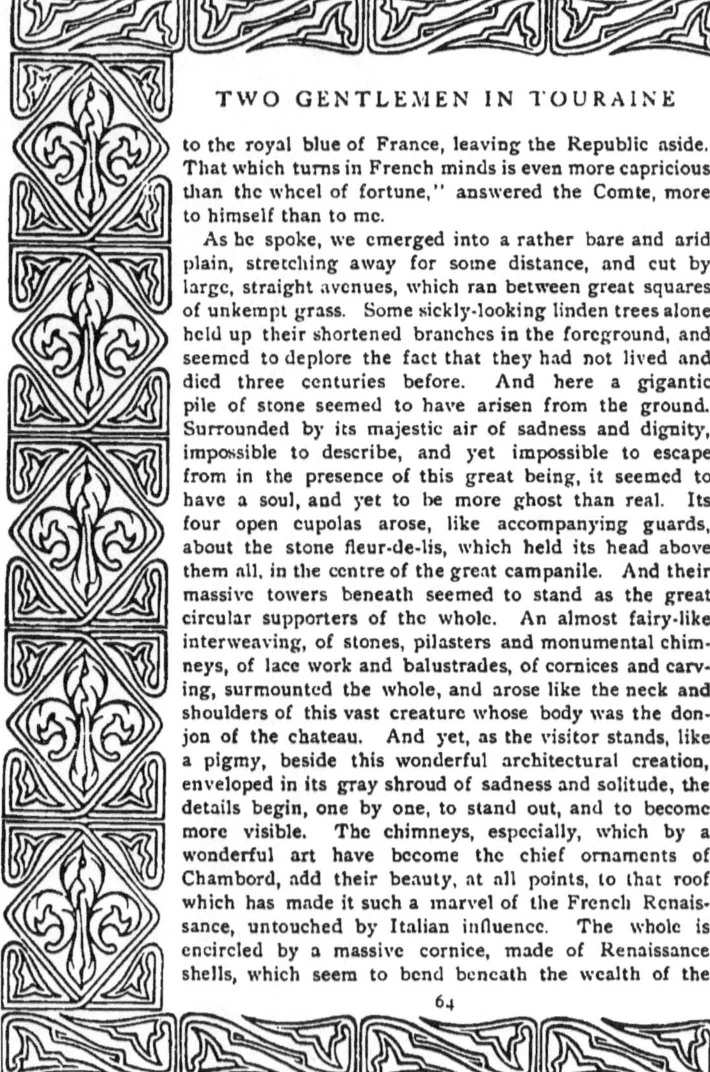

to the royal blue of France, leaving the Republic aside.
That which turns in French minds is even more capricious
than the wheel of fortune," answered the Comte, more
to himself than to me.

As he spoke, we emerged into a rather bare and arid
plain, stretching away for some distance, and cut by
large, straight avenues, which ran between great squares
of unkempt grass. Some sickly-looking linden trees alone
held up their shortened branches in the foreground, and
seemed to deplore the fact that they had not lived and
died three centuries before. And here a gigantic
pile of stone seemed to have arisen from the ground.
Surrounded by its majestic air of sadness and dignity,
impossible to describe, and yet impossible to escape
from in the presence of this great being, it seemed to
have a soul, and yet to be more ghost than real. Its
four open cupolas arose, like accompanying guards,
about the stone fleur-de-lis, which held its head above
them all, in the centre of the great campanile. And their
massive towers beneath seemed to stand as the great
circular supporters of the whole. An almost fairy-like
interweaving, of stones, pilasters and monumental chimneys, of lace work and balustrades, of cornices and carving, surmounted the whole, and arose like the neck and
shoulders of this vast creature whose body was the donjon of the chateau. And yet, as the visitor stands, like
a pigmy, beside this wonderful architectural creation,
enveloped in its gray shroud of sadness and solitude, the
details begin, one by one, to stand out, and to become
more visible. The chimneys, especially, which by a
wonderful art have become the chief ornaments of
Chambord, add their beauty, at all points, to that roof
which has made it such a marvel of the French Renaissance, untouched by Italian influence. The whole is
encircled by a massive cornice, made of Renaissance
shells, which seem to bend beneath the wealth of the

carving above them. A little lower down, and to the
right and left, come the straight lines of the roofs which
join the donjon to the round, corner towers. And lower
still come the walls, hard and dry, not even softened by
the gray hues of time. They are cold and bare, cut by
high windows close together, and divided at each story
by the strong horizontal lines which alone endeavor to
relieve their nudity. It is strange that as the eye falls
lower and lower toward the ground, this bare simplicity
shows in stronger contrast to the warmth and artistic
wonders of the roofs. The roofs of Chambord! What a
note the words strike upon the heart! What a magic
they hold for all those who know them, or who have
seen them! What a thrill of artistic and historic greatness they contain! What a world they are within themselves, high up above the head, as we stand before the
castle gate, high and higher every moment, as we
approach, till they seem almost to hang upon the air in
the soft light of the departing day!

Thus appears the south façade: nearly forty metres
high and one hundred and fifty-six metres long.

The Comte began speaking to himself as we stood, still
gazing at the chateau.

"And here it has been standing for more than three
hundred years," said he, breaking in upon my revery.
"Here it has been since 1523, when Francois I ordered it
to be erected by Trinquaux, an architect of Blois, as a
hunting lodge—a royal hunting lodge, in the midst of
the wilderness of Sologne, close to a little stream called
le Cosson, whose yellow, muddy waters wind in and out
among the surrounding trees! What a curious idea!
But I suppose that 'le Roi Chevalier' required change
and diversion, so that his love for hunting led him to
choose the best country for hunting rather than the most
beautiful. In 1538 Chambord was nearly completed.
How beautiful it must have been then! And no wonder

that it caused 'Charles-quiut' to utter a cry of admiration.
It is both curious and interesting to note how the walls
grow richer and richer as they approach the roofs, where
they reach the climax of their art and their perfection.''

Here I could not refrain from remarking: ''I fear, my
dear friend, that curiosity and interest are so tenderly
amalgamated in your mind that I shall soon have to
invent a new name for the resulting combination of these
two predominant qualities in your character. Curiosity and
interest! How much they mean to Frenchmen in general and to you in particular! Hereafter, when you wish
to speak of them both say only 'interest,' and I promise
you I will always take the other for granted. You will
forgive my little interruption, I am sure.'' And the
Comte continued in as forgiving a manner as was possible
under the circumstances:

''Chambord was built as a hunting lodge, and so it was
constructed with a view to overlooking the chase in the
park. Thus the roofs became the most important part,
since they were to be used as a rendezvous for the court
to watch the huntsmen in the distance. It is for this
reason that the richness of decoration is centered there,
rather than upon the walls of the castle. Another
strange thing, of which Chambord is an exponent, is the
fact that the architects and the architectural schools in
the time of French Renaissance seem to have fallen into
strange insignificance, considering the importance of that
architectural period. Indeed, the Italian influence was so
strongly felt in everything at that time, that it has even
ascribed the conception of Chambord to the great Italian,
le Primatice, although this seems well-nigh impossible,
for the latter was not in France at the time, as there was
a war between France and Italy. It is extraordinary,
however, how strong the Italian feeling is, in all that
architecture which we call French Renaissance. Italy
and Italian art seem to have been embraced, on all sides

and at all points, throughout these chateaux of Touraine.
I suppose, of course, that Catherine de Medici was
largely responsible for it, and it is in this perhaps that
she impressed her existence, and its after effects, upon
France, more than in anything else. It is wonderful to
think how much art Henry II brought into his nation
and among his people when he asked the famous Italian
princess to be "la Reine de France." It is wonderful to
think of the power which one human being may possess
and may exercise upon people and peoples yet unborn,
upon a nation whose age and position may impress that
power throughout the civilized world, and hand it down
to posterity. And what is it, my dear friend, which has
created this wonderful power in the past and present of
history and which still continues to create it wherever it
chances to exist to-day? What? Why, it is Royalty!
Royalty alone has been able to do it in the past, and
Royalty alone is capable of doing so to-day, and of doing
so to-morrow. Run over the greatest individual influences of the world in your mind, taking their lasting
effects upon art, architecture, religion, politics, government, manners, customs, or institutions, anything, in
short, which goes to make a nation great among its
neighbors, and you will see more than a little truth in
what I say."

As the Comte was speaking we left the south façade of
the castle and walked along by the great west walls, leaving upon our left the little church, situated some hundred
yards away. Its newly repaired façade was half hidden
by the trees around, and its miniature steeple—the exact
copy of one of the monumental chimneys of the castle—
threw its shadows over the nave, to give a softening, gray
effect to the milk-white stone. Before us and still a
little to the left stood our hotel, a building like a thousand others all over France, looking suspiciously like a
square box, covered with white mortar. "Hotel du

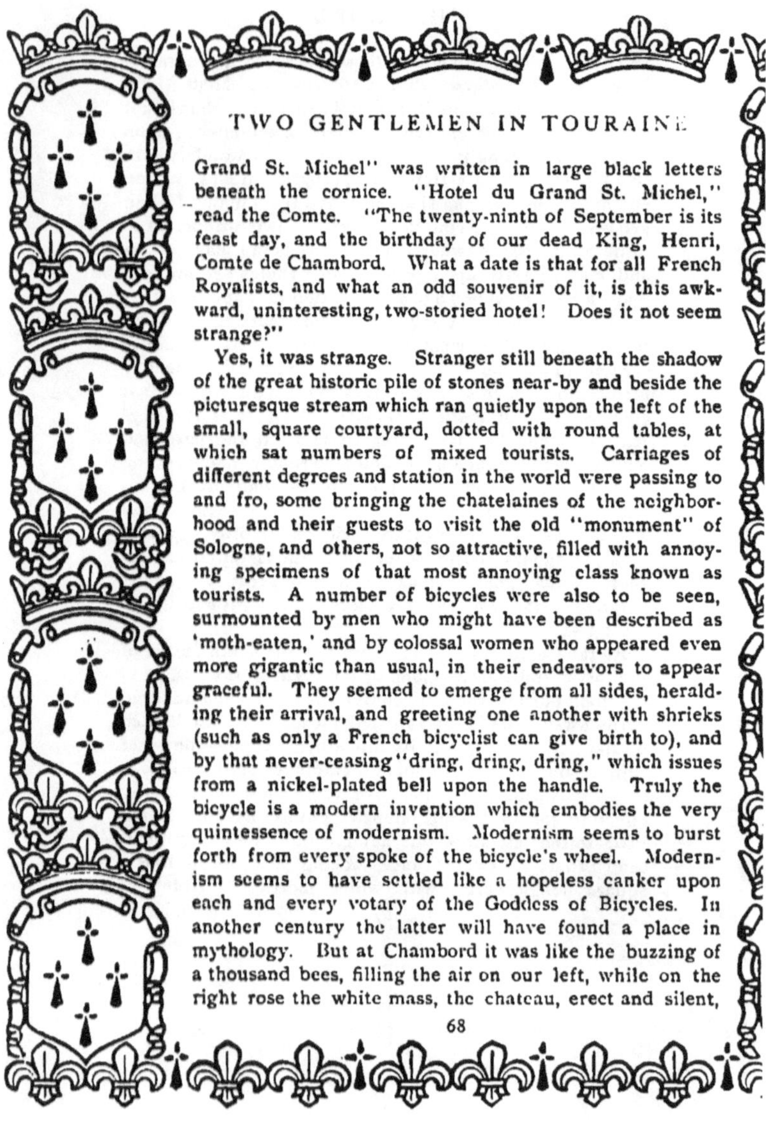

Grand St. Michel" was written in large black letters beneath the cornice. "Hotel du Grand St. Michel," read the Comte. "The twenty-ninth of September is its feast day, and the birthday of our dead King, Henri, Comte de Chambord. What a date is that for all French Royalists, and what an odd souvenir of it, is this awkward, uninteresting, two-storied hotel! Does it not seem strange?"

Yes, it was strange. Stranger still beneath the shadow of the great historic pile of stones near-by and beside the picturesque stream which ran quietly upon the left of the small, square courtyard, dotted with round tables, at which sat numbers of mixed tourists. Carriages of different degrees and station in the world were passing to and fro, some bringing the chatelaines of the neighborhood and their guests to visit the old "monument" of Sologne, and others, not so attractive, filled with annoying specimens of that most annoying class known as tourists. A number of bicycles were also to be seen, surmounted by men who might have been described as 'moth-eaten,' and by colossal women who appeared even more gigantic than usual, in their endeavors to appear graceful. They seemed to emerge from all sides, heralding their arrival, and greeting one another with shrieks (such as only a French bicyclist can give birth to), and by that never-ceasing "dring, dring, dring," which issues from a nickel-plated bell upon the handle. Truly the bicycle is a modern invention which embodies the very quintessence of modernism. Modernism seems to burst forth from every spoke of the bicycle's wheel. Modernism seems to have settled like a hopeless canker upon each and every votary of the Goddess of Bicycles. In another century the latter will have found a place in mythology. But at Chambord it was like the buzzing of a thousand bees, filling the air on our left, while on the right rose the white mass, the chateau, erect and silent,

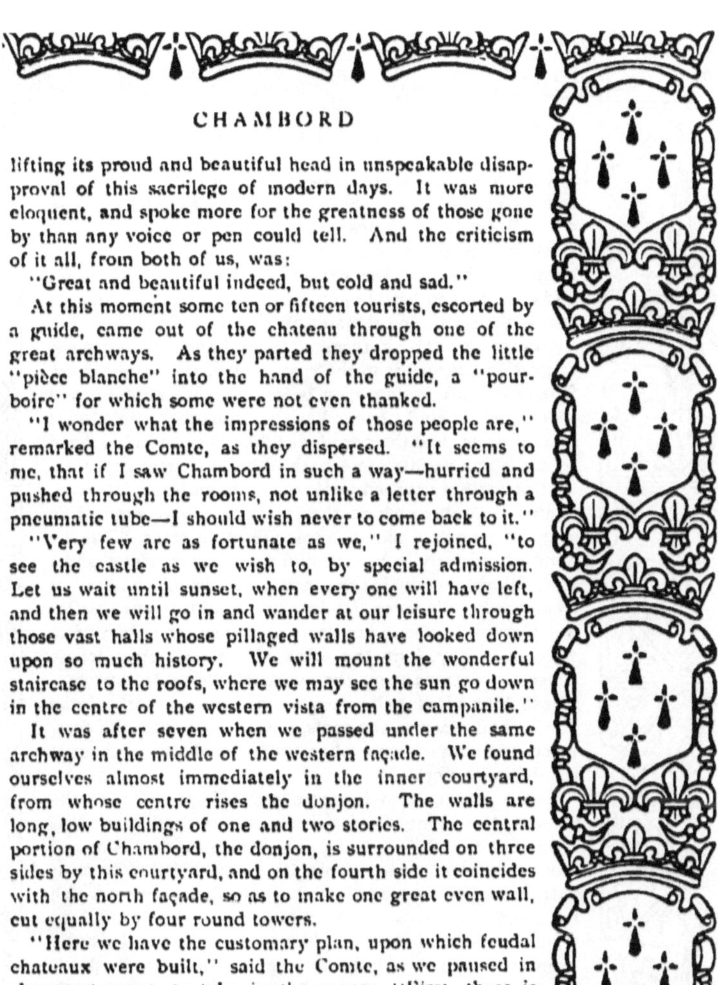

lifting its proud and beautiful head in unspeakable disapproval of this sacrilege of modern days. It was more eloquent, and spoke more for the greatness of those gone by than any voice or pen could tell. And the criticism of it all, from both of us, was:

"Great and beautiful indeed, but cold and sad."

At this moment some ten or fifteen tourists, escorted by a guide, came out of the chateau through one of the great archways. As they parted they dropped the little "pièce blanche" into the hand of the guide, a "pourboire" for which some were not even thanked.

"I wonder what the impressions of those people are," remarked the Comte, as they dispersed. "It seems to me, that if I saw Chambord in such a way—hurried and pushed through the rooms, not unlike a letter through a pneumatic tube—I should wish never to come back to it."

"Very few are as fortunate as we," I rejoined, "to see the castle as we wish to, by special admission. Let us wait until sunset, when every one will have left, and then we will go in and wander at our leisure through those vast halls whose pillaged walls have looked down upon so much history. We will mount the wonderful staircase to the roofs, where we may see the sun go down in the centre of the western vista from the campanile."

It was after seven when we passed under the same archway in the middle of the western façade. We found ourselves almost immediately in the inner courtyard, from whose centre rises the donjon. The walls are long, low buildings of one and two stories. The central portion of Chambord, the donjon, is surrounded on three sides by this courtyard, and on the fourth side it coincides with the north façade, so as to make one great even wall, cut equally by four round towers.

"Here we have the customary plan, upon which feudal chateaux were built," said the Comte, as we paused in the great court, to take in the scene. "First, there is

always a great square mass, with its proverbial round towers, enclosing the whole chateau. Then there comes a smaller pile of stones, with towers also—the donjon. Custom has preserved these plans and their ancient names, so that if, in the sixteenth century, we find towers and donjons and battlements, they are only as ornaments and as the beautified remains of past feudality.''

Our guide, taking from a large bunch of keys the largest one, turned it in the rusty lock of the donjon door. The heavy oak swung open before us. We entered, and it banged behind, banged with a moaning, an almost tearful noise, like the cry of a child. The sound, echoed by the stone vaults, came back to us, ten times repeated. Instinctively we turned as if to depart, to leave this cold, damp atmosphere where the frosts of winter seemed no more to penetrate than the warmth of summer. But the door was already locked behind us, and my friend and I were alone; alone in the great, deserted chateau of Chambord. We were standing in one of the four "Salles des Gardes.'' These are forty feet long and thirty feet wide, and they form the arms of a Greek cross whose centre is occupied by the wonderful, double staircase. These four giant halls occupy the greater part of the donjon and reach to the roofs, except, as is now the case, where they have been broken by floors which cut them at the different stories.

Before we realized it, our surroundings had torn the present, the living present, from us, and had carried us back to the dead, the dying past, which fascinates one so that one cannot escape from its grasp. We were as if petrified. We seemed riveted to the flagstone on which we stood. Perhaps we feared to move, lest each step taken by us should be brought back in a thousand echoes, from the vaulted ceilings of the "Salles des Gardes.'' As we looked up at them we could see those compartments into which the stone was furrowed to encase the salamander of François I, which, according to some, is able to exist in fire and, according to others, extinguishes it by its very coldness. In every other compartment appeared the royal F, surmounted by the crown of France, and surrounded by the "Cordon de St. François." "St. François was the founder of the Franciscan fathers, who still wear the same cordon about their waists," said the Comte to me, almost in a whisper.

A ray of light, dimmed by the growing twilight, reached us, through the crack of a door which stood ajar upon the left. As if drawn on by an enchanted hand, we crept toward it, entered, and found ourselves in a large, square room. Some six or eight state coaches caught the eye, in unexpected brilliancy. The panelings and trappings were of dark blue. In the centre of the boxes shone the three golden fleurs-de-lis, upon azure—the royal arms of France. They were surrounded by the lilies of France, painted upon blue. A royal crown surmounted the whole, while at the upper corners of the coach and at intervals along the top were smaller crowns of silver. The hammer cloth was dark blue also, heavily fringed with gold; and the state coach of the king was lined with white satin, quilted with gold.

"And this is all that is left of Royalty," the Comte broke in on the impressive silence, "eight carriages, ordered by le Comte de Chambord from a Paris carossier. And they have remained here ever since, untouched, unused, as if waiting in a sort of stupor for something which will never be. Each morning they are dusted carefully, as if the king were to drive out in them that day. How long will it last? We know not. Once a presumptuous man dared to ascend the king's carriage, and there ruffle the white satin of the cushions. Since that day the door of this room has been locked, and the carriages stand, untouched, unseen, except by a few who, by special favor, may look at them without touching."

We turned from the coaches, and were once more in one of the "Salle des Gardes" and standing at the foot of the wonderful staircase, the climax of Chambord in beauty and in conception, a chef d'œuvre of art, of execution, and of wealth of detail. The staircase is completely isolated, and runs, like one great shaft, intricately chiseled into two winding stairs which unfold themselves, within the lacework of the whole, up to the roof. These two staircases, twisted into one, twined about one another like a braid of hair, make it possible for two persons to start from the bottom and to mount to the very top, without once meeting, although they are visible to one another, through the lacework of the ornamental carving.

We started in this way, feeling our way up the white stone steps, for it was now almost dark. When I had lost sight of my companion, who had ascended the other staircase, it seemed as if the last link which held the present to the past had parted. And as I mounted, the past seemed to surround me more and more at every step. At last I was forced to stand aside, so as to allow the people to pass, the crowds of people who inhabited the chateau and who were ever passing and repassing over the great staircase. Soldiers, valets, gentlemen and ladies of the court were meeting one another and passing me at every turn. Some were descending to fulfil an order; others were proudly ascending to the private apartments of the king. All were beautifully attired, and greeted one another with a nod of the head, with a smile. Priceless tapestries hung from the walls, and drowned the sounds of their steps. The "frou-frou" of silks, the "cliquetis" of swords, the "chuchotments" of love—it was all there, the life of Chambord. And to-day? . . . The walls are bare and damp. The sounds are uncanny. Our voices, half restrained in our throats by some unconscious fear, come back to us nevertheless, increased and rendered harsh by the echoing of the stone. It is the death of Chambord.

We have reached the top. The network of stones is lost within the furrowed vaults. The double staircase has become a single mass, that springs up into the air over the roofs, one hundred feet above the ground. And still higher up, lost almost in the fleeting light, the great, central "campanile" crowns the whole edifice, and ends in the stone fleur-de-lis that blooms over all. We tread the topmost stair; we pass through a little door, which causes us to bend the head, and we come out, at last upon the roofs—the famous roofs of Chambord.

Is it possible to forget our first impressions of bewilderment, of ecstasy, when we set foot upon those roofs, upon those hanging avenues and streets, lined with the fairest jewels of architecture? The four principal avenues start from the central crowning of the staircase, and run, north, east, south and west, to the stone balustrade, which surrounds the entire roof. On either side of these four aërial avenues, which are really but the roofs of the four great chambers of the chateau, through which we entered, and which are the continuance of the motive of the Greek cross, arise pile upon pile of rich decorative detail. Windows, whose massiveness and ornaments would alone make a miniature chateau, burst forth from the roofs, around, above, at each new turn. And higher still the chimneys of the roofs of Chambord seem to grow from the very midst of this wealth of ornament and beauty. Here, even more predominant than in the smaller pilasters, is seen the motif of stone lozenges inlaid with black slate. It is indeed impossible to tell this slate from marble, although it would seem otherwise.

"The original plans provided for black Italian marble," said the Comte to me, as we stood in silent admiration of this detail, "but it was impossible to obtain this at the moment of construction, owing to the war between

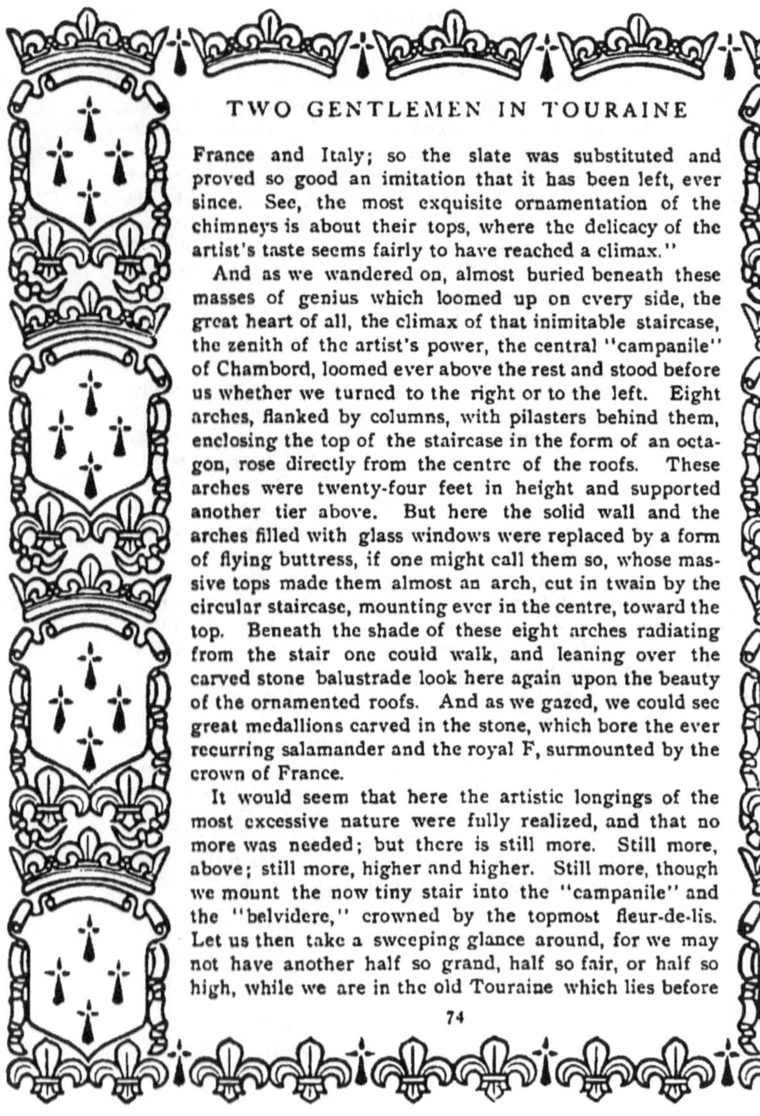

France and Italy; so the slate was substituted and proved so good an imitation that it has been left, ever since. See, the most exquisite ornamentation of the chimneys is about their tops, where the delicacy of the artist's taste seems fairly to have reached a climax.''

And as we wandered on, almost buried beneath these masses of genius which loomed up on every side, the great heart of all, the climax of that inimitable staircase, the zenith of the artist's power, the central ''campanile'' of Chambord, loomed ever above the rest and stood before us whether we turned to the right or to the left. Eight arches, flanked by columns, with pilasters behind them, enclosing the top of the staircase in the form of an octagon, rose directly from the centre of the roofs. These arches were twenty-four feet in height and supported another tier above. But here the solid wall and the arches filled with glass windows were replaced by a form of flying buttress, if one might call them so, whose massive tops made them almost an arch, cut in twain by the circular staircase, mounting ever in the centre, toward the top. Beneath the shade of these eight arches radiating from the stair one could walk, and leaning over the carved stone balustrade look here again upon the beauty of the ornamented roofs. And as we gazed, we could see great medallions carved in the stone, which bore the ever recurring salamander and the royal F, surmounted by the crown of France.

It would seem that here the artistic longings of the most excessive nature were fully realized, and that no more was needed; but there is still more. Still more, above; still more, higher and higher. Still more, though we mount the now tiny stair into the ''campanile'' and the ''belvidere,'' crowned by the topmost fleur-de-lis. Let us then take a sweeping glance around, for we may not have another half so grand, half so fair, or half so high, while we are in the old Touraine which lies before

us, there in the last orange glow of the departed sun.
And if we follow these avenues of the roof below us, if
we wind our way around these great towers, around the
high and pointed roofs of slate, we may well imagine ourselves in some fairyland. This maze of cupolas, of
domes, of towers, appears more bewildering to us than
ever. And we lean against the stone, in an artistic intox-
ication, so overpowering is it.

Oh, matchless evening of an August day! You have
already covered the ground with a mantle of sleepiness,
which seems to hang over everything and to cast its
shadow. The green trees in the plain, a hundred feet
below, seem to slumber in the shade. Wearied looking
and dark, they scarcely show against the ground. A
long line of silvery gray winds its way amidst the trees.
It is the tiny river Cosson, catching the reflected rays of
the starry heavens. But we, who are so high above, we
still catch the mauve tint of the last hour of the day. It
is a faint glimmer which gives not strength enough to
live by itself, but only to form the subject and the surroundings of a dream.

The day is at an end, and we are left, still leaning
against the "campanile," whose wings look like those of
some great firefly. The long shadows around us are of
the same pale color as the sky. No sound, no breath disturbs the silence. These marvels of artistic genius alone
speak to us from every side. Their splendor is brought
out the more by the very contrast of flowering beauty
with the fading of decay. Here a lace-work colonnade,
here a stone tower arises, before unnoticed. The faces
of the gargoyles make strange grimaces at us in the evening light. Caryatids, with features that express strange
thoughts and strange emotions, look down upon us in the
gloom. One might well give them the names of mistresses and courtiers and monarchs that have passed, for
they are surrounded by the air of other days. Indeed,

under the weight of such overpowering beauty as they support, our own eyelids close, and we are in another world, with scenes and characters surrounding us that have long passed into history.

A strange, dreamy atmosphere attends us. The faint sounds of distant music reach the ear. The hand of some fairy seems to have placed a light in the open campanile, beneath the fleur-de-lis. It is "le feu du roi." It burns only when the king is present. Lines of Venetian lanterns and tiny lamps, of stained glass, are hung across the avenues, above the head, or twined about the towers. Large orange trees, brought recently from Italy, are planted in wooden boxes, and perfume the air with the intoxicating odor of bridal flowers. They are grouped here and there, in clusters, about the windows of the roofs or of the great towers. In the shadows of their branches there are tables spread out, laden with fruits and wines and flowers in gold and silver dishes. Valets and servants hover around, and give last touches to the decorations. And it is not difficult to see that some large entertainment will take place. Soon the murmur of voices, coming as if from the court below, reaches the ear. The murmur increases in a crescendo, like the ninth wave of a summer sea, till it breaks and falls upon us. The door leading from the double staircase onto the roofs opens, and an endless stream of gentlemen and ladies pours forth. They wear costumes of the sixteenth century, and as they emerge from the staircase, two by two, their eyes and faces tell us of what they must be thinking. They move slowly forward, lingering beneath the orange trees, or stopping at the tables. They walk toward the balustrade, and look through the park.

They seem to be watching, as if waiting to detect some light, some unknown object, in the forest. But the night has spread its dark wings over all, and there is nothing to be seen. They turn from the stone balustrade, discouraged by their unsuccessful attempts, and wander once more around the towers and in and out among the orange trees. Suddenly a voice is heard above the murmurs of conversation, "Le Roi! le Roi!" And all turn toward the door from whence it comes, hushed and with bowing heads. A tall, thin figure wearing a velvet "pourpoint," with puffed sleeves, appears in the midst of a respectful court. It is François I. At his side walks another figure. And we can hear those about us whispering: "Charles-quint, the Emperor."

The laughter and talking is replaced by a silence so profound that the steps of the Emperor and the King may be heard distinctly, as they move slowly through the crowds of courtiers.

They stop, here and there, to speak to a favorite, or to some dignitary. "Le Roi Chevalier" gives a smile, a compliment, to the beauties of his court. They receive them with a bow of respect and admiration. One of them, a woman of extraordinary beauty, receives more than a bow from the King. He looks at her in a peculiar way; we do not understand, for we know not the secrets of the court. And as he lifts his finger, to command her attention, we can hear him say: "Descend to my private apartments, and look upon the windows. For on one of the panes of glass I have written, with the diamond of my ring, what I have learned through your inconstancy. Stay, I will repeat it now:

'Souvent femme varie,
Bien fol est qui s'y fie.'

"And now adieu."

He passes on, and leans over the stone balustrade with Charles-quint. They look, with the others, in the direction of the park, and endeavor to pierce the darkness of the night. But nothing is to be seen.

77

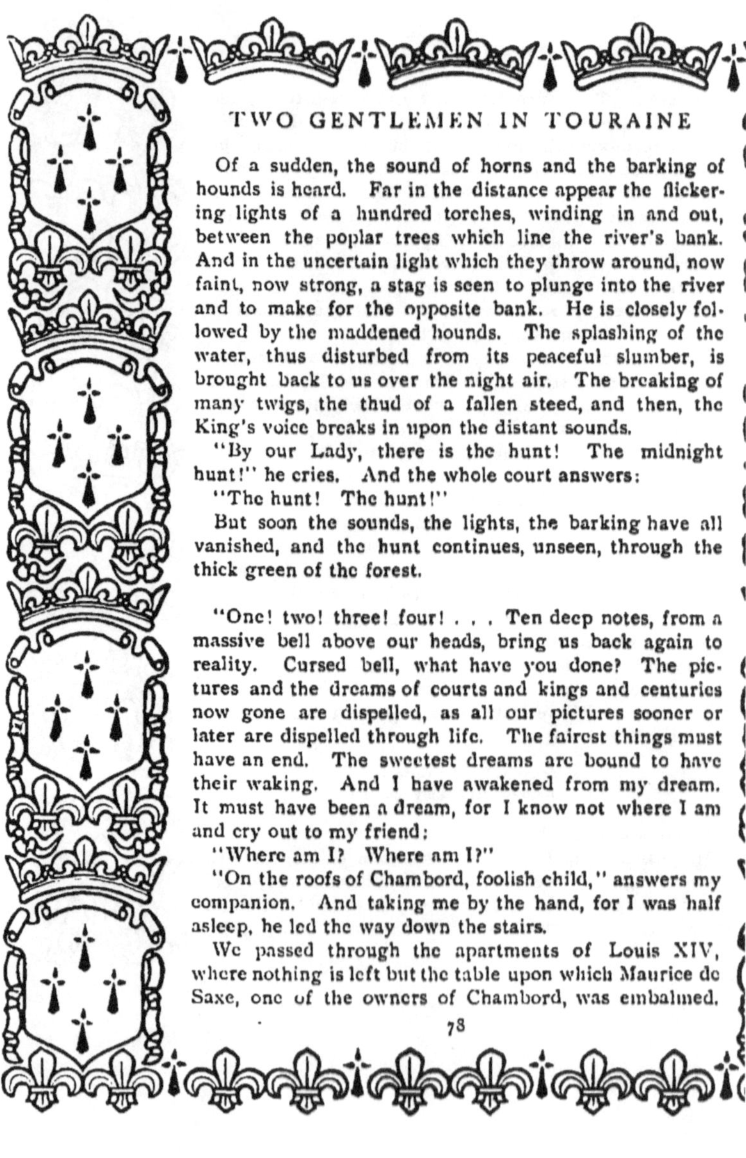

Of a sudden, the sound of horns and the barking of
hounds is heard.   Far in the distance appear the flicker-
ing lights of a hundred torches, winding in and out,
between the poplar trees which line the river's bank.
And in the uncertain light which they throw around, now
faint, now strong, a stag is seen to plunge into the river
and to make for the opposite bank.   He is closely followed by the maddened hounds.   The splashing of the
water, thus disturbed from its peaceful slumber, is
brought back to us over the night air.   The breaking of
many twigs, the thud of a fallen steed, and then, the
King's voice breaks in upon the distant sounds.

"By our Lady, there is the hunt!   The midnight
hunt!" he cries.   And the whole court answers:

"The hunt!   The hunt!"

But soon the sounds, the lights, the barking have all
vanished, and the hunt continues, unseen, through the
thick green of the forest.

"One! two! three! four! . . . . Ten deep notes, from a
massive bell above our heads, bring us back again to
reality.   Cursed bell, what have you done?   The pictures and the dreams of courts and kings and centuries
now gone are dispelled, as all our pictures sooner or
later are dispelled through life.   The fairest things must
have an end.   The sweetest dreams are bound to have
their waking.   And I have awakened from my dream.
It must have been a dream, for I know not where I am
and cry out to my friend:

"Where am I?   Where am I?"

"On the roofs of Chambord, foolish child," answers my
companion.   And taking me by the hand, for I was half
asleep, he led the way down the stairs.

We passed through the apartments of Louis XIV,
where nothing is left but the table upon which Maurice de
Saxe, one of the owners of Chambord, was embalmed.

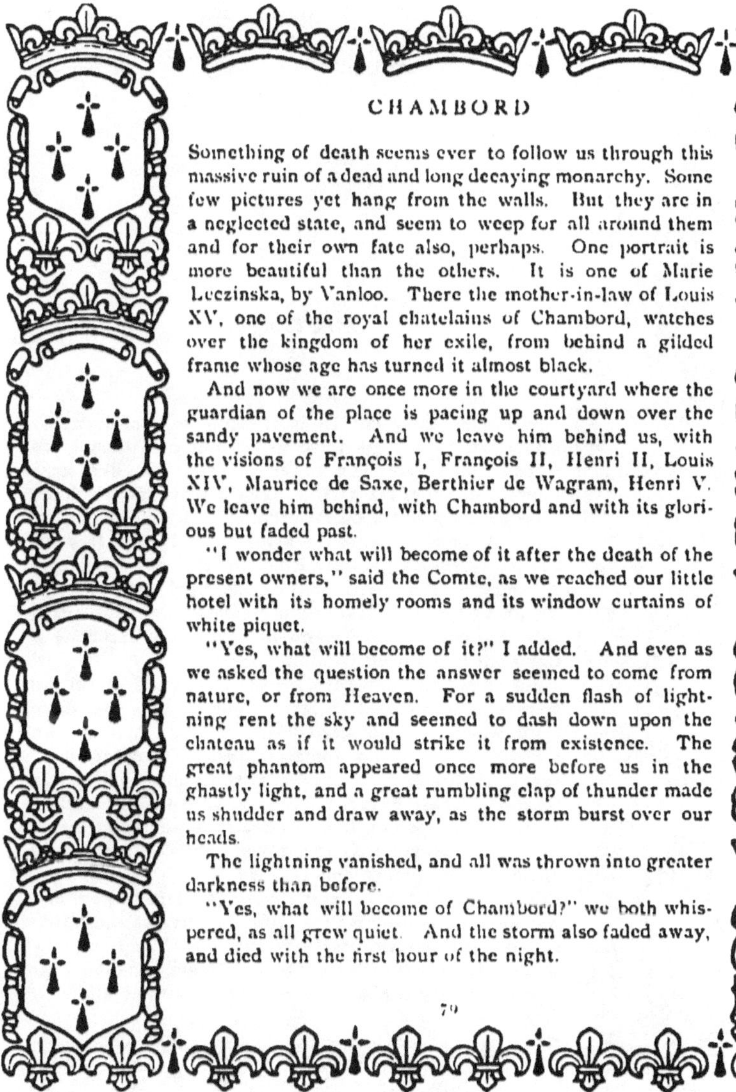

Something of death seems ever to follow us through this massive ruin of a dead and long decaying monarchy. Some few pictures yet hang from the walls. But they are in a neglected state, and seem to weep for all around them and for their own fate also, perhaps. One portrait is more beautiful than the others. It is one of Marie Leczinska, by Vanloo. There the mother-in-law of Louis XV, one of the royal chatelains of Chambord, watches over the kingdom of her exile, from behind a gilded frame whose age has turned it almost black.

And now we are once more in the courtyard where the guardian of the place is pacing up and down over the sandy pavement. And we leave him behind us, with the visions of François I, François II, Henri II, Louis XIV, Maurice de Saxe, Berthier de Wagram, Henri V. We leave him behind, with Chambord and with its glorious but faded past.

"I wonder what will become of it after the death of the present owners," said the Comte, as we reached our little hotel with its homely rooms and its window curtains of white piquet.

"Yes, what will become of it?" I added. And even as we asked the question the answer seemed to come from nature, or from Heaven. For a sudden flash of lightning rent the sky and seemed to dash down upon the chateau as if it would strike it from existence. The great phantom appeared once more before us in the ghastly light, and a great rumbling clap of thunder made us shudder and draw away, as the storm burst over our heads.

The lightning vanished, and all was thrown into greater darkness than before.

"Yes, what will become of Chambord?" we both whispered, as all grew quiet. And the storm also faded away, and died with the first hour of the night.

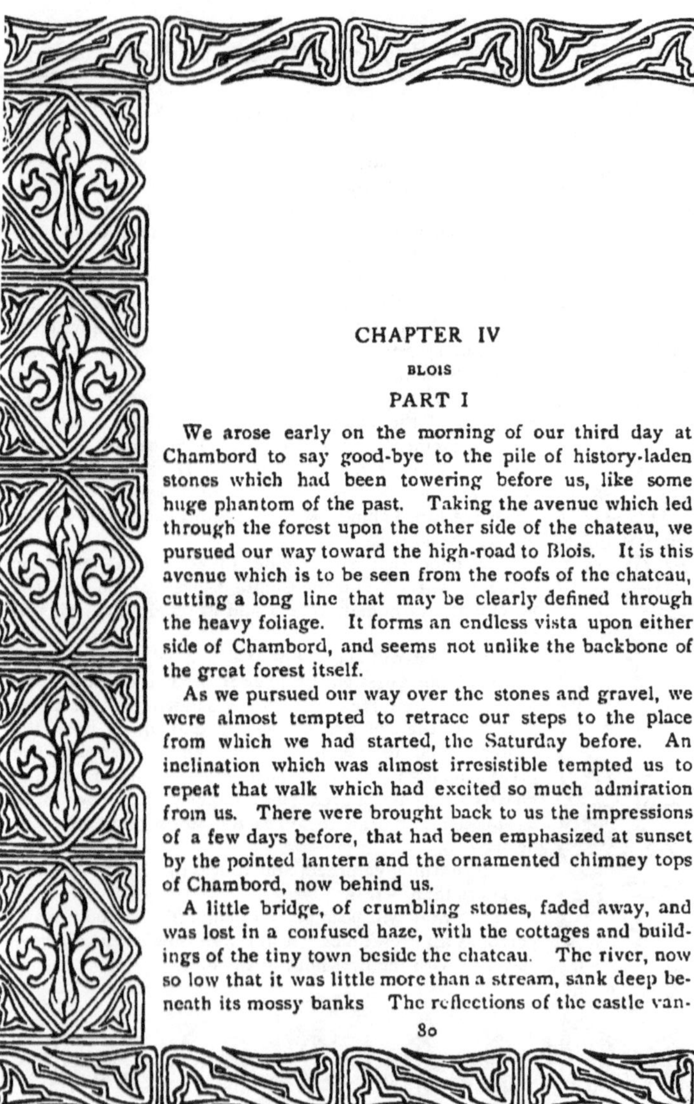

CHAPTER IV

PART I

We arose early on the morning of our third day at
Chambord to say good-bye to the pile of history-laden
stones which had been towering before us, like some
huge phantom of the past. Taking the avenue which led
through the forest upon the other side of the chateau, we
pursued our way toward the high-road to Blois. It is this
avenue which is to be seen from the roofs of the chateau,
cutting a long line that may be clearly defined through
the heavy foliage. It forms an endless vista upon either
side of Chambord, and seems not unlike the backbone of
the great forest itself.

As we pursued our way over the stones and gravel, we
were almost tempted to retrace our steps to the place
from which we had started, the Saturday before. An
inclination which was almost irresistible tempted us to
repeat that walk which had excited so much admiration
from us. There were brought back to us the impressions
of a few days before, that had been emphasized at sunset
by the pointed lantern and the ornamented chimney tops
of Chambord, now behind us.

A little bridge, of crumbling stones, faded away, and
was lost in a confused haze, with the cottages and buildings of the tiny town beside the chateau. The river, now
so low that it was little more than a stream, sank deep beneath its mossy banks The reflections of the castle van-

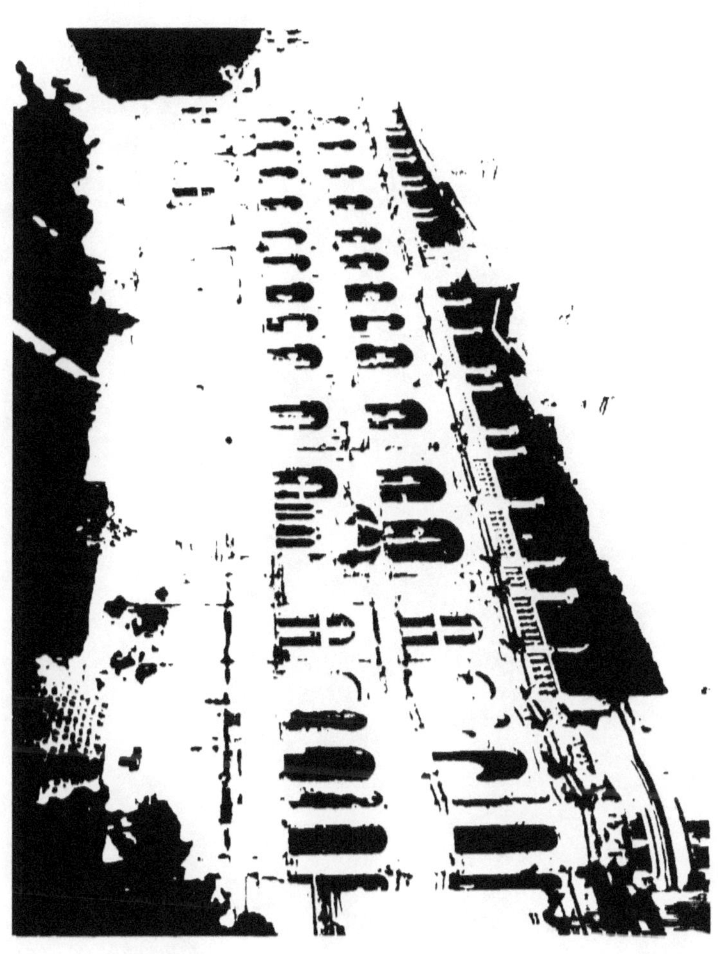

ished with it, and the trees shut in a small, square picture
in which the chateau occupied the chief position. Wearied
of the saddening aspect of the roofs and ever fading
"campanile" behind us, we turned from the beaten track
of fallen kings and courts of France, this avenue where,
not long ago, the cracking whips and the shouts of postilions announced the arrival of some courtier to the
chateau, this avenue which to-day is used but once a year
by its present master, the Duc de Parme. Leaving the
road, we wandered through the paths and alleys of the
park. The faint mist of the summer morning lent a
mystic charm to the foliage, around and overhead. The
trees and bushes met in some places, to form a canopy of
green leaves. Tiny vistas caught the eye at a distance,
and near at hand, others still distracted the attention in a
series of ever changing pictures. The mossy bed on
which we walked was strewn with flowers. The trunks
of trees were often covered by a thin coat of ivy, which
grew everywhere in profusion. The silence was broken
only by the clear note of a skylark, high above the head.
One could almost realize the winged forms of a fairy
host, flitting hither and thither amid the trees and flowers.

The deep bay of a hound sounded afar off, and then
nearer. The noise of cracking branches and of rustling
leaves was followed by the sound of horses' footsteps and
the winding of a hunter's horn. Suddenly a blast of
cold air blew against our startled faces, and from the
trees emerged a spectral huntsman, dressed in black, riding madly a jet black steed and followed by a pack of
hounds, black also. The ghostly cavalcade covered the
open space and disappeared around the angle of an alley,
before we knew whether it was a reality or not. Could it
have been but a passing picture of the mind, or had we
unconsciously wandered through that part of the forest
which is haunted by the famous Thibault de Champagne,
called "The Cheat"? The Solognots know it well, for it

is covered by the long green grass they call "l'herbe qui égare"—meaning the grass which misleads unwary travelers through this haunted spot. The legend runs that the spectral huntsman is to be seen returning, early in the morning, from the pavilion of Montfrault to the ruins of Bury. Perhaps, after all, we had seen the vision so much spoken of, but which no Solognot had ever cared to verify for himself. And yet, who knows whether we had not been allowing our imaginations to form poetic visions in these fairy-like surroundings?

By and by, the forest and its scenes had given place to open country, fields and lanes. Chambord had disappeared, and we had laid aside its legends, its history, and its wonders of architecture, to think of Blois, which was before us, and to picture to ourselves the details of that central figure in this unrivaled group of royal monuments. A walk of some six or eight miles, broken here and there by a picturesque village, with roses hanging from the cottage walls, brought us, after a steep incline, to the banks of the Loire.

Here the road turned sharply to the left, to follow for a hundred miles this wonderful river, whose banks are fortified by a long line of dikes crowned by the winding road. Across the river, an almost endless row of clipped linden trees, a white wall (nearly brown with age), and a long slate roof among the green told us that we were not far from the beautiful Chateau de Ménars. In the seventeenth century this chateau was inhabited by Stanislas Lesinski, King of Poland, and the father-in-law of Louis XV. Madame de Pompadour rebuilt it, as it stands to-day, and lived in it for some time with her brother, the Marquis Poisson de Marigny. As might be expected, Louis XV paid all the bills, which was no light obligation even for him to meet, for both Madame de Pompadour and her brother had exquisite taste, which they did not hesitate to satisfy at the expense of the king. Dur-

ing the revolution, however, the chateau was sold; but it was bought finally by the Duc de Bellune. During his ownership of Ménars the episode took place on which Scribe presumably founded his social drama "Malheurs d'un Amant Heureux." The chateau has since been owned respectively by the Prince Joseph de Chimay, the Princesse de Beauffremont, and lastly by M. Vatel, an "entrepreneur de construction."

Some distance further on it appeared in full view—a simple but exceedingly good bit of Louis XV architecture. The long, flat façade, the two wings, the flower-grown terraces, reaching almost to the river's edge, and a little classic summerhouse with Ionic columns, all blended gracefully in the mist. The whole scene, of a deep green relieved only by the white stone of the buildings and statues, made one think of one's ideals of French chateaux, as depicted in a stage setting, or upon some noted canvas.

And still the road-crowned dike wound on and on, following the snake-like curves and turnings of the river to which it owes its "raison d'être." Forests, chateaux, villas, appeared in the distance, became momentary realities and faded away behind us. The third shower of the morning broke over our heads, to be succeeded shortly by the ever recurring sunshine, whose intensity now announced it to be not far from midday. An old stone bridge with enlarging arches appeared in view, stretching across the river. The central arch, which was much wider than the others, culminated in a carved pedestal surmounted by an iron cross. Green fields and trees and country scenes gave place to plaster houses and paved streets. A large town appeared upon the opposite bank, with countless slate roofs growing up the hill, like so many mushrooms that were black instead of white, by some sad chance. The whole was crowned by a larger mass of slate than those below. This must then be the

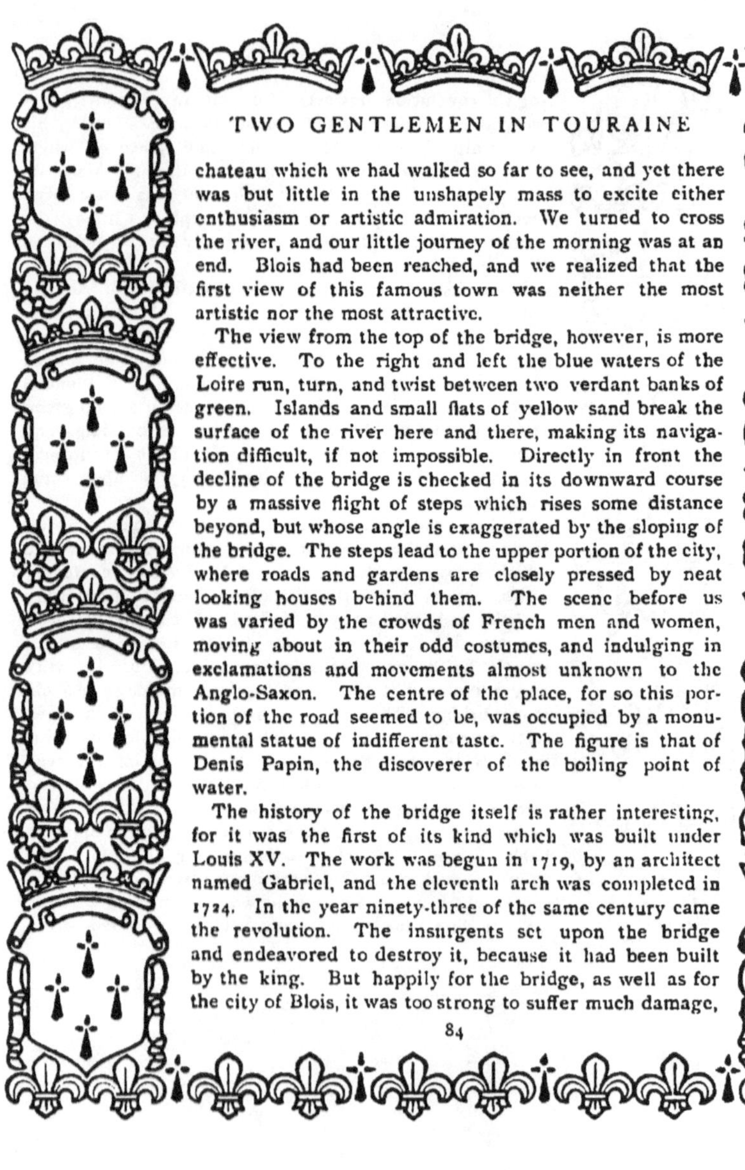

chateau which we had walked so far to see, and yet there was but little in the unshapely mass to excite either enthusiasm or artistic admiration. We turned to cross the river, and our little journey of the morning was at an end. Blois had been reached, and we realized that the first view of this famous town was neither the most artistic nor the most attractive.

The view from the top of the bridge, however, is more effective. To the right and left the blue waters of the Loire run, turn, and twist between two verdant banks of green. Islands and small flats of yellow sand break the surface of the river here and there, making its navigation difficult, if not impossible. Directly in front the decline of the bridge is checked in its downward course by a massive flight of steps which rises some distance beyond, but whose angle is exaggerated by the sloping of the bridge. The steps lead to the upper portion of the city, where roads and gardens are closely pressed by neat looking houses behind them. The scene before us was varied by the crowds of French men and women, moving about in their odd costumes, and indulging in exclamations and movements almost unknown to the Anglo-Saxon. The centre of the place, for so this portion of the road seemed to be, was occupied by a monumental statue of indifferent taste. The figure is that of Denis Papin, the discoverer of the boiling point of water.

The history of the bridge itself is rather interesting, for it was the first of its kind which was built under Louis XV. The work was begun in 1719, by an architect named Gabriel, and the eleventh arch was completed in 1724. In the year ninety-three of the same century came the revolution. The insurgents set upon the bridge and endeavored to destroy it, because it had been built by the king. But happily for the bridge, as well as for the city of Blois, it was too strong to suffer much damage,

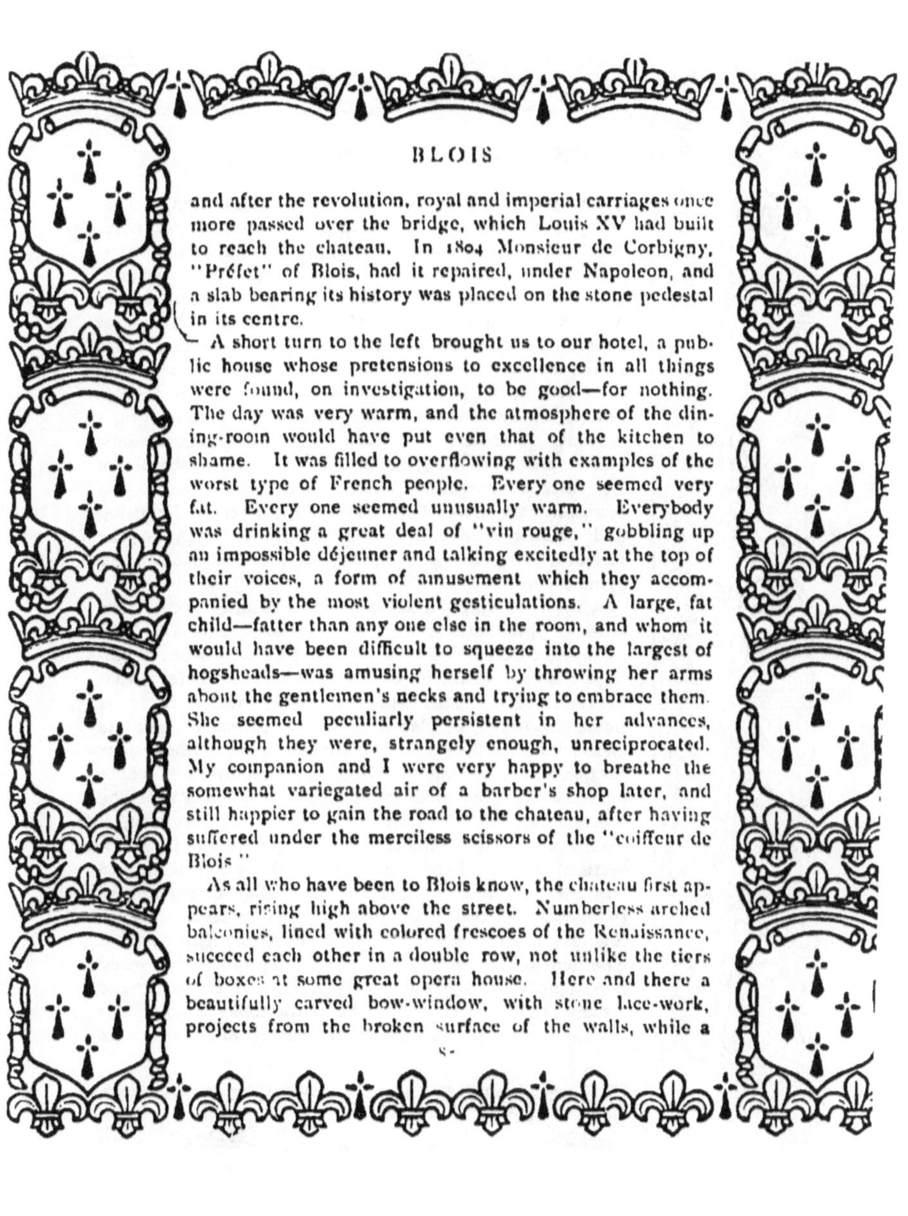

and after the revolution, royal and imperial carriages once more passed over the bridge, which Louis XV had built to reach the chateau. In 1804 Monsieur de Corbigny, "Préfet" of Blois, had it repaired, under Napoleon, and a slab bearing its history was placed on the stone pedestal in its centre.

A short turn to the left brought us to our hotel, a public house whose pretensions to excellence in all things were found, on investigation, to be good—for nothing. The day was very warm, and the atmosphere of the dining-room would have put even that of the kitchen to shame. It was filled to overflowing with examples of the worst type of French people. Every one seemed very fat. Every one seemed unusually warm. Everybody was drinking a great deal of "vin rouge," gobbling up an impossible déjeuner and talking excitedly at the top of their voices, a form of amusement which they accompanied by the most violent gesticulations. A large, fat child—fatter than any one else in the room, and whom it would have been difficult to squeeze into the largest of hogsheads—was amusing herself by throwing her arms about the gentlemen's necks and trying to embrace them. She seemed peculiarly persistent in her advances, although they were, strangely enough, unreciprocated. My companion and I were very happy to breathe the somewhat variegated air of a barber's shop later, and still happier to gain the road to the chateau, after having suffered under the merciless scissors of the "coiffeur de Blois."

As all who have been to Blois know, the chateau first appears, rising high above the street. Numberless arched balconies, lined with colored frescoes of the Renaissance, succeed each other in a double row, not unlike the tiers of boxes at some great opera house. Here and there a beautifully carved bow-window, with stone lace-work, projects from the broken surface of the walls, while a

quantity of grinning gargoyles crane out their long necks, and peer down upon the intruder from the heavy cornice. The Italian Renaissance is a strong element in the architecture of this portion of the chateau, and the delicately chiseled pilasters, everywhere dividing the balconies and windows, are among its chief characteristics. The roof especially savors of the Italian, and it is flatter than those which we are accustomed to in France. It projects over the great cornice, not unlike a huge villa, and is supported by shortened columns, forming a long upper balcony. The roof is broken by a Renaissance window and several massive ornamented chimneys, which pierce its surface irregularly, like seeds which have just sprouted in a flower bed. The whole effect is imposing and artistic, beautiful in detail rather than in the ensemble, which is irregular and often lacking in symmetry.

A flight of steps, a steep avenue, leading around the massive foundations of the wing of François I, and an open place, bring one face to face with what is perhaps the most beautiful façade of the whole chateau, that of Louis XII. This wonderful wing, which takes its name from its founder and which forms a complete chateau in itself, is but one side of a court whose four portions boast as many styles of architecture, and whose character is unrivaled in France. The beauty of the whole effect of this court is indescribable. Indeed, it would afford a complete study of perfection in architectural detail. From the outside, the pinnacle-capped windows, the red and black brick walls, culminating in the elaborate carving and the "statue équestre" of Louis XII, are a soft and happy mélange of exquisite details. The fleur-de-lis, appearing everywhere, and the crowned porcupine (the sign of Louis XII), are characteristic ornaments in this façade. The gentle tones of color, the genius in the proportions, the master hand which is

felt at every point, transport the spectator and silence
the critic. Indeed, the first view of this façade is a
wonderful introduction to the great splendor of the
Chateau of Blois.

Passing through the deeply chiseled archway, the
visitor finds himself suddenly in the great court of the
chateau. At the first view the sight seems difficult to
realize. It appears rather like the massive "mise-en-
scène" to some opera than the actual setting of the
history of France; and we wait, almost expecting the
tenor to spring from some low window upon the right,
and to hold us entranced by an impassioned love song.
Again it is like the square of an enchanted city whose
four palaces stand before us, all distinctly different and
yet all blending into a marvelous ensemble. Yes, it is
not a dream but a grand reality, the far-famed court of
the Chateau de Blois, the scene of so many pageants and
displays in the history of France, this incomparable spot
where are clustered such marvels of the Renaissance.
Behind and to the right are the interior façades of the
two wings that are seen from without, and in admiring
the unbounded richness, the perfect taste, and the
extraordinary beauty of both, it is well-nigh impossible to
lay the laurel wreath upon the steps of the François 1
wing and yet refrain from doing likewise to that of Louis
XII. A low cloister stretches along the entire length of
this last façade, making a delicate foundation to the
beautiful work above. It is in the transition period, or
that prior to the Italian Renaissance. The high slate
roof, broken by five richly ornamented windows and surmounted by a heavy stone railing, is higher even than
the two stories below it. Yet the lines and proportions
are so perfect that they form an ensemble more pleasing
to the eye, if anything, than the beauties of the François
1 wing, beside it. A square tower of brick and stone
(like all of the Louis XI and Louis XII portions of Blois)

divides this cloister from another upon the left. The columns are foreshortened and extremely simple in the cloister of Louis XI; but in that of Louis XII they are richly carved. They are alternated, round and square, the round ones being studded with fleur-de-lis.

The chapel of Louis XI, upon the left, is half hidden, from where we stand, by the cloister and the rather heavy work above it. A beautiful bit of stone detail, with a huge gargoyle at the climax of a corner buttress, tempts one to peer around still further, to be rewarded by a large gothic window over the door of the chapel. The top to the door itself is a fine bit of carved stonework and extends in a point up against that of the window. It bears the letters L and A, with the escutcheons of Louis and Anne, surmounted by the royal crown of France. Within, the chapel is rich in frescoes, copied after those of the fifteenth century. The effect outside is not unlike that of the famous Sainte-Chapelle in Paris, with its laceworked spire, rising against the sky from the top of the pointed roof. The chapel and the rest of this wing were the work of Louis XI, and are the oldest parts of the chateau, after the "Salle des Etats" opposite.

The Louis XII wing forms an harmonious second link, in this marvelous sequence of architectural studies. The styles of these two are so much alike as to blend almost into one, at the first glance; but we soon notice the more graceful and elaborate finish of the details. The carving of the windows assumes the most exquisite and artistic convolutions. The ornaments and accessories of the two towers show, with the long wing between them, the superiority and advance of this period over that of Louis XI.

I was standing in the centre of the court, and had turned about to take in, to their fullest extent, the beauty of the buildings just described. I must have lost myself in the enchantment of their lines, for I was

LOUIS XI WING. CHÂTEAU DE BLOIS

aroused from my dreams and criticisms by my friend the Comte, who touched my arm, and said:

"Let us go into this portion of the chateau, before even looking at the outside of the rest of it. Let us dip into the life and the surroundings of Louis XII and of Anne de Bretagne, and fill our minds with more knowledge of their own period, before passing on to the home of François I and of Catherine de Medici."

"You are right," I replied. "I always like to go to the bottom of one thing, or one monument, if it happens to be one, before going to another. It seems more of a duty than a pleasure, if one is hurried along from one set of thoughts, or the masses of historical stones which produce them, to the next, without time to sit down and to study something about them. Whereas, if one is only permitted to wander peacefully about, to enjoy those things which most appeal to the senses, and to pick up something of the time-laden air that hangs about and lurks in dusty corners, a feeling of charm and poetry unconsciously takes hold of one. To-day, especially, I feel in just such a mood, and as I am aware that you know as much of Blois as many of these guides, we will dispense with them, and you shall tell me of Louis XII and his portion of Blois."

"Eh bien," said the Comte, delighted at my proposal, "we are now in the guard chamber of Anne de Bretagne. I will not slight your French history by telling you that she was the wife of Louis XII. See how triste and gloomy these state apartments are. I have always wondered why they have never cut some windows upon the side of the cloisters here; these seem so small and so insufficient. There is a very good example of those wonderful chimney-pieces, which have lent their fame and beauty to the chateau." And the Comte pointed out an elaborate specimen. "See with what art and taste the richness of the carving is still kept delicate

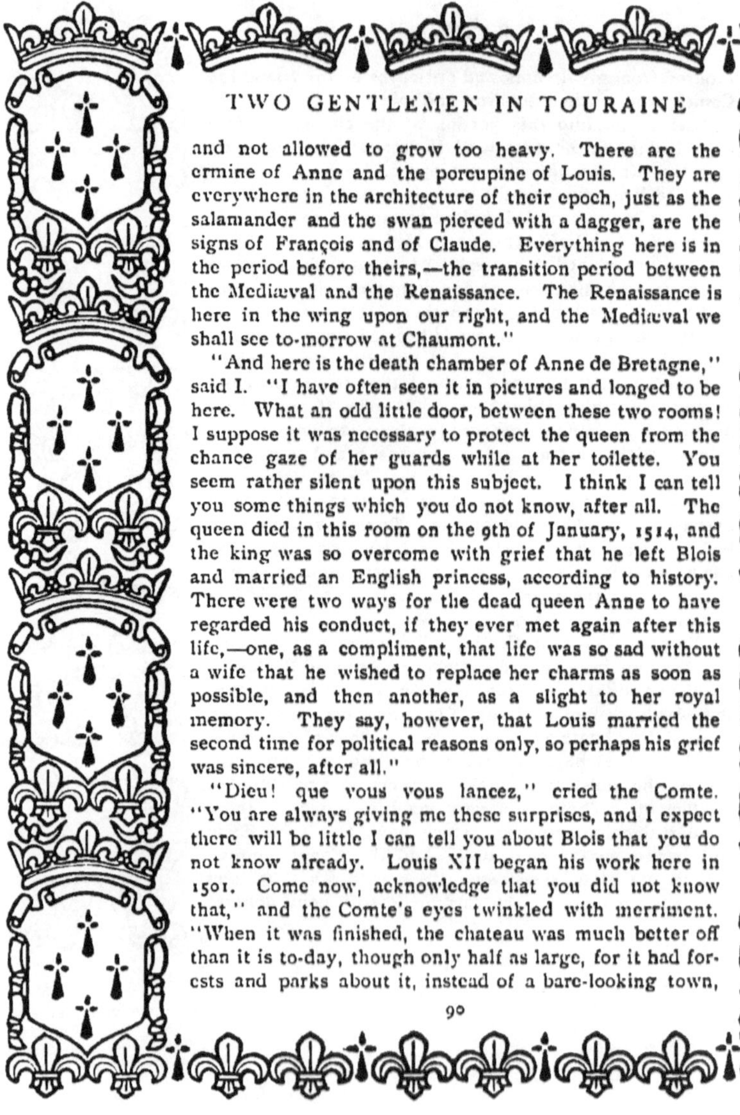

and not allowed to grow too heavy. There are the
ermine of Anne and the porcupine of Louis. They are
everywhere in the architecture of their epoch, just as the
salamander and the swan pierced with a dagger, are the
signs of François and of Claude. Everything here is in
the period before theirs,—the transition period between
the Mediæval and the Renaissance. The Renaissance is
here in the wing upon our right, and the Mediæval we
shall see to-morrow at Chaumont."

"And here is the death chamber of Anne de Bretagne,"
said I. "I have often seen it in pictures and longed to be
here. What an odd little door, between these two rooms!
I suppose it was necessary to protect the queen from the
chance gaze of her guards while at her toilette. You
seem rather silent upon this subject. I think I can tell
you some things which you do not know, after all. The
queen died in this room on the 9th of January, 1514, and
the king was so overcome with grief that he left Blois
and married an English princess, according to history.
There were two ways for the dead queen Anne to have
regarded his conduct, if they ever met again after this
life,—one, as a compliment, that life was so sad without
a wife that he wished to replace her charms as soon as
possible, and then another, as a slight to her royal
memory. They say, however, that Louis married the
second time for political reasons only, so perhaps his grief
was sincere, after all."

"Dieu! que vous vous lancez," cried the Comte.
"You are always giving me these surprises, and I expect
there will be little I can tell you about Blois that you do
not know already. Louis XII began his work here in
1501. Come now, acknowledge that you did not know
that," and the Comte's eyes twinkled with merriment.
"When it was finished, the chateau was much better off
than it is to-day, though only half as large, for it had forests and parks about it, instead of a bare-looking town,

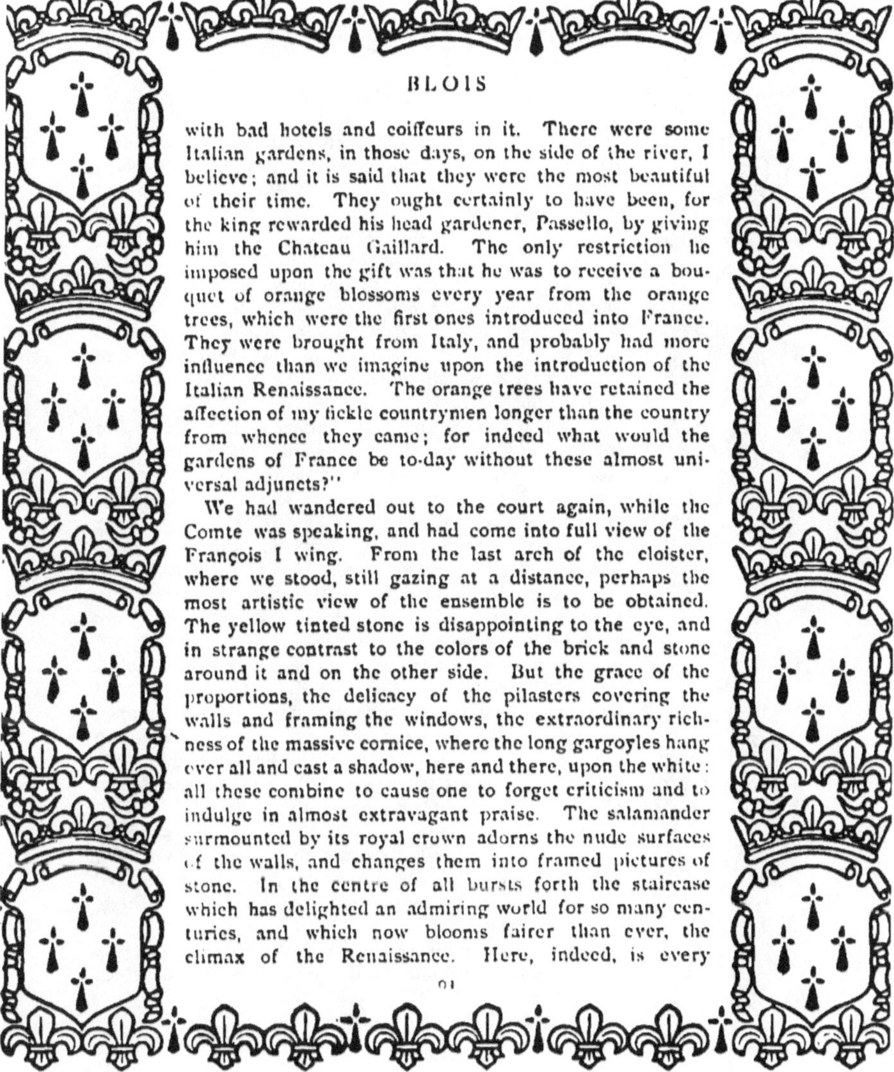

with bad hotels and coiffeurs in it. There were some Italian gardens, in those days, on the side of the river, I believe; and it is said that they were the most beautiful of their time. They ought certainly to have been, for the king rewarded his head gardener, Passello, by giving him the Chateau Gaillard. The only restriction he imposed upon the gift was that he was to receive a bouquet of orange blossoms every year from the orange trees, which were the first ones introduced into France. They were brought from Italy, and probably had more influence than we imagine upon the introduction of the Italian Renaissance. The orange trees have retained the affection of my fickle countrymen longer than the country from whence they came; for indeed what would the gardens of France be to-day without these almost universal adjuncts?''

We had wandered out to the court again, while the Comte was speaking, and had come into full view of the François I wing. From the last arch of the cloister, where we stood, still gazing at a distance, perhaps the most artistic view of the ensemble is to be obtained. The yellow tinted stone is disappointing to the eye, and in strange contrast to the colors of the brick and stone around it and on the other side. But the grace of the proportions, the delicacy of the pilasters covering the walls and framing the windows, the extraordinary richness of the massive cornice, where the long gargoyles hang over all and cast a shadow, here and there, upon the white: all these combine to cause one to forget criticism and to indulge in almost extravagant praise. The salamander surmounted by its royal crown adorns the nude surfaces of the walls, and changes them into framed pictures of stone. In the centre of all bursts forth the staircase which has delighted an admiring world for so many centuries, and which now blooms fairer than ever, the climax of the Renaissance. Here, indeed, is every

artistic longing of the French temperament satisfied. Here the genius of a taste-gifted race has forced its chisel, with a master hand, into the soft and shadow-covered stone, to create a chef d'œuvre of the art of architecture. Here richness and delicacy go hand in hand, mounting the ever-winding stair to drop their fairest jewels upon each step, and to vie with one another in their gifts. Detail and ensemble meet one another in a harmony so seldom found that it adds a tenfold charm. Shades and shadows blend in a softening tone, and throw a cloak of beauty over something which is more than our own eyes at first appreciate.

As we look at the staircase of Blois, framed by the two columns of the cloister, darkened by heavy shadows, it seems to fascinate the whole being as only perfection and beauty have the power to do. And we are tempted to say: "Why has the New World left so long untouched a design and an inspiration that deserve to find reproductions in a hundred forms and combinations? Why, when it has such marvelous examples and incentives in France and in the whole of Europe, has it not more improved such opportunities?"

"You must not go in there yet," said the Comte, pointing to the staircase. "You must allow the beauty of that wonderful piece of architecture to dawn more fully upon you, and to sink deeper into your mind, before entering the door which leads to the scenes of history within. We will cross the court and examine the most recent portion of the chateau, the last side of this inimitable quadrilateral. There it is, as you see, a cold and pure example of Louis XIII's period. It was built by Gaston d'Orleans, who was exiled to Blois for many years, and who died in 1660. His heart, by the way, is in the Jesuit Fathers' church of Blois.

"He had always intended to tear down the rest of the chateau and to rebuild it all in the style of this wing;

THE STAIRCASE, CHÂTEAU DE BLOIS

but, mercifully for those who have lived since, his death prevented him from destroying these stones, which have been such a standard of beauty in architecture ever since.''

"What a contrast," said I, "to the beauty of the architecture surrounding it! How could any one have been so dead to artistic value as to think of destroying such creations as that staircase, or the wing behind us?"

"You know what the poet says, do you not?" said the Comte.

> 'Breathes there a man with soul so dead,
> Who never to himself hath said:
> "This is my own, my native land"'?

Gaston d'Orleans might have paraphrased:

> 'There breathes a man with soul so dead,
> Who never to himself hath said:
> "This is indeed true, noble art,
> And from its lines I may not part."'

But he did not, as you see. Let us go inside, and look at the great staircase, reaching to the heavily ornamented roof. It is a noble work, one cannot deny the fact; but what a contrast to its neighbors!" And the Comte shook his head sadly, while I bowed a silent assent.

Turning from the rather overshadowed beauties of this massive wing, we crossed once more the sandy court, and mounted the winding staircase.

Here, in the days of Claude, the wife of François I, and in those of the famous Catherine de Medici, the soldiers and officers of the court stood on its many winding balconies, outside the ever-winding stairs, to welcome their king and queen. Here, royal persons of history, whose names stand out in bas-relief against centuries of time, wound their way, in state processions, to their apartments above. Here they gathered in the morning, in the evening, for a casual

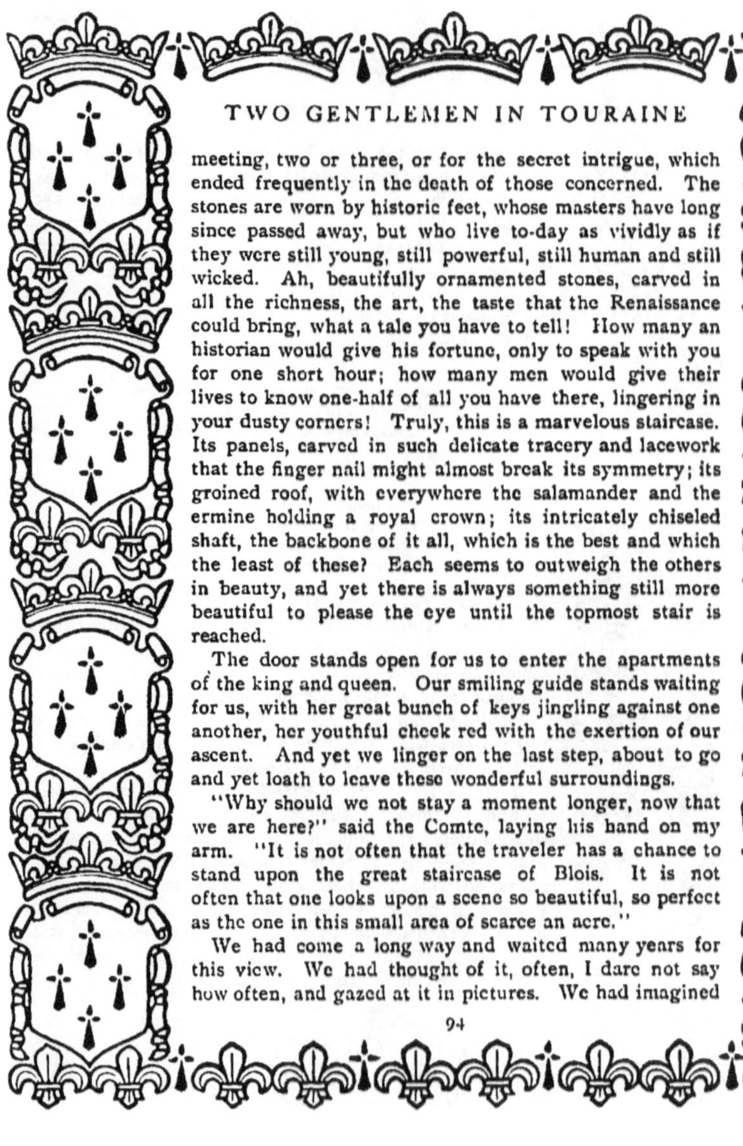

meeting, two or three, or for the secret intrigue, which ended frequently in the death of those concerned. The stones are worn by historic feet, whose masters have long since passed away, but who live to-day as vividly as if they were still young, still powerful, still human and still wicked. Ah, beautifully ornamented stones, carved in all the richness, the art, the taste that the Renaissance could bring, what a tale you have to tell! How many an historian would give his fortune, only to speak with you for one short hour; how many men would give their lives to know one-half of all you have there, lingering in your dusty corners! Truly, this is a marvelous staircase. Its panels, carved in such delicate tracery and lacework that the finger nail might almost break its symmetry; its groined roof, with everywhere the salamander and the ermine holding a royal crown; its intricately chiseled shaft, the backbone of it all, which is the best and which the least of these? Each seems to outweigh the others in beauty, and yet there is always something still more beautiful to please the eye until the topmost stair is reached.

The door stands open for us to enter the apartments of the king and queen. Our smiling guide stands waiting for us, with her great bunch of keys jingling against one another, her youthful cheek red with the exertion of our ascent. And yet we linger on the last step, about to go and yet loath to leave these wonderful surroundings.

"Why should we not stay a moment longer, now that we are here?" said the Comte, laying his hand on my arm. "It is not often that the traveler has a chance to stand upon the great staircase of Blois. It is not often that one looks upon a scene so beautiful, so perfect as the one in this small area of scarce an acre."

We had come a long way and waited many years for this view. We had thought of it, often, I dare not say how often, and gazed at it in pictures. We had imagined

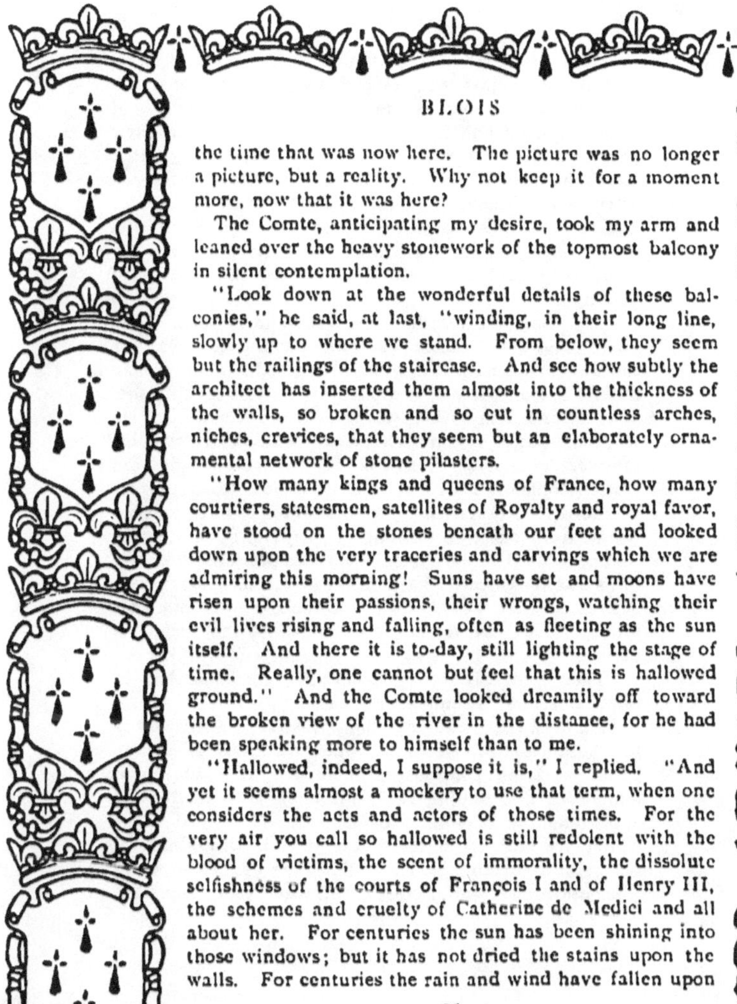

the time that was now here. The picture was no longer
a picture, but a reality. Why not keep it for a moment
more, now that it was here?

The Comte, anticipating my desire, took my arm and
leaned over the heavy stonework of the topmost balcony
in silent contemplation.

"Look down at the wonderful details of these balconies," he said, at last, "winding, in their long line,
slowly up to where we stand. From below, they seem
but the railings of the staircase. And see how subtly the
architect has inserted them almost into the thickness of
the walls, so broken and so cut in countless arches,
niches, crevices, that they seem but an elaborately ornamental network of stone pilasters.

"How many kings and queens of France, how many
courtiers, statesmen, satellites of Royalty and royal favor,
have stood on the stones beneath our feet and looked
down upon the very traceries and carvings which we are
admiring this morning! Suns have set and moons have
risen upon their passions, their wrongs, watching their
evil lives rising and falling, often as fleeting as the sun
itself. And there it is to-day, still lighting the stage of
time. Really, one cannot but feel that this is hallowed
ground." And the Comte looked dreamily off toward
the broken view of the river in the distance, for he had
been speaking more to himself than to me.

"Hallowed, indeed, I suppose it is," I replied. "And
yet it seems almost a mockery to use that term, when one
considers the acts and actors of those times. For the
very air you call so hallowed is still redolent with the
blood of victims, the scent of immorality, the dissolute
selfishness of the courts of François I and of Henry III,
the schemes and cruelty of Catherine de Medici and all
about her. For centuries the sun has been shining into
those windows; but it has not dried the stains upon the
walls. For centuries the rain and wind have fallen upon

the roof and tried to purify this hallowed atmosphere, and yet they have not washed away those stains, that must remain as long as the mortar holds the stones of Blois together and as long as those stains retain their particles. Call it hallowed, if you like, this ground, which has stayed the fall of many a murdered victim of intrigue and jealousy. I fear all history must be so then, and that we must take those men who figured in it as they came, judging them only for their good and for what they have left behind them for the benefit of mankind."

"Are you not a little hard upon men and women of the past?" said the Comte. "You must consider, you know, the circumstances under which they lived. Poor human nature, it seems to me, is capable of only so much resistance against temptation, just as it is capable of so much work and power of comprehension. I think, if you come to a careful analysis of natural desires, you will find the worst people of the world to be in almost exact proportion to their temptations. We are all too fond of judging people from our own standpoints, neglecting to consider that perhaps they have desires and temptations unknown to us and of which we have never tasted the bitterness— desires that are so unknown to us and temptations that are so strong as to be irresistible to the strongest natures."

"Then I take it that you consider good and bad as relative terms?" I replied.

"Hardly that," said my friend, his face lighting up as he continued in a strain in which he loved so well to speak. "I am considering more the impossibility of human nature judging itself properly, with its limited data, than the possibility of being good or bad. Our bodies are nothing more or less than intricate, natural machines expressing actions. They are gauged to stand a certain amount of pressure, and after that they must give way. Temptation is the pressure, and the people who are called bad in this world, are almost always those who have had more temptation than they could bear. In the same way, the good ones are more often those who have not experienced temptation, and less often, alas, those whose resistance is the greatest. A great many people in this world have forces, evil forces, working upon them to such an extent that the strongest nature even must succumb. The world calls them bad. Others there are, who have never had even the semblance of such a force brought to bear upon them, and so it is not surprising that they never give way to it. And these the world calls good.

"For all we know, Catherine de Medici was of the former class. But how is it possible to decide whether one of these classes is better or more culpable than the other? Human beings have not the power of discovering this exact ratio between the opposite forces of temptation and resistance; and therefore it is impossible for them to judge one another correctly."

PART II

The conversation on the staircase was interrupted by our guide, who had been waiting patiently while we indulged in philosophical speculations, which had wandered somewhat from the overhanging gargoyles of the roof. We turned, with some reluctance, from the scene without and the thoughts which it had inspired, to enter the apartments of Henry III. These occupy the whole of the upper floor; and if they are barren of their former furniture, they may at least boast a wealth of old and historical associations connected with the times and doings of Catherine de Medici. The whole suite, consisting of rooms, of private closets and galleries overlooking the town, is in a perfect state of restoration. The French government has devoted much time and money to the preservation and reproduction of old designs and styles of decoration. Everywhere the blue and yellow polished tiles, representing the or and azure of heraldry, are noticeable, in their everchanging design, upon the floor. The thick beams of the ceiling, decorated in the thousand patterns and brilliant coloring peculiar to the Renaissance, blend with that of the walls, and make us believe almost that it is yesterday in which we are living rather than to-day. A beautiful little chamber leads out of the private chapel of the king. It is entirely lined with tiny wooden panels, two hundred and forty in number, which are all of different design and highly ornamented in gold and brown. The ceiling is so similar to the walls that it gives to the whole the appearance of a little jewel box built to enclose some royal gem. And indeed it did once, long ago, for hard by is a window leading to the famous balcony where Marie de Medici, the cousin of Catherine and the wife of Henry IV, escaped, after twenty two years of captivity in this chamber. The secret cavities, behind their symmetrical panels, bring vividly to mind the terrible reality of those Mediæval days, when a chance mistake in court diplomacy might mean ruin or even death. Then an injudicious remark, a word too much, or a look misunderstood, might bring the fatal consequences of an angry sovereign or of a scheming mother. A note discovered, intercepted perhaps, the paper of a courtier, might be as dangerous as a cup of poison. So a secret panel, opening with an invisible spring, was, in the days of Blois, of Chambord, or of Chenonçeau, a valuable necessity, rather than an idle plaything in which to hide one's jewels.

A little door leads to a balcony of stone, winding around a tower to the dungeon where the Cardinal de Lorraine, the ill-fated brother of the Duc de Guise, passed his last night on earth. It was during the morning that he was taken out upon some false pretense and

murdered at a place not far distant. The dungeon is the same to-day as when the Cardinal was imprisoned in it. A large, iron-grated window looks out toward the garden of the king, high up on the Mediæval walls, and across a narrow gateway. In the distance, are the baths of his persecutor, Catherine de Medici. As one looks out upon all this from behind the bars of iron, one may well imagine the despair of the Cardinal, the agony of anticipation in which he must have passed that last night in prison. With what terrible sufferings of mind and soul must he have looked first at the beautiful scene without, thinking the while of all that it embodied, of life, of freedom, of everything that is precious to a human being! And with what a sickening dread must he have turned to the iron door, or the round hole in the centre of his royal cell, where on the morrow his body might be precipitated into the bowels of the castle, from which no link or memory of him ever could return! A shudder passed over my companion and myself as we turned to one another and exclaimed, almost in the same breath: "And of such were the Mediæval days."

"The present days are bad," said I, "far worse than they should be; but I think we have a few advantages over those that are left behind, in spite of telegraph poles, electric cars and modern so-called conveniences."

"It is, indeed, difficult to combine advanced civilization with the early simplicity and taste," the Comte remarked, musingly. "The modern education seems to teach rich men nothing of this principle and to teach poor men still less. At present, apparently, everything is considered useful if only it is made cheap and ugly. In the olden times everything was made to please the eye and to satisfy the taste, without the least idea of its convenience. Take these old chateaux of the Loire, for instance. They are wretchedly inconsistent and impracticable to live in. But they are perfectly beau-

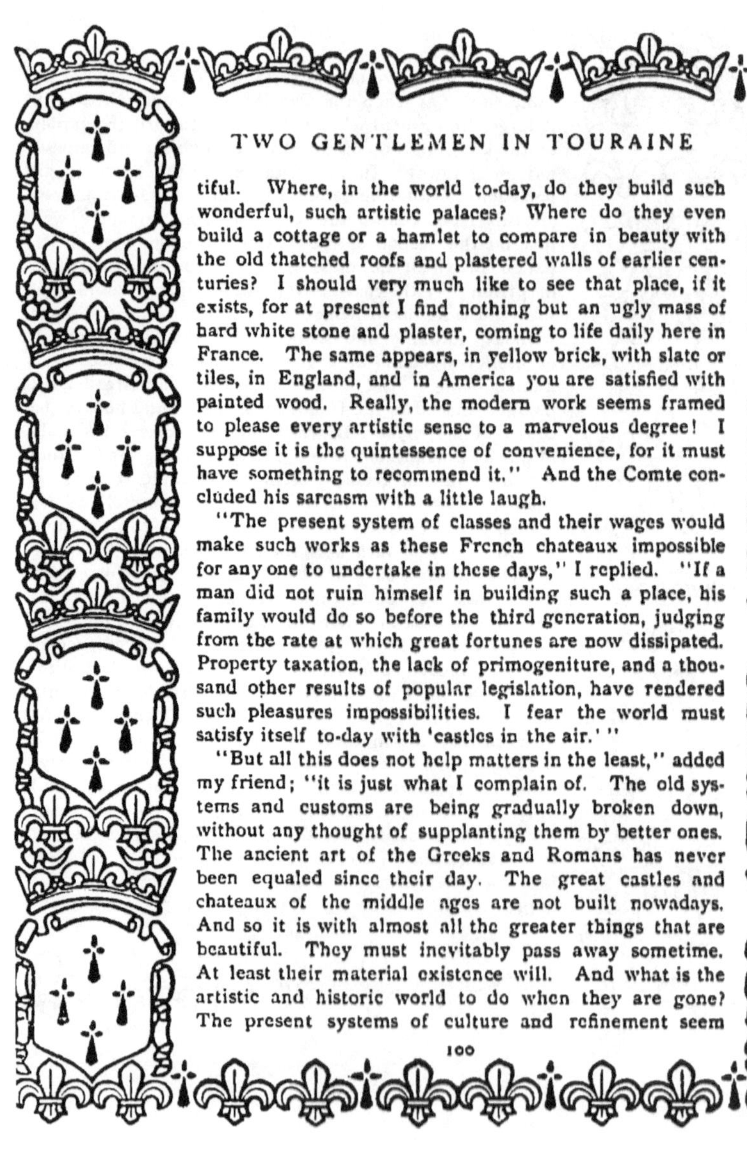

tiful. Where, in the world to-day, do they build such wonderful, such artistic palaces? Where do they even build a cottage or a hamlet to compare in beauty with the old thatched roofs and plastered walls of earlier centuries? I should very much like to see that place, if it exists, for at present I find nothing but an ugly mass of hard white stone and plaster, coming to life daily here in France. The same appears, in yellow brick, with slate or tiles, in England, and in America you are satisfied with painted wood. Really, the modern work seems framed to please every artistic sense to a marvelous degree! I suppose it is the quintessence of convenience, for it must have something to recommend it." And the Comte concluded his sarcasm with a little laugh.

"The present system of classes and their wages would make such works as these French chateaux impossible for any one to undertake in these days," I replied. "If a man did not ruin himself in building such a place, his family would do so before the third generation, judging from the rate at which great fortunes are now dissipated. Property taxation, the lack of primogeniture, and a thousand other results of popular legislation, have rendered such pleasures impossibilities. I fear the world must satisfy itself to-day with 'castles in the air.'"

"But all this does not help matters in the least," added my friend; "it is just what I complain of. The old systems and customs are being gradually broken down, without any thought of supplanting them by better ones. The ancient art of the Greeks and Romans has never been equaled since their day. The great castles and chateaux of the middle ages are not built nowadays. And so it is with almost all the greater things that are beautiful. They must inevitably pass away sometime. At least their material existence will. And what is the artistic and historic world to do when they are gone? The present systems of culture and refinement seem

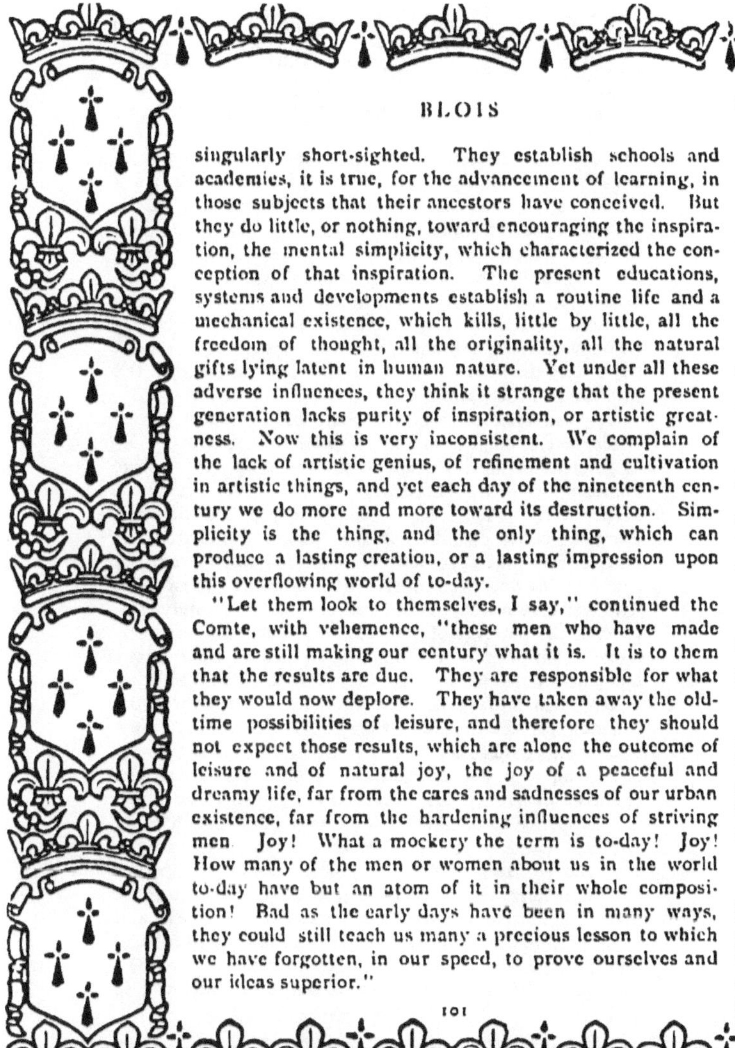

singularly short-sighted. They establish schools and academies, it is true, for the advancement of learning, in those subjects that their ancestors have conceived. But they do little, or nothing, toward encouraging the inspiration, the mental simplicity, which characterized the conception of that inspiration. The present educations, systems and developments establish a routine life and a mechanical existence, which kills, little by little, all the freedom of thought, all the originality, all the natural gifts lying latent in human nature. Yet under all these adverse influences, they think it strange that the present generation lacks purity of inspiration, or artistic greatness. Now this is very inconsistent. We complain of the lack of artistic genius, of refinement and cultivation in artistic things, and yet each day of the nineteenth century we do more and more toward its destruction. Simplicity is the thing, and the only thing, which can produce a lasting creation, or a lasting impression upon this overflowing world of to-day.

"Let them look to themselves, I say," continued the Comte, with vehemence, "these men who have made and are still making our century what it is. It is to them that the results are due. They are responsible for what they would now deplore. They have taken away the old-time possibilities of leisure, and therefore they should not expect those results, which are alone the outcome of leisure and of natural joy, the joy of a peaceful and dreamy life, far from the cares and sadnesses of our urban existence, far from the hardening influences of striving men. Joy! What a mockery the term is to-day! Joy! How many of the men or women about us in the world to-day have but an atom of it in their whole composition! Bad as the early days have been in many ways, they could still teach us many a precious lesson to which we have forgotten, in our speed, to prove ourselves and our ideas superior."

"My dear friend," I replied, at the conclusion of these reflections, "you must remember that you are a Conservative, but that the world of the present day is Radical, yea, and more than Radical. Entre nous, I coincide with many if not all of your opinions, and I hope sincerely that some day we shall obtain the much desired 'golden mean' of which the poets speak, between Radicalism and Conservatism, between poetry and practicality, between ornament and use. I say, let us indeed hope that the future may be such a medium between the present and the past."

Our conversation was cut short by the voice of our guide, exclaiming, as she threw open a door, with the air of one who is offering the best she has to an appreciative audience: "This, Messieurs, is the bed-chamber of Henry III." And, indeed, this was the bed-chamber, the famous bed-chamber, of that dissolute monarch. It looked not unlike several other royal bed-chambers in the castle. The floor was covered with blue and yellow tiles. The walls were hung in painted canvas, elaborately frescoed in the patterns of that period. The windows overlooked the town below, and the arches of their heavy balconies were painted in the same brilliant coloring which is so noticeable from without. Everywhere the salamander, crown and coronet appeared, amid a mass of blue and gold and yellow, adding richness to the whole, and beauty to one another. Yes, this was indeed the chamber of Henry III, the chamber in which so much had happened to be handed down to history, the chamber and perhaps the very spot where the famous murder of the Duc de Guise had taken place. Scenes and names and characters well up and overflow the mind as we stand here, in the room that has witnessed so much and between these four walls that have so many histories to tell if they could only speak. The tragic death-scene of the Duc de Guise seems to stand out, especially, and to

present its vivid picture to our imaginative fancy. Catherine de Medici, hard and pitiless, moved only by her jealousy and pride, passes before the eyes, and sinks behind the tapestries of an adjoining apartment. Henry III, inflamed by his intriguing mother and thinking only of how to rid himself of this cousin, who had incurred the jealousy of Catherine, waits in his private room, to hear the Duc de Guise come toward his door, and fall beneath a murderer's hand. The room is separated by a portière of tapestry, only, and as the king waits for the sounds, which are soon to tell him that his treacherous commands have been fulfilled, the scowl upon his brow haunts us, and we shudder as the Duc de Guise enters the fatal chamber. The walls are lined by armed gentlemen of the court, and we are surrounded by them and crushed in by those who push forward to bow to the Duc. He advances unsuspectingly, holding his drageoir in his hand, and smiling upon those who are around him. Suddenly a footstep from behind surprises him. An expression of alarm overspreads his countenance, as he realizes, for the first time, his danger. Another step, nearer and nearer. It is an enemy, a murderer, and he may not show his fear, lest all be lost. Another sound, close to him now, tells him instinctively that he must defend himself, or die by the assassin's hand. He turns, he is about to draw his sword; but another hand is too swift, too fatal, in its aim. Ah, unhappy cousin of an angry king, you are too late; the hour is at hand, and nothing can avail. Ah, noble victim of a jealous queen, you are betrayed, and naught can save you now. The poignard is at your heart; and enemies abound. Fall, there, upon the cold blue tiles. The "bleu de France" has neither aid nor pity for you, in this last hour. Your life is cut down in a moment, and you lie writhing amid a pool of royal blood.

And has the king no word, no act of pity or of mercy,

for his murdered kinsman? Has he no feelings of remorse nor consciousness of crime within his heart? It would seem not, for methinks that we can see him, issuing from among the tapestries, in the confusion of this dreadful scene, to stop before the dying man and kick the bleeding brow that is turned toward him. Another and another "coup de pied" fall in relentless wrath upon the body, from which life has been so foully driven, and from which it is now fast fleeing, as from an outraged shrine.

And has the royal pleasure been fulfilled; is the monarch satisfied? Is His Majesty unmoved by conscience, or by a solitary feeling of humanity? Alas, it is difficult for us to see, the courtiers hover so around the king, the scene becomes confused. Forms and faces grow dim. The curtain of Time drops softly over all; and we are once more in an empty chamber, filled only with the recollection of a former century.

Many winding passages and stairs, worn by the deep ruts of time, bring one at last from the apartments of Henry III to those of Catherine de Medici. They are upon the lower story, and are much the same, in plan and in decoration, as the ones above. The visitor is not a little impressed, as he passes through these rooms and guard-chambers, by their massive chimney pieces of carved stone. Still larger rooms open out of antechambers, decorated in the manner of the rest of Blois, and the long line of apartments ends in the private closet and bed-chamber of the most famous member of a famous family. Although our guide tells us but little of the historic associations of these rooms, inhabited by the Queen of France, the imagination is fain to picture sights and scenes which must have been there in her time. Near at hand, a beautifully ornamented little door, carved in French Gothic, and perfectly restored in colors, leads into one of the guard chambers. And here again we find

another door of equal beauty, while the massive chimney
piece of carved stone, might well be called a chef d'œuvre.
Again the life and characters of Blois come vividly to the
imagination in these royal chambers which have enclosed
so many chapters of French history.   Almost do the faces
of the soldiers, courtiers, generals and statesmen, rise
and live, until we expect to hear them exchange a word,
a salutation, or an order.   Here is a group about the
fire.   There is another by the window, looking out upon
the court.   Each and all are the satellites, the servants of
a queen who is there behind the ornamented door, there
in the recesses of the tapestry-covered boudoir, the corridor or the closet, there behind it all, invisible and yet
holding all within her iron grasp.   For Catherine de
Medici is no visionary queen, but an august reality, before
whom all tremble, all bow down.   Within her hand she
holds the reins of a kingdom, and directs a power, that is
second to none other of the Mediæval world.   What a
life, indeed, is hers, what a power, what a past!   And
yet when all is said of it, all written, was not the power
of the life of Catherine de Medici more like a living
death, so tinged was it with blood, and so covered was it
by a cloak of crime and cruelty?

A great door swings to, upon our departing footsteps.
A modern staircase brings us to a great hall whose domed
ceiling is covered with golden fleurs-de-lis upon a ground
of royal blue.   We wander in and out among the pillars,
which are but slender bands to uphold so vast a chamber
as is this.   It is the ancient "Salle des Etats" of the
Chateau of Blois, and we are wafted back to the very
beginning of its history, to mingle with the company of
nobles assembled here who rule the land.

At last our dreams of other days come to an end,
and we are once more under the beautiful tower of Louis
XII and in the cloister, where again we look back upon
the home of so many of the kings and queens of France

We cast a last look at the tower, ere we part, and breathe a silent prayer that we may once more return. The shadows of the archway are succeeded by the steps, the avenue, the town; and Blois, in all its beauty, all its grandeur, all its history is left behind. And as the haunts of Catherine, of Henry, of François, Louis, Claude and Anne fade out of our sight, their memories, both good and bad, seem to come out more strongly, and to remain imprinted upon the mind.

CHAPTER V

A long, straight road leads from Blois to Chaumont, ending in a street between two rows of plaster-covered houses. A high cliff, covered with trees and shrubs, rises a hundred feet above the street and seems almost to over-hang the roofs of slate. The deep, blue waters of the Loire are darkened by the shadows of the cliff that are made longer by the setting sun, and they wash the garden walls. Such is the village of Chaumont. Pointed roofs and pinarets, standing against the sky, crown the cliff and tell of the presence of the castle.

We draw up at the Hotel Méchin, occupying a humble position at one end of the village street. It is half past seven, and in spite of the pleasures of the afternoon, we welcome the hour for dinner. The dining-room of this diminutive public-house is approached through the principal apartment of the establishment, the billiard room. Its dingy walls are decorated in lugubrious frescoes, of an indifferent character. The cobwebs in the corners look as if laden down, with years, and the accumulated dust of ages. The blackened ceiling bears signs of many a bowl of tobacco, smoked beneath it. In short, this is the banqueting hall of the Hotel Méchin. We, however, are not deemed worthy of being honored with a banquet here, and we sit down—though none the less contentedly—to eat our "poulet de fondation," and to turn our thoughts toward the Chateau of Chaumont.

TWO GENTLEMEN IN TOURAINE

The evening is one of those soft and mild ones that are to be found so frequently in August. The sky overhead is spangled with a myriad of stars that culminate, at last, in the long "milky way," which seems to cut the heavens with an avenue of silvery light. After our dinner, we are tempted, before bringing the day to an end, to stroll through the village street, out toward the river, beside which we had been lingering during the last days. The little houses looked even smaller in the moonlight. They seem to be positively shriveled up, in fear of the covered cliff, which is threatening to fall upon them. The modern village church looms up beside the road, and its pointed spire is lost in the soft shades of the night. The "Presbytère," built in the shadows of the church, seems to be gazing at itself in the great, moving mirror by its side— the water, that is sometimes blue and dark, sometimes light and clear, sometimes yellow, as it runs over a bed of golden sand. The houses disappear one by one, and a little square comes into view, overlooking the river. Linden trees are planted here and there upon it, and beneath them the village children play a last game of hide and seek. Their childish cries, their protestations to their mothers' calls, alone break the peaceful calmness of the river's bank. One by one the children leave the game and seek their homes. The waters, flowing smoothly on their course, splash against the bank. A horse and cart, delayed by some unknown cause, pass us hastily upon the village road, to gain the town beyond. These are the last sounds which disturb the tranquillity of the summer's evening, lighted by the stars.

And as the hour strikes, from the village church, we return to our hotel. We cross the long, low billiard room, whose darkened walls are made still darker by the night without; we pass the kitchen, with its large, square table, where the men are drinking; we ascend the steep flight of stairs, leading from the kitchen itself, and

at last lay our heads down to rest in rooms as small
as they are uncomfortable. The bursts of laughter
from the men below reach us through the cracks of the
old tiled floors, and mingle with the dreams of a day that
has been filled with Chambord, Blois, and the approach
to Chaumont.

Early the next morning we left our hotel to enter the
park of Chaumont by an iron gateway, which was almost
directly across the street. This entrance is, however, far
from being one's ideal of the principal approach to a
chateau so renowned as this. The gate itself, which is
painted black, has an indescribable air about it which
suggests something less grandiose than Chaumont, and it
seems more appropriate to a side entrance than to the
chief approach. A steep avenue, cut into the side of the
cliff, leads from it toward the chateau. On the left
shrubberies and English ivy hide a stone wall, built there
to protect the land from sliding away. The high trees
upon the right half disclose and half conceal the panorama of the Loire, which, as we ascend, becomes more
and more beautiful.

At the end of half a mile, the avenue opens upon the
park above. Lawns, that are left untrimmed and allowed
often to grow half wild, are dotted here and there
with trees, and they stretch off with a rolling effect, due
partly to the long grass. At the edge of the cliff they are
lost in evergreens and bushes. The pointed slate roofs,
the towers and the gray walls of the chateau, appear in
front, while the park spreads out behind. And yet the
park itself is disappointing. It seems too cramped and
narrowed for the dignity of the chateau in its midst.
The trees seem small, as if the earth in which they grew
could not afford to give them their necessary food, or as
if they were beaten by a harsh wind. The stables are too
prominent and too near the chateau. The gardens, which,
strange as it may seem, are too much filled with flower-

beds, near together, lose in effect by their great number and by their odd shapes. They remind one more of that acre of ground which surrounds a villa in the Paris suburbs.

An effect of simplicity and grandeur would be more in keeping with the massive pile of stone which rises now before us, flanked by its great round towers. Large trees and straight avenues, which lose themselves in the distance, would have been preferable here to this overtaxed originality and misunderstood variety. The matchless situation of the chateau calls for natural beauty made by nature itself, and not for any human creation, which bears always testimony of the imperfection of man. For we are no longer standing in front of a chateau of the French Renaissance, whose delicate lacework and carving would allow more liberty to the imagination, would call for exterior embellishments more properly termed pretty than beautiful.

Chaumont has nothing of the fairy-like grace of a Renaissance chef d'œuvre. It is rather stately than graceful, rather imposing than alluring, borrowing its beauty, as well from its position, as from its construction. From the first moment, the castle appears as a very good example of that architectural period which preceded the awakening of the Renaissance. If Chenonçeau and Azay le Rideau picture to the mind, as we shall see before long, the refinements and pleasures of luxurious courts, Chaumont awakens an impression perhaps unknown until now. It brings a feeling, more of respect than admiration, a souvenir of feudal life, of pride and ancient might, inherent in a period preceding that of the Renaissance. It has, in addition to the historical interest of the other chateaux of the Loire, that, of having had a life which is now lost in the night of bygone centuries. We feel that Catherine de Medici and Diane de Poitiers have had predecessors within these walls and that they have left something of interest behind

CHÂTEAU DE CHAUMONT-SUR-LOIRE

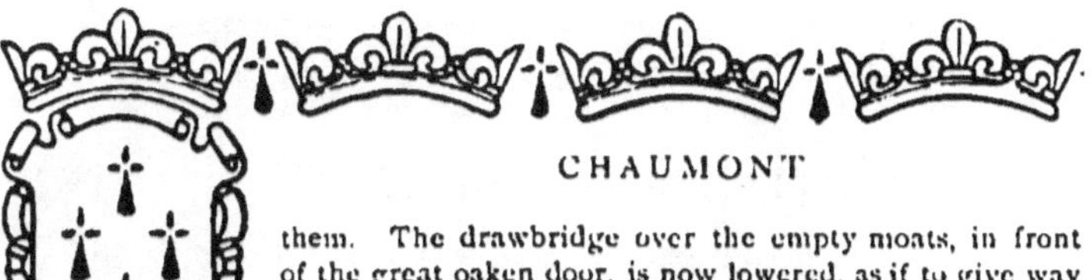

them. The drawbridge over the empty moats, in front of the great oaken door, is now lowered, as if to give way to chevaliers clothed in steel and silver armor, returning from a long war. The African hounds, belonging to the Princess, seem to watch for these knights, that they may announce their master's arrival to their mistress.

Our imaginations would induce us to believe that it is night, and that the chateau is plunged in darkness. A light, here and there, is the only thing that tells of life behind the heavy walls. The large cedar trees hide behind their heavy cloak of leaves a young chevalier, perhaps a page, watching in the night his lady-love, who stands beyond, behind the small lozenges of glass joined together in their leaden frames. She opens the window and comes out upon the balcony, where, leaning upon the stone rail, she watches the stars shining, bright and clear, in a cloudless sky. Now her eyes wander down to the Loire, which looks like an endless riband, set with the diamond reflections of the stars. Now she strains them in an endeavor to absorb the matchless panorama, glittering in the moonlight, a hundred feet below. It is half hidden in the mantle of night—midnight—and as the new day finds her still in contemplation of the scene, it hears also the plaintive note of an unseen guitar. The soft harmony is borne to her upon the summer wind. It hovers among the leaves of the trees and is echoed by the hills.

The night and its vision of a beautiful woman have both vanished in the glare of the morning sun. But we are still in front of the castle, which appears like a gigantic fan whose handle is the drawbridge. The fan is opened evenly, toward the right and left, and is pointing toward the Loire. Both ends of it are flanked by two large towers, while two more guard the narrow portion close to the handle. Between these last two towers is the great entrance door, with its ancient portcullis still

hanging above it, though centuries have passed since it
was used. Charles d'Amboise, the founder of the present
chateau, has given his name to the tower upon the left,
while the cabalistic signs which adorn the battlements of
the tower on the right have given that the name of
Catherine de Medici. A cordon of stone, almost as
wide as a cornice, encircles the two towers above the
first-story windows. The C in cipher and the monogram
of Charles de Chaumont are carved in the stone and
alternated with the emblem of the chateau's name,
miniature volcanoes—"Chaud Mont"—warm mountain.
The great door has the medallions of the Twelve Apostles
carved in the oak, while in the stone above, appear the
"L" of Louis XII on a semé of fleur-de-lis, and the
"A" of Anne de Bretagne, on a semé of ermines. The
rather barren walls of the towers are adorned with a
Cardinal's chapeau of George d'Amboise, a minister of
Louis XII, who was called "the friend of the people."
The coat of arms of his nephew, Charles, is also to be
seen, "paly of six, gold and gules," with two naked wild-
men as supporters.

If we cross the bridge, and pass through the vaulted
archway, we shall find ourselves in what is called "la cour
d'honneur." Some hundred and fifty years ago, this was
surrounded on all sides by the wings of the chateau; but
that portion overlooking the river has since been torn
down by Berties de Vauguyen, one of the chatelains of
Chaumont, and replaced by an esplanade enclosed with an
iron rail. From this is to be seen an almost unrivaled
panorama. The cliff here is so steep and high that we
seem to hover above the valley spreading beneath. And
for more than ten miles the Loire spins its graceful thread
through what is called "the garden of France." High
upon the other side rise the hills, dotted with clusters of
trees, or green, with the well-known vineyards beyond,—
"les coteaux de la Loire." The even rows of vines stretch

away for miles in straight, dark lines. Here and there, patches of reddish brown grapes are mingled with the white and green. In some places the sulphate, sprinkled upon the leaves to protect the plant from a much-feared disease, looks like a silvery spot upon this green of emerald hue. Such landscapes, seen by the light of a sun so clear that all things seem to shine, awaken in one an impression of contentment and peace to be found only in nature, and which nature only may retain.

Behind us, the castle rises, upon three sides of an imperfect quadrilateral. The fan-like effect has remained without; and on entering the court, another wing, before unseen, changes the shape of its contour. The construction here is also of the period preceding that of the Renaissance. The walls look like the skeleton of that architecture on which the following period was to add the carvings, the delicate art, the highest development, in fact, of its knowledge and capacity. An arcade of some beauty stretches along the façade, to the left of the entrance. A tower, or the three sides of one, at this end of the arcade, encloses a circular staircase, and its carved buttresses, more like pilasters in their appearance, add to the effect. Beds of flowers grow in straight lines along the walls, while a stone well-top, brought from Italy, completes the ornamentation of the court.

We had been standing there some time, when a woman, dressed in black and wearing the small white cap of the peasant woman of Touraine, came toward us and asked us if we wished to visit the interior. We expressed a desire to do so and followed her to the tower and its cloister. Some twelve or thirteen steps—the exact number is not of vital importance—brought us to a heavy oaken door through which we were ushered into a long room, called "la Salle des Gardes." Here the walls are hung with Flemish tapestries of the fifteenth century, framed in oak panelings. The ceiling is high and made of black oak beams crossed by smaller ones, while the floor is paved in ordinary tiles painted brown.

"This is 'la Salle des Gardes,' " said our guide, glancing around the room to see if all was in order. "The tapestries are old; but they have been placed here only recently. The furniture, as you may see, is all of old oak, and it is authentic. Monsieur le Prince and Madame la Princesse, who are both connoisseurs, take pleasure in buying a great deal of old furniture and bringing it here to decorate Chaumont. Every year they make some new improvement. This year, for instance, we are to have some old, stained windows put into the historical rooms. If ces Messieurs wish to take a look at the stone chimney here, they may enter, and come close to it." And we entered. The chimney, which occupies the centre of the further end of the great room, is all of stone and painted according to the period, while the escutcheon of the present master adorns the centre of it.

As we walk through the room, stopping here and there to admire and examine, the Comte tells me that once or twice a year (in September as a rule, when the chateau is filled with guests), private theatricals are performed in this room. The more talented guests at the chateau take part, and the excellence of the acting and management has given them no little reputation throughout the neighborhood. "These entertainments are the signal for great rejoicings, picnics, shooting parties, etc.," he added. "The princess, who is a delightful hostess, is always ready for something new to entertain her guests. As an instance the following anecdote is told: Wednesday is the day allowed for strangers to visit Chaumont during the residence of family at the chateau. And one day some of the guests took it into their heads to dress up as maids or servants, and to act as guides. They showed all the rooms to the strangers, and some rooms that they ought not to have shown, I believe, also. Some were

very clever and spirituelle, and told such funny stories that the poor visitors did not know what to believe and what to disregard, and were completely mystified."

Our guide had heard some of the Comte's remarks, and seeing that he was a friend of the house, she took pains to tell us more about the place.

"Here," she said, pointing to a table near a window on the left, "here is a case containing some very interesting medallions of terra cotta. They represent the profiles of a great number of personages who lived during the eighteenth century. The best medallion, both in its likeness and its finish, is that of Benjamin Franklin, who was a frequent visitor at Chaumont. He was a great friend of Monsieur Leray, who then owned the chateau, and it was doubtless he who induced the son to go on an expedition to America; for it is well known that young Monsieur Leray went to the United States, and tried to colonize on the banks of the Ohio. But it is also a well-known fact that he did not succeed, and came back to Chaumont after his father's death about the year 1815.

"Ces Messieurs will admire the medallions even more when they have learned how much the present chateau owes to them. The greater part of the furniture and perhaps the walls themselves were saved from destruction and pillage by these medallions, now resting peacefully under this glass case.

"In 1750, forty-three years before the revolution of 1793, Chaumont was bought by Monsieur Leray, whose name, 'sauf votre respect,' I have already mentioned. He started, in the park, a factory of pottery and ceramic products, including medallions, which were made out of the clay of Chaumont. These bear testimony to the talent of Nini, an Italian, who superintended the factory and who gave it great renown. Thus, industry came to take possession of a castle which had always been the

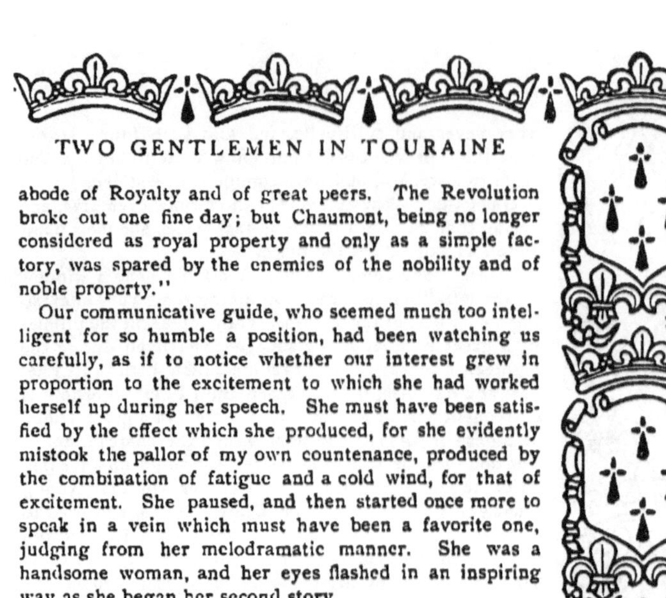

abode of Royalty and of great peers. The Revolution broke out one fine day; but Chaumont, being no longer considered as royal property and only as a simple factory, was spared by the enemies of the nobility and of noble property."

Our communicative guide, who seemed much too intelligent for so humble a position, had been watching us carefully, as if to notice whether our interest grew in proportion to the excitement to which she had worked herself up during her speech. She must have been satisfied by the effect which she produced, for she evidently mistook the pallor of my own countenance, produced by the combination of fatigue and a cold wind, for that of excitement. She paused, and then started once more to speak in a vein which must have been a favorite one, judging from her melodramatic manner. She was a handsome woman, and her eyes flashed in an inspiring way as she began her second story.

"May I beg ces Messieurs to come close to the window and take a look at this scene below. It was here that an interesting circumstance took place, at the beginning of this century,—in 1810, I believe.

"A very great lady, no less a person than Madame la Baronne de Staël, the daughter of Necker, the minister of Louis XVI and wife of the ambassador whose christian name was Magnus, was traveling one day by the white stone dike which runs along the bank of the Loire, and which you see now shining in the morning sun. The great lady was on her way back from exile, where she had been sent by Napoleon, who, according to her own opinion, could never appreciate her truest value. She was driving in a 'chaise de poste,' and as she passed Chaumont, she caught sight of the chateau, standing out of its bed of trees on the opposite bank, and ordered her postillion to stop.

" 'Postillion, this is a superb chateau.'

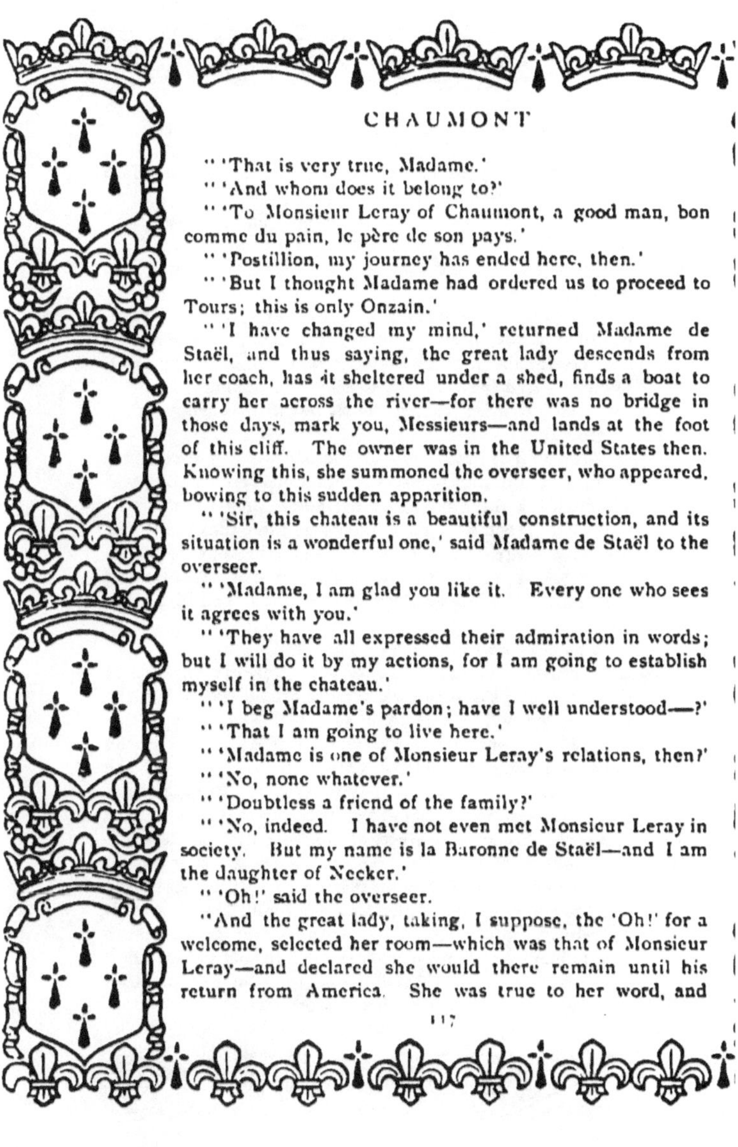

" 'That is very true, Madame.'

" 'And whom does it belong to?'

" 'To Monsieur Leray of Chaumont, a good man, bon comme du pain, le père de son pays.'

" 'Postillion, my journey has ended here, then.'

" 'But I thought Madame had ordered us to proceed to Tours; this is only Onzain.'

" 'I have changed my mind,' returned Madame de Staël, and thus saying, the great lady descends from her coach, has it sheltered under a shed, finds a boat to carry her across the river—for there was no bridge in those days, mark you, Messieurs—and lands at the foot of this cliff. The owner was in the United States then. Knowing this, she summoned the overseer, who appeared, bowing to this sudden apparition.

" 'Sir, this chateau is a beautiful construction, and its situation is a wonderful one,' said Madame de Staël to the overseer.

" 'Madame, I am glad you like it. Every one who sees it agrees with you.'

" 'They have all expressed their admiration in words; but I will do it by my actions, for I am going to establish myself in the chateau.'

" 'I beg Madame's pardon; have I well understood—?'

" 'That I am going to live here.'

" 'Madame is one of Monsieur Leray's relations, then?'

" 'No, none whatever.'

" 'Doubtless a friend of the family?'

" 'No, indeed. I have not even met Monsieur Leray in society. But my name is la Baronne de Staël—and I am the daughter of Necker.'

" 'Oh!' said the overseer.

"And the great lady, taking, I suppose, the 'Oh!' for a welcome, selected her room—which was that of Monsieur Leray—and declared she would there remain until his return from America. She was true to her word, and

stayed until—by order of Napoleon—she was forced to remove to a further exile."

"Delightful!" said the Comte, who had listened with interest to the story. "If you really want anything, there is nothing like taking it and keeping it, and that without asking."

"Ah ça, c'est bien vrai," replied our guide, and turning toward me, probably to see if I took in the joke, she noticed for the first time that I was looking very tired. In fact, I had been forced to seek the support of one of the hard, wooden chairs, more beautiful perhaps than comfortable.

"Monsieur is ill? Too bad, too bad. But never mind, I will give him a good glass of brandy when we go down. We must see the room of Catherine de Medici first."

With a great deal of dignity she then took from her pocket a large bunch of keys. Selecting one of them, she turned it in the lock with a great deal of noise and creaking. The heavy door swung open, and she cried out:

"Chambre de Catherine de Medici!"

"I must apologize," she added, "for the absence of the stained glass windows. They are in Paris, for the present, but will be here again soon. The chimney, which you see in front, is remarkable only as being that of the queen's room. But please notice the doorway on the right, which leads into Ruggieri's room. Ruggieri was the astrologer and confidant of this superstitious Italian princess. Some time since, we found a little stone staircase, concealed in the thickness of the walls. It winds up to Ruggieri's observatory in the tower. If we stop here and look into Catherine de Medici's room, ces Messieurs will notice the old carved bed, with its four twisted posts and its canopy. The coverlet is modern, but copied from an ancient pattern. As you may see, the moss-colored cloth is covered with various colored silk applications,

just as the original stuffs were. Madame la Princesse
had it made recently, but she was so dissatisfied with the
coloring that she wrote me to put it near the window
that the sun might fade it to a softer tone. It was very
expensive, and Madame regrets having spent so much
upon it."

At this point, our guide drew herself up in great
majesty, walked to the window, and turning towards us
once more, she continued, with the same inspired air
which she had assumed before:

"The queen is here, sitting close to the window and in
the recess within which I now stand. Her countenance
is that of a woman greatly preoccupied. Her body is
bent forward, her forehead resting upon her hand, and she
leans toward the door which leads to Ruggieri's room.
She is listening intently, as if to catch the faintest sound.
Suddenly she hears the noise of a door, opening and closing again. Footsteps sound upon the stone staircase, and
the noise grows faint and fainter as the steps are lost in
the distance. The queen rises to her feet in an endeavor
to call, but her lips close without framing the sound;
she falls back upon her chair and sighs deeply. For she
knows that the steps she hears must be those of her
astrologer, ascending the winding stairs which lead to
his observatory. She knows that he has gone to fulfil
her orders, to consult the stars as to the destiny of her
children. Cruel and depraved as it is, her mother's heart
has shrunk from the ordeal at the last moment, and she
has already risen to stay the fulfilment of the order; but
pride and superstition have overcome her softer feelings,
and she awaits the issue. Ruggieri is already upon the
platform of the highest tower of Chaumont, communing
with the stars.

"The night has fallen clear and cold—a night of Octo-
ber, lighted by a silver crescent in the east and stars so
brilliant that they seem the inevitable vanguard of a

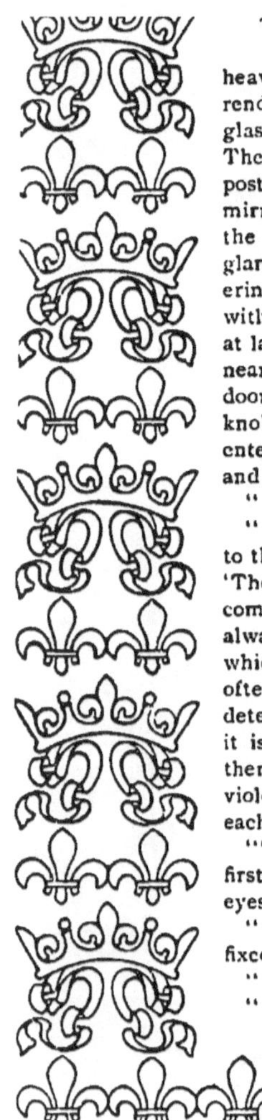

heavy frost for the next morning. The pale, cold light, rendered still softer and more indistinct by the stained glass window, spreads a dismal sadness through the room. The chairs, the table, and the bed with its four twisted posts, blend with the dark hangings of the wall. A mirror hanging opposite the stone chimney alone catches the rays of the moon, and reflects them in a metallic glare against the dark surroundings. The queen, Catherine, is still sitting in the oaken chair, leaning forward with her forehead upon her hands. Footsteps are heard at last upon the stairs, and they grow loud as they come near. The queen rises and walks hurriedly to the door. She lifts the heavy portière of tapestry, turns the knob, and a man clad in the long robes of a magician enters. The queen locks the door carefully behind him, and follows him to the chair.

" 'What have you seen?' she enquires, eagerly.

" 'I have drawn four themes of nativity, corresponding to the four sons of your Majesty,' replied the astrologer. 'These themes are the result of astronomic observations, combined and drawn according to fixed rules. They are always followed by a series of necessary consequences, which may be sometimes fortunate, though they are more often unfortunate. Thus human destiny is known and determined beforehand. I read it in the heavens, where it is written in letters of fire. And according to these themes, the four princes, your Majesty's sons, will die violent deaths. They will die without posterity, and will each wear, successively, a royal crown.'

"The haughty queen cast down her eyes, and for the first time in her whole life, perhaps, tears rolled from her eyes.

" 'These observations are, alas, combined according to fixed rules?' she enquired.

" 'Yes, your Majesty.'

" 'Fatal consequences follow them?'

" 'Yes, your Majesty.'

" 'Then let us ascertain if you could not have been mistaken in reading the words written in letters of fire upon the heavens. Let us consult the magic art, and see if it will confirm the language of the stars.'

" 'Amen—so let it be,' replied Ruggieri, solemnly; and leading the queen by the hand to the mirror shining in the night, he said:

" 'Look into this enchanted mirror and you will see a large room. It is not the one in which we stand. Those who shall cross that room will reign—and their reign will last as many years as they shall cross the mirror.'

"The reigning king, François II, the husband of Marie Stuart, came first. His features were contracted by illness. His body seemed too heavy to be sustained, and his cheeks were burned with fever. He walked a few steps across the room and soon vanished, without even completing the first year's passage. He remained just long enough for Catherine to recognize the reigning king, just enough to learn that before the end of a year she would mourn for her eldest son.

"Charles IX appeared next, and after having crossed the room thirteen and a half times, he vanished, leaving a bloody cloud behind him.

"The Duc d' Anjou, who was to be Henry III, crossed fifteen times and then vanished.

"Henry IV, young and healthy, entered and crossed twenty times, disappearing at the beginning of the twenty-first. He was immediately followed by a boy, eight or nine years old, who crossed thirty-seven times.

"The queen, pale with fear and anguish, covered her eyes with her hands, and begged to see no more. The mirror ceased to reflect the visions, and all things became invisible again.

"If ces Messieurs wish to see the famous Ruggieri's room, here it is," said our dramatic guide, and we awoke

from the dream which her story had produced, to leave
this haunted chamber and to pass on to its neighbor.
Yes, here it is! Let us look hastily through the ancient
and historically haunted apartment and see the cabalistic
signs above the chimney. Let us take in, at a glance,
the tapestries and walls, and let us leave these rooms, so
sad in aspect and in recollections.

The door is closed carefully behind us, a new one
opened, and we find ourselves in the gallery overlooking
the chapel.

A feeling of admiration, of sanctity almost, impresses
itself upon the visitor as he enters this graceful and
impressive chapel of Chaumont. The light, softened by
the old stained-glass windows, spreads a mysterious and
haloed charm over all. The carved altar rises in front,
almost at the feet, as we stand in the balcony overhanging
the whole. On the right is an oaken throne with its
canopy above, while over it hangs the red cardinal's
chapeau of George d'Amboise. On the left, facing the
throne, is a very fine ivory Christ of a Spanish or
Italian school. It stands out in relief against a deep red
velvet ground. Large silk banners of many families
hang from the walls above, like flags taken from an
enemy and brought there as an ex-voto—a votive offering
to God. Benches and prie-Dieu are arranged below, on
either side of the central aisle, and are covered with pearl
gray velvet, on which the two C's of Chaumont (OC)
stand out in crimson. Venetian lanterns made of gold
stand high above these benches, and must, when evening
comes, spread a softer light even than that which now
harmonizes the effect, enhancing the stone carvings and
their purity of style by the shadows, here deep, here light.

The Comte could not help saying to me in a subdued tone how much he admired the chapel. "It is
the most perfect," he said, "if not in detail at least
taken as a whole, of all the private chapels of

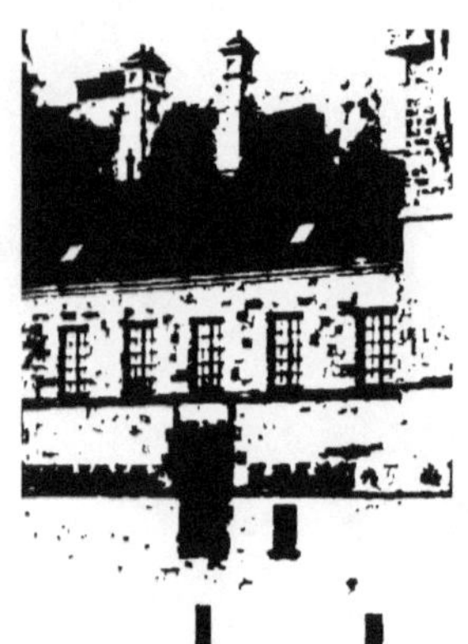

IONT-SUR-LOIRE

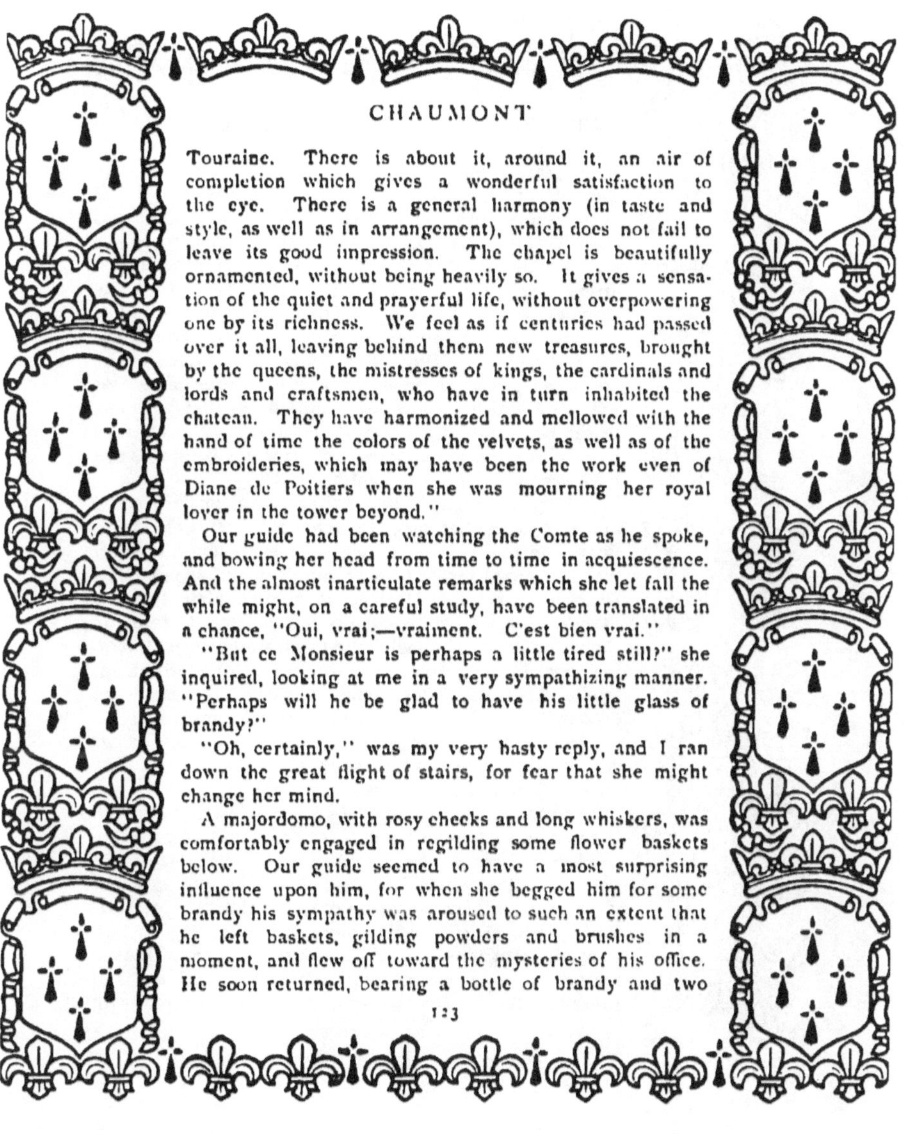

Touraine. There is about it, around it, an air of completion which gives a wonderful satisfaction to the eye. There is a general harmony (in taste and style, as well as in arrangement), which does not fail to leave its good impression. The chapel is beautifully ornamented, without being heavily so. It gives a sensation of the quiet and prayerful life, without overpowering one by its richness. We feel as if centuries had passed over it all, leaving behind them new treasures, brought by the queens, the mistresses of kings, the cardinals and lords and craftsmen, who have in turn inhabited the chateau. They have harmonized and mellowed with the hand of time the colors of the velvets, as well as of the embroideries, which may have been the work even of Diane de Poitiers when she was mourning her royal lover in the tower beyond."

Our guide had been watching the Comte as he spoke, and bowing her head from time to time in acquiescence. And the almost inarticulate remarks which she let fall the while might, on a careful study, have been translated in a chance, "Oui, vrai;—vraiment. C'est bien vrai."

"But ce Monsieur is perhaps a little tired still?" she inquired, looking at me in a very sympathizing manner. "Perhaps will he be glad to have his little glass of brandy?"

"Oh, certainly," was my very hasty reply, and I ran down the great flight of stairs, for fear that she might change her mind.

A majordomo, with rosy cheeks and long whiskers, was comfortably engaged in regilding some flower baskets below. Our guide seemed to have a most surprising influence upon him, for when she begged him for some brandy his sympathy was aroused to such an extent that he left baskets, gilding powders and brushes in a moment, and flew off toward the mysteries of his office. He soon returned, bearing a bottle of brandy and two

small glasses, on a silver tray, engraved with princely
coronets and coats of arms. In the meantime we had
been ushered into the vaulted dining-room, which has
been recently repaired. It is long and narrow, more like
a gallery or closed cloister than like a dining-room. It
opens upon the park, as well as upon the inner court. The
chimney, which occupies the whole of the further end, is
perhaps the most interesting portion of this restoration;
for it is truly beautiful. For the rest, the tables, chairs
and other pieces of furniture, whether for ornament or
use, were a little below the standard, so that we must
beg to be excused from their description, as the bottle of
brandy, the glasses and the tray are now before us and
have yet to restore us to health.

"I hope Monsieur is better," asked our guide, putting
her face, only her face, through the half open door.
Poor woman! I saw in her glance an expression of
fear, a thought that may have run through her mind, lest
we should take the silver as an accompaniment to our
brandy. And I could scarcely refrain from turning to
the majordomo, who had retired to his gilding, and quot-
ing one of my countrymen—I have forgotten whom:
"John, the Count has come to call. Put away the
spoons." But I refrained, and answered simply:

"Much better, thank you, and if you will permit us, we
will continue our visit through the other rooms." I
was now somewhat refreshed.

The part of the chateau we were now passing through
is one which has been lately furnished with every modern
comfort. Some of the furniture is old, but most of it is
new, and the whole has that air of habitation about
it, which awakens an instinctive feeling of cosiness.
Perhaps the artistic feeling loses something by it. Perhaps the artistic eye runs laboriously over these rooms,
taking in at a glance the new-looking velvets and
brocades, the modern screens, the tables covered with

plush and ornaments. Perhaps it may find too many palms and flowers and photographs about. We know not. But the feeling of home is certainly a pleasant one; at least my companion found it so, for he immediately ensconced himself in one of the velvet arm-chairs, which looked even more comfortable than they actually were, after the stiff Renaissance furniture of the opposite wing. A quantity of photographs were hanging upon screens, standing upon small tables, or filling large bowls of old china. A beautiful picture of a woman in a ball dress, with a quantity of diamonds about her neck, attracted our attention.

"Dear me," said the Comte, enchanted to find an old acquaintance. "Why, this is the Vicomtesse de ——! I haven't seen her for three years. How she has changed since her marriage! Dear me, dear me!"—and he passed on to the next.

"What a good likeness this is of the Comte de X. There is no mistaking him," he continued. "How photographs bring back old faces, old associations, almost forgotten but for these drawing-room reminders! Do you see this large group here, taken upon a terrace? And this other one on the coach, and the other upon the lawn? I put a name to each face, and they remind me of a world of thoughts and pleasures,—a picnic, a hunting party, a coaching drive, a theatrical performance, may be. All these photographs bring back the thousand recollections of an ideal, though, it may be, idle life in the midst of people with whom we have been thrown, who have drifted in various directions, and who now repass before our eyes, like the glasses of a magic lantern,— representing a good share of what is called 'la societé Française.' "

The Comte was in his most amusing mood, looking over the bibelots in the large salon, and caused no little amusement to our guide, who was smiling and looking

over his shoulder, as if she knew the originals of the
photographs as well as he. Each little corner of the
room, each screen and chair, shaded by a tall palm,
seemed to remind him of something or some one. He
might have picked up each photograph, I suppose,
brought them to life, set them in the "coins à flirter," as
they are called there, and told us word for word the conversations held by them when they were last there. As
he passed from one place to another, he was smiling,
shrugging his shoulders and skipping about, as only a
Frenchman knows how to do, giving himself heart and soul
to the performance of the smallest action and lending an
apparently vital importance to the most trivial gossip.

"How soon will you have finished your inspection?"
said I at last.

"As soon as you wish," replied my friend. "But
I do not see why you are in so great a hurry to leave
Chaumont. There is much here which is worthy of
notice. You will hardly find another historical chateau
in France, at least among those which are noted as 'historical monuments,' that belongs to the proper people
and is inhabited in the right manner. You may as
well be noticing all this, while I renew acquaintance
with these photographs. You must remember that for
those Frenchmen who are so unfortunate, or so fortunate,
as you like, to belong to that class which cannot work
without breaking with the prejudices of centuries, you
must remember, I say, that the most interesting part of
their lives is in making, losing and renewing acquaintances. As a rule, all these acquaintances belong to
the same class and to the same society. They might
even be compared to a great family, the members of
which (although they may sometimes hate one another
inwardly from envy or jealousy), are still glad to meet
again, because they are tied to one another by an
unbreakable bond, that of birth. Well, I suppose

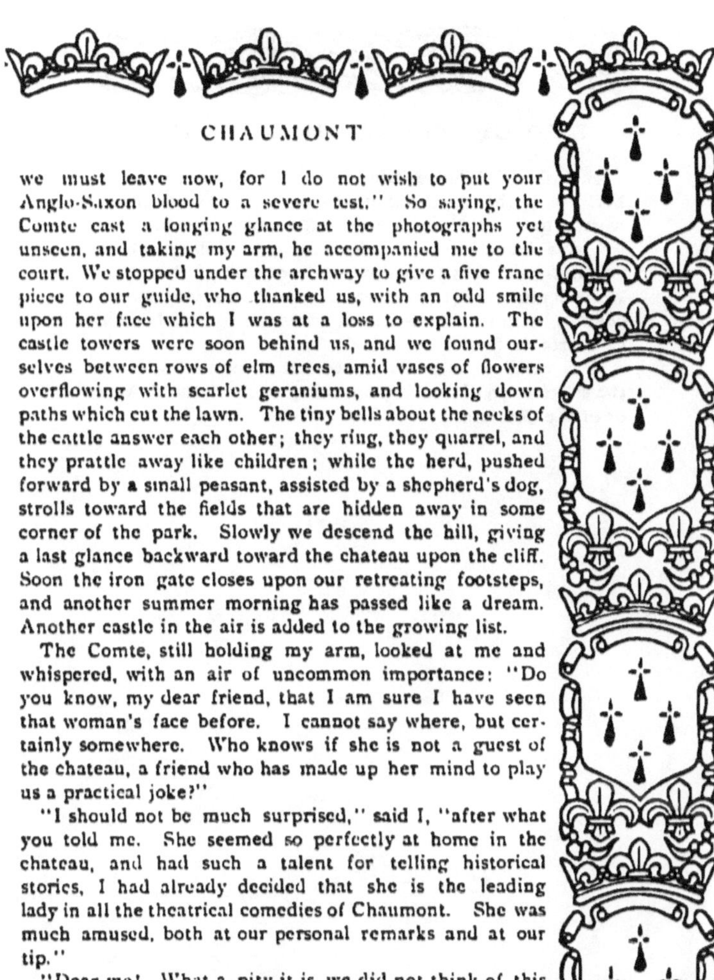

we must leave now, for I do not wish to put your Anglo-Saxon blood to a severe test." So saying, the Comte cast a longing glance at the photographs yet unseen, and taking my arm, he accompanied me to the court. We stopped under the archway to give a five franc piece to our guide, who thanked us, with an odd smile upon her face which I was at a loss to explain. The castle towers were soon behind us, and we found ourselves between rows of elm trees, amid vases of flowers overflowing with scarlet geraniums, and looking down paths which cut the lawn. The tiny bells about the necks of the cattle answer each other; they ring, they quarrel, and they prattle away like children; while the herd, pushed forward by a small peasant, assisted by a shepherd's dog, strolls toward the fields that are hidden away in some corner of the park. Slowly we descend the hill, giving a last glance backward toward the chateau upon the cliff. Soon the iron gate closes upon our retreating footsteps, and another summer morning has passed like a dream. Another castle in the air is added to the growing list.

The Comte, still holding my arm, looked at me and whispered, with an air of uncommon importance: "Do you know, my dear friend, that I am sure I have seen that woman's face before. I cannot say where, but certainly somewhere. Who knows if she is not a guest of the chateau, a friend who has made up her mind to play us a practical joke?"

"I should not be much surprised," said I, "after what you told me. She seemed so perfectly at home in the chateau, and had such a talent for telling historical stories, I had already decided that she is the leading lady in all the theatrical comedies of Chaumont. She was much amused, both at our personal remarks and at our tip."

"Dear me! What a pity it is we did not think of this before we gave it to her," exclaimed the Comte, with true

French thrift. "But, of course! Why did I not recognize her? It is the Comtesse de P—— and a very clever woman too. And now, quick! We must show her that we have found her out." Rushing to a gardener whose establishment was flourishing on the bank of the river, we ordered a large bouquet of roses to be sent to the chateau, with the Comte's card, addressed to "Madame la Comtesse de P——."

It is needless to add that we left Chaumont without the satisfaction of hearing anything more of the flowers or of the Comtesse.

CHAPTER VI

AMBOISE

Tired of waiting for the carriage which was to carry us
from Chaumont to Amboise, we set out on foot over the
picturesque road which borders the beautiful banks of the
Loire. If not as verdant here as it was from Blois to
Chaumont, the scenery is far from uninteresting. The
towers of the chateau beetle, high above the head, over
the cliff on our left. Our road runs along a pretty hillside which grows higher and higher as we proceed. On
the other side of the river and parallel to it, the railroad
follows its bank, like a band of steel that turns and twists
with the stream. A cloud of white smoke, like a tuft of
feathers, now visible between the trees, now hidden by
the foliage, heralds the advent of a train. The long line
of shaky white is lost in the distance, and another one
appears in its place, to follow it in wild pursuit.

We walk along, admiring the countryside, so smiling
and fertile that it extends like an immense English
garden, planted by a master hand. Great bunches of
trees are dotted about here and there between the farms
of diminutive proportions, with their pointed roofs of
sombre red. Little white cottages play at hide and seek
behind their hollyhocks and sunflowers. The pastures
are dotted with cattle, and in the distance the church
spires seem to rise, like needles from an ivory case.
Everything seems made to please the eye, and everything

is in such perfect harmony that we feel transported almost into a sphere above, into a higher world.

Before entering the little village of Rilly, we threw ourselves down on the edge of a slope to contemplate the scene, and to think unconsciously of those things which come naturally to the mind when, lulled by an irresistible reverie, the body seems to fall asleep. Under such circumstances and in such a mood, nature seems to contain infinite things—ideals, which at another hour, at another moment perhaps, might pass unnoticed. A harmony of notes is heard, discordant if separated, but of which the combination forms a perfect symphony. The sound of horses' footsteps on the hard sandy road, the tinkling of the tiny bells about their necks, the rattle of a distant wheel, the wind among the trees, the song of a bird perched above the head, all contribute. Herds of cattle moving slowly on the green below, men, flowers, and even the humming of a bee, join in this rural symphony; and each sound adds to the effect. Perfumes, at the same time sweet and aromatic, such as only summer and a summer's day do give, still the bodily faculties, only to awaken and intoxicate the more those of the mind. And as we dream and dream, in this peaceful hour, a voice seems often to whisper in the ear: "What, indeed, has life to offer equal to this perfect harmony? Ambitions of the world? Worldly loves? Worldly gains, that after all are little gained, when they are added up? What ambition, what worldly love is more satisfied or satisfying than this natural harmony of a summer day? What moment in our lives more happy than this spent in an idle dream?"

The cracking of a whip sounds in our ears, to break the dream. A horse, at full gallop, stops suddenly, in the middle of the road, and our carriage has caught up with us, so that in climbing up into the cart we descend from our ideals to reality.

There is no livery stable at Chaumont, and the butcher profits by the fact to act as a substitute (at a very high price). The horse is good; but the cart, perched upon two large wheels, innocent of springs, and with a wooden seat hanging from four leather straps, is not as comfortable as it might be. And three on a seat are a little crowded. Our driver in his blue blouse and black cap might have been twenty, judging from a face which was frank, open and full of good will, not in the least in keeping, be it said, with his station in life. His physiognomy was characterized by a poetic melancholy, which interested an observer, and seemed to invite a search beneath the surface. Even apart from this, we were tempted to speak with him, the better to study the characteristics of a peasant who was so evidently superior to his station.

I opened conversation by praising the qualities of his horse. It is always a sensitive point to those who often find the horse their sole companion. The attempt succeeded more easily than I had imagined, and before many minutes we were friends.

"Monsieur likes this part of the country?"

"Yes, very much. One cannot help admiring it."

"Oh, yes, Monsieur, it is a fine country. Everything looks so green and fresh, and at this time of the year all the gardens are in flower and it makes the air as sweet as honey. Then the river here is a great thing, and the chateaux, too, make a great deal of difference; they are so fine. Monsieur has been to visit Blois and Chambord?"

"It is strange," thought I, "to find so appreciative a nature in the butcher's assistant." That he should have noticed the artistic points about him, which are usually overlooked, if not unknown, by the members of his own class, was somewhat curious.

"And are you of this country?" I continued, with some

growing interest in a character that seemed so much above its surroundings.

"No, Monsieur, I am from Sologne, where my mother and father still live. There is a country that is wild and picturesque—forests everywhere, and ponds and lakes! I am always glad when I can go back, every two years, to see my parents. I have a brother, too, in this part of the country. He is a butcher's assistant at Asay."

"Oh. And does he like it there?"

"No, Monsieur; we miss our country people. They are nicer than they are here—much nicer. And then, they are not so curious to see strangers and to stare at them. Ma foi, if I were a stranger here I should not much like to be so stared at. Did you notice it, Monsieur?"

"Yes," I replied, "and I was about to ask the reason for it. So you do not like it, either? I am glad to hear you say so. Are there many chateaux near by? I am rather interested to know."

"A great many, Monsieur," replied the boy; and his countenance lighted up as he thought of them, with evident pleasure. "There is one at Rilly, and also some bourgeois houses and villas. One of them is very pretty. I was passing it a week ago, and I stopped to have a look at it and to smell the roses. They were falling down almost into the road. Ma foi, I couldn't resist picking one or two;" and our poetic companion smiled as the thought returned to him. "There, Monsieur; there is the very house, now," said he, as we turned a corner in the road. We looked in the direction to which he had pointed, and saw in the centre of a lot of land (less than half an acre), a diminutive villa whose walls, newly covered with pink plaster, were relieved by the shutters of the windows, painted a brilliant green. In the little garden and on the grass, which looked as if it were clipped at least once a day, stood several statues of painted terra cotta. A soldier, as large as life, stood guarding a minia-

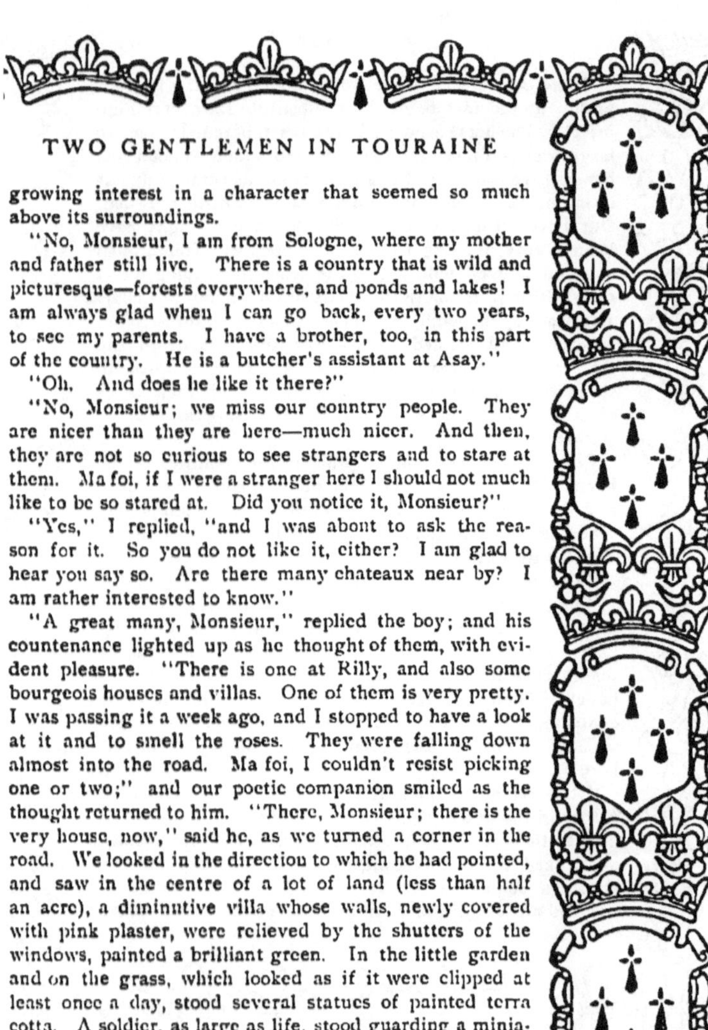

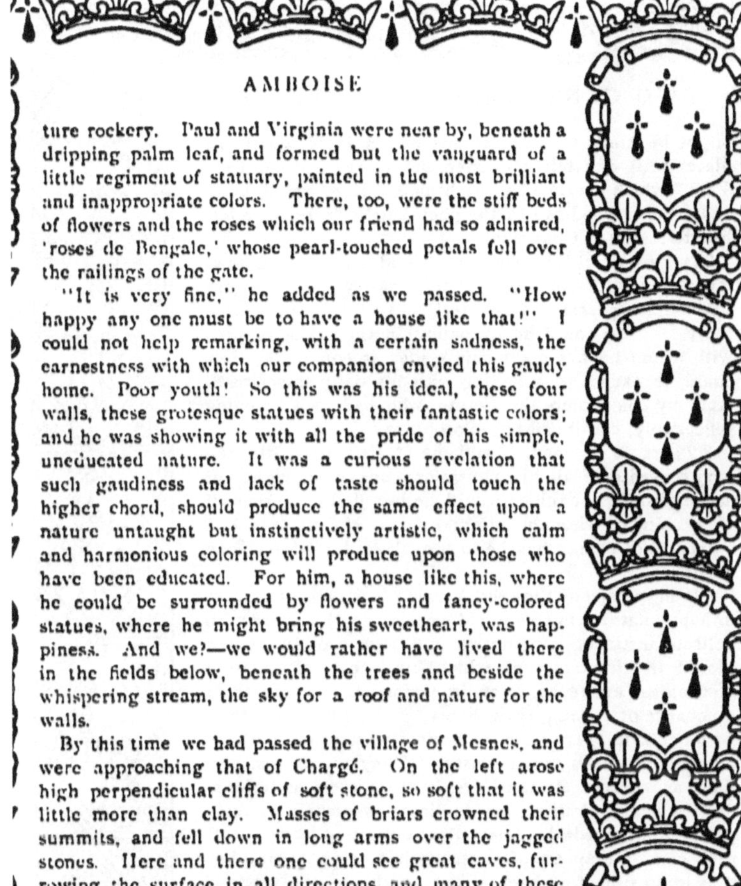

ture rockery. Paul and Virginia were near by, beneath a
dripping palm leaf, and formed but the vanguard of a
little regiment of statuary, painted in the most brilliant
and inappropriate colors. There, too, were the stiff beds
of flowers and the roses which our friend had so admired,
'roses de Bengale,' whose pearl-touched petals fell over
the railings of the gate.

"It is very fine," he added as we passed. "How
happy any one must be to have a house like that!" I
could not help remarking, with a certain sadness, the
earnestness with which our companion envied this gaudy
home. Poor youth! So this was his ideal, these four
walls, these grotesque statues with their fantastic colors;
and he was showing it with all the pride of his simple,
uneducated nature. It was a curious revelation that
such gaudiness and lack of taste should touch the
higher chord, should produce the same effect upon a
nature untaught but instinctively artistic, which calm
and harmonious coloring will produce upon those who
have been educated. For him, a house like this, where
he could be surrounded by flowers and fancy-colored
statues, where he might bring his sweetheart, was happiness. And we?—we would rather have lived there
in the fields below, beneath the trees and beside the
whispering stream, the sky for a roof and nature for the
walls.

By this time we had passed the village of Mesnes, and
were approaching that of Chargé. On the left arose
high perpendicular cliffs of soft stone, so soft that it was
little more than clay. Masses of briars crowned their
summits, and fell down in long arms over the jagged
stones. Here and there one could see great caves, fur-
rowing the surface in all directions, and many of these
were built up, either as cellars to hold the wine which is
made from the grapes above, or as houses for the peasants. In the distance, a mass of buildings looked as if it

might be Amboise, and yet one was in doubt about the place until one fairly stopped before the "Hôtel Lion d'Or," which overlooked the bridge. Here we alighted, and bidding good-bye to the poet butcher's boy, we left him to return to Chaumont.

"Is he happy?" I asked my friend, as we stood looking at his retreating figure, "this man whose tastes are so much the opposite of his life?" "No," was our mutual reply. "How could he be happy in the midst of men with whom he has not a single idea in common? How could he exchange a feeling with his daily associates?" And my companion, the Comte, who had been listening reflectively, continued to philosophize.

"There is a man," said he, "tied to a life the very opposite of all his aspirations, one who might yet accomplish better things, could he but find a single soul about him to whom he might express his ideals. And what sort of chance has he to rise above his life? None whatever."

"I have often thought," said I, "that the most unhappy natures in this world were those, that, born with delicate instincts, imagination and high aspirations, are placed in circumstances which bind them down to a mechanical existence, in an iron grasp that leaves them no chance of gaining their liberty. We find these temperaments in every stage of society, and often, perhaps most often, in its upper classes. They are as unhappy there as in other states of life, because their ambitions, desires and aspirations are in direct proportion to their position in the world. They are so delicately formed, and their constitutions are often strung in so high a vein, that it is impossible for them to pursue the beaten track of common men. They must needs wander from it, and often they are like the bird which flies from branch to branch, so that it ends by losing the way back to its nest."

"What you say is very true," replied the Comte. "I

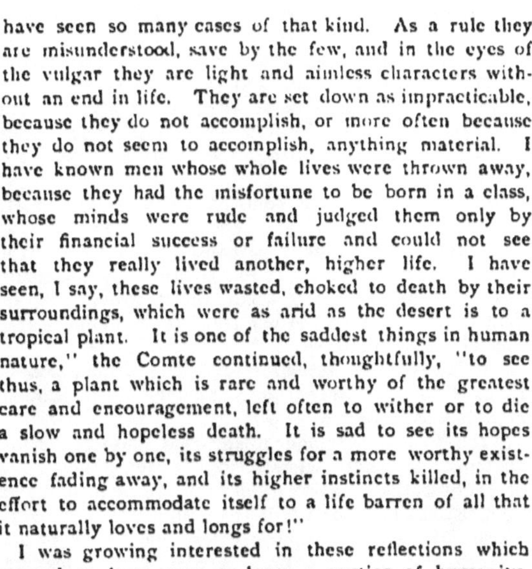

have seen so many cases of that kind. As a rule they are misunderstood, save by the few, and in the eyes of the vulgar they are light and aimless characters without an end in life. They are set down as impracticable, because they do not accomplish, or more often because they do not seem to accomplish, anything material. I have known men whose whole lives were thrown away, because they had the misfortune to be born in a class, whose minds were rude and judged them only by their financial success or failure and could not see that they really lived another, higher life. I have seen, I say, these lives wasted, choked to death by their surroundings, which were as arid as the desert is to a tropical plant. It is one of the saddest things in human nature," the Comte continued, thoughtfully, "to see thus, a plant which is rare and worthy of the greatest care and encouragement, left often to wither or to die a slow and hopeless death. It is sad to see its hopes vanish one by one, its struggles for a more worthy existence fading away, and its higher instincts killed, in the effort to accommodate itself to a life barren of all that it naturally loves and longs for!"

I was growing interested in these reflections which seemed to bear upon so large a portion of humanity. The nature of our hypothetical man—or woman, it mattered not, the cases were the same—as well as his position in the world, had awakened thoughts and inquiries in both our minds. This example of a soul born in an alien soil, this simple youth and his chance remarks, had been enough to bring to my mind, as well as to that of the Comte, a state of existence which we had both observed. I thought, with pity, of this nature, which was thus forced to suffer for its position as well as its education. For the education of the French lower classes gives, as in the case we have just seen, enough to tell of better things.

But it leaves the poor peasant, or workman, without the means of procuring them, and yet dissatisfied. As we drew closer to the little table, with its stiff glasses filled with rum and water, I could not refrain from laying before the Comte a question, a theory, which I had often considered myself.

"What if one of these souls of which we have been speaking," said I, "a soul made for better things,—things which remain latent, perhaps, while it battles with the world alone, what if it find another kindred soul? What if it discovers, by some kindly Providence, in another human being the complement of all its aspirations, all its ambitions?"

The Comte looked at me for some time without speaking, as if to thoroughly take in my hypothesis. But at length he answered:

"Then I should say undoubtedly that these two souls had found happiness. They will, if circumstances permit, join together in a sort of immaterial marriage, if one might use the term, and will go through this world arm in arm. It will probably lose for them much of its harshness and its insincerity. They will find (if they are as you have described them in your hypothesis) that good which lies latent in all things. For they must inevitably search for it, since they long for a more perfect and a higher existence than the one around them. They will, if time permits, become great together, while either one alone might have lived and died unknown. For such is the force of a pure affection (which must be the necessary result of two such natural affinities), that it is bound to produce greatness, if only from its very power. These two natures, these beings, these souls, as you have termed them, will become great together; tasting not alone of that greatness which the world recognizes, but of that which is great in itself and for itself, the greatness that is found in the child who goes straight toward its

settled end because the opinions of men do not exist for it nor influence its decisions."

"I have often wondered," I replied, "whether this would be so or not. I have often argued in my own mind whether, in the case of such a possible affinity of two minds—such a Platonic friendship, be it in any class of society or life—whether these souls might not become intellectually satisfied with one another, and end by being sufficient to themselves. They would find, it is true, a great contentment in one another's company. They would have a progressing influence upon one another, which might become, in time, almost sublime, but which, for its very purity and light, the world would certainly misunderstand. Therefore, in arguing with myself upon this ideal relationship, I have often thought that the misunderstanding of the world, in this self-absorption of the two minds, might defeat its own object rather than produce greatness, as you have said."

"They must not allow the world to misunderstand them," returned the Comte, "for then they would be unable to accomplish much of what they would do. Yet how many men who have stood out upon the pinnacles of the world's history have been misunderstood for this very reason! True greatness will never be thoroughly understood until the mind of the world is great enough to realize and to recognize that which is often overlooked, or, as you say, misunderstood."

"You are right," said I, "and yet, if one is misunderstood by those around one—I care not whether you take the butcher's boy who is going back there to a sphere for which he is not created, or if you take the statesman and his own class—it must always be the same; it must always be difficult to be useful to society. For in fact society in itself would become insupportable to the individual. How many of us have felt in different ways a certain distaste for the noise of town and for the society

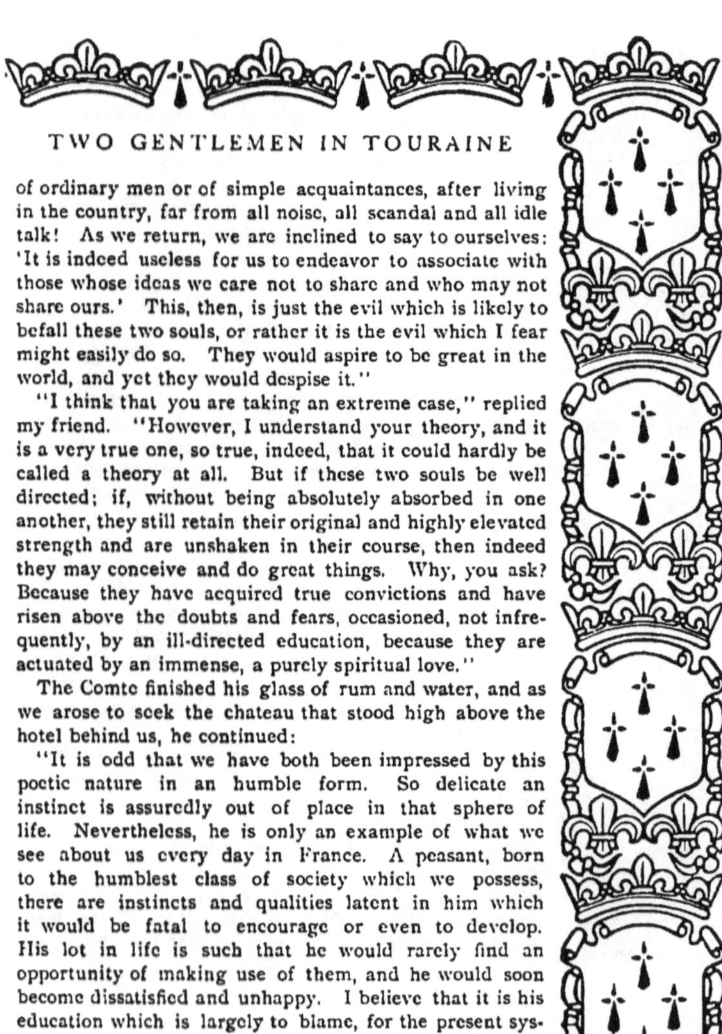

of ordinary men or of simple acquaintances, after living in the country, far from all noise, all scandal and all idle talk! As we return, we are inclined to say to ourselves: 'It is indeed useless for us to endeavor to associate with those whose ideas we care not to share and who may not share ours.' This, then, is just the evil which is likely to befall these two souls, or rather it is the evil which I fear might easily do so. They would aspire to be great in the world, and yet they would despise it."

"I think that you are taking an extreme case," replied my friend. "However, I understand your theory, and it is a very true one, so true, indeed, that it could hardly be called a theory at all. But if these two souls be well directed; if, without being absolutely absorbed in one another, they still retain their original and highly elevated strength and are unshaken in their course, then indeed they may conceive and do great things. Why, you ask? Because they have acquired true convictions and have risen above the doubts and fears, occasioned, not infrequently, by an ill-directed education, because they are actuated by an immense, a purely spiritual love."

The Comte finished his glass of rum and water, and as we arose to seek the chateau that stood high above the hotel behind us, he continued:

"It is odd that we have both been impressed by this poetic nature in an humble form. So delicate an instinct is assuredly out of place in that sphere of life. Nevertheless, he is only an example of what we see about us every day in France. A peasant, born to the humblest class of society which we possess, there are instincts and qualities latent in him which it would be fatal to encourage or even to develop. His lot in life is such that he would rarely find an opportunity of making use of them, and he would soon become dissatisfied and unhappy. I believe that it is his education which is largely to blame, for the present sys-

tem gives to him only the knowledge of things which he cannot obtain, and leaves him there, without the desire to return to the plow or the shovel, and yet unfitted to proceed. I believe that such an education is often a great evil in our lower classes. You may start at hearing me denounce knowledge in this manner, but I think our forefathers had more wisdom in their ignorance than we have often in our new-fangled notions and our excessive education. Educate those who are in the proper position to use knowledge for their fellow men, and leave those to their natural occupation who are better at the plow than at the pen!"

As my friend finished speaking, it began to rain, and yet we had lingered so long over our rum and our speculations, that the chateau still remained above, unvisited, unseen.

"Where was it, indeed? There, straight above the head, and if we had taken the trouble to look over the roof of our hotel, we would have seen its ornamented windows and its pointed roofs. A great mass of walls and fortifications rises out of the narrow, picturesque streets of the town. A steep and rather shabby avenue winds up to a gateway in the walls, seeming almost like a giant's ladder. The details of a Gothic chapel rise up against the sky on our right, and, in short—we are disappointed. Is it the rain? We cannot say; but Amboise, though in a matchless situation upon the Loire, seems sad and dirty, like a beautiful face covered with spots and freckles. This castle, like a crowning coronet to the little town, seems, in a way, almost out of tune. It is patched with stones as yet too white for those which have been left behind. And it is almost with regret that we mount the steep incline leading to the inner court of the chateau.

The chapel first attracts the attention. It is one of the "chef d'œuvres" of Gothic art; but it seems to strike us,

we hardly know why, as if cut (like some forms of lace) in a point that is too delicate, somewhat too fine. The flounces of the stone lacework lining the walls of the interior seem especially to be woven in a detail almost too light for a chapel—almost too frivolous, if one may use the term. They resemble Valenciennes lace, though perhaps the imitation more than the real. They strike one as too white at first, in spite of the wonderful purity of the whole interior. One would have suggested, perhaps, a bath in some softening dye, to turn their whiteness into a darker hue.

A black marble slab beneath the feet bears the inscription: "A Leonard de Vinci." Beneath these stones his body is supposed to lie, and yet in looking at them one is inclined to think of legends rather more than of reality. The whole chapel gives one the unusual impression of a modern work in ancient garb. Moreover a tree, whose thick and clumsy branches burst out on every side, stands in front of the doors—for there are two of these, one beside the other. As if determined to impede the view, it succeeds in hiding almost completely the bas-relief above them, which represents St. Hubert hunting the deer, and the apparition of the cross between two antlers. The chapel itself is one of the creations of Charles VIII, and is interesting, apart from its perfection, as being an example, and a remarkable one, of French architecture before it had felt the influence of the Italian school. As it was dedicated to St. Hubert and intended as a hunting chapel, where the king might hear a hasty mass of an autumn morning, the carving everywhere is suggestive of its object. The Gothic detail branches out like the antlers of a deer. And in fact, this is the chief characteristic of the decoration. The art with which these emblems are adroitly disguised in the graceful ensemble has given to the chapel, more than anything else, its importance.

AMBOIS

AMBOISE

An indifferent postern, with a few scattered flowers around its wall, looks, in comparison with the beauty of the chapel, more like the public square of a provincial town. But we will be impartial and say that the panorama which unfolds itself below the terrace is indeed fairylike. To-day, especially, it looks as if a gentle covering of gauze had been thrown over its luxuriant face, and as we stand on this historic terrace, we see the first vanguards of the "brouillard de la Loire," so well known in this region, already veiling the distant horizon. Perhaps it was just such a day as this when a young and brilliant princess, whom the world has known as Marie Stuart, standing on this same terrace and looking at the scene before us now, cried, as she gazed upon it: "France! France! Doux pays de France!" The words were uttered on the eve of her return to Scotland, when she was already the widow of François II, though but seventeen years old. Well might she exclaim in admiration at this sight! The soft mist harmonizes with the varied shades of green. It brings each object nearer to the eye, and mingles land and water, while it envelopes all, as in the first kiss of love. The sharp outlines of the landscape fade away. The eyes grow heavy with their foggy weight. They fall, half closed, and distinguish only a vague ensemble of gray and green.

The linden trees above the head grow like some Gothic gallery, supported upon shortened columns of a darker marble. Their branches, closely clipped, and on which the butterflies of a summer have now left but fragments of shapeless leaves, rival even the lacework and the carving of the chapel. The fog has changed to rain, which adds to their effect, while it falls in a heavy drenching downpour—a perfect deluge that wets one through and through. The long gargoyles of the roof catch the falling water, spouting it far from the wall, and as they drip, they dig deep circular basins in the sand.

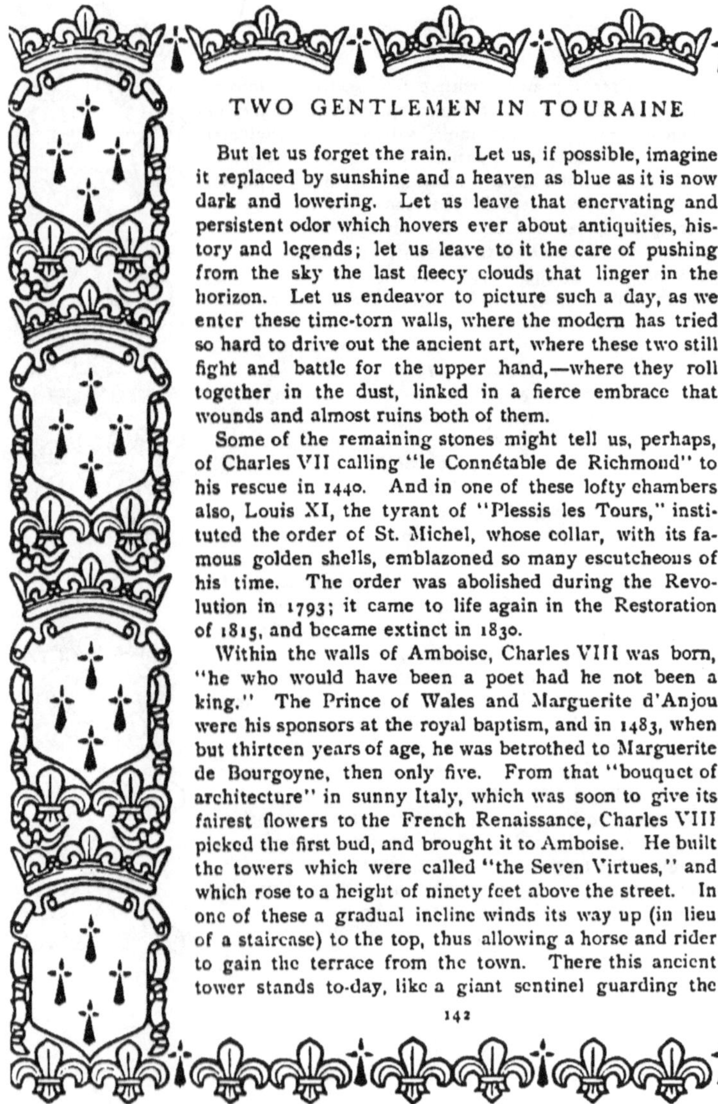

But let us forget the rain. Let us, if possible, imagine it replaced by sunshine and a heaven as blue as it is now dark and lowering. Let us leave that enervating and persistent odor which hovers ever about antiquities, history and legends; let us leave to it the care of pushing from the sky the last fleecy clouds that linger in the horizon. Let us endeavor to picture such a day, as we enter these time-torn walls, where the modern has tried so hard to drive out the ancient art, where these two still fight and battle for the upper hand,—where they roll together in the dust, linked in a fierce embrace that wounds and almost ruins both of them.

Some of the remaining stones might tell us, perhaps, of Charles VII calling "le Connétable de Richmond" to his rescue in 1440. And in one of these lofty chambers also, Louis XI, the tyrant of "Plessis les Tours," instituted the order of St. Michel, whose collar, with its famous golden shells, emblazoned so many escutcheons of his time. The order was abolished during the Revolution in 1793; it came to life again in the Restoration of 1815, and became extinct in 1830.

Within the walls of Amboise, Charles VIII was born, "he who would have been a poet had he not been a king." The Prince of Wales and Marguerite d'Anjou were his sponsors at the royal baptism, and in 1483, when but thirteen years of age, he was betrothed to Marguerite de Bourgoyne, then only five. From that "bouquet of architecture" in sunny Italy, which was soon to give its fairest flowers to the French Renaissance, Charles VIII picked the first bud, and brought it to Amboise. He built the towers which were called "the Seven Virtues," and which rose to a height of ninety feet above the street. In one of these a gradual incline winds its way up (in lieu of a staircase) to the top, thus allowing a horse and rider to gain the terrace from the town. There this ancient tower stands to-day, like a giant sentinel guarding the

souvenir of its king. As years of time have thrown a sombre cloak over the straight and martial lines—a cloak which, owing to the restoration above, seems now to have fallen from the shoulders—it has assumed a soul of poetry, like him who gave it birth. The "machicoulis" still remain above, uncovered; but they no longer flow with boiling oil, to burn the heads of mediæval enemies. They live, to-day, an idle life and are but souvenirs of the past.

Close to the linden trees, which cover the terrace on this side of the chateau, and overlooking the river, is a low doorway, whose massive framework of stone makes it look peculiarly heavy. The crowned porcupine of Louis XII is above it, in bas-relief, and was placed there shortly after the doorway had become famous, as the cause of Charles VIII's death. At that time the game of racquets was a favorite pursuit at Amboise. The racquet courts were situated in the empty moats, which were reached only by a staircase leading from this doorway. One day the king, on his way to them, passed under the doorway, and struck his head so violently against the top, that he fell, unconscious, upon the steps. On hearing the noise occasioned by the king's fall, the valets and gentlemen-in-waiting hurried to the scene, but only to find their master mortally wounded. The dying king was carried into one of the galleries of the chateau and laid upon a couch. He expired shortly afterwards. Thus a brilliant future and a reign that had promised many things were cut suddenly in twain by his untimely death. It is said that his wife, Anne de Bretagne, was in such an agony of grief at his death that she neither ate nor drank for three days, and wished to follow him to the tomb. But we fear that the ill-fated king carried with him to the tomb the shadow only of his lamenting queen, for the next year Anne de Bretagne married Louis XII, king of France.

Louis XII carried on the work of his predecessors, at

Amboise, and built the great gallery and the balcony which faced "le Couvent des Minimes." François I, called often the "king of chivalry," is responsible for the apartments of the king and queen, and Catherine de Medici added an isolated chamber built upon four columns. This was said to have been the result of Ruggieri's prophecy at Chaumont that "Catherine should fear the fall of a great edifice." She built this isolated chamber, without even an aperture, thinking to be safe there from the fall of Amboise. But little did she dream, in her literal translation of the astrologer's words, that the "great edifice" he referred to was none other than the House of Valois.

Amboise, situated upon the butting cliff, and surrounded on three sides by the forest, was a favorite hunting place of François I. Indeed, he was wounded there once by a large thorn, which pierced his boot while in the forest. It occurred during the festivities in honor of the marriage of the Duc de Lorraine with Reneé de Bourbon. The court was assembled in all its brilliancy and pomp, and the king, then but twenty years of age and in the first flush of his youthful power, amused himself daily by keeping up the interest of the court with some new entertainment. One day, a wild boar was taken in the forest, and the king, on learning it, gave orders for the captured animal to be brought into the inner court of the chateau and there let loose. He gathered about him the élite of his youthful court, and began the hunt amid the blowing of the hunters' horns and the applause of the ladies from the apartments overlooking the court. The boar, at first confused and dazed by this unaccustomed scene, remained immovable. "By St. Hubert!" quoth the king, "we would say the boar were frightened, were he not, like my lords perhaps, held victim to the ladies' glances from the windows!" But it appeared that he was neither one nor the other. For maddened by the dogs and men, he

became so fierce that at last he broke through the door leading to the apartments where the ladies were clapping their hands and encouraging their favorites. Excited by the frightened cries, he burst into the interior of the castle, and would have done some mischief had not the king, though he was still wounded, anticipated him. Placing himself in front of the boar, "with an energy worthy of a king," he transfixed the animal with his sword, so that he fell dead at his very feet.

A balcony runs along the façade of the chateau, overlooking the Loire, between the carved stone gallery and those beautiful windows which have been lately restored. Its square bars of cast-iron cross each other in a long network of links or squares, stretching away for a distance of twenty-five metres. It follows, in its course, the windings, turnings, recesses and reliefs of the castle walls.

On a certain night, in the year 1560, the boatmen sailing up and down the river might have seen some masses of black and sombre tatters hanging from the balcony in the pale moonlight. The midnight breeze fanned them to and fro; they seemed like massive bundles, hung out there to dry. But when the breeze was fanned a little also—ever so little, so as to drive away the clouds from the face of the watery moon, livid faces, stiffened limbs and lifeless bodies—that is what the boatmen would have seen as they pursued their tranquil way up or down the Loire. It was the "Conjuration d'Amboise," and its conspirators were paying for their treason.

During the seventeenth century Royalty abandoned Amboise, and in 1764 the Duc de Choiseul bought Chanteloup and the Baronie d'Amboise. The Duc brought back to it somewhat of its former character, and the court, to show its displeasure at the triumph of "la du Barry," passed often over the road from Chanteloup to Amboise. The Duc de Penthière was the next owner, and through him Amboise passed into the

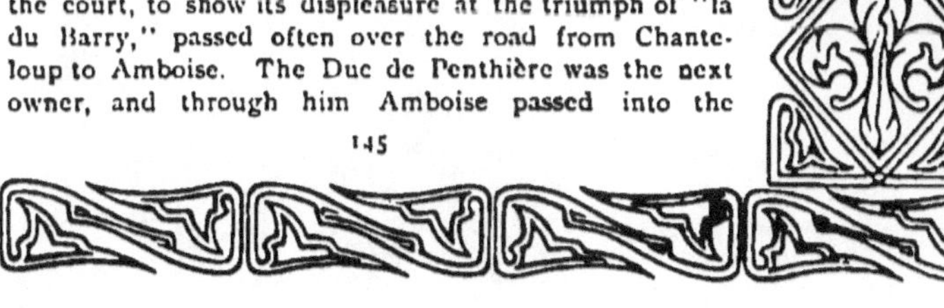

d'Orleans family.   Napoleon III confiscated the chateau
and used it as a prison for Abd-el-Kader, the Arabian
chief.   In later years he came himself and set the Emir
at liberty.   By the decree of 1892 Amboise came back to
the Comte de Paris, and after his death it was sold by the
Duc d'Orleans to the latter's uncle, the Duc d'Aumale.
The Duc d'Aumale has left it to the nation as a hospital
for retired soldiers,   That little which the centuries and
revolutions have left of this royal chateau is being slowly
restored.   It will be just enough to become a feature in
the landscape and to attract the eye to an effective union
of the Gothic and the Renaissance, just enough to keep
alive its interest of to-day.   But, in spite of all, it reminds
us of a cripple that has just begun to walk.   It must
always have one of its limbs shorter than the other; but
its doctors and its friends still trust that it may one
day walk alone, with only the inevitable limp.

As we wind our way down the steep path leading to
the "Hôtel Lion d'Or," while the mists float over the
ancient walls, Amboise seems to be, more and more,
"a castle in the air."   High above the little town its
pointed windows scrape the sky itself.   Its ruined walls
and half restored galleries and chambers seem to be more
in keeping with a legend, or a fancy of the mind, than with
reality.   As we look once more upon this strange, though
beautiful, painted picture, we are unable to conceal from
ourselves a faint fear that what has been so long delayed
may perhaps be abandoned altogether.   For it seems as
if Amboise might soon become, as it must one day, a
castle of the past, a ruin of the Mediæval glory.

CHAPTER VII

FROM AMBOISE TO CHENONCEAU

A sudden "bang! bang! bang!" aroused me from a
dream, and I was brought to consciousness by a knock at
my door, no ordinary knock, alas, but one such as only a
Frenchman may give and a French door endure; a knock,
in short, which dispels all thoughts of dreams or castles
in the air, and calls us back to the most unattractive of
realities.

"Cinq heures—et demi!" echoed a voice, in very good
French. "Time to gaet hup"—in very bad English—
"Monsieur le Comte 'as geeven horders to wake Monsieur
hup at deess hour."

"Then this hour is altogether too early," I thought to
myself, and fell back once more into silence and sleep. I
endeavored to recall my dream so inopportunely broken.
But, alas, it was gone; it had departed forever. My
half-closed eyes were but just making the acquaintance
of the faint light floating in at my window when I was
aroused by a second knock, which would certainly have
disturbed the repose of a dead man's soul, had there
been one in the room. This time the knocking came,
not from the door, but from the wall between my room
and that of the Comte. And through this wall I could
hear him say:

"Hurry up! Hurry up! We are late. We should
have left by this time." No answer was vouchsafed to

this, for I knew how wrong I was, as I had promised to be ready at that hour. And I endeavored to make up for lost time, by dressing as fast as possible.

Another knock, to which I answered: "Entrez!" brought in the garçon, the "café-au-lait," steaming in its cafétière, and a huge cup and saucer. It looked peculiarly tempting, with rolls and butter beside it, all on a tray covered with a snow-white napkin. I was glad to see it.

"Put it on the table near the window, if you please," said I, and as soon as the waiter had closed the door behind him, I finished dressing and sat down to my petit déjeuner. "Rather early to enjoy it," I thought. Oh, how I wished the Comte were not such an early riser nor so fond of walking at sunrise! I was quietly buttering my hot rolls when the door was thrown open—this time without even a preliminary knock—and the Comte came flying into the room.

"This is really too much! Six o'clock, and you are still breakfasting. I am surprised that you are not still sleeping. Indeed, you are worse than those animals—I forget what you call them—that sleep six months in the year, for I think you must certainly sleep eleven out of twelve. You left me last evening at nine, and you cannot be ready by six. It is rather hard."

"Nine hours of sleep, you know," I put in, "only nine hours. That is not a very great hardship to bear. But pray, what is the matter with you this morning? I have never seen you in such a state. The flowers of the Comtesse must have been sent back from Chaumont. Sit down, and drown your sorrows in a bowl of my coffee. It is an excellent antidote for the temper."

"No, certainly not," replied the Comte. "I am in my ordinary state, though I have several good reasons for losing my temper."

"My dear friend," I replied, "nothing is worth the

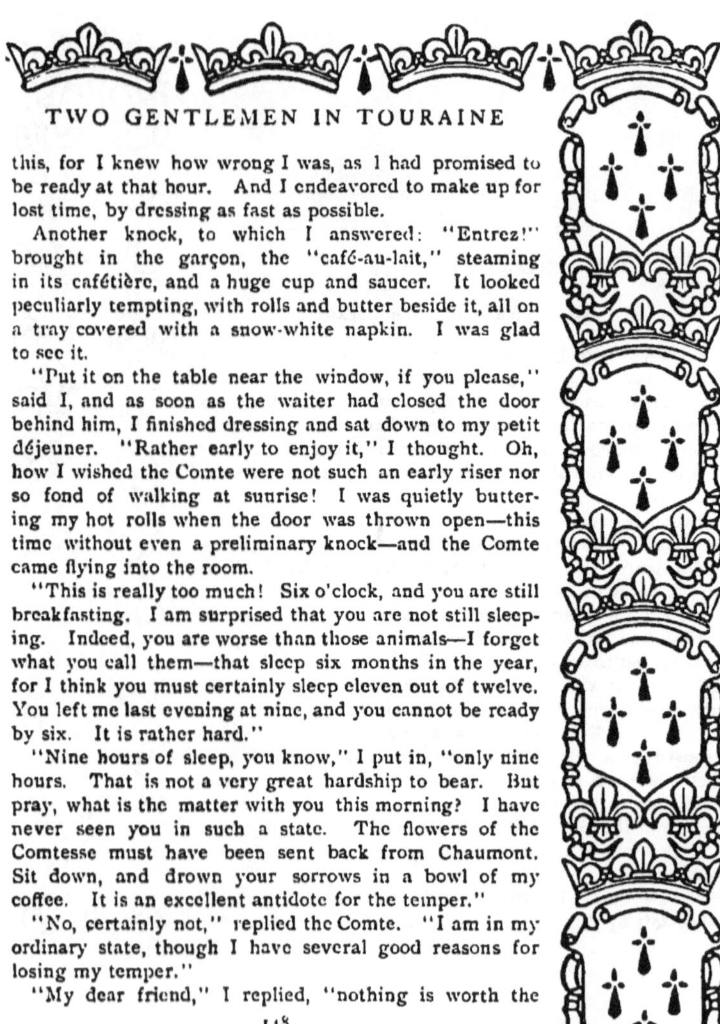

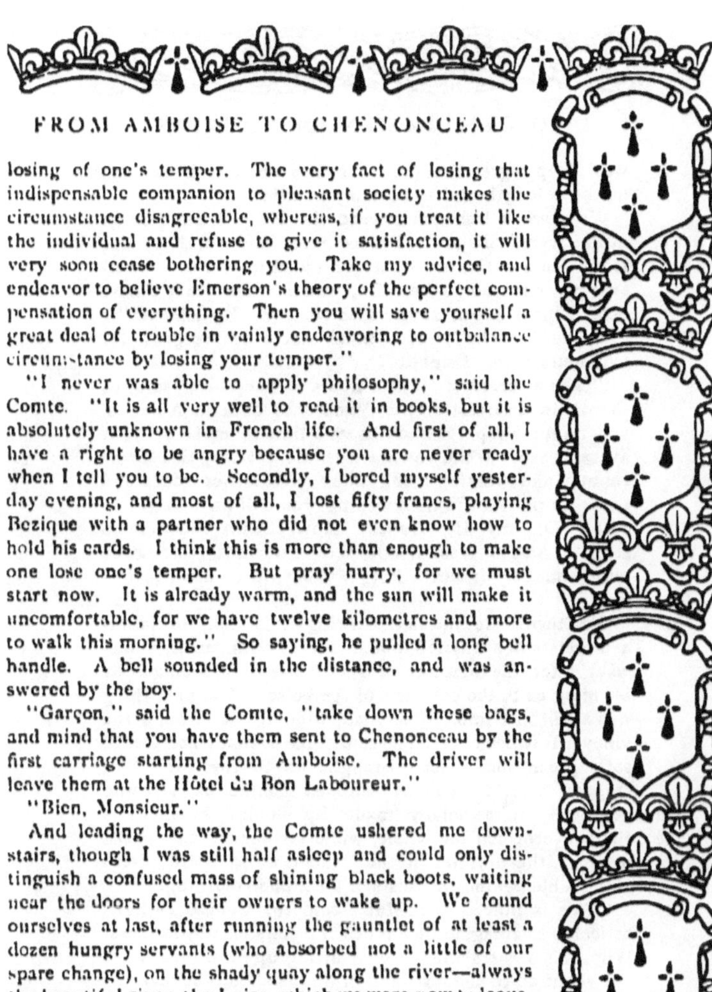

losing of one's temper. The very fact of losing that indispensable companion to pleasant society makes the circumstance disagreeable, whereas, if you treat it like the individual and refuse to give it satisfaction, it will very soon cease bothering you. Take my advice, and endeavor to believe Emerson's theory of the perfect compensation of everything. Then you will save yourself a great deal of trouble in vainly endeavoring to outbalance circumstance by losing your temper."

"I never was able to apply philosophy," said the Comte. "It is all very well to read it in books, but it is absolutely unknown in French life. And first of all, I have a right to be angry because you are never ready when I tell you to be. Secondly, I bored myself yesterday evening, and most of all, I lost fifty francs, playing Bezique with a partner who did not even know how to hold his cards. I think this is more than enough to make one lose one's temper. But pray hurry, for we must start now. It is already warm, and the sun will make it uncomfortable, for we have twelve kilometres and more to walk this morning." So saying, he pulled a long bell handle. A bell sounded in the distance, and was answered by the boy.

"Garçon," said the Comte, "take down these bags, and mind that you have them sent to Chenonceau by the first carriage starting from Amboise. The driver will leave them at the Hôtel du Bon Laboureur."

"Bien, Monsieur."

And leading the way, the Comte ushered me downstairs, though I was still half asleep and could only distinguish a confused mass of shining black boots, waiting near the doors for their owners to wake up. We found ourselves at last, after running the gauntlet of at least a dozen hungry servants (who absorbed not a little of our spare change), on the shady quay along the river—always the beautiful river, the Loire, which we were now to leave,

with deep regret that our four days upon its banks had not been lengthened to as many months.

We gave a last look toward the Hôtel Lion d'Or—I think every village in France must have at least one Hôtel Lion d' Or, for we never failed to find one, wherever we chanced to be. Oh, how I wished that I were behind those green shutters in what the French call "la Chapelle Blanche"! How much would I have given for two hours more of sleep!

"Take a record of all your hours of sleep lost," said the Comte, in a sarcastic tone, "and once back in America, you might sleep for months at a time to make up your average. But while you are with me, crossing this lovely country and walking along these picturesque roads and paths, so pleasant in the morning, you will have to get up early. Oh, my fifty francs! How I wish I had them still!" And I was tempted to exclaim, "Oh! away with your fifty francs! Forget them; they are lost forever."

We turned to the left, during this talk, to follow a street which twisted about for several turns, somewhat after the manner of a corkscrew, and ended by bringing us to the outskirts of Amboise. The next thing was a hill to climb. The road, winding up through the vineyards which covered its slope, like so many hectares of soft, green moss, soon brought us to the top. We stopped here, to look at Amboise behind us, sleeping peacefully in a hollow made by sloping hills. The chateau crowned the whole, while farther on, and in the distance, the outlines of the "vallée de la Loire" were just visible behind the mists of a summer morning.

"This is indeed beautiful," said the Comte, enthusiastically. "Imagine how much travelers lose by laziness. Why, this scene alone is worth sitting up for all night."

I ventured to suggest that all things should be taken in moderation, and that I was more than contented to arise

at six in order to see it.   But my suggestion was not very well received.

"I must call it an unpardonable lack of artistic and poetical feeling, by which one certainly loses half of the pleasures of life."

"I fear the 'pleasures of life,' even as Sir John Lubbock has so ably painted them, would lose a great deal of their charm under such conditions.   But I suppose that we should not stop indefinitely here, so let us pursue our road through the forest, which looks as if it had lowered its green curtain in front to arrest us on our walk."

"This is the forest of Amboise, and it belongs to the state," said my friend, who was regaining his good humor by degrees.   "Some hundred years ago it was part of the great estate of Chanteloup, which belonged to the Duc de Choiseul, one of the ministers of Louis XV. The castle itself was a beautiful palace, built by the Princess des Ursins, who played such a poetical part, as you know, in the "affaires d'Espagne," under Louis XIV. The stables, however, were the only portion of the chateau that was ever completed.   The Duc de Choiseul made it the rendezvous of the discontented members of the court, and they must have been numerous, for we still hear of the great number of state coaches and of the old carrosses which furrowed, night and day, the very road upon which we are walking."

"That time, then, has certainly passed," said I, "for we have not met a single carriage, nor even a peasant, this morning.   But it is, of course, too early for any one but enthusiasts to be up and out."

"Chanteloup is a thing of the past," the Comte continued, without heeding my interruption.   "It has now been bought by 'la bande noire,'* which has destroyed

* A company, so-called because it has bought historical monuments throughout the country, and torn them down in order to sell the stone.

it completely and sold the stone. The only thing left of it is a tower, built by Choiseul, in the middle of this forest. It was in the Chinese style, which was then 'à la mode,' and is called 'la pagode de Chanteloup.'"

We now found ourselves before three roads, without having the least idea which to take; so that we were forced to produce our map, "d'état major," which was always at hand, but which, nevertheless, it needed a liberal education to make head or tail of. As this failed to give us the desired information, we waited for some one who should go by, to tell us. Soon the rattle of wheels was heard in the distance, and a peasant woman, with a short pinafore and white cap, appeared upon the road, pushing forward in front of her a hand-cart in which two rows of high tin cans were rattling merrily together. She was a farmer's wife about to sell her milk at Amboise. The Comte stopped her, and after the customary, "Bon jour, ma brave femme," he inquired the road to Chenonceau.

"Je ne sais vraiment pas," answered the peasant woman. "Perhaps it is the middle one, and then the turn on the right at the first road you meet, then on the left afterwards, and on the right or on the left after that. Je ne sais vraiment pas."

"Is it far from here?"

"Je ne sais vraiment pas. Perhaps six kilometres. Bon jour, Messieurs;" and she went rattling off on her way.

"What a very unsatisfactory answer!" said I.

"You must get accustomed to it, for you will never find a peasant who will answer your question directly, or in a direct manner, although she could perfectly well tell you what you ask her. That woman knew the road as well as her name; but I could not have got her to tell it to me if I had asked her from now until Doomsday."

"How strange!" I replied. "Why is it?"

"Why? Because he is always afraid of committing himself."

"An I are all the members of your lower class influenced in the same way?"

"That depends upon whether you consider the lower class to be made up entirely of peasants. If so, I must answer that they are. But we subdivide our lower class in France into two branches, the peasants and the working people, as well of villages as towns. And here we find a great difference between the two branches."

"This is very interesting to me," I replied. "The more so as I should never have thought it to be the case. For, on the contrary, I should have thought that the peasant, from his very ignorance, would have been far more easy to influence than the workman. The latter has often tasted the bitterness of the new principles, inculcated in him, and he is consequently embittered against the present conditions of society."

"We have a word which expresses exactly, I think, our peasant's mood. He is 'têtu.' It means, that if he has once an idea in his head, you cannot get it out again. He has inherited the idea from his forefathers that every one is his enemy, and that he is the only person who can help himself, and he still believes this. It is a consequence of atavism, against which nothing but generations of education, properly applied, can fight with success. The older generation of peasants is too ignorant to know better, and keeps to its old inheritances of defiance and slyness. The new generation, dissatisfied with the ignorance of their fathers, has tried another channel, that of throwing off the occupations of their parents and embracing some trade or employment. And this is because they have tasted the bitterness and the deceptions that are to be found in those principles which, once instilled into them, give ambitions without the means of gratifying them. So they cling to the first one whom they may meet, who

seems to understand them, or to be likely to do them some good by advice or influence."

"I can understand what you mean," I replied. "But how is it about religion? Ought it not to help matters in one way or another? I notice such strong expressions of religious feeling at every turn, that, even allowing for the additional forms of the Roman Catholic Church, I should have thought its influence would be felt in this direction."

"Oh, religion in the peasantry, I fear, comes after what they call their 'self-interest'; and the village church is crowded only because the master of the chateau near by employs only those people who go to church. Very often a church only a few miles distant will be almost empty, because the chatelains do not care either one way or the other. I believe that there is still to be found in Brittany and in Normandy a true and deep faith at the root of the peasant's nature. But there also, as in Sologne and Touraine, the faith is founded upon superstition, rather than upon truer principles."

"And what is the reason for this, do you suppose?" I asked.

"I should say the principal reason was to be found in the ignorance of the peasants, ignorance inherited and deeply rooted because it is an inheritance. And then perhaps it is in the priests also, for, finding the impossibility of making the peasants understand the principles, even the most elementary principles, of religion, they have learned that the only way of making them come to church is by frightening them, and they have themselves awakened and developed those superstitious instincts which are latent in all of us."

"And do you approve of this?"

"Of course not. But it has been the work of many centuries, and it will need many centuries to break up these superstitions. Knowledge alone will do it, and a good education, only, can replace the superstition. But

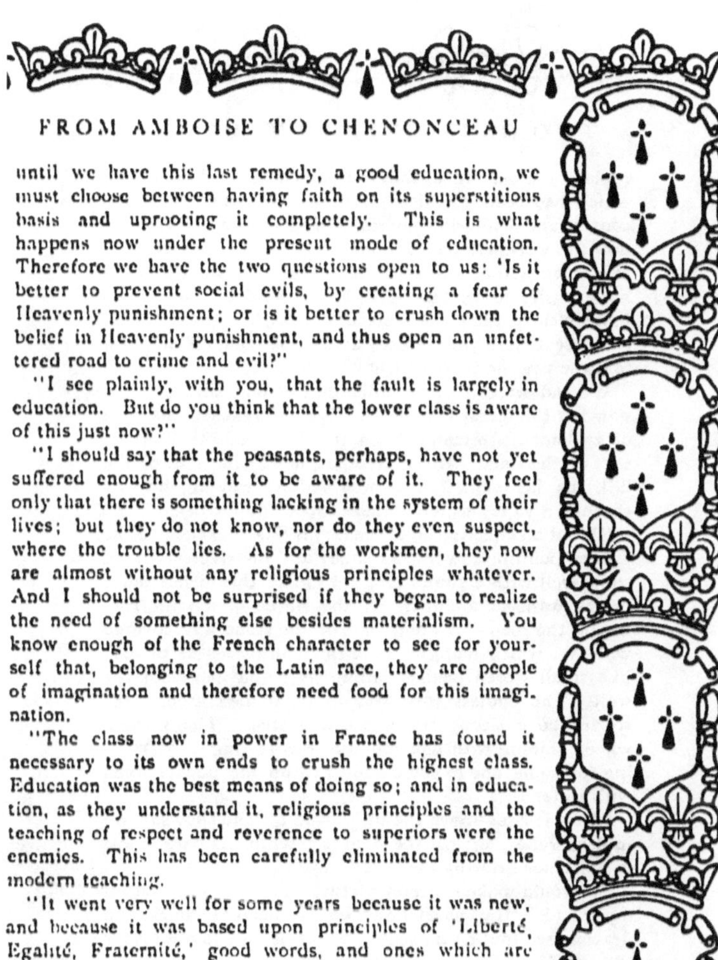

until we have this last remedy, a good education, we must choose between having faith on its superstitious basis and uprooting it completely. This is what happens now under the present mode of education. Therefore we have the two questions open to us: 'Is it better to prevent social evils, by creating a fear of Heavenly punishment; or is it better to crush down the belief in Heavenly punishment, and thus open an unfettered road to crime and evil?''

"I see plainly, with you, that the fault is largely in education. But do you think that the lower class is aware of this just now?''

"I should say that the peasants, perhaps, have not yet suffered enough from it to be aware of it. They feel only that there is something lacking in the system of their lives; but they do not know, nor do they even suspect, where the trouble lies. As for the workmen, they now are almost without any religious principles whatever. And I should not be surprised if they began to realize the need of something else besides materialism. You know enough of the French character to see for yourself that, belonging to the Latin race, they are people of imagination and therefore need food for this imagination.

"The class now in power in France has found it necessary to its own ends to crush the highest class. Education was the best means of doing so; and in education, as they understand it, religious principles and the teaching of respect and reverence to superiors were the enemies. This has been carefully eliminated from the modern teaching.

"It went very well for some years because it was new, and because it was based upon principles of 'Liberté, Egalité, Fraternité,' good words, and ones which are always popular. But now, those who have the highest sense of reason find that no new creed has come to

replace the old creed, that the golden ages without God, which had been promised, have never turned up. Discontent and disillusion have increased, more and more, and now the workman has become conscious of the necessity of a creed and of a truth to help him. This is why he is more easily to be managed, for he understands things more clearly than the peasant. I wish I could set an example before your eyes," added my companion, "just to show you the truth of what I am saying."

We had walked some miles during our talk, and had now left the forest behind us. We had reached the edge of a plateau, stretching from the valley of the Loire to that of the Cher. In front of us, and at the foot of the hill, the last-named river was visible, winding its way through a valley which is there especially fertile.

"What an effective bit of scenery is this!" exclaimed the Comte, pointing toward the valley and the river. An old stone well with a round top, not unlike the niches made in the walls of a church for the statue of a saint, rose beside the road. A great part of the stone was covered with ivy, which had grown so thick in places as to look like small green bushes falling over the mouth of the well. The endless rope was there, twined around the roller like a sleepy snake about a tree. The wooden wheel, shining with age and use, was resting as if waiting for some one to come and draw up the bucket filled with water.

"How it rises above the hill," said I, "and shows there, in dark relief, against the blue sky, while its base is lost in the vines growing about it!"

"It would make a pretty picture, would it not?" added my friend. "Let us sit down on this heap of stones, and draw a few lines on a sheet of paper, if only to remember the spot."

"I wish one could put down also upon paper that feeling, not of existence but of life, which completes the pleasure of watching or of drawing such bits of land-scape even imperfectly."

"I agree with you," asserted the Comte absently, for he was already busy drawing. "There is a wonderful peace and at the same time a buoyant life in everything around us just now. Look down the slope there," and he paused in his work to point with his long pencil, "look down into the valley itself and at the cottages, the villas, and the chateaux, hanging in a cluster of trees, or resting near the river; how they seem to slumber in the shade and to breathe peace and happiness. But, alas, when one thinks of all that goes on under those roofs, under those towers of the chateau! I think one is tempted to be more satis-fied with one's own lot, as being, in reality, more peaceful than those which we see at that distance which always lends enchantment. We do not have to go as far as those houses to realize that the struggle for life is here, as well as everywhere. Listen to the deep, harmonious voices of those men, calling the women who are working in the neighboring fields. The sound is pleasant enough, and the picture is full of poetry and charm, as we watch them. But see how soon it is dispelled by the answers that come in high, shrill tones, to tell of something not in harmony —something that brings us back again to reality. What a busy world it is! They work to live, here in this quiet spot, as truly as the struggling laborer in a swarming city, as truly as the bees which have stayed a long time in the valley, sipping the heart of the flowers for their existence. See, they are hovering over our heads, on their return to the stone well, filled with honey. They are pretty pictures also to look at; but they have their work, nevertheless. In short, walls and appearances may tell of peace and smiles and poetry; but underneath them there is life and a struggle."

"You see how good it is for us both," answered my friend the Comte, "to get up early; for it allows one to

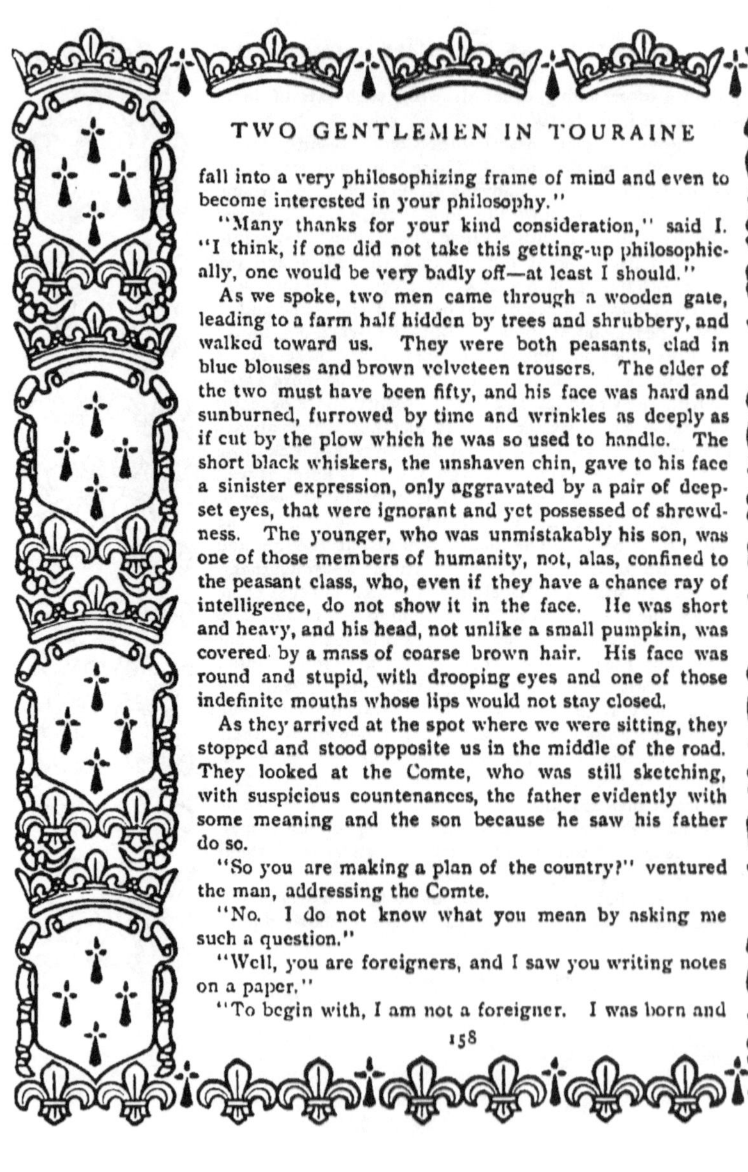

fall into a very philosophizing frame of mind and even to become interested in your philosophy."

"Many thanks for your kind consideration," said I. "I think, if one did not take this getting-up philosophically, one would be very badly off—at least I should."

As we spoke, two men came through a wooden gate, leading to a farm half hidden by trees and shrubbery, and walked toward us. They were both peasants, clad in blue blouses and brown velveteen trousers. The elder of the two must have been fifty, and his face was hard and sunburned, furrowed by time and wrinkles as deeply as if cut by the plow which he was so used to handle. The short black whiskers, the unshaven chin, gave to his face a sinister expression, only aggravated by a pair of deep-set eyes, that were ignorant and yet possessed of shrewdness. The younger, who was unmistakably his son, was one of those members of humanity, not, alas, confined to the peasant class, who, even if they have a chance ray of intelligence, do not show it in the face. He was short and heavy, and his head, not unlike a small pumpkin, was covered by a mass of coarse brown hair. His face was round and stupid, with drooping eyes and one of those indefinite mouths whose lips would not stay closed.

As they arrived at the spot where we were sitting, they stopped and stood opposite us in the middle of the road. They looked at the Comte, who was still sketching, with suspicious countenances, the father evidently with some meaning and the son because he saw his father do so.

"So you are making a plan of the country?" ventured the man, addressing the Comte.

"No. I do not know what you mean by asking me such a question."

"Well, you are foreigners, and I saw you writing notes on a paper."

"To begin with, I am not a foreigner. I was born and

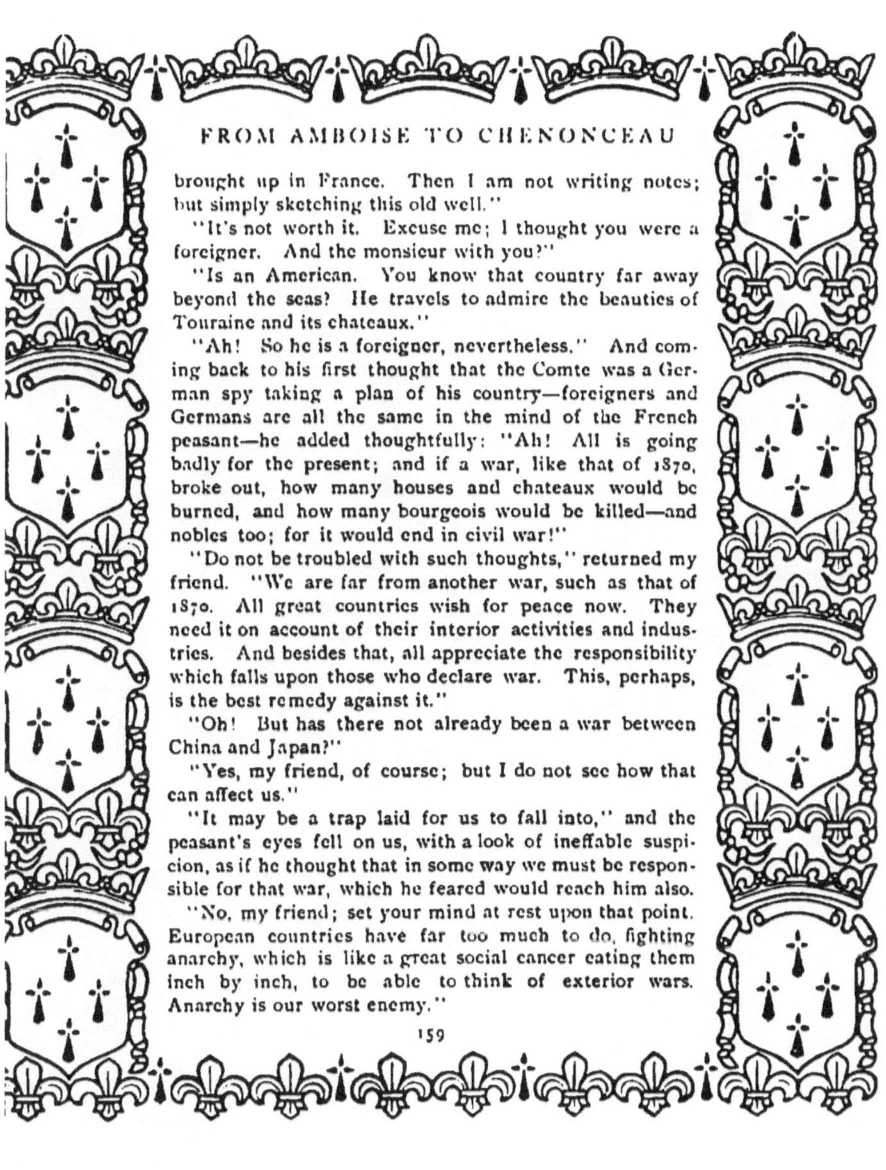

brought up in France. Then I am not writing notes; but simply sketching this old well."

"It's not worth it. Excuse me; I thought you were a foreigner. And the monsieur with you?"

"Is an American. You know that country far away beyond the seas? He travels to admire the beauties of Touraine and its chateaux."

"Ah! So he is a foreigner, nevertheless." And coming back to his first thought that the Comte was a German spy taking a plan of his country—foreigners and Germans are all the same in the mind of the French peasant—he added thoughtfully: "Ah! All is going badly for the present; and if a war, like that of 1870, broke out, how many houses and chateaux would be burned, and how many bourgeois would be killed—and nobles too; for it would end in civil war!"

"Do not be troubled with such thoughts," returned my friend. "We are far from another war, such as that of 1870. All great countries wish for peace now. They need it on account of their interior activities and industries. And besides that, all appreciate the responsibility which falls upon those who declare war. This, perhaps, is the best remedy against it."

"Oh! But has there not already been a war between China and Japan?"

"Yes, my friend, of course; but I do not see how that can affect us."

"It may be a trap laid for us to fall into," and the peasant's eyes fell on us, with a look of ineffable suspicion, as if he thought that in some way we must be responsible for that war, which he feared would reach him also.

"No, my friend; set your mind at rest upon that point. European countries have far too much to do, fighting anarchy, which is like a great social cancer eating them inch by inch, to be able to think of exterior wars. Anarchy is our worst enemy."

"Yes. Monsieur is right; but if a war like that of 1870 were to break out, the chateaux would be burned, and the proprietors with them."

"And why this?" I put in.

"I will tell you," took up the Comte. "Because the judgment of the peasant has been falsely made. He forgets that if the chateau is inhabited by the right 'noble,' as he calls 'him, it makes the one and only wealth of the country and of the peasants around it. Take, for instance, this particular village—Chenonceau. What would it be without its chateau?"

"Monsieur is right; the village would be nothing. It would crumble to ruin, and the inhabitants would die of poverty."

"Eh bien," said the Comte, "you forget it too easily; and because for centuries a particular family has been beloved in a place and made every one around it comfortable, you have become accustomed to this family and wish for a change. Why? Because the love of change is innate in our French blood. The old chatelains have left, and new ones have come, who may remain within the chateau and allow no visitors to see it or to walk in the park. In a word, they have stopped short the channel which brought the visitors, and consequently the wealth to the place. So, for this reason, you say: 'If 1870 came back nobles and chateaux would be burned.' You forget, the peasant forgets, that he has brought upon himself what is happening now; he forgets that if he had not had a master at the chateau to assist him, he would have been unable to carry the burden of cares that fall upon him."

"Yes, yes, monsieur is right. But everything is getting on so badly. The grape vine itself does not ripen. So monsieur is not taking a plan of the country? So monsieur is really French?"

"Yes, I am; but with this difference, that I am not like

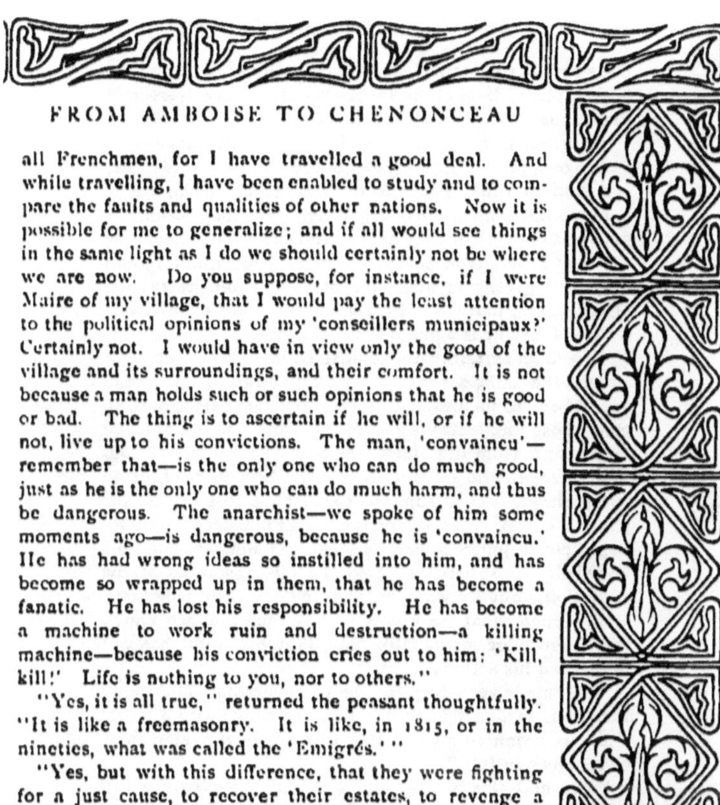

all Frenchmen, for I have travelled a good deal. And while travelling, I have been enabled to study and to compare the faults and qualities of other nations. Now it is possible for me to generalize; and if all would see things in the same light as I do we should certainly not be where we are now. Do you suppose, for instance, if I were Maire of my village, that I would pay the least attention to the political opinions of my 'conseillers municipaux?' Certainly not. I would have in view only the good of the village and its surroundings, and their comfort. It is not because a man holds such or such opinions that he is good or bad. The thing is to ascertain if he will, or if he will not, live up to his convictions. The man, 'convaincu'—remember that—is the only one who can do much good, just as he is the only one who can do much harm, and thus be dangerous. The anarchist—we spoke of him some moments ago—is dangerous, because he is 'convaincu.' He has had wrong ideas so instilled into him, and has become so wrapped up in them, that he has become a fanatic. He has lost his responsibility. He has become a machine to work ruin and destruction—a killing machine—because his conviction cries out to him: 'Kill, kill!' Life is nothing to you, nor to others."

"Yes, it is all true," returned the peasant thoughtfully. "It is like a freemasonry. It is like, in 1815, or in the nineties, what was called the 'Emigrés.'"

"Yes, but with this difference, that they were fighting for a just cause, to recover their estates, to revenge a father, a mother, a sister, a brother, or some other victim of the revolution. The anarchists fight, however, for a cause which is thought just only by them, and to revenge themselves for having been born to an age which has failed them in its promises."

"And whose fault is it, then, if our children do not like to work the soil we have worked all our lives?" The words of the Comte had touched the vital chords of the peasant's constitution, and a revolution of ideas was taking place, behind those black eyes, which were still suspicious, though less so than before.

"Your own fault, my friend," the Comte answered; "your own fault, because you believed in those who came, and said to you: 'There is no distinction of classes, no more nobility, no more bourgeoisie. You may become as fine, and finer, than they are.' And you have believed it; and you have given them charge of your children, and they have given you back 'des messieurs,' and pretty sorts of messieurs, too! All this comes from your education."

"So Monsieur is against education, then?"

"No, I am certainly not against education in itself; but against the same sort of education given to all. How can you expect to inculcate doctrines, the same doctrines, to men whose intellects vary from the brute's to the average man's, and from this down again to the brute's? You, for instance, who do not know even how to read, or to write either, do you suppose that I have less respect for you? No. A cross is enough to sign a deed; and we ought not to judge a man by what he knows (because his knowledge is subordinated to the circumstances of his education), but by what he does by his own judgment, acting upon what he knows. It is then that we know, that knowledge, artificially placed in his mind, has not influenced his actions."

"All this is very deep for me to understand, Monsieur; but what is a fact is that I sign my name with a cross, and that I wanted my children to know how to sign their own names in full."

"Yes, and this is why you have sent your children to the 'école primaire communale' to be brought up under the care of a schoolmaster, whom you know nothing about, whom you accept because he is the only one, and because he has been sent by the Ministre de l'Instruction Public. Now as a matter of fact, the Ministre, who

sends the school teacher, seldom knows as much about him as you do. How could he? Did you ever think of that? You either do not take the trouble, or you cannot, to inquire what sort of a person the Ministre is, what are his principles, or what are the interests which move his actions. You accept his choice, because the halo of power which surrounds him renders his judgment infallible in your eyes, and you hand over your children to this instruction because everybody does it. There you will find a teacher, imbued with the principles of the new school, who by conviction, by fashion, or more probably, by fear of losing his position, will have no moral principles, will not go to church, and will never mention the name of God, because, as he says: 'Ce n'est plus la mode.' He will crush out the last atom of religion which may have chanced to linger in your child's heart, by calling it 'a superannuated superstition.' Mind, I do not advocate any one faith in favor of another; for according to my ideas, all men who lead an honorable life, obeying the voice of their conscience or creed, have a religion, and a religion which is worthy of respect."

"Oui, oui! . . ."

"This teacher, if not by words, at least by his own personal example, will persuade your son that the peasant and the farmer are nonentities, that the work of the soil is a work worthy only of brutes, that the seed, sown, fermenting, growing, flowering, ripening and nourishing the world, is not worthy of a natural study. They place in your children's minds the idea that a city, with all its advancement and distraction, its pleasures and possibilities, is the only place worthy of a man. They tell them that nobles and bourgeois have "had their time," and that now it is somebody's else turn. Your children leave their school, thinking to be teachers themselves, to go to the town or the city, and they are ashamed of their old father, who lives yonder in the country on the hillside,

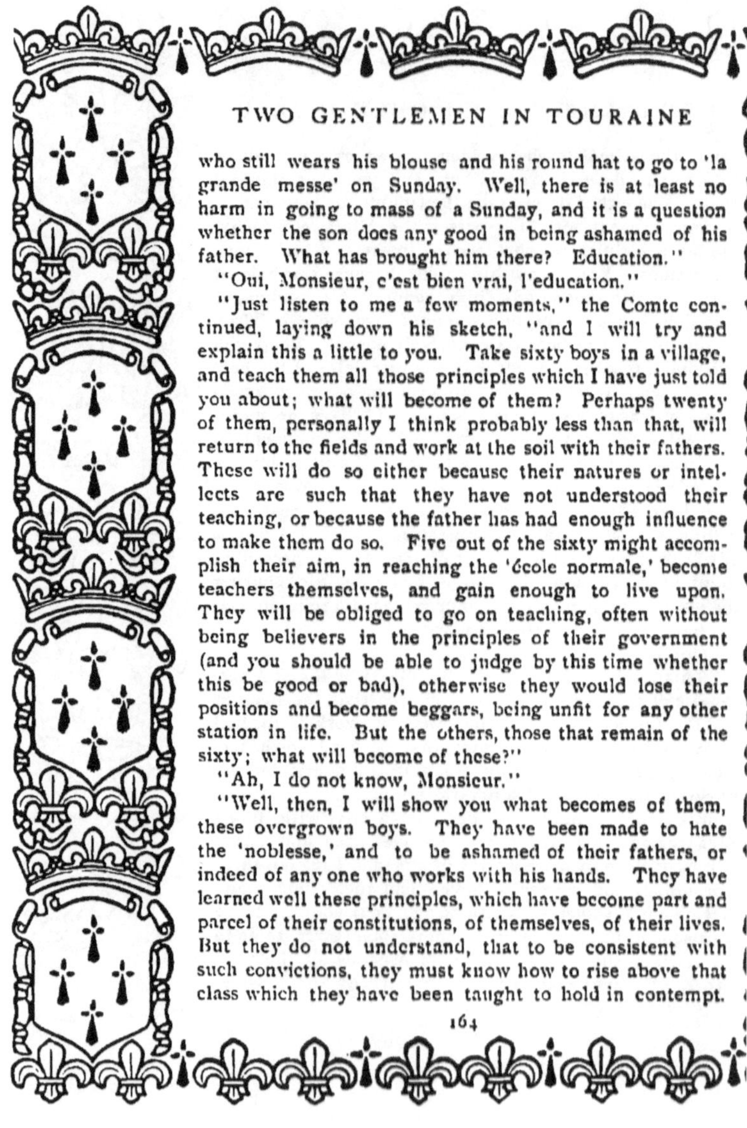

who still wears his blouse and his round hat to go to 'la grande messe' on Sunday. Well, there is at least no harm in going to mass of a Sunday, and it is a question whether the son does any good in being ashamed of his father. What has brought him there? Education."

"Oui, Monsieur, c'est bien vrai, l'education."

"Just listen to me a few moments," the Comte continued, laying down his sketch, "and I will try and explain this a little to you. Take sixty boys in a village, and teach them all those principles which I have just told you about; what will become of them? Perhaps twenty of them, personally I think probably less than that, will return to the fields and work at the soil with their fathers. These will do so either because their natures or intellects are such that they have not understood their teaching, or because the father has had enough influence to make them do so. Five out of the sixty might accomplish their aim, in reaching the 'école normale,' become teachers themselves, and gain enough to live upon. They will be obliged to go on teaching, often without being believers in the principles of their government (and you should be able to judge by this time whether this be good or bad), otherwise they would lose their positions and become beggars, being unfit for any other station in life. But the others, those that remain of the sixty; what will become of these?"

"Ah, I do not know, Monsieur."

"Well, then, I will show you what becomes of them, these overgrown boys. They have been made to hate the 'noblesse,' and to be ashamed of their fathers, or indeed of any one who works with his hands. They have learned well these principles, which have become part and parcel of their constitutions, of themselves, of their lives. But they do not understand, that to be consistent with such convictions, they must know how to rise above that class which they have been taught to hold in contempt.

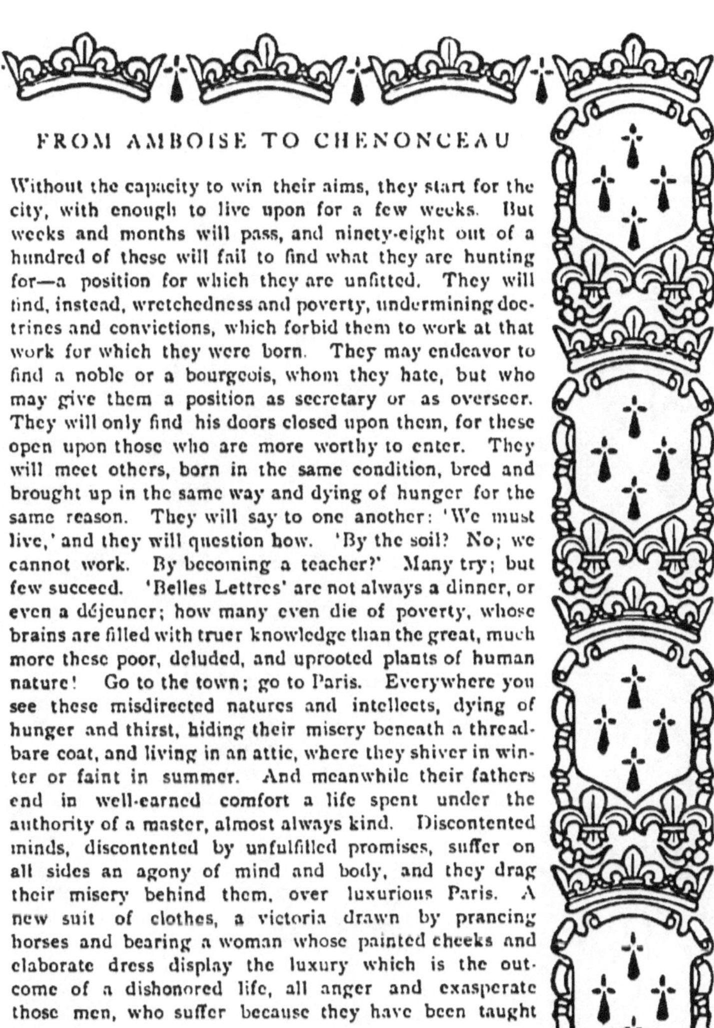

Without the capacity to win their aims, they start for the city, with enough to live upon for a few weeks. But weeks and months will pass, and ninety-eight out of a hundred of these will fail to find what they are hunting for—a position for which they are unfitted. They will find, instead, wretchedness and poverty, undermining doctrines and convictions, which forbid them to work at that work for which they were born. They may endeavor to find a noble or a bourgeois, whom they hate, but who may give them a position as secretary or as overseer. They will only find his doors closed upon them, for these open upon those who are more worthy to enter. They will meet others, born in the same condition, bred and brought up in the same way and dying of hunger for the same reason. They will say to one another: 'We must live,' and they will question how. 'By the soil? No; we cannot work. By becoming a teacher?' Many try; but few succeed. 'Belles Lettres' are not always a dinner, or even a déjeuner; how many even die of poverty, whose brains are filled with truer knowledge than the great, much more these poor, deluded, and uprooted plants of human nature! Go to the town; go to Paris. Everywhere you see these misdirected natures and intellects, dying of hunger and thirst, hiding their misery beneath a threadbare coat, and living in an attic, where they shiver in winter or faint in summer. And meanwhile their fathers end in well-earned comfort a life spent under the authority of a master, almost always kind. Discontented minds, discontented by unfulfilled promises, suffer on all sides an agony of mind and body, and they drag their misery behind them, over luxurious Paris. A new suit of clothes, a victoria drawn by prancing horses and bearing a woman whose painted cheeks and elaborate dress display the luxury which is the outcome of a dishonored life, all anger and exasperate those men, who suffer because they have been taught

to consider themselves as victims. 'Why may we not afford new clothes; why are we not rich also? It was promised to us that, all being equal, we too should be rich.' And these wretched beings vow death to society and to men. They are those who have given to France and to Europe the word anarchy. Are they guilty? They are most certainly; but less so, I think, than those who have taken them as children and brought them, little by little, to their present condition. If these men had only remained in their own sphere of life, they would have been happy, and happier than many who live within their castle walls. They are like seeds which have been planted in a fertile soil, but have afterwards been dug up and allowed to dry in the sun, without nourishment. And should we be angry with such men? No; we may only deplore their state of mind and fight against them for the defense of society. They, alas, are 'convaincu' that death is better than life, which they would end; and it is here that the danger lies.''

"What is the remedy?'' I asked, as the two peasants were still motionless and endeavoring to take in all that the Comte had been telling them.

"Time; alas, time alone. One cannot destroy the poisoned fruit which the present generation bears. The remedy is in the education of the coming generation, in an education well understood and well applied, proportionately to the need, the intellect and the station in life of the peasant.''

"The trouble seems to be in a lack of convictions and in the self-interested purposes of those who govern,'' said I.

"Monsieur a bien raison; but remember, if another war of 1870 broke out now many chateaux and chatelains would be burned. It would be a civil war.''

"Yes, perhaps, and that by your own fault. You might not even be spared yourself, because your children

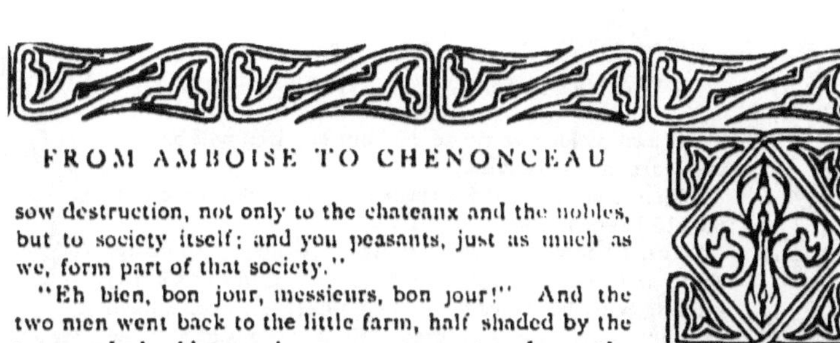

sow destruction, not only to the chateaux and the nobles, but to society itself; and you peasants, just as much as we, form part of that society."

"Eh bien, bon jour, messieurs, bon jour!" And the two men went back to the little farm, half shaded by the trees and shrubbery. A woman came out as far as the gate to meet them, and we heard her say:

"You have lost a famous time gossiping with those messieurs."

But the elder man, in a subdued voice, and looking around as if he feared we might hear him, answered:

"Stop, my wife. Stop talking nonsense. I have spoken with these messieurs who are sitting near the well. I believe in the truth of what they told me, and never will any one lose time in listening to their advice. Don't you think so, my son?" . . .

I looked at the Comte and asked him if he had heard.

"Yes, I have," he answered, with an earnest and rather sad expression. "Yes, I have. But the seed has been sown in a very hard and unfruitful soil. To-morrow, this evening perhaps, any good influence he may have received from our talk will have vanished forever."

"But why?" I persisted, hardly agreeing with the Comte's pessimism.

"Oh, because no one will come to water the seed. No one will come to talk the matter over with him. The bad ones alone take the trouble to work up the peasant to their ways of thinking, because they are convinced, not of the truth of their doctrines, but of the necessity of having them believed by others, in order that they may gain their aim and power."

"But why do you not all work together and fight against such a power? It would be self-defense. If you do not, you will end by being overpowered by the mob, and brought to ruin, if all that you say is true."

"Oh, we know it; but we are so few. Then, besides,

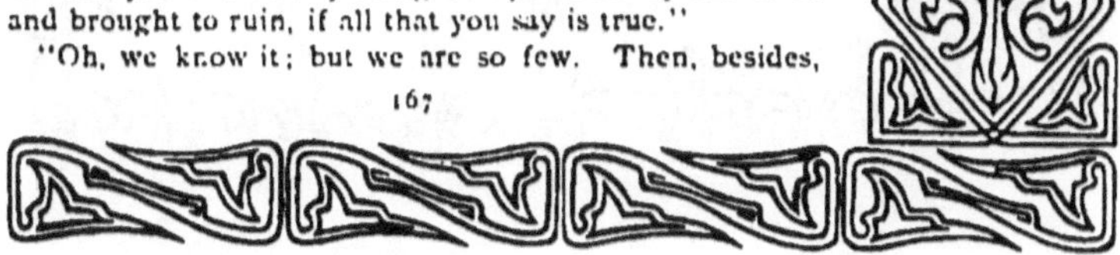

it will last as long as we do, and our children will have to take care of themselves."

"That is an unworthy answer from one who represents the old French blood," said I.

"Yes, I know; but what are we to do against so many? Time and God will make it all right." And the Comte, walking with bent head, fell into a deep silence, broken only by these words uttered with a deep sigh: "The trouble! We are not convaincu."

"No, you are not convaincu."

We crossed an avenue at the further end of which could be distinguished a small, white spot. It was Chenonceau; and we were entering the village. We were soon to stop in front of a small white plaster house, two stories high, standing at the corner of the village street. Above the door and windows hung festoons of grape vines, already laden with the ripening fruit. A sign which bore the words, "Au Bon Laboureur," in gold letters, hanging from an iron rod, swung to and fro in the wind, and played with the rays of the sun. A neat-looking old lady, dressed in black, with a white lace cap on her head, came out to meet us with a pleasant smile, and asked us, with many airs and graces, if we were the messieurs whose bags had arrived from Amboise. We told her that we were, and were soon led upstairs to a large room, overlooking the street and a little garden opposite, whose trees and flowers blended with the purpled roof of the cottages it surrounded. A lovely, peaceful scene was this, to look at from our window flooded by the morning's sun.

"I hope you will be very comfortable," said the old lady. "This is my best room and you will find a small private dining-room, near by, where you will be served alone. I shall try to give you my best cuisine, and shall superintend it myself. Ces messieurs need nothing for the present? If they wish for anything they will please to call for it, and I will send somebody up immediately." And Madame Desert shut the door behind her—and we were really at Chenonceau.

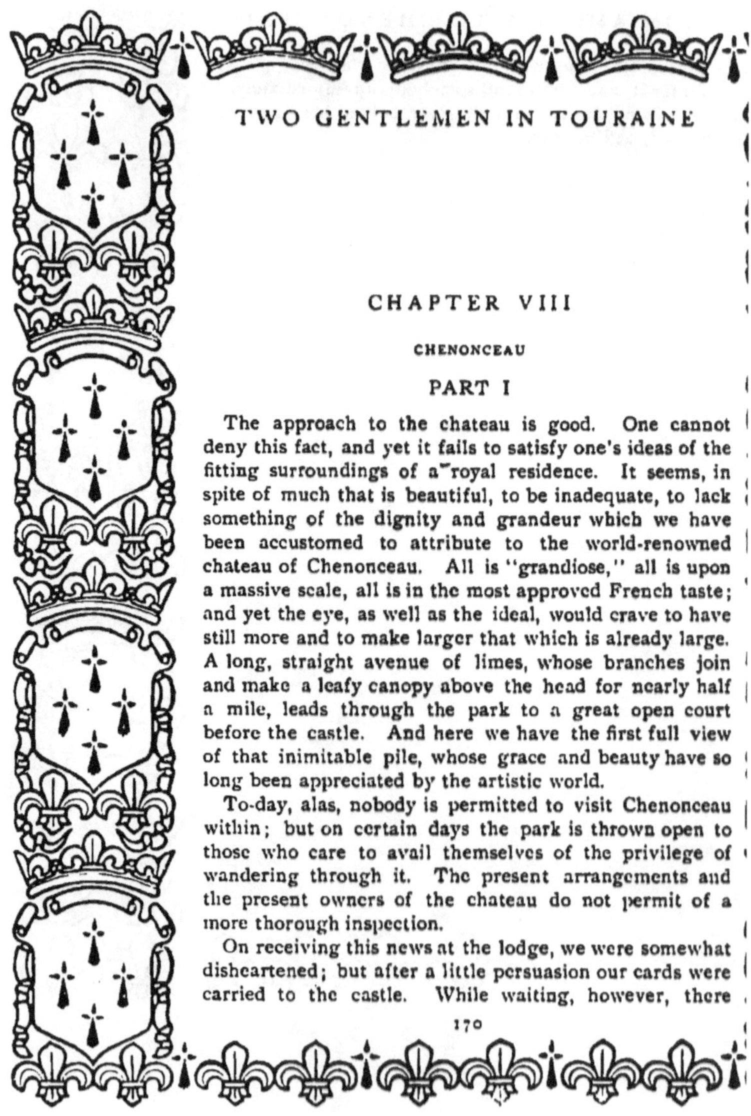

CHAPTER VIII

CHENONCEAU

PART I

The approach to the chateau is good. One cannot deny this fact, and yet it fails to satisfy one's ideas of the fitting surroundings of a royal residence. It seems, in spite of much that is beautiful, to be inadequate, to lack something of the dignity and grandeur which we have been accustomed to attribute to the world-renowned chateau of Chenonceau. All is "grandiose," all is upon a massive scale, all is in the most approved French taste; and yet the eye, as well as the ideal, would crave to have still more and to make larger that which is already large. A long, straight avenue of limes, whose branches join and make a leafy canopy above the head for nearly half a mile, leads through the park to a great open court before the castle. And here we have the first full view of that inimitable pile, whose grace and beauty have so long been appreciated by the artistic world.

To-day, alas, nobody is permitted to visit Chenonceau within; but on certain days the park is thrown open to those who care to avail themselves of the privilege of wandering through it. The present arrangements and the present owners of the chateau do not permit of a more thorough inspection.

On receiving this news at the lodge, we were somewhat disheartened; but after a little persuasion our cards were carried to the castle. While waiting, however, there

CHÂTEAU DE CHENONCEAU

was plenty to occupy the attention and to draw forth admiration. Upon the right of the great court, before mentioned, stretched the stables, a long line of white stone buildings, which have been recently restored on the original lines of Philibert Delorme. Directly in front, the castle arose out of the river in all its beauty, while the picturesque lodge of the overseer, hung with vines and wall roses still in flower, the vast "parterre de Diane de Poitiers," looking like a giant oriental rug with its thousand patterns and colors, all of flowers, occupied the left of this exceptional scene. A courteous invitation followed our cards, and by the exceptional kindness of the present owners we were thus enabled to visit in detail the most private as well as the most historic apartments.

So familiar is the world with the appearance as well as the history of Chenonceau, that it seems almost an impertinence to criticise its architecture. However, before availing ourselves of the kindness within, it is difficult to refrain from stopping at the first drawbridge to examine the architectural beauties of this famous chateau. There is an irresistible impulse to detain one's panion, if only for a moment, upon the threshold of the highly ornamented door, with a few of its impressions— impressions which sink deeply into the mind of one who has often studied Chenonceau in pictures and who finds himself, at last, face to face with all that it has to tell of art and history.

We are now standing in the centre of a large square terrace entirely surrounded by a moat, the waters of which are let in from the river. At the further, right hand corner of the terrace stands that well-known piece of feudal architecture, "la Tour des Anglais," all that now remains of the original fortress of the ancient family of the Marques, who were the founders of Chenonceau. This was originally a large castle, and covered the whole of the terrace; but Thomas Bohier swept it all away to give place to the present chateau.   He spared this tower, however, and embellished it by a pointed roof and a small, hanging turret, to which he added some good carving about the doors and windows.   Thus it stands to-day, an old and picturesque vanguard to the fine and delicate work behind.   That part of Chenonceau which was built by Thomas Bohier and his wife, Catherine Bryçounet — or what is known as "le pavillon," the chateau proper—is by far the most beautiful in architecture.   The façade, especially, is worthy of a careful study, for it is here that the richness of the ornamentation is at its height.   The door, which has been restored in the brilliant colors of the Renaissance, is surmounted by a heavy balcony of carved stone, flanked by two semicircular brackets which seem to hang, almost like lanterns, from the wall.   These form a striking feature of this façade, and we shall find them recurring again in the round corner towers and upon the stonework of the drawbridge.   The battlements and machicoulis at the tops of the former were of but little use in the luxurious and peaceful times of the Renaissance, and here they are replaced by delicate entablatures and pointed roofs. Their pinarets of ironwork rise to-day like shortened spires above the roof between them, and the beauty of their symmetry is enhanced by a high grating of intricately-wrought iron.   The tall Gothic windows of the chapel are as perfect and as fine as lace; but the pilasters which divide them disappoint the eye, in that they are perfectly bare.   Their flat and glaring surfaces are a shock, after the delicate ornamentations of the roof, after the richness of the windows which they accentuate. We had almost anticipated a wealth of carving after seeing their surroundings.

The three windows in the roof of the pavillon are more satisfying, and they stand out at once as the most effective portions of the façade.   Their points and

corners of white stone, are in strong relief against the
dark slate behind them, and they make a worthy climax
to the walls beneath. One feature of the architecture that
is impressive is the symmetry of the whole. And it is
curious to remark how this symmetry is always to be found
in the ensemble though the detail everywhere is of a
wonderfully varying character.

Let us retrace our footsteps for a little and turn to the
left, that we may thus obtain a view of the chateau from
the "parterre de Diane." If we walk along the edge for
some distance, and lean over the wall against an earthen
jar drooping with flowers, we shall see in perspective the
castle and its long galleries over the river. It was here
that the artist wisely stood when he drew his picture for
that scene in the opera of Les Huguenots, and here we
will stand a moment also, noticing the scene before us.
The first portion of the chateau is the pavillon, built over
two massive stone piers and the arch which joins them.
Behind it stretch the galleries entirely across the river.
They are built upon the five arches of a bridge constructed by Diane de Poitiers to connect the chateau with
the park behind it. In later years Catherine de Medici
finished the two galleries, as they stand to-day, one on top
of another and surmounted by a high slate roof that is
broken by eight ornamented windows. The architecture
here is that of Henry II and Henry III, inferior in its
contour, as well as in its detail, to that of Thomas Bohier.
But it is safe to say that without these galleries Chenonceau would lose much of its character and its beauty.
Let us therefore treat this portion of the chateau with
respect, judging it from its good points, which are not to
be despised. The pillars of the bridge project beyond
the walls and are pointed, in order to withstand more
easily the current of the stream. These are carried up to
the second story, in tower-like form, and there they end
in miniature terraces. It is perhaps a question whether

this was a happy method of breaking the even surface of this façade. The semicircular projections are a little lacking in ornamentation, and the effect is enhanced by windows which divide their centres. The four windows between them strike one as being a little inadequate, both in size and in decoration, and they contrast strongly with the double rows above. But we are glad to recognize, here as elsewhere, that sign of all good architecture, namely, the strong horizontal lines which assume almost the importance of cornices between the different stories. The double row above the first story is especially prominent; and the cornices of the roofs are at all points in keeping with them.

The more we gaze at this engrossing picture the more we are tempted to pause, the more we are inclined to criticise it. The roofs in front draw forth our admiration. Their harsher lines are broken at the points by iron pinnacles, by gratings standing out against the sky, by graceful towers, by the stone lacework of a window, or by an ornamental chimney—that often hideous necessity which Chevalier has so aptly termed "le désespoir des architectes." And yet, as we contemplate the whole, we do not hide from ourselves a certain disappointment. Perhaps we have idealized this monument too greatly before beholding it. Perhaps (like some people) it is better in a picture than in reality. But whence is it? Are those stones, which have borne the atmospheres of so many centuries, still too bright? And is the richness of the door, the balconies, the windows, in spite of all their decoration, insufficient? Is Chenonceau, with all that it has to boast, with all its points and minarets, its carvings and its cornices, still too bare? We long, even in spite of so much beauty, for a more elaborate design. We long to force our chisel deeply into the glaring surfaces of the many pilasters. We crave a bit of tracery, a cornice ornament, a thousand little things, in short, to soften and

to finish so beautiful a beginning. Were the stones but of a softer, deeper hue; were brightness and the glare of day but drowned in shades and shadows, this in itself would be enough. In so brilliant a light, however, more carving seems almost a necessity to give to it that artificial mystery to be found only in darkened crevices and dusty corners, to give, especially to the galleries, that ancient air of poetry which its age, as well as its unique position, seems to court.

This last has made it impossible to give to the chateau those surroundings which it would otherwise have possessed. The shade of trees, the lawns and gardens, which lent their softening notes to other castles, are at a distance here. They are separated by the moat-encircled area upon which "la Tour des Anglais" stands. The sun pours down its summer rays, unhindered, upon the castle walls. The glare of day intrudes itself where the privacy of shade were better placed. The air of poetry, of something yet unseen, is lost to Chenonceau. We gaze upon the whole at once, and with the whole we wish for more.

PART II

The interior of the Chateau is more than interesting. Shall we call it beautiful? Shall we call it artistic? It would be wiser to leave these questions unanswered until we have seen and judged it for ourselves. On the other side of the door before us — looking not unlike the plumage of some tropical bird, with its greens and yellows, its reds and blues, and the arms of royal masters joining with the humbler ones of those who have inhabited the chateau—a door and vaulted corridor lead to the lower gallery. It is lined with stone and is comparatively pure in style, save that the ancient tiles are now replaced by modern imitations copied from an ancient pattern. The vaulting of the roof is perhaps too

brilliant in its lately restored escutcheons, from which the colors of the Renaissance proclaim, "à haute voix," their recent coats of paint. Time will mellow them, as it will the brightness of the recent restorations.

The first room of interest upon the left is the ancient "Salle des Gardes." At present it is used as a dining-room, and has been elaborately restored in the richest period of Renaissance. The chimney-piece is worthy of at least a passing glance, and it reminds one, in its varied detail and its heavy carving, of those that we have seen at Blois. The walls are decorated with a series of portraits, let into painted panels, which are rich in coats-of-arms. They form, in all, a complete collection of the former masters of Chenonceau, and have been admirably copied from old portraits. Here these noted characters look down upon the fates and the fortunes of their ancient chateau. Some of them are scowling at the doings here, while others smile, happily or contemptuously, according to their moods. First upon the wall is Catherine de Medici, proud and cruel as in life. François I is not far from her, looking not unlike Henry VIII of England with his "manches à gigots" and his flat velvet cap, a long ostrich feather flowing almost to his shoulder. Henry II and Henry III are also in their places, and the famous mistress, Diane de Poitiers, watches over the present revels of Chenonceau, revels which can never equal those of former days.

Let us leave this room, whose brilliant restoration is almost too dazzling, and let us open the door into the chapel. A carving upon it of the apparition of our Saviour to St. Thomas, after the Resurrection, stands in relief, to-day, as clearly as when it was first chiseled. The interior of the chapel beyond cannot fail to satisfy the artistic sense. Its lines and its general effect are distinctly Gothic, and they are in strong contrast to the character of the room behind it. The windows, which

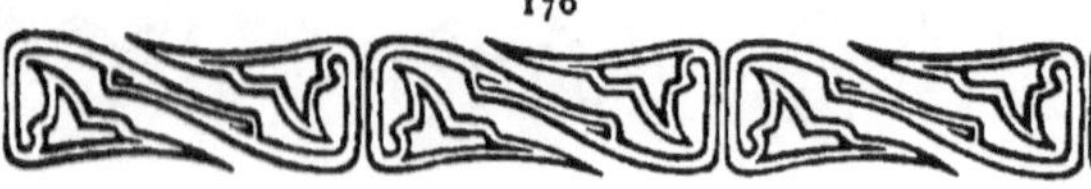

we have already seen from without, are flamboyant in their groining and their tracery, being built of pure white stone, still in perfect condition. The stained glass within them is very good; but we have not time to pause, or to admire it in detail. The altar and its reredos are simple, and behind them a small circular staircase, ornamented with black marble, inlaid, winds a tortuous descent into the crypt.* Preparations for an elaborate restoration are in process here; but the refinement of detail is rendered strangely inconsistent by a fantastic drawing in charcoal of a huge woman. It is evidently a sketch for some future carving; the woman is represented as reclining in an easy manner above the door. Upon closer examination the details of the chapel above prove to be of the Renaissance, although the effect of its ensemble is Gothic—ogival.

These private chapels are interesting features of the royal chateaux of Touraine, and they are so bound up with the history of their masters that they are frequently of more importance than the rooms themselves. As a whole, they are in a wonderfully perfect state of preservation, especially when we pause to consider the number of pillages that they have experienced. For in spite of the fear which the Roman Catholics have always entertained for their church's wrath, they seldom left a private chapel in peace when they attacked the chateau.

A little door leads from the chapel to a terrace or balcony connecting it with the ancient library. Catherine de Medici originally built two chambers over this terrace; but they were out of keeping with the façade, and have since been torn down. At one time the terrace was used as a summer dining-room. It must have been a pleasant spot to feast upon, for the view of le Cher is very picturesque from here, ending in a stone bridge surrounded

---

* The chapel has since been restored, this description having been written during a visit in the summer of 1894.

by the distant trees. Here at least we forget that barrenness which was so harsh in front. Here at least the air
is filled with poetry and pictures, and upon a summer's
evening, by the light of a "ver-luisant," we may almost
distinguish faces and figures of history in the running
waters beneath the stone balcony.

We turn from this romantic corner to visit the principal
drawing-room of the chateau, situated on the other side
of the hall. The waving palms and cooling walls give
out a faint suspicion of the atrium of some Roman or
Pompeiian house, and they form a strong relief to the
richly decorated rooms upon either side of it. The drawing-room itself is almost entirely modern, though furnished in great luxury, and is very florid. But the
pictures are among the best of the wonderful and almost
priceless collection at Chenonceau. In spite of the
changing fortunes of the chateau, it has always remained
intact, and is said to be so valuable as to be worth everything else put together. The portrait of the Duchesse de
Chateauroux, by Nattier, is the most beautiful picture in
this room.

At the foot of the hall, a door built at an angle leads
into the lower gallery. The fate of this enormous hall is
indeed a sad one to-day. Its large, square tiles of black
and white marble no longer echo the footsteps of a tyrant
queen, a royal mistress, or a luxurious monarch. No
longer do the medallions upon the walls look down upon
those fêtes, those banquets, those orgies, with the fame
of which the world has since been filled. No longer
is this river-cellared gallery the haunt of a court whose
excesses outrivaled even those of the Roman emperors for
splendor and extravagance. To-day the gallery is left,
unhindered, to live in the recollections of the past. One
corner of it, however, is not entirely neglected. It is
evidently used as a children's nursery; for cups and
saucers on a kitchen table tell of "café au lait," of bread

and milk. A sad descent, indeed, is this juvenile repast from the royal feasts of other days. We have no doubt that it is less injurious to bodily health, and perhaps to morals; but we may not refrain from regret that this historic hall does not serve to-day some nobler purpose.

Turning from the gallery, we gain the hall, and mount that beautiful staircase of white stone which is much in the Italian style, so popular at that period. Its steps are worn into deep furrows by the thousands of historic feet which have passed over it to reach the hall, or vestibule, above. The ceiling is vaulted, and decorated with panels of white stone, and upon this have been carved human heads, fruits, flowers and other motifs of ornamentation which were new at that epoch.

The walls of the vestibule above, which in reality are those of a large gallery, have been hung recently with pieces of magnificent Flemish tapestry. They have perhaps been too freshly repaired, like all around them, "mais que voulez vous?" as my companion replied to a similar criticism. And he proceeded to discuss the interior of the chateau.

"It is impossible to inhabit a castle without furniture in it. Of course, the proper furniture for such a place as this was the original period—the Renaissance. But alas, all that has been lost—sold by the creditors of the last proprietor. It is now floating over the world in a thousand channels—beyond the reach of any one. Therefore we find at Chenonceau modern furniture, though often well copied from the old and set off by original decorations upon the walls, still in their ancient beauty. Sometimes these are oddly accentuated by the newer effect of all that they enclose; but on the whole, it must be said that the restoration of the interior shows much care and knowledge."

The ancient state apartments lead out of the gallery and occupy this part of the chateau. The only room

among them, however, which has retained its historic
interest is the bed chamber of Catherine de Medici.   The
walls of the apartment are decorated in the manner so
much in vogue at that period, the painted canvas.
Though the colors are darker, they remind one of those
at Blois.   In fact, these canvas decorations of the walls
are almost a study in themselves.   It is said that they
were made at a special establishment some distance
from the chateau, and put into a remarkable preparation
which has preserved them ever since almost in perfection.   The ceiling of this particular chamber is decorated
in square oak panels, painted.   Crowned ciphers of the
letters C and H abound, and these are interspersed with
the monograms of Catherine's children surmounted by
their royal crowns or ducal coronets.   The ceiling was
probably painted about the year 1570, when this famous
daughter of the de Medicis was already advanced in years.
The arms of her family are also to be found among the
decorations, and their six balls, or globules (palle),
remind one of the various discussions and comments that
have been made in regard to the escutcheon of the historical Florentine family.   There have been many theories
as to the heraldic significance of the globules and their
origin, and some have even gone so far as to consider
them as pills, significant of the original occupation of the
family (who were said to have been chemists).   How
much truth there is in this theory we do not know,
although the origin of the family was undoubtedly
plebeian.

Turning from the room just described, we cross once
more the vestibule, and enter the climax of the whole
interior, the great picture gallery over the river.

Never have the aesthetic senses received a more violent
or unexpected shock than they experience upon issuing
from the sombre rooms of "le pavillon" into this
extraordinary, this incongruous apartment.   Never were

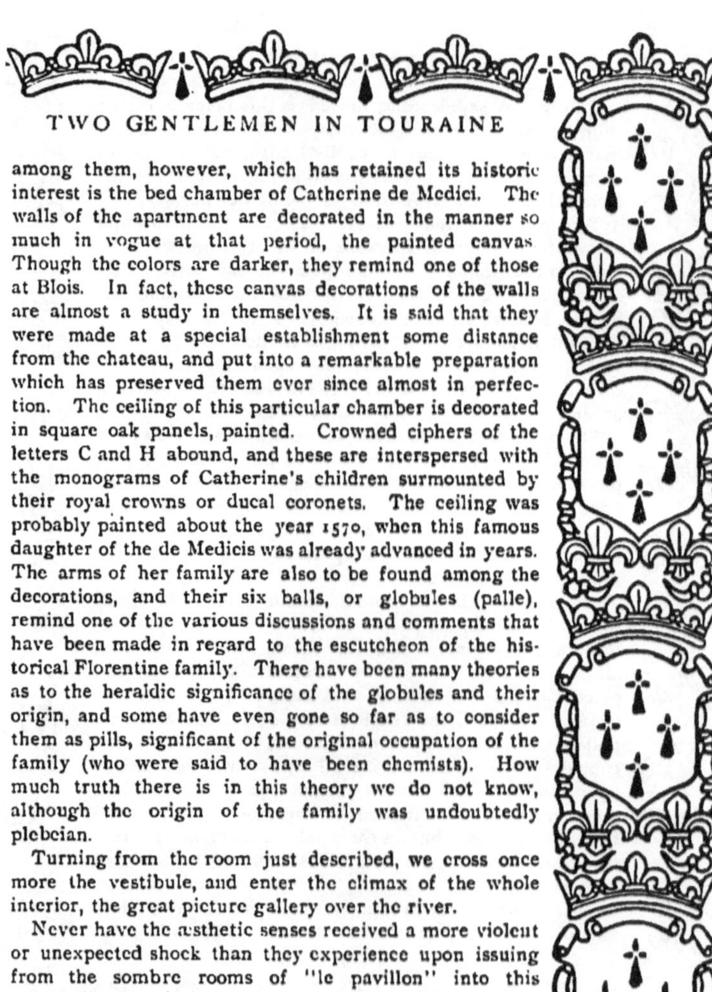

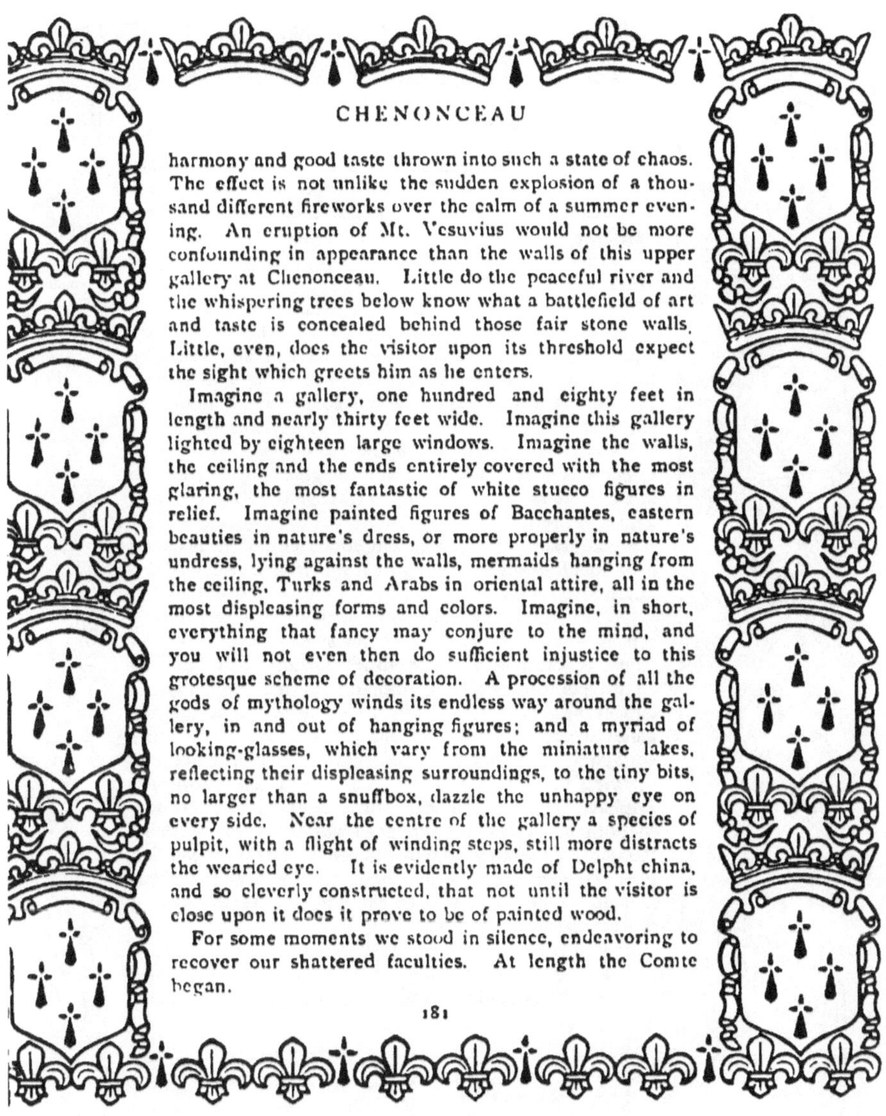

harmony and good taste thrown into such a state of chaos. The effect is not unlike the sudden explosion of a thousand different fireworks over the calm of a summer evening. An eruption of Mt. Vesuvius would not be more confounding in appearance than the walls of this upper gallery at Chenonceau. Little do the peaceful river and the whispering trees below know what a battlefield of art and taste is concealed behind those fair stone walls. Little, even, does the visitor upon its threshold expect the sight which greets him as he enters.

Imagine a gallery, one hundred and eighty feet in length and nearly thirty feet wide. Imagine this gallery lighted by eighteen large windows. Imagine the walls, the ceiling and the ends entirely covered with the most glaring, the most fantastic of white stucco figures in relief. Imagine painted figures of Bacchantes, eastern beauties in nature's dress, or more properly in nature's undress, lying against the walls, mermaids hanging from the ceiling, Turks and Arabs in oriental attire, all in the most displeasing forms and colors. Imagine, in short, everything that fancy may conjure to the mind, and you will not even then do sufficient injustice to this grotesque scheme of decoration. A procession of all the gods of mythology winds its endless way around the gallery, in and out of hanging figures; and a myriad of looking-glasses, which vary from the miniature lakes, reflecting their displeasing surroundings, to the tiny bits, no larger than a snuffbox, dazzle the unhappy eye on every side. Near the centre of the gallery a species of pulpit, with a flight of winding steps, still more distracts the wearied eye. It is evidently made of Delpht china, and so cleverly constructed, that not until the visitor is close upon it does it prove to be of painted wood.

For some moments we stood in silence, endeavoring to recover our shattered faculties. At length the Comte began.

"Have you ever seen a more fantastic sight?" said he.

"Never," I replied. "It looks more like the unpleasant dream of an excited imagination than anything in real existence. The effects are more worthy of a theatrical extravaganza than the interior of a chateau of the Renaissance."

"And what is more, you cannot imagine the cost of all these decorations," the Comte continued. "The lady who is responsible for them was ruined as completely by their creation as the gallery has been by their existence. It is said that in the end, she was so steeped in debt that she was obliged to live in the miserable apartments of 'la Tour des Anglais,' until the chateau was finally sold to her creditors. You may well imagine this, as you look at the endless details of this extravagant mixture of art. You will probably realize it more fully, however, when I tell you that each workman employed either in frescoing or in molding the stucco figures, received a salary of one hundred francs a day."

"Where could one conceive of such an idea, and having conceived it, how could one allow such things to be executed, at the cost of one's entire fortune? But here is an oil painting," said I, stopping in front of a mythological figure carrying a banner—in reality a painted panel which enframed a beautiful old picture. Truly enough! And this wretched mythological subject was carrying in this banner no less a prize than an original Raphael. There it hung, in silent disapproval of its surroundings. The effect produced was as inconsistent as a Passion Play at a circus, save that in this case the Passion Play was so remarkable and so engrossing that the circus seemed to sink almost into the insignificance which it deserved.

At first invisible, there appeared upon a close investigation, a collection of pictures by old masters, seldom to be met with anywhere, and certainly never to be found

under similar circumstances. One by one, they gradually
unfolded themselves from their grotesque frames—frames
of every form and shape that could possibly be imagined
—frames which were now a banner, now an animal, now
a building, anything, in fact, but what they should be,
any color but the one most suitable. The art of Rubens
was surrounded by a mass of painted wood or stucco, up-
held by graceless Graces or by gods in fancy costume.
Some of the most beautiful, the most artistic portraits of
Nattier or Philippe de Champagne were tucked up into a
cluster of clouds, or placed in some still more inconsistent
setting. The inspiration everywhere—if one could even
call such fantasies an inspiration—was more appropriate to
some drinking saloon than to the setting of a master's
work. Priceless gems of Poussin and other famous artists
were almost lost in this barbaric luxury of ill-placed
ornament.

But let us not be ill-natured. Let us rather endeavor
to forget the settings and enjoy the pictures themselves,
for they at least are worthy of admiration. Famous
kings and queens, royal dukes and duchesses, with other
persons of historical distinction, hang in silent honor to a
master's hand. Well-known faces, far more beautiful than
beauty's hand had ever made them, hold us here in an
embracing gaze. Originals that we have seen before in
copy, copies that are sometimes better than originals,
follow one another in a bewildering succession. Perhaps
the finest picture of the whole collection is the "Descent
from the Cross," by Ribera. The force and coloring of
this marvel of painting are engrossing, and hold the spectator in rapt admiration, to leave a deep impression
upon the mind. Another picture worthy of attention is
a pastel of Mme. Dupin, by Latour. The artistic grace
and coloring of this portrait give to the student something of the same sensation which a beautiful passage of
music will produce upon an artistic or an appreciative

nature. It gives, in short, that exquisite pleasure to the higher senses which perfect art, perfect music, or the results of perfect genius, only may produce. Few things have more power to please the eye than a good pastel of a good subject, by a truly great master. We remember seeing some by Greuze, both in France and England, which are of surpassing beauty, as well in their wonderful freshness of tints as in the delicacy of their treatment. His fastidious talent seems to have absorbed in his colors something of that mist which hovers, in a bluish gray or green, over the forests, the rivers and the scenery of France. Greuze must have inhabited and loved Touraine, for the poetic beauty of the "brouillard de la Loire" is the same which characterizes all his work. One pastel of his especially we have in mind. It is a noval portrait of Mme. de Pompadour;* and those who are so fortunate as to see it once will not easily lose the remembrance of it.

A beautiful picture of the Three Graces, screwed into the wall on the right, seduces our thoughts away from Greuze, leaves them to mourn the fact that this picture, like all of its companions, is so injured by its frame. At last the now famous portrait of Mme. Pelouse looms up before us. It cannot be denied that the picture is a fine one, though we fear that the artist's name has rendered criticism less impartial than it might otherwise have been.

But let us now return to the beginning of the gallery, and take a last survey of this remarkable collection. It impresses us more and more, at every turn, for there is seldom gathered together in a private collection such a representative mass of famous masters. Some private galleries in England or in Italy may possess more works of a single artist, may contain more "chefs-d'œuvres" of

---

* The pastel hangs in the South Kensington Museum, London, and is part of the remarkable collection of various objects of art, known as "the Jones collection."—*Author.*

a particular master, but very few in France, and certainly no other chateaux of the Loire, have such an array as there is at Chenonceau. It is difficult, then, to realize that any one, appreciating the value of such beautiful works of art, could have been induced to consign them to their present surroundings. It is difficult to realize such apparent vagaries as seem to have controlled the ideas of those who are responsible for the decoration of this gallery. It is safe to say that if it were only dismantled and redecorated, in the dignified manner appropriate to its architecture, if the works of art, now screwed into its redundant walls, were rehung in gilded frames, the gallery would be one of the best of its kind in the world. Certainly to-day it is unique—but, alas, to be unique is not to be perfection, nor even the approach to it. As it is, one can but close the eyes to what is bad, and open them upon what is really good and beautiful. One can but give indulgent reins to the imagination, and pray that one day an artistic fairy-godmother may transform the gallery of Chenonceau into what it should be.

With this let us bid farewell to what we have seen. Let us leave these galleries, these halls, these rooms, to weave their own futures, year by year and century by century, until one day — who knows? — they may pass again into the hands of kings and queens and mistresses unborn. For who shall tell what Time has yet in store for this favored haunt of history? One might well spend an idle hour wandering through the flowers of the famous parterre and weaving, in an idle skein, an imaginary future for the castle. A fertile brain would need but little more than these surroundings (now that the sombre rooms and all that they contain have given place to sunlit stones), to picture personages and events to come, equal to the many that have passed into history. Certainly there is no better place than this to cause the thoughts to fly backward, back amid the trees and the

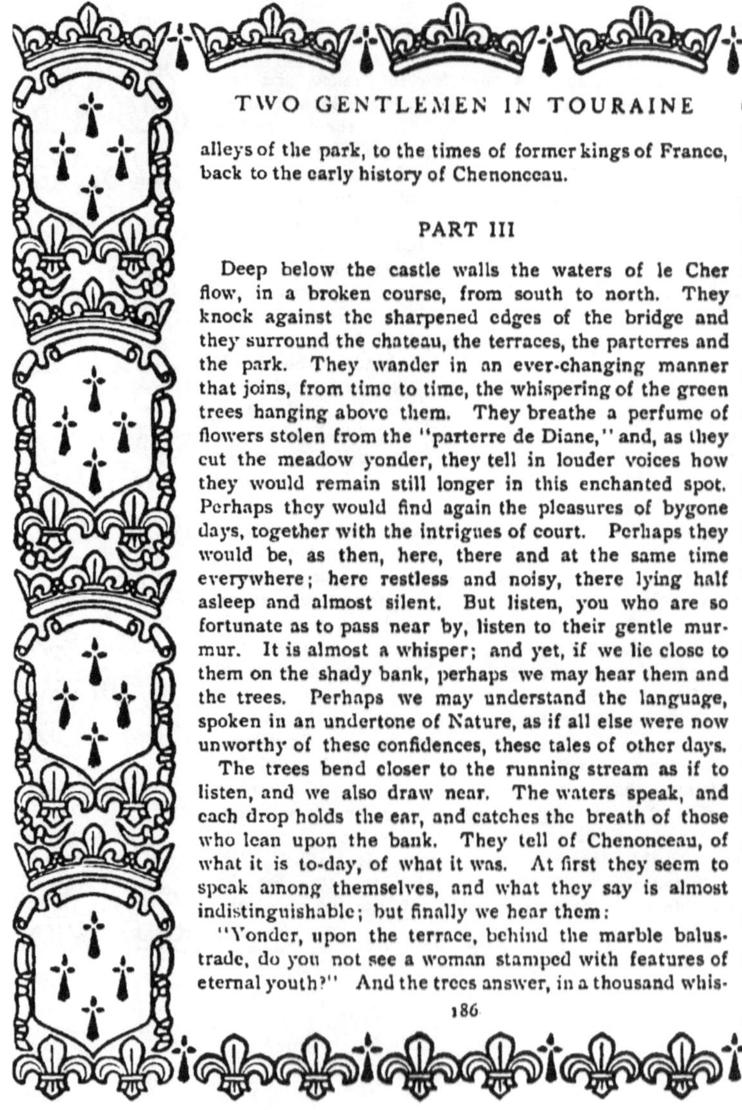

alleys of the park, to the times of former kings of France, back to the early history of Chenonceau.

PART III

Deep below the castle walls the waters of le Cher flow, in a broken course, from south to north. They knock against the sharpened edges of the bridge and they surround the chateau, the terraces, the parterres and the park. They wander in an ever-changing manner that joins, from time to time, the whispering of the green trees hanging above them. They breathe a perfume of flowers stolen from the "parterre de Diane," and, as they cut the meadow yonder, they tell in louder voices how they would remain still longer in this enchanted spot. Perhaps they would find again the pleasures of bygone days, together with the intrigues of court. Perhaps they would be, as then, here, there and at the same time everywhere; here restless and noisy, there lying half asleep and almost silent. But listen, you who are so fortunate as to pass near by, listen to their gentle murmur. It is almost a whisper; and yet, if we lie close to them on the shady bank, perhaps we may hear them and the trees. Perhaps we may understand the language, spoken in an undertone of Nature, as if all else were now unworthy of these confidences, these tales of other days.

The trees bend closer to the running stream as if to listen, and we also draw near. The waters speak, and each drop holds the ear, and catches the breath of those who lean upon the bank. They tell of Chenonceau, of what it is to-day, of what it was. At first they seem to speak among themselves, and what they say is almost indistinguishable; but finally we hear them:

"Yonder, upon the terrace, behind the marble balustrade, do you not see a woman stamped with features of eternal youth?" And the trees answer, in a thousand whis-

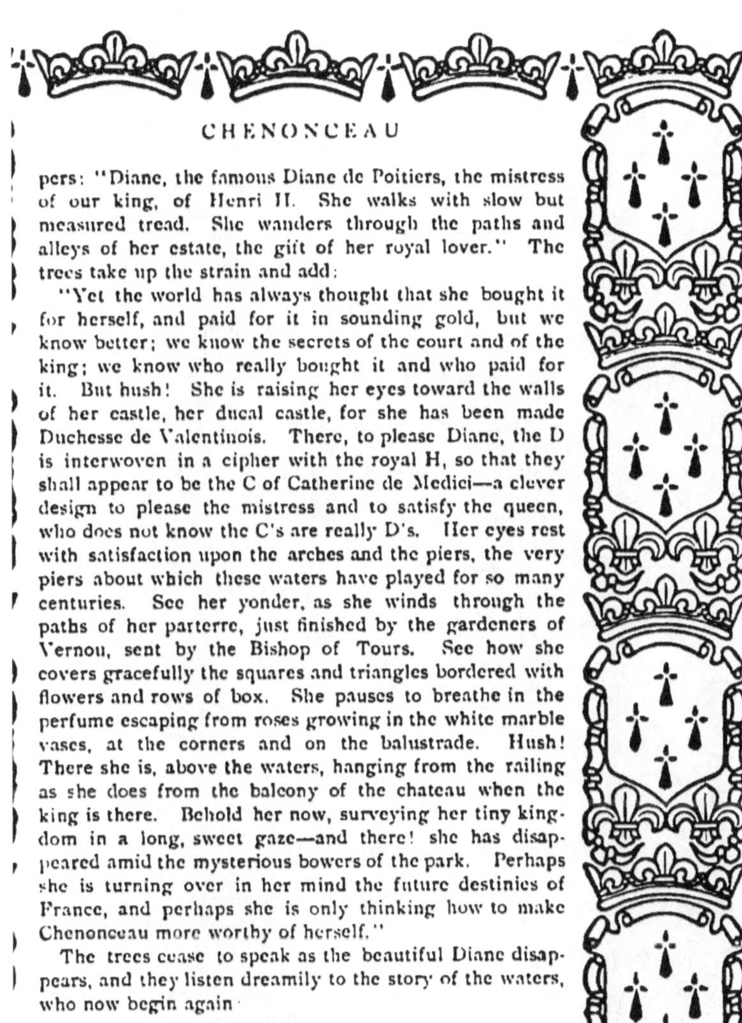

pers: "Diane, the famous Diane de Poitiers, the mistress of our king, of Henri II. She walks with slow but measured tread. She wanders through the paths and alleys of her estate, the gift of her royal lover." The trees take up the strain and add:

"Yet the world has always thought that she bought it for herself, and paid for it in sounding gold, but we know better; we know the secrets of the court and of the king; we know who really bought it and who paid for it. But hush! She is raising her eyes toward the walls of her castle, her ducal castle, for she has been made Duchesse de Valentinois. There, to please Diane, the D is interwoven in a cipher with the royal H, so that they shall appear to be the C of Catherine de Medici—a clever design to please the mistress and to satisfy the queen, who does not know the C's are really D's. Her eyes rest with satisfaction upon the arches and the piers, the very piers about which these waters have played for so many centuries. See her yonder, as she winds through the paths of her parterre, just finished by the gardeners of Vernou, sent by the Bishop of Tours. See how she covers gracefully the squares and triangles bordered with flowers and rows of box. She pauses to breathe in the perfume escaping from roses growing in the white marble vases, at the corners and on the balustrade. Hush! There she is, above the waters, hanging from the railing as she does from the balcony of the chateau when the king is there. Behold her now, surveying her tiny kingdom in a long, sweet gaze—and there! she has disappeared amid the mysterious bowers of the park. Perhaps she is turning over in her mind the future destinies of France, and perhaps she is only thinking how to make Chenonceau more worthy of herself."

The trees cease to speak as the beautiful Diane disappears, and they listen dreamily to the story of the waters, who now begin again·

"Henri II is wounded by Montgomery. Diane leaves Chenonceau to hasten to the side of her royal lover; but she is kept from him, and after ten days of agony the king dies on the 10th of July, 1559. The mistress, but yesterday a queen, must now seek the protection of her son-in-law, the Duc d'Aumale. Luckily for her, he is one of the four de Guises, and the cousin of Henry III, for her life is already in danger. Thavannes has offered the queen to 'cut off the nose of the mistress,' and Chenonceau is lost forever to Diane de Poitiers; for Catherine de Medici has forced her to exchange it for the high towers of Chaumont. What days were those when Catherine de Medici lived in the chateau, as the queen dowager! From 1559 to 1589, were over thirty years of continual feasts for Chenonceau! The royal chatelaine hid there, beneath a brilliant court, its fêtes and pleasures, the crimes which she committed at a distance. Chenonceau, itself, was mercifully spared these crimes, for it was never to be the scene of bloodshed. It was born of love and has always remained an abode of pleasure." The trees bend closer to the river, and the talking waters are lost beneath the lilies.

Later, they are heard again whispering, and speaking louder, the waters ask the trees a question whose answer we can hear:

"Who is the young queen and her royal husband, coming later, coming after Diane, and with another? Who is this fairy godmother who weaves a mantle of pleasure which the castle wears for them?"

"But do you not remember, O forgetful waters? Have you so easily forgotten those memorable days; have you forgotten Mary Stuart and François II? And do you not recognize in the fairy godmother Catherine de Medici, the proud and haughty Catherine whom we have known of old? These must be golden ages returned to Mediæval days, for the gods of Olympus sit at feasts. Mythology

walks arm in arm with rural deities. Columns of stone, hung with great wreaths of flowers and ever-greens, spring from every bower and grove. Altars have been erected beneath the shade of trees and are already laden with fruits and flowers, sacrifices to love and pleasure. Triumphal arches, obelisks and antique statues rise toward the skies, in the wide avenue, or upon the lawns. Long streamers bearing inscriptions, taken from the poets of Rome and Greece, flutter like dragon-flies between the trees. The murmur of a gushing fountain, the crystal notes upon the water, as the drops fall like pearls upon the marble basin, lend an imposing note to the songs of Bacchus upon the green.

"And do you remember the Sunday, following the 2d of May, 1577, when Catherine gave the most beautiful of all her feasts? It was given in honor of her two sons, Henri III and the Duc d'Alençon, who had won the victory of 'la Charité.' The table was laid upon the lawn of the gardens, behind the tower, for the banquet was to take place out of doors. The king appeared, dressed as a woman, as was his custom. His doublet, open, left bare his throat, which was covered with three rows of pearls. He wore three collars made of linen, two of which were ruffs, and the third turned down, according to the custom of the ladies at his court.

> " 'Si qu'au premier abord chascun etoit en peine
> S'il voyait un roy-femme ou un homme-reyne.'*

"Around him gathered his parrots, his monkeys, his dogs, all who partook their master's pleasures. Below the king, at his table, sat his 'mignons' and his favor-ites, with curled hair and painted faces like their master. They too wore ruffs about their necks, twelve inches wide. And lastly came the queen dowager,

---

* Quotation from a contemporary poet.

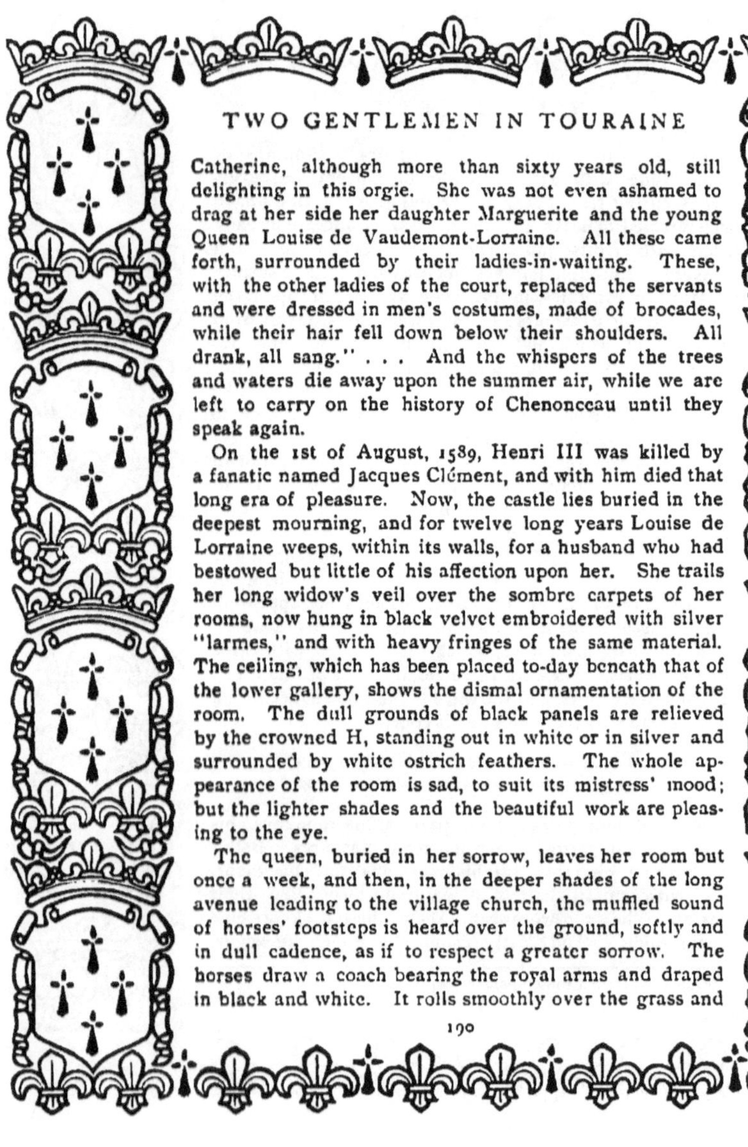

Catherine, although more than sixty years old, still delighting in this orgie. She was not even ashamed to drag at her side her daughter Marguerite and the young Queen Louise de Vaudemont-Lorraine. All these came forth, surrounded by their ladies-in-waiting. These, with the other ladies of the court, replaced the servants and were dressed in men's costumes, made of brocades, while their hair fell down below their shoulders. All drank, all sang." . . . And the whispers of the trees and waters die away upon the summer air, while we are left to carry on the history of Chenonceau until they speak again.

On the 1st of August, 1589, Henri III was killed by a fanatic named Jacques Clément, and with him died that long era of pleasure. Now, the castle lies buried in the deepest mourning, and for twelve long years Louise de Lorraine weeps, within its walls, for a husband who had bestowed but little of his affection upon her. She trails her long widow's veil over the sombre carpets of her rooms, now hung in black velvet embroidered with silver "larmes," and with heavy fringes of the same material. The ceiling, which has been placed to-day beneath that of the lower gallery, shows the dismal ornamentation of the room. The dull grounds of black panels are relieved by the crowned H, standing out in white or in silver and surrounded by white ostrich feathers. The whole appearance of the room is sad, to suit its mistress' mood; but the lighter shades and the beautiful work are pleasing to the eye.

The queen, buried in her sorrow, leaves her room but once a week, and then, in the deeper shades of the long avenue leading to the village church, the muffled sound of horses' footsteps is heard over the ground, softly and in dull cadence, as if to respect a greater sorrow. The horses draw a coach bearing the royal arms and draped in black and white. It rolls smoothly over the grass and over the sand; it is scarcely heard. A woman dressed in the purest white sits alone upon the cushions, like a ghostly vision. It is Louise de Lorraine, on her way to the church, there to pray for the repose of the soul of Henri III of France. And the peasants, as they see her pass, whisper to each other, "C'est la Reine Blanche." And the waters, too, seem to awaken at the name, and they answer, telling us what they have seen and known.

"If the night is clear—not too clear; if the stars shine brightly—not too brightly, as if half-hidden in the milky way, and if the midnight breeze is so soft that it does not drown our murmuring flow as we run on, yonder, through the moat and through the Cher, as we drip from the bronze or marbled basins, you will see a woman all in white. She is beautiful and young, and her figure hovers through the midnight air, over that grass which was once pro-faned by royal orgies, but which is now grown with summer flowers. The grass is bending beneath the soft step of 'la Reine Blanche,' who, driven from Chenon-ceau by the creditors of Catherine de Medici, returns by night to visit her abode. The walls that were born of love and made for pleasure have rung with the voices of sheriffs, selling at a pittance the jewels which have hung about the neck of Catherine, and the dresses of brocade or velvet which have been worn by both the mother and the son.

"Now Louise is dead; but still she haunts the castle by night. She wanders along the avenues and lawns, at times stopping suddenly, and casting down her eyes, as if in search of something. Perhaps she still seeks, in vain, the king's love, there in the tomb beneath the ground;—or is it only a souvenir, a trifle hidden in the grass, which has escaped the sheriff's eye?"

One evening—one winter's night—in an obscure corner of a tavern of St. Denys rested a coffin. A black

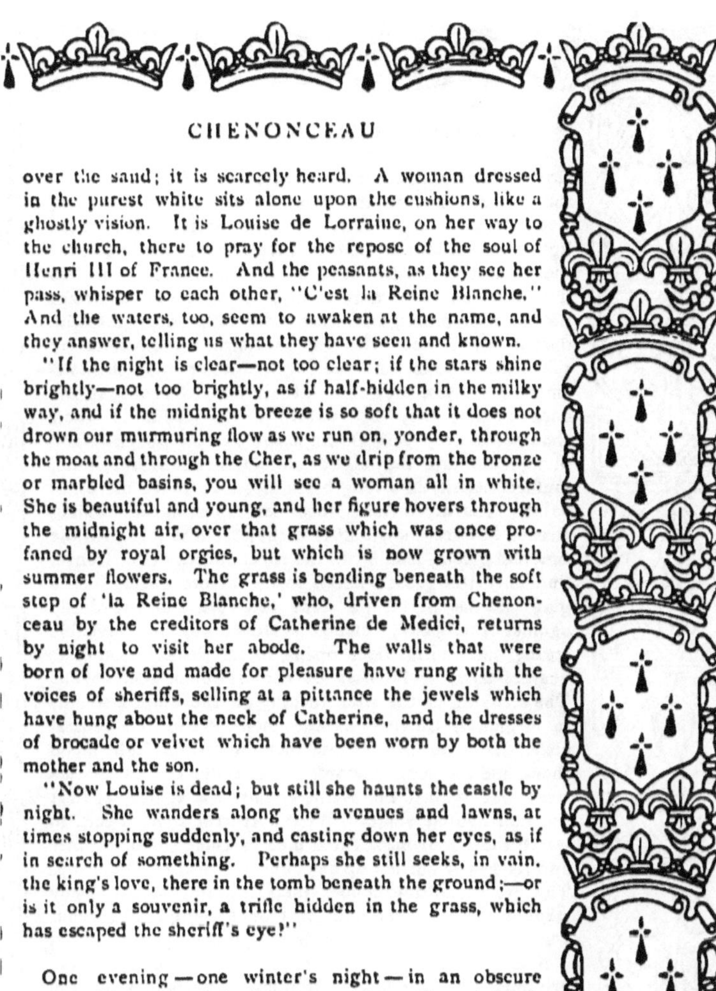

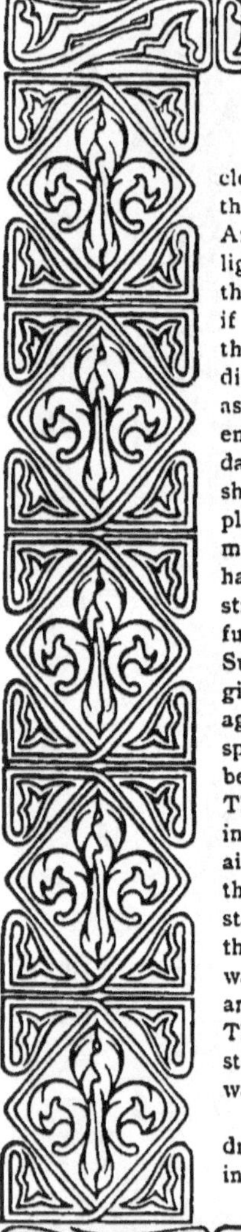

cloak dotted with fleur-de-lis of tarnished silver, covers the bier and sweeps the damp, musty tiles of the floor. Around a greasy table sit four valets, their faces lighted by a tallow candle, their heads bending over their game of cards. And as they play they drink, as if to kill the time more easily. A distant clock strikes the hour of midnight. Each note falls deeply into the dismal night, and with the last stroke the valets lay aside their cards, and leaving the table with its half-emptied glasses, they rise to their feet. Turning to the dark corner, they lift painfully the coffin to their shoulders; they pass through the narrow doorway and plunge out into the night. A single stranger follows, muffled heavily in a long black cloak, to cover his other habit. The mysterious procession is lost in the winding streets, so dark and silent that they seem to join with the funereal gloom, leading to the royal church of St. Denys. Suddenly the great church looms before them, like a giant in the night, its stone lacework showing dimly against the heavy clouds. Moved by an invisible spring, the central door opens, to let the coffin and its bearers pass, and closes once more upon their heels. The creaking of the iron, turning on the hinges, sounds in a ghostly cadence as the men ascend the central aisle. Four torches throw their uncertain light upon them, and the long shadows of the coffin and its bearers stand out against the walls, against the tombs, against the half-lighted vaults. What a fearful sight is this, to watch those four intoxicated men carrying the black bier and its heavy burden up the church's aisle! They stop. The great vaulting echoes their faltering steps. They stagger to their feet and start once more. The coffin wavers; it loses its balance, but regains it again.

A crash, like that of some exploding substance, like the dry burst of a thunderbolt dropping at one's feet, like the indescribable cracking of the bones. . . . Ah! cursed

men, . . . what have you done? . . . Alas, it is too
late; the coffin falls upon the ground; it rolls over and
over upon itself, and breaks! The black pall is torn in
twain; the fleurs-de-lis, unfastened, fall upon the flagstones and mix with the gray dust escaping from the
floor. Ah, dust of kings! Another heap is added to
your growing pile. And this is all that remains of
Henri III. And this stranger, bending to the ground,
collecting with his hands the broken fragments, to hold
them in his shriveled clasp, as if they were the most
precious of relics—this is Epernon, the last surviving
favorite of a departed king. He who had partaken of the
pleasures of his beloved master while at Chenonceau was
endeavoring, after many years of religious wars, to give
to him a last resting-place beneath the royal vaults of
St. Denys. Nine years before, in January, 1601, Louise
de Vaudemont-Lorraine had died. God had spared her
the horrors of this ghastly scene.

From 1601 to 1733 Chenonceau belonged to the Duchesse
de Mercœur and to the Vendome and Condé families.
Vendome (the rival of Turenne and Condé, if not their
equal in military success and fame) inhabited Chenonceau for a short time only. The peace and calm of a
castle, far from any town and surrounded by unfre-
quented roads, the liveliness of nature in its fairy-like
frame, could be of little attraction to a man so dissolute as
was Vendome. The noise of camps, the expeditions to
Italy,—"where he could conceal his excesses behind the
screens of easy victories and false dispatches to King
Louis XIV," as St. Simon tells us in "Les Memoires,"
—were better suited to a general whose life was given up
to every form of vice. He married, not inappropriately,
Mademoiselle d'Enghein, who was known as the richest,
as well as the ugliest heiress of her time, and shortly
afterwards he left for Madrid at the head of an expedition sent by Louis XIV to help his grandson, Philip V

of Spain. Vendome was over-fond of dinners and the pleasures of the table, and he is even reported to have used the same means as the Roman emperors to enable him to satisfy these tastes more fully. One night, after an unusual orgie, he was taken ill, and died of indigestion. As soon as it was known that he would not recover, his valets and his servants abandoned him, stealing everything that they could lay their hands upon, even to the sheets upon his bed, so that the great Vendome, who had lived in luxury and in excess, was left to die upon a simple mattress. Thus ended the worthy successor to Catherine de Medici as owner of Chenonceau.

In 1733 the Duc de Bourbon sold the castle and its estates to Monsieur Dupin, who belonged to an old noble family. He had served as a captain in the army, and had left it, on account of an "affair of honor," to become Fermier General. This position was a most remunerative one during the old regime, and was much sought after. In fact, if we should take the trouble of traveling through France and of noticing its most historic chateaux, we should find almost invariably that they were bought, at some time or another, by a Fermier General. This office was usually held by financiers who leased the right to collect the taxes of the various provinces. It was small wonder that every one wished to be a Fermier General, for that dignitary often raised, for his own benefit, double or triple the amount paid into the public treasury. The office was suppressed, however, in 1790.

Dupin owed his position to the great financier Samuel Bernard, who gave it to him as a reward for marrying an illegitimate daughter by Mlle. de Fontaine. This daughter was as good as she was beautiful, and under her care and influence, for more than half a century Chenonceau became the rendezvous of the highest representatives of literature and good manners, from 1733 to 1799. Fontenelle, Buffon, Montesquieu, St. Aulaire, Lord

Bolingbrooke, Voltaire, and Rousseau, all brought the mind, the intellect and the principles of a new school. Besides these, Madame de Luxembourg, Madame de Rohan-Chabot, Madame de Forcalquier, Madame de Mirepoix, Madame de Tençin, all belonging to ducal or to princely houses, all known as the most distinguished and fascinating women of their day, all known as "per.fections," if one does not scrutinize their morals too severely, all gave the fitting crown, the worthy setting to this royal chateau.

At the further end of the upper gallery, Madame Dupin installed a private theatre, with the aid of Jean Jacques Rousseau. There the author of "Les Confessions" acted some of his plays before an audience well calculated to appreciate them. For many years this relic of ancient times was left untouched, and would have remained in existence to-day, had not a woman of artistic but more modern taste replaced the theatre by the wooden pulpit which has already been described.

In 1769 Monsieur Dupin died, and each year his wife stayed longer at Chenonceau, where she was greatly beloved on account of her generosity to the poor. In 1793 the Revolution found her still at Chenonceau, and in those days the waters of the Cher must have been tinged to a reddish hue with the blood of victims that was flowing in them. As they passed beneath the great stone arches, they must have whispered many a sad tale of ruin and revenge, and on the stones of the piers, perhaps, might have seen the stains of blood which centuries could not wipe away. And during those violent days a woman more than eighty years of age was spending, in the rooms above those arches, the last days of an edifying life. She was left alone of all those who had surrounded her. Her husband and her sons were dead; her nephew, de Villeneuve, the only member of so large a family remaining, had fallen, one of the first victims of the

Revolution, and Chenonceau had even been appropriated as national property. It was easily proved, however, that Diane de Poitiers had bought it of Thomas Bohier in an unlawful manner, and that, therefore, it could not be considered as a royal estate, so that Madame Dupin was safely reinstalled in the chateau.

In 1799 she died, and the eighteenth century closed upon a freshly filled grave. A strange coincidence—a century of revolutions, of new ideas, of principles, ends in chaos, dies in reality to live in the memory of men as the most terrible period of French history. A woman, whose life had been one of sweetness and of generosity, dies peacefully; and her body rests, to this day, beneath the very spot where, in the shade of trees, far from the dazzling rays of a summer's sun, Voltaire and Rousseau must have ripened those ideas which were to foster the Revolution itself. Her memory lives, too, in harmony with the calm and peaceful surroundings.

The nineteenth century opens, and with it René Vallet de Villeneuve, the grand-nephew of Madame Dupin, inherits Chenonceau when only twenty years of age. Until 1814 Monsieur de Villeneuve was engaged in the fulfilment of several diplomatic missions; but afterwards he came to live at Chenonceau. The careful restoration of the chateau then became his chief occupation. Unfortunately for his purpose, however, architecture in France was then undergoing a period prejudicial to the Renaissance, and owing to this, some errors were undoubtedly committed. Monsieur de Villeneuve fortunately understood that above all things the character of the monument was to be respected. Madame de Villeneuve took charge of the gardens, whose taste and style she borrowed from "la Malmaison," while lady-in-waiting to Queen Hortense. The park and flower gardens became the pleasure grounds of the rustic inhabitants of the village, and of a Sunday they would all

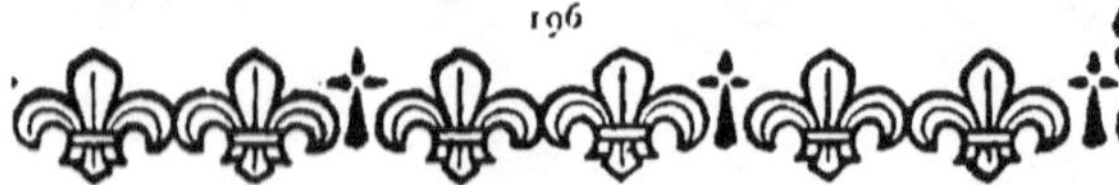

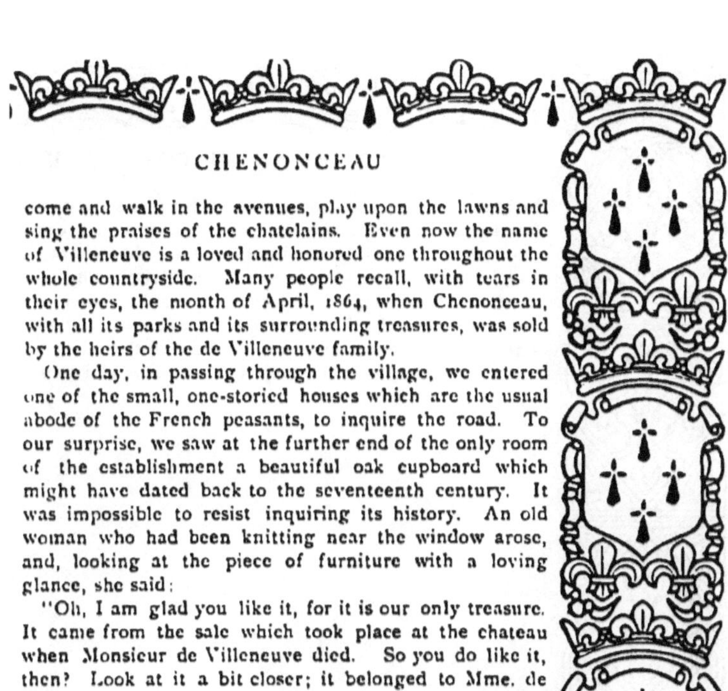

come and walk in the avenues, play upon the lawns and sing the praises of the chatelains. Even now the name of Villeneuve is a loved and honored one throughout the whole countryside. Many people recall, with tears in their eyes, the month of April, 1864, when Chenonceau, with all its parks and its surrounding treasures, was sold by the heirs of the de Villeneuve family.

One day, in passing through the village, we entered one of the small, one-storied houses which are the usual abode of the French peasants, to inquire the road. To our surprise, we saw at the further end of the only room of the establishment a beautiful oak cupboard which might have dated back to the seventeenth century. It was impossible to resist inquiring its history. An old woman who had been knitting near the window arose, and, looking at the piece of furniture with a loving glance, she said:

"Oh, I am glad you like it, for it is our only treasure. It came from the sale which took place at the chateau when Monsieur de Villeneuve died. So you do like it, then? Look at it a bit closer; it belonged to Mme. de Villeneuve; she hung her dresses in it. Yes, yes, this is all that is left of our dear master's." And her husband added: "Never mind; the chateau never will be again what it has been under the good de Villeneuve family."

Nevertheless, it must be acknowledged that if the later restorations of the interior of Chenonceau have not been successful in every way, it has been a wonderful undertaking, and certainly well carried out on the exterior of the chateau. Perhaps the best portion of the work has been the tearing down of the rooms built by Catherine de Medici above the terrace adjoining the library, for it brings out the façade of the latter, and keeps the purity of style unbroken. Those who did all this, as well as those who decorated the upper gallery, have departed, victims of the undertaking, and the waters which have

looked upon the past, for centuries, from the moats and fountains, have departed also. New waters have come; but they are silent. They have lost their cheerful tattle, and have ceased to speak to us by the river. The trees have lost their tongues, and the stories, the visions and the characters of other days have faded as in a dream. The present weaves out its own unfinished threads, while the past remains a silent majesty that never will return.

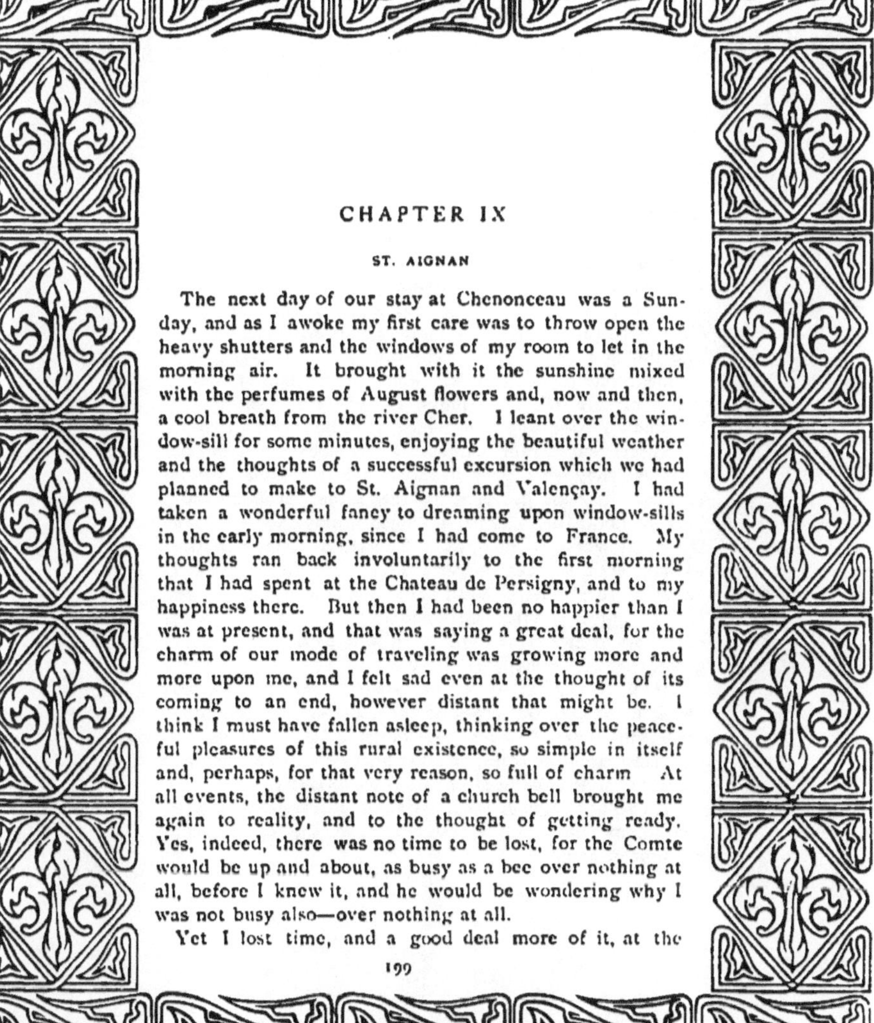

CHAPTER IX

ST. AIGNAN

The next day of our stay at Chenonceau was a Sunday, and as I awoke my first care was to throw open the heavy shutters and the windows of my room to let in the morning air. It brought with it the sunshine mixed with the perfumes of August flowers and, now and then, a cool breath from the river Cher. I leant over the window-sill for some minutes, enjoying the beautiful weather and the thoughts of a successful excursion which we had planned to make to St. Aignan and Valençay. I had taken a wonderful fancy to dreaming upon window-sills in the early morning, since I had come to France. My thoughts ran back involuntarily to the first morning that I had spent at the Chateau de Persigny, and to my happiness there. But then I had been no happier than I was at present, and that was saying a great deal, for the charm of our mode of traveling was growing more and more upon me, and I felt sad even at the thought of its coming to an end, however distant that might be. I think I must have fallen asleep, thinking over the peaceful pleasures of this rural existence, so simple in itself and, perhaps, for that very reason, so full of charm At all events, the distant note of a church bell brought me again to reality, and to the thought of getting ready. Yes, indeed, there was no time to be lost, for the Comte would be up and about, as busy as a bee over nothing at all, before I knew it, and he would be wondering why I was not busy also—over nothing at all.

Yet I lost time, and a good deal more of it, at the

window.   I could not resist the temptation, for the picture
was so engaging.   The single street of the village, that
ran beneath me, was wonderfully silent, and wonderfully deserted too, I thought.   The only sound was
that caused by the sabots of a peasant, going to
la première messe, no doubt, that he might pray for
some one or something near at heart.   And now the silence was again broken by two church bells, one, that of
Chenonceau, near by, the other that of the little village of
Cirray, two miles distant.   The one, in a shrill and high-
pitched note, the other in a deep and mellow tone, called
the respective villages to worship.

At last the little door of the hotel opened and the
Comte appeared.   He was going toward the little church
and did not see me.   I held my peace, and left him
to his Sunday meditations.   Some time elapsed, and I
found myself still lingering at the window, gazing into
the small garden opposite, which was filled with all kinds
of flowers and shrubs.   I could see a large collection of
peonies; they were very beautiful.   Later I discovered
that the garden belonged to the father of our landlady, a quaint old character whose kindly face bespoke
too many years to mention.   The little cottage in the
garden, with its trees and shrubs on every side, possessed
an air of rural poetry, and I could not help thinking that
if Washington Irving had come to Chenonceau, instead
of going to the Alhambra, he would have left even a
greater legacy perhaps behind him.

"It is breakfast time, monsieur," called Madame
Dessert, through the crack of the door—a very generous
crack, in spite of locks and bolts.   "If ce monsieur
wishes to catch the train, he must hurry.   Ça part bientôt,
bientôt," added she in a tone of great anxiety.

"All right," I answered, "I shall be ready in a very
few moments.   But please to have my café-au-lait
brought in here."

"Oh, no, monsieur; that is impossible. I could not have allowed ces monsieurs to start on such a journey with café-au-lait simply, so I have prepared a good déjeuner for them. Voyons donc," continued Madame Dessert, meditatively, still on the other side of the door, while I was endeavoring to finish my toilet. "Voyons donc; there are eggs, sausages, boudin, and cotelettes au cresson, with a bottle of my best white wine 'Mousseux.' It is all in the little dining-room on this floor, and Monsieur le Comte has already finished his eggs. Ça qu'il faut se depecher." And I could hear Madame Dessert trotting off down the entry and felt sure that she was shaking her head over the thoughts of her unappreciated déjeuner. I must say, however, that it did not long remain so, for the boudin and the "vin mousseux" sounded particularly inviting.

"At last!" exclaimed the Comte, as I entered the little dining-room. "Hurry, hurry. Gobble your breakfast quickly, or we shall be late." And he proceeded to suit the action to the word.

"But, my dear friend," I returned, "the train does not leave for an hour. At all events, you will not be late, for I saw you up and out and ready to start, I suppose, an hour ago at least. Your energy, this hot weather, is really extraordinary."

"Well, I am French in that way, you see," the Comte continued, hastily drinking a glass of the "mousseux" as if his life depended upon it. "We are a fidgety sort of people, and if we are going anywhere we always hear the whistle of the train leaving the station, a good two hours before it is even due. We love to be ahead of time, as much as you do to squeeze in at the last minute." And the Comte had finished his breakfast, and I, alas, had only just begun.

"I am sorry to disturb ces messieurs," said Madame Dessert, again poking her head, with its lace cap and

strings, in at the door. "I am sorry; but the omnibus will not wait."

"Quick, quick!" shouted the Comte, rising hurriedly. "Are the bags strapped? Are the umbrellas tied together? Mon Dieu! Mon Dieu! I have left my brush behind. Madame Dessert, tell the omnibus to wait a moment longer."

"But, my dear friend," I put in, "the omnibus has not yet even arrived." It was no use. The Comte had disappeared and was busy, frantically busy, with his bags and his brush.

"Nah!" said he, in an odd little tone that he was very fond of, as he returned. "We are ready at last. Surely you have forgotten something. Nothing? Well, I have never seen such a person. Do you never forget anything? There; here is the omnibus." And the Comte pushed me before him into the vehicle, for fear lest I should escape him, and Madame Dessert turned the handle of the door and fastened it herself, for fear (the good soul) lest we should fall out of the door.

"Allez, cocher!" I felt as if I were back in Paris in the Faubourg St. Honore.

"Au revoir; bon voyage!" And off we went. Ten minutes later we were at the station.

The train came in at last, puffing and whistling even more than usual. It seemed to me that everything created more disturbance in starting this morning than ever before. Perhaps, I thought, because it was Sunday. That was the only reason that I could think of. At all events, we jumped into the first carriage near us. Our only companion was certainly not prepossessing. He wore a long black beard which had not been trimmed to its best advantage. He had taken off his large straw hat and replaced it by a cotton handkerchief of many hues. His limbs seemed to hang, indifferently, from a huge, an almost circular body, as if they were in some

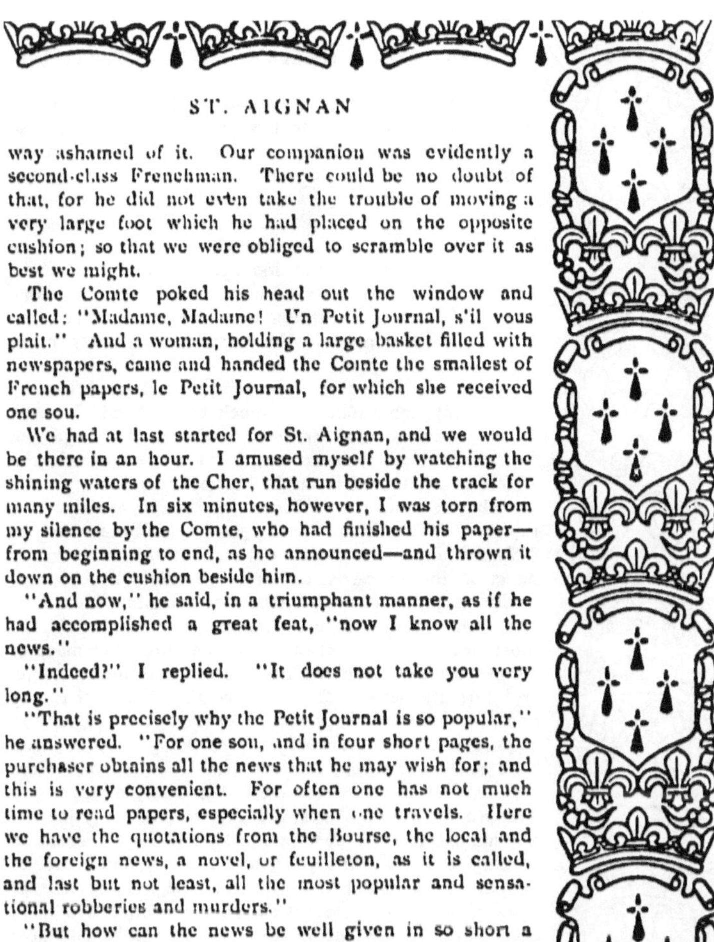

way ashamed of it. Our companion was evidently a second-class Frenchman. There could be no doubt of that, for he did not even take the trouble of moving a very large foot which he had placed on the opposite cushion; so that we were obliged to scramble over it as best we might.

The Comte poked his head out the window and called: "Madame, Madame! Un Petit Journal, s'il vous plait." And a woman, holding a large basket filled with newspapers, came and handed the Comte the smallest of French papers, le Petit Journal, for which she received one sou.

We had at last started for St. Aignan, and we would be there in an hour. I amused myself by watching the shining waters of the Cher, that run beside the track for many miles. In six minutes, however, I was torn from my silence by the Comte, who had finished his paper— from beginning to end, as he announced—and thrown it down on the cushion beside him.

"And now," he said, in a triumphant manner, as if he had accomplished a great feat, "now I know all the news."

"Indeed?" I replied. "It does not take you very long."

"That is precisely why the Petit Journal is so popular," he answered. "For one sou, and in four short pages, the purchaser obtains all the news that he may wish for; and this is very convenient. For often one has not much time to read papers, especially when one travels. Here we have the quotations from the Bourse, the local and the foreign news, a novel, or feuilleton, as it is called, and last but not least, all the most popular and sensational robberies and murders."

"But how can the news be well given in so short a space?" I asked.

"I do not know how; but it is very well given. And

the details and descriptions are so accurate that the social danger of such a paper lies in its very accuracy of detail; for it teaches others, who may have been ignorant before, how to commit crimes."

"And what kind of persons buy this paper?" I inquired.

"Almost every one," the Comte replied. "The poor, because it is cheap and sensational; the rich, because the political opinions are not too decided; and the ladies, because of the feuilleton. I know many a grande dame who would not for anything miss the pleasure of reading her Petit Journal at the regular hour every morning."

"I had no idea that this rather sensational looking paper held such a place in French hearts," said I. And as the Comte seemed inclined to discuss the subject of French journals at some length I ventured to ask him which he considered to be the best of them.

"That is rather a difficult question to answer," he replied. "For the political opinions in France are so different, and so firmly adhered to, that we seldom read a paper of another party, and have therefore little opportunity to judge our newspapers as a mass. Nevertheless, I should say that le Temps was, upon the whole, the most impartial and reliable. To be sure, it is more or less republican. But its literary worth is indisputable, and I really believe, Conservative that I am, that any one who reads le Temps every day for a year is bound to acquire a certain knowledge by so doing. There; you have extracted a very fair criticism from me, and more than you would have received from many of my kind, who would think it almost a heresy to praise any journal not upholding their own political doctrines. I speak of reading le Temps for a year; and you will find plenty of people who consider that if a man begins the first of January and reads it every day, his education will have been completed by the next Christmas. It is odd how many countries possess a leading newspaper called 'The Times.' The Times of London must, I think, head the list, but they seem all to be good and serious journals. I have yet to live to see a bad Times." The Comte paused a moment in his soliloquy on the journals of France and of other countries, and then turning to me, he remarked:

"In your country they are very fond of 'Heralds,' are they not? Almost every city seems to require at least one Herald as well as its Times, for self-respect if nothing else. And I have heard that one city, especially, not content with these two alone, has combined them both, by way of change, and now rejoices in a 'Times-Herald.' I have always thought it such an aristocratic sounding name for a journal, and indeed," added the Comte, always afraid of giving offense without meaning to, "and indeed, I have every reason to believe that in every way it lives up to the high standard of its name."

As I knew the "Times-Herald" which he referred to merely by reputation, I could do nothing but smile at the Comte's remark and wait for him to proceed, which he did almost immediately.

"As a Conservative paper, I think the Gaulois must be considered the best. It has often a very good editorial, signed by some man of literary note. An excellent article, signed 'Tout, Paris,' speaks of people, places and customs in a pleasant way, and tells also of contemporary celebrities. Under the heading 'Mondanités' are detailed the doings, the marriages and deaths of what we are pleased to call 'le Monde,' which in reality is nothing but that small fraction of people whose names are forever in the public print. Then, above all, it gives on its last page the 'Déplacements et Villégiatures,' a column or more, in which the names of all the principal subscribers are noted, with the place where each one is stopping at that present moment. You cannot imagine

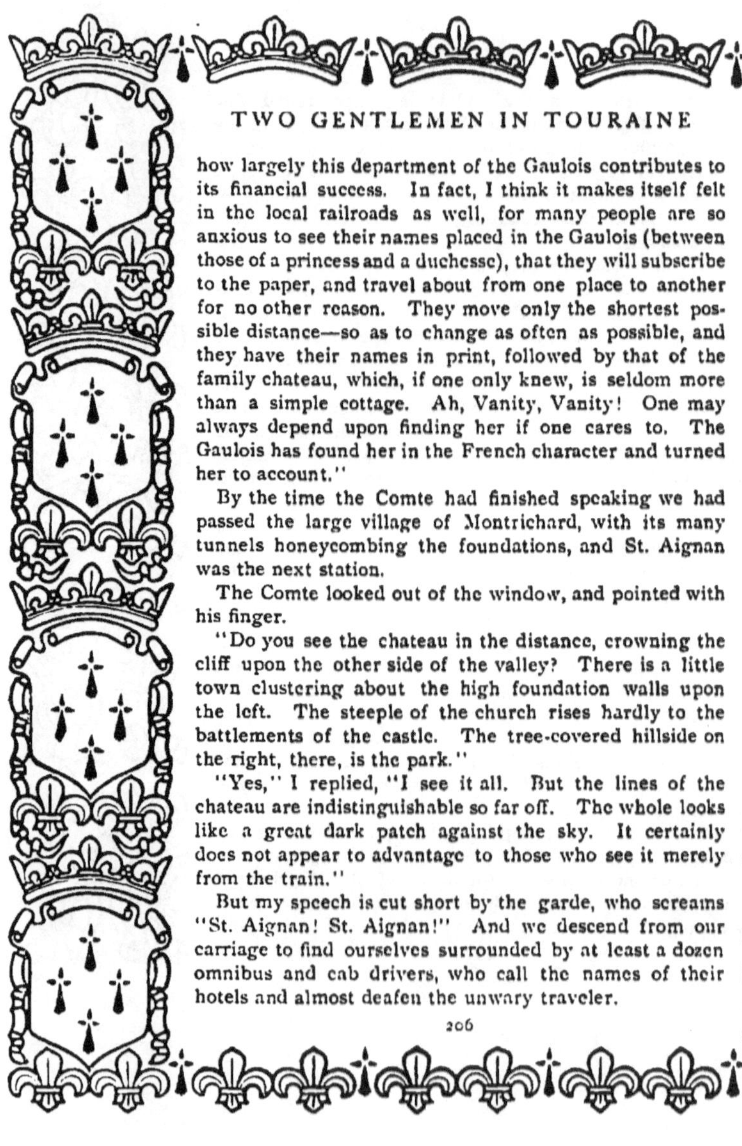

how largely this department of the Gaulois contributes to its financial success. In fact, I think it makes itself felt in the local railroads as well, for many people are so anxious to see their names placed in the Gaulois (between those of a princess and a duchesse), that they will subscribe to the paper, and travel about from one place to another for no other reason. They move only the shortest possible distance—so as to change as often as possible, and they have their names in print, followed by that of the family chateau, which, if one only knew, is seldom more than a simple cottage. Ah, Vanity, Vanity! One may always depend upon finding her if one cares to. The Gaulois has found her in the French character and turned her to account."

By the time the Comte had finished speaking we had passed the large village of Montrichard, with its many tunnels honeycombing the foundations, and St. Aignan was the next station.

The Comte looked out of the window, and pointed with his finger.

"Do you see the chateau in the distance, crowning the cliff upon the other side of the valley? There is a little town clustering about the high foundation walls upon the left. The steeple of the church rises hardly to the battlements of the castle. The tree-covered hillside on the right, there, is the park."

"Yes," I replied, "I see it all. But the lines of the chateau are indistinguishable so far off. The whole looks like a great dark patch against the sky. It certainly does not appear to advantage to those who see it merely from the train."

But my speech is cut short by the garde, who screams "St. Aignan! St. Aignan!" And we descend from our carriage to find ourselves surrounded by at least a dozen omnibus and cab drivers, who call the names of their hotels and almost deafen the unwary traveler.

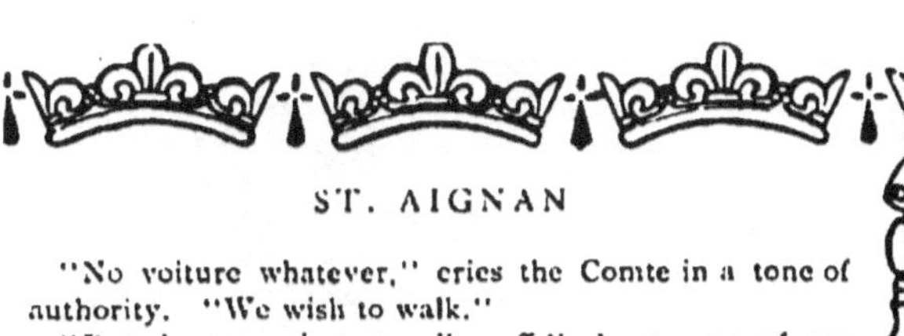

ST. AIGNAN

"No voiture whatever," cries the Comte in a tone of authority. "We wish to walk."

"But the town is two miles off," shouts one of our persecutors.

"Three," shouts a second.

"Four!"

"Five!"

"Six!" shout others almost in a chorus.

"Une voiture, messieurs, une voiture; seulement dix sous. Allons; une voiture!" And we are almost torn to pieces by our anxious tormentors.

"No—o—o—o! I told you no," the Comte cries in decisive tones, while we struggle against children, boys, drivers and women who seize the bags, the umbrellas and the brush, carrying them all in different directions.

At last we have fought clear of them, and are off upon the road to St. Aignan. The conventional avenue of lime trees stretches before us in a straight line that seems almost lost in infinity. This is, indeed, the land of limes and poplars. And as we walk briskly along, in the soft morning air, I try to recall how many chateaux we have approached before in just this way, and wonder how many more we shall find ere we have left the dark green shades and the gray mists of this fairy-like Touraine. At length we have reached the little town, and are pausing, here and there, in the quaint old streets where the artistic hand of time is oddly linked with that of modern innovation. It seems, indeed, as if the three thousand inhabitants who form it would affect the importance of a township of ten times that number. And the result may be seen in a mélange of electric lights and telegraphic wires, hanging against houses of the sixteenth century or crumbling buildings of an even earlier period.

Shops appear, with showy windows, built into some ancient house that looks ill at ease in these surroundings.

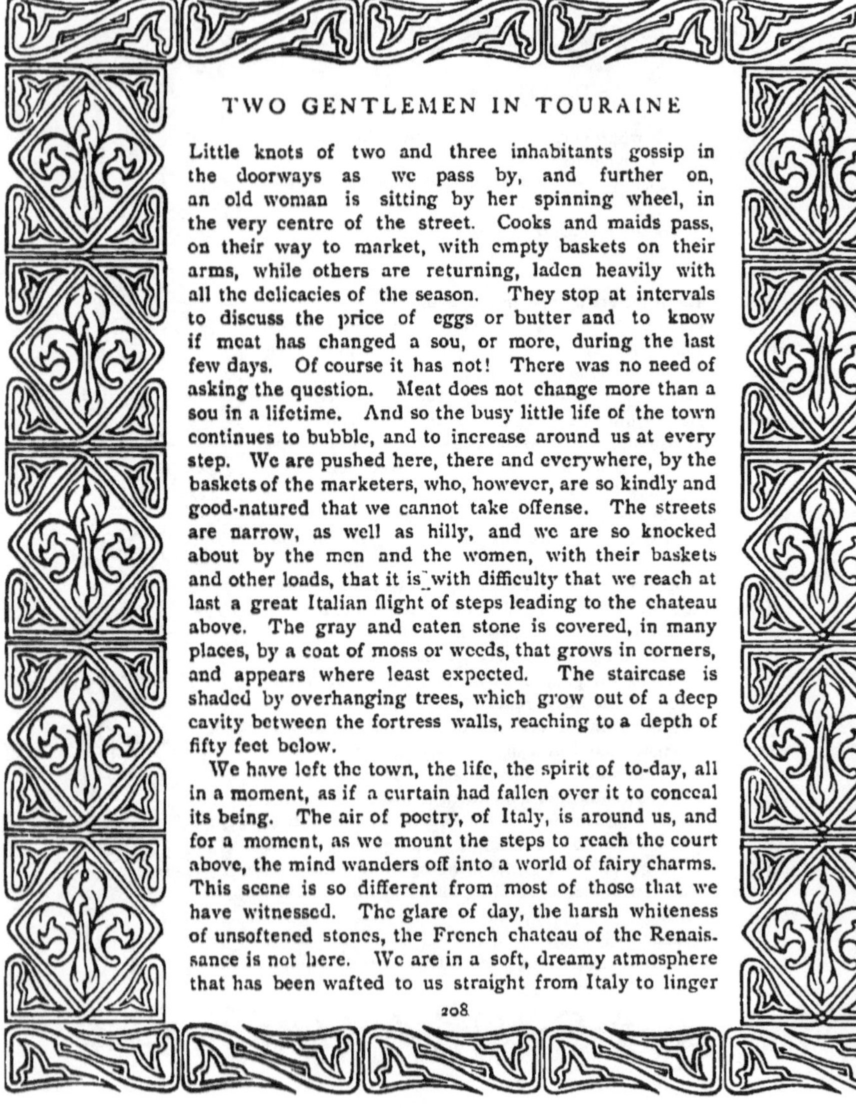

Little knots of two and three inhabitants gossip in
the doorways as we pass by, and further on,
an old woman is sitting by her spinning wheel, in
the very centre of the street. Cooks and maids pass,
on their way to market, with empty baskets on their
arms, while others are returning, laden heavily with
all the delicacies of the season. They stop at intervals
to discuss the price of eggs or butter and to know
if meat has changed a sou, or more, during the last
few days. Of course it has not! There was no need of
asking the question. Meat does not change more than a
sou in a lifetime. And so the busy little life of the town
continues to bubble, and to increase around us at every
step. We are pushed here, there and everywhere, by the
baskets of the marketers, who, however, are so kindly and
good-natured that we cannot take offense. The streets
are narrow, as well as hilly, and we are so knocked
about by the men and the women, with their baskets
and other loads, that it is with difficulty that we reach at
last a great Italian flight of steps leading to the chateau
above. The gray and eaten stone is covered, in many
places, by a coat of moss or weeds, that grows in corners,
and appears where least expected. The staircase is
shaded by overhanging trees, which grow out of a deep
cavity between the fortress walls, reaching to a depth of
fifty feet below.

We have left the town, the life, the spirit of to-day, all
in a moment, as if a curtain had fallen over it to conceal
its being. The air of poetry, of Italy, is around us, and
for a moment, as we mount the steps to reach the court
above, the mind wanders off into a world of fairy charms.
This scene is so different from most of those that we
have witnessed. The glare of day, the harsh whiteness
of unsoftened stones, the French chateau of the Renaissance is not here. We are in a soft, dreamy atmosphere
that has been wafted to us straight from Italy to linger

among the leaves and branches, and we breathe enchantment in this poetry-laden air.   In another moment it has
passed, and we stand upon the platform upon which the
chateau is built.

A mass of ornamented towers, some dismantled, others
white and new, rises up before us.   Windows with
Renaissance carving about them stand out at all points,
while their side-stones are inlaid with black Italian
marble.   Side by side with these are modern windows,
harsh and without style, with freshly painted iron shutters.   Orange trees stand half-buried in their painted
boxes, and hide the lower portion of this façade, whose
architecture but faintly suggests that of the sixteenth
century.   A parterre covered with beds of flowers leads
to a long terrace shut in by a stone parapet which overlooks the Cher.   At the further end of this terrace is one
of the façades of the chateau, white and new, and
which, notwithstanding a coronet and monogram, and
Renaissance windows in the roof, looks more like a
modern Italian pavilion.   A chapel near by of the sixteenth century has been restored with taste and care.
On the southeast of the chateau there stands a tower in
modern imitation of the fifteenth century.   The three
escutcheons rising above its battlements produce an effect
more curious than happy.   The door, however, is a good
example of the flamboyant detail of that period.

This chaos of stones, so new and white, beaten by the
winds and eaten by the frosts and rain, this strange
mixture of the harsh and the rude with the soft and the
poetic, these modern lines placed side by side with Gothic
minarets, this tower—called "the tower of Agar," the last
remains of the castle of the Barons of Donzy—this collection of buildings of every period, from the fifteenth to
the seventeenth centuries, on which Time has left the
deepening signs of its passage unassisted by art—all these
attract the eye, as they mislead the taste.   Unconsciously

we admire it, although we are constrained to feel how much more beautiful it might have been.

We turn from the chateau, and pass through an archway whose gray stones have been clad in ivy. We cross a wooden bridge thrown over a deep ravine, and a few steps bring us to a park, thus separated from the chateau. It has been laid out by a master's hand and is, beyond doubt, one of the most graceful as well as one of the most perfect ones in all Touraine. Though small in its proportions, it has been made, through the cleverness of its designs, to appear much larger than it is in reality. On entering this park we find ourselves at one end of an oblong terrace cut into the hillside. So long is this terrace that the trunks of the tree at its furthest end are almost indistinguishable; and it is so wide that a person walking on one side of it cannot be recognized by those upon the opposite.

A broad, graceful path runs along the curved outline of the left. It is shaded by a wall of laurels, meadow sweets and other shrubs, themselves enshadowed by the higher trees behind. This is cut sharply, here and there, by a path, an alley, or an avenue of grass leading to unknown bowers. It is shaded by the soft foliage around and above it. The ivy-covered ground is like a softened carpet beneath the feet, and in the distance it is lost in this maze of green. The alley itself seems to have been made for love and poetry, and inspires romantic pictures in the mind.

"Let us take one of these paths," said I to my companion. "This one in which we stand seems to be without limit, without end. What a place to linger in, surrounded by all those things that tend to please and soften the heart, and to fill it with thoughts of the loves and enchantments of other days that would last as long as the path itself—forever! See, the shadows fan the ground, moved to and fro by the soft air that fades away, even

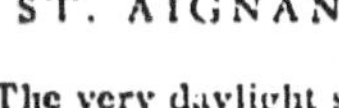

while we speak. The very daylight seems to respect the sanctity of this enchanted spot."

"Come," said the Comte, laying his hand gently on my arm. "Come and see how short a thing your love would be if it lived no longer than this deceiving path. Alas, this wall of leaves is not impenetrable, though it appears as solid as if made of stones. See, the sunlight already makes its way through the green. The leaves and foliage grow thin. Soon the shades and shadows of the poetry and love of those long past will have faded altogether, and all will change. And the maze also, as we pass on, has only the depth of a curtain. Do but draw it apart, and you will find the hilltop covered with vineyards. The trees have disappeared. The path has vanished, suddenly, as it appeared. How sad, indeed, is the delusion! But the passing hand of poetry has nevertheless left its love-jewel in the heart; that remains, and we cling to it as we pass onward."

The Comte spoke with a show of feeling that any one less sensitive to nature might have questioned. But to me it seemed only in keeping with my thoughts and mood. And as we turned from the spot where we had stood some moments while he spoke, I found myself saying, half to my companion and half to the trees that now appeared once more: "How wrong was I thus to test the depths of this beautiful gem, which seemed to me so truly a jewel that it could not perish! However, it is only one more dream, one more illusion, exposed by that cold reality that one learns to dread as one grows older day by day. Let us return. Let us re-enter our dream and forget that it is only half imagination, and that it has an end."

"You are right," said the Comte. " 'Le mieux est l'ennemi du bien.' Let us retrace our steps lest we lose even that which we would covet the more."

We find ourselves once more upon the terrace, stand-

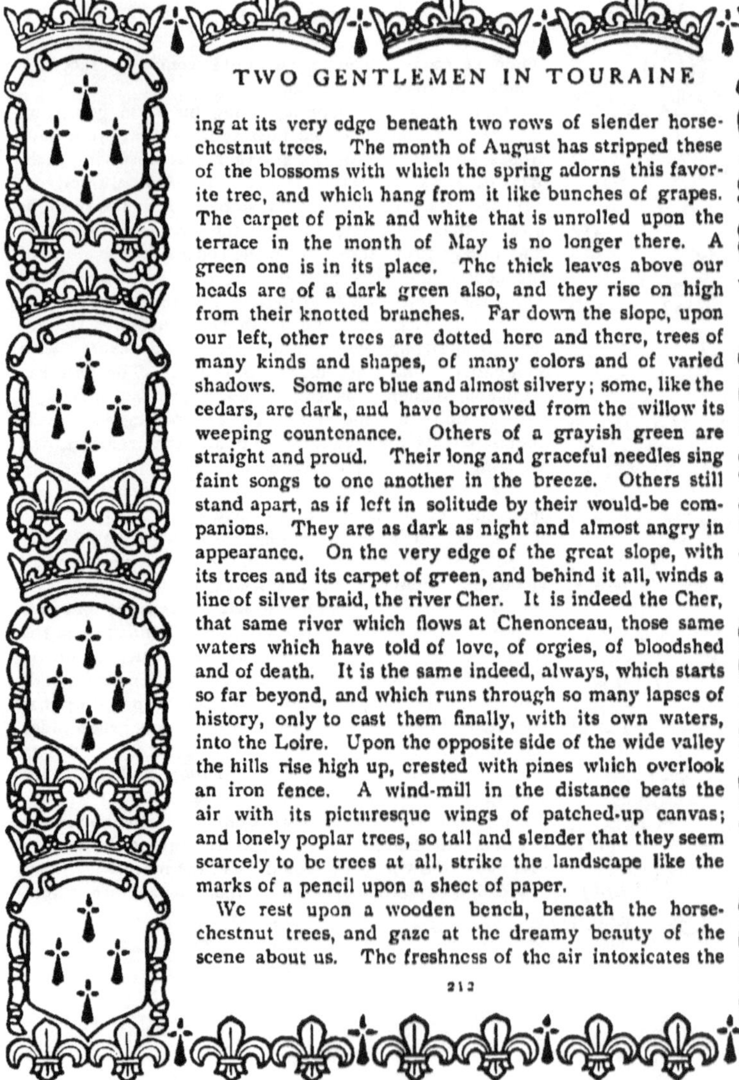

ing at its very edge beneath two rows of slender horse-chestnut trees. The month of August has stripped these of the blossoms with which the spring adorns this favorite tree, and which hang from it like bunches of grapes. The carpet of pink and white that is unrolled upon the terrace in the month of May is no longer there. A green one is in its place. The thick leaves above our heads are of a dark green also, and they rise on high from their knotted branches. Far down the slope, upon our left, other trees are dotted here and there, trees of many kinds and shapes, of many colors and of varied shadows. Some are blue and almost silvery; some, like the cedars, are dark, and have borrowed from the willow its weeping countenance. Others of a grayish green are straight and proud. Their long and graceful needles sing faint songs to one another in the breeze. Others still stand apart, as if left in solitude by their would-be companions. They are as dark as night and almost angry in appearance. On the very edge of the great slope, with its trees and its carpet of green, and behind it all, winds a line of silver braid, the river Cher. It is indeed the Cher, that same river which flows at Chenonceau, those same waters which have told of love, of orgies, of bloodshed and of death. It is the same indeed, always, which starts so far beyond, and which runs through so many lapses of history, only to cast them finally, with its own waters, into the Loire. Upon the opposite side of the wide valley the hills rise high up, crested with pines which overlook an iron fence. A wind-mill in the distance beats the air with its picturesque wings of patched-up canvas; and lonely poplar trees, so tall and slender that they seem scarcely to be trees at all, strike the landscape like the marks of a pencil upon a sheet of paper.

We rest upon a wooden bench, beneath the horse-chestnut trees, and gaze at the dreamy beauty of the scene about us. The freshness of the air intoxicates the

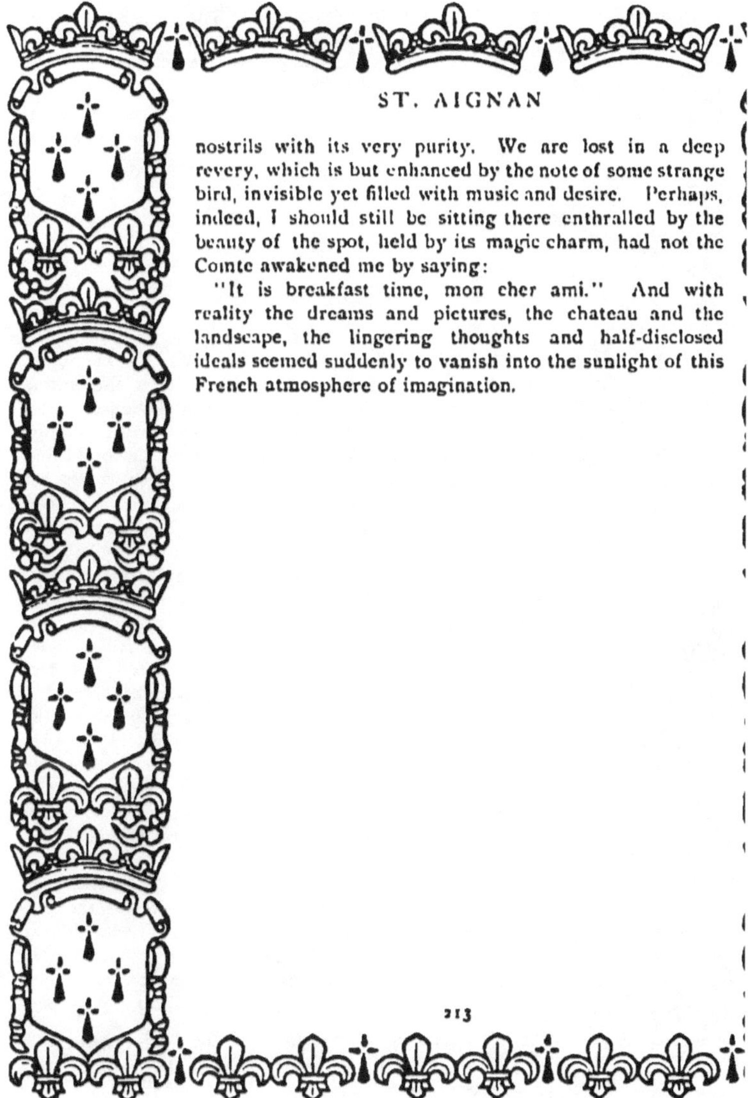

nostrils with its very purity. We are lost in a deep revery, which is but enhanced by the note of some strange bird, invisible yet filled with music and desire. Perhaps, indeed, I should still be sitting there enthralled by the beauty of the spot, held by its magic charm, had not the Comte awakened me by saying:

"It is breakfast time, mon cher ami." And with reality the dreams and pictures, the chateau and the landscape, the lingering thoughts and half-disclosed ideals seemed suddenly to vanish into the sunlight of this French atmosphere of imagination.

CHAPTER X

The chateau of St. Aignan was behind us, spreading
its wings, like a giant bird, over the cliff. We wound our
way down the tortuous hill, through steep and uncon-
ventional streets lined with picturesque old houses whose
pointed gables of beams and bricks projected high
above the narrow sidewalk. Before long we found ourselves at the banks of the Cher, whose deep waters are
here bounded on one side by the white stones of a pier,
and on the other by the green fields. The stone bridge
leading to the railway station guards it, upon the left, and
a large mill—not so large as to be unsightly—seems as if
it were holding an intimate conversation with the waters,
whose result concerns the miller's welfare. We turned,
however, to the right, following the quay, and stopped,
before many yards, at what is considered the best
hotel of the place. The stir which our arrival created in
the ménage of the hotel was such as to bring the master,
the wife, the servants, the men and the maids, all away
from their work to hover about us like so many flies, and
to take, each, an individual and fee-anticipating part in
the setting of a diminutive table—by the window of the
table d'hôte which overlooked the river. Our breakfast
began by a series of attacks from the various officers of
the household, who came marching in, one by one, bearing the details of our meal. First, there was the proverbial omelette of a French inn. Then, the cold chicken
(the fifteenth that we had eaten during our journey), the
potatoes en robes de chambres, grapes which would have

needed at least a month of summer sunshine to make
them eatable, peaches (bought at a high price from the
fruit seller at the corner and sold to us for twice their
value), and, in short—you may imagine the rest. Finally,
the coffee, which had nothing in common with that deli-
cious beverage except the name, ended, not inappropriately, this inferior déjeuner.

Quarter of an hour later we are jogging along the
road to Valençay. Our victoria, perhaps inferior to
those which we were accustomed to see in the avenues of
the Bois de Boulogne, perhaps less brilliant in its paint
and varnish, and a little out of fashion in its superannuated lining, is at least comfortable. My companion
goes fast asleep, accommodating his afternoon dreams
to the rocking of the springs, and taking to himself
more than three-quarters of the carriage. Tucked up
in my corner, and wide awake myself, I find the drive
delightful. A hill on the right has forced the road to
nestle itself close beside it, and to follow its contour,
while on the left the valley of the Cher is flat and open,
much wider than at Chenonceau. It seems as if the
river had kept its liveliness and its smiling surroundings
for Diane de Poitiers, for here it flows between two barren
banks. The grass of the fields is hardly green, and it
looks as if it were forever covered with the gray fog of a
September dawn. Here the water-willows, with their
bushy branches, clipped every year, are the only trees to
be found. They grow, short and round, by the side of
the river, or in the ditches which divide the fields. Those
that are planted by the roadside have longer branches;
and often, behind the trembling leaves, a spire, crowned
by its cross and weather-cock, and a few white houses
covered with vines, slumber peacefully in the shade and
tell of some little village not far distant.

We turn at right angles, leaving the departmental
road and the Cher, to take a communale, and proceed

along the banks of a tiny tributary to the river. The
Department of Loire et Cher is now behind us and we
are in that of l'Indre. Behind us the last line of the
distant hill is lost in the mist, but the sun is now burn-
ing away and making all about us shine. Suddenly a
large, deep-colored cloud casts a shadow over the scene.
It grows larger and deeper, as the cloud ascends into the
sky, and finally it covers the sun, at a moment when we
plunge into the shade of green trees that are growing in
a deep vale, where around us nature is dark and sad.
The dust of the road is caught up in a whirlwind by the
coming storm, and it almost blinds our horse. The men-
acing wind whistles through the trees, as if to battle
against the coming rain and to drive it away. But it comes
at last, and the first drops fall upon us as large as coins.

The Comte, awakened by the noise, rubbed his eyes,
and scarcely realizing the nightmare which had succeeded
his dreams, he jumped unconsciously out of the carriage.
Once upon the road, he put up the top of the victoria,
which had now come to a standstill, and the driver, holding the reins in one hand, endeavored with some difficulty
to put on his rubber overcoat. I alone, quiet and peaceful in my corner, untied the leather apron to cover our
knees, and fell back in silent contemplation of the storm.
The Comte returned to the victoria and we started once
more. The horse, frightened by the first clap of thunder,
quickened his pace to a marvelous degree, and plunged
deeper and deeper into the heavy rows of poplar trees—
always poplar trees, extending in avenues without end,
poplar trees as yet untouched by the yellow tints of
autumn. From time to time a peasant, driving a herd
of cows, would cross our path, pushing her indolent animals forward to reach the farm before the drenching
rain should come. And looking at them, one could but
wonder how it was that the woman with her knitting (for
it is almost always the woman who tends the cows in

France) could spend her days by the roadside or in the pastures with no other company than this. Strange, indeed, to think that sometimes a whole life may be passed in this manner, without the knowledge of better things; and yet how often is it happier than the lives of those who know grander conditions which they may not attain! For the simple peasant kens not the painful contrasts of the world: she heeds not the pains and anguish born of hopeless longings for some condition which she may not reach. Yet as the picture of the peasant, and her sabôts, and her cows, fades behind us, we are tempted to think that often, as in her case, ignorance is indeed a blessing. For there is little in life which causes more unhappiness than unattained ambition.

Suddenly the sun shines—more brilliantly than ever— through a break in the clouds, and its sharp rays reveal startlingly some trees in the distance. In front of us the storm is raging more than ever, and the inky clouds throw darkness over everything beneath them. At a turning of the road an outline, a flash of lightning, tears the sky. It remains and grows more and more distinct as we approach. What is it? The lines cut one another at sharp angles, rising here and falling there. They show in the lightning-color of the clouds. They are lost, in fact, in the clouds. The deep color about them is as dark as night and the whole scene mysterious and strange.

"Do you see that curious phenomenon?" said the Comte. "I should say it was an apparition in the heavens. See how it seems to move to and fro, as if pushed by wind."

"Pardon me," I replied, "if you will but gauge it by some steady object you will see that it is motionless."

As we approached, the lines stood out more distinctly and were more clearly marked. Gradually they assumed different shapes, and finally some high, dismantled

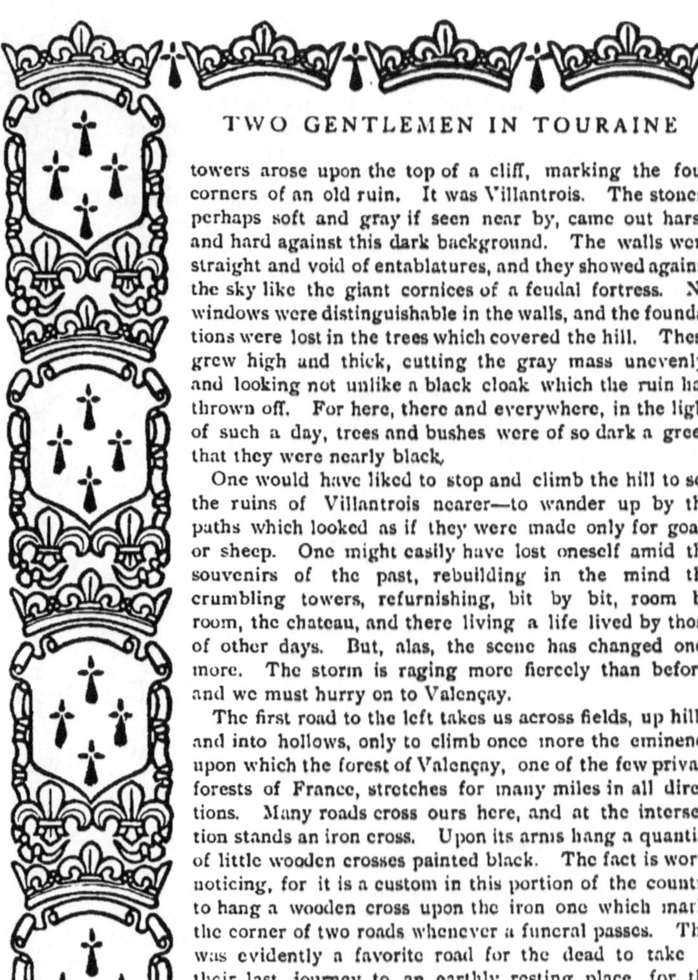

towers arose upon the top of a cliff, marking the four corners of an old ruin. It was Villantrois. The stones, perhaps soft and gray if seen near by, came out harsh and hard against this dark background. The walls were straight and void of entablatures, and they showed against the sky like the giant cornices of a feudal fortress. No windows were distinguishable in the walls, and the foundations were lost in the trees which covered the hill. These grew high and thick, cutting the gray mass unevenly, and looking not unlike a black cloak which the ruin had thrown off. For here, there and everywhere, in the light of such a day, trees and bushes were of so dark a green that they were nearly black.

One would have liked to stop and climb the hill to see the ruins of Villantrois nearer—to wander up by the paths which looked as if they were made only for goats or sheep. One might easily have lost oneself amid the souvenirs of the past, rebuilding in the mind the crumbling towers, refurnishing, bit by bit, room by room, the chateau, and there living a life lived by those of other days. But, alas, the scene has changed once more. The storm is raging more fiercely than before, and we must hurry on to Valençay.

The first road to the left takes us across fields, up hills, and into hollows, only to climb once more the eminence upon which the forest of Valençay, one of the few private forests of France, stretches for many miles in all directions. Many roads cross ours here, and at the intersection stands an iron cross. Upon its arms hang a quantity of little wooden crosses painted black. The fact is worth noticing, for it is a custom in this portion of the country to hang a wooden cross upon the iron one which marks the corner of two roads whenever a funeral passes. This was evidently a favorite road for the dead to take in their last journey to an earthly resting place, for the number of tributes was very large.

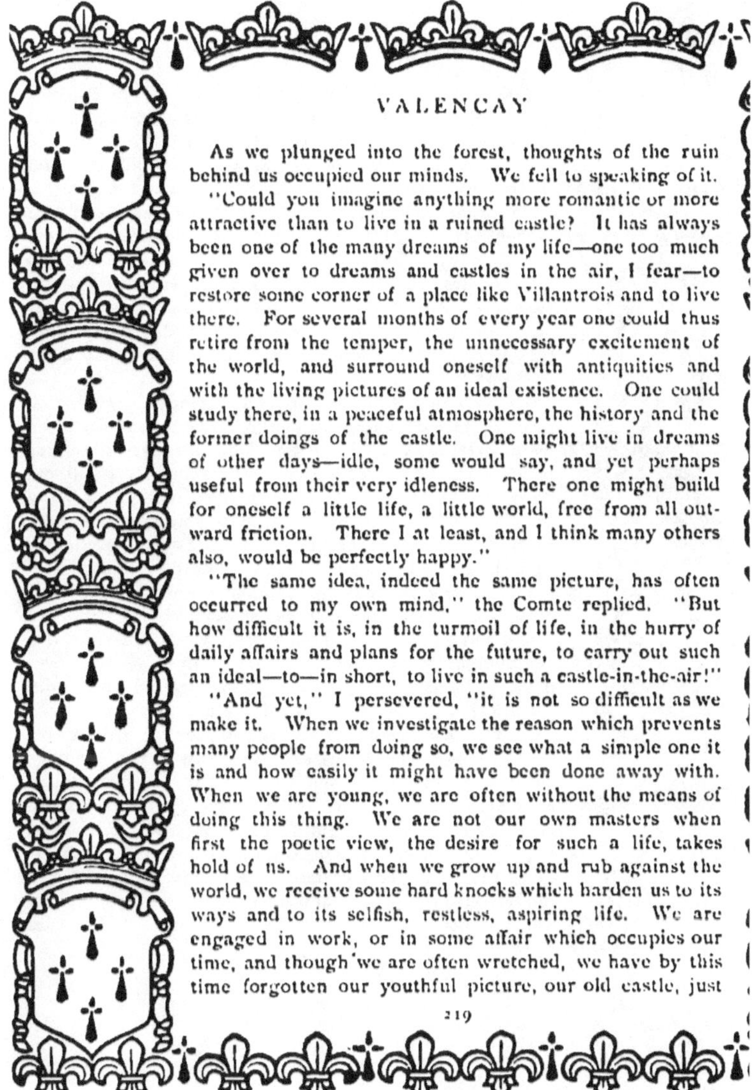

As we plunged into the forest, thoughts of the ruin behind us occupied our minds. We fell to speaking of it.

"Could you imagine anything more romantic or more attractive than to live in a ruined castle? It has always been one of the many dreams of my life—one too much given over to dreams and castles in the air, I fear—to restore some corner of a place like Villantrois and to live there. For several months of every year one could thus retire from the temper, the unnecessary excitement of the world, and surround oneself with antiquities and with the living pictures of an ideal existence. One could study there, in a peaceful atmosphere, the history and the former doings of the castle. One might live in dreams of other days—idle, some would say, and yet perhaps useful from their very idleness. There one might build for oneself a little life, a little world, free from all outward friction. There I at least, and I think many others also, would be perfectly happy."

"The same idea, indeed the same picture, has often occurred to my own mind," the Comte replied. "But how difficult it is, in the turmoil of life, in the hurry of daily affairs and plans for the future, to carry out such an ideal—to—in short, to live in such a castle-in-the-air!"

"And yet," I persevered, "it is not so difficult as we make it. When we investigate the reason which prevents many people from doing so, we see what a simple one it is and how easily it might have been done away with. When we are young, we are often without the means of doing this thing. We are not our own masters when first the poetic view, the desire for such a life, takes hold of us. And when we grow up and rub against the world, we receive some hard knocks which harden us to its ways and to its selfish, restless, aspiring life. We are engaged in work, or in some affair which occupies our time, and though we are often wretched, we have by this time forgotten our youthful picture, our old castle, just at the moment when we might really obtain it. We grow older; sometimes the castle comes of itself; but not until we are too old or too tired to enjoy it."

"I wish that more of us might retain our youthful desires and ideas in after life," the Comte answered. "We forget youth very quickly, and with it much that makes our life attractive." And he concluded the conversation by adding: "You are right in your ideals, and your castles-in-the-air. Cling to them as long as possible, for they will melt away all too soon. Restore your old ruin if you should ever find it, and I shall count myself as lucky if I am permitted to come and stay there with you."

We were now forced to turn our attention to the beauties of the surroundings. The avenue upon which we were driving cut a straight line through the very heart of the forest for nearly three miles. Up hill and down dale it ran, but never turned so much as a hair's breadth to right or left—"a most excellent example for human nature to profit by," as the Comte facetiously remarked. Oaks and elms and pines lined themselves upon either side, making an almost impenetrable wall around us. Here and there at regular intervals we would come upon a small open place where the road was cut at right angles—or often diagonally—by other avenues. The customary wooden gates, painted white, told plainly that the forest was a private one, and their closed bars bore testimony that the hunting season had not yet opened. For many miles these grass-grown avenues cut through the forest and were lost in the distance, in a faint vista of rather leaden sky. At one of these rendezvous de chasse eight avenues met one another, and a white post in the centre bore on its sign the names of "de Dino," "de Talleyrand," "de Sagan," or others of the famous family who then inhabited Valençay.

"Is it not impressive?" said the Comte. "Here the

CHÂTEAU DE VALENÇAY

owners have met, for well nigh a century, upon their hunting parties, within these walls or avenues, and among these trees. Before the days of the famous Prince de Bénévent, the great diplomat and statesman under Napoleon, perhaps even the Emperor himself has hunted in the forest."

I saw by the way in which the Comte had settled himself against the cushions of the carriage that he was preparing himself for a long and serious talk, and as I knew that he would give me some interesting information I listened to him quietly, without attempting to disturb his train of thought.

"These beautiful trees, these avenues and this aristocratic air of grandeur," he continued, "tell us in places like this that if the Monarchy and the Empire of France have passed away the families and the places that they inhabit do still exist—to die perhaps to-morrow!—how can we tell in these uncertain days?—but to live another hundred years, I hope, that those around may learn to profit by the taste and grandeur of our French refinement." The Comte was warming to his subject.

"Aristocracy!" he continued. "Where is the class and what does the word mean to-day? Not, alas, what it should. And why do we find it in the sad state in which it is? I think it is because, first from fear, and then from jealousy, and then from hatred—not altogether uncalled for—the bourgeoisie, or second class, have inflamed and misdirected and wrongly educated themselves. Not contented with the disorder which they had already created, they incited those beneath them to contempt for and rebellion against those to whom they owed often their very happiness and maintenance. Alas, revolutions, wars and radical reforms have brought changes to the old customs, the old associations, and the old noblesse, which would to-day have been less chaotic had they been left alone to rectify themselves.

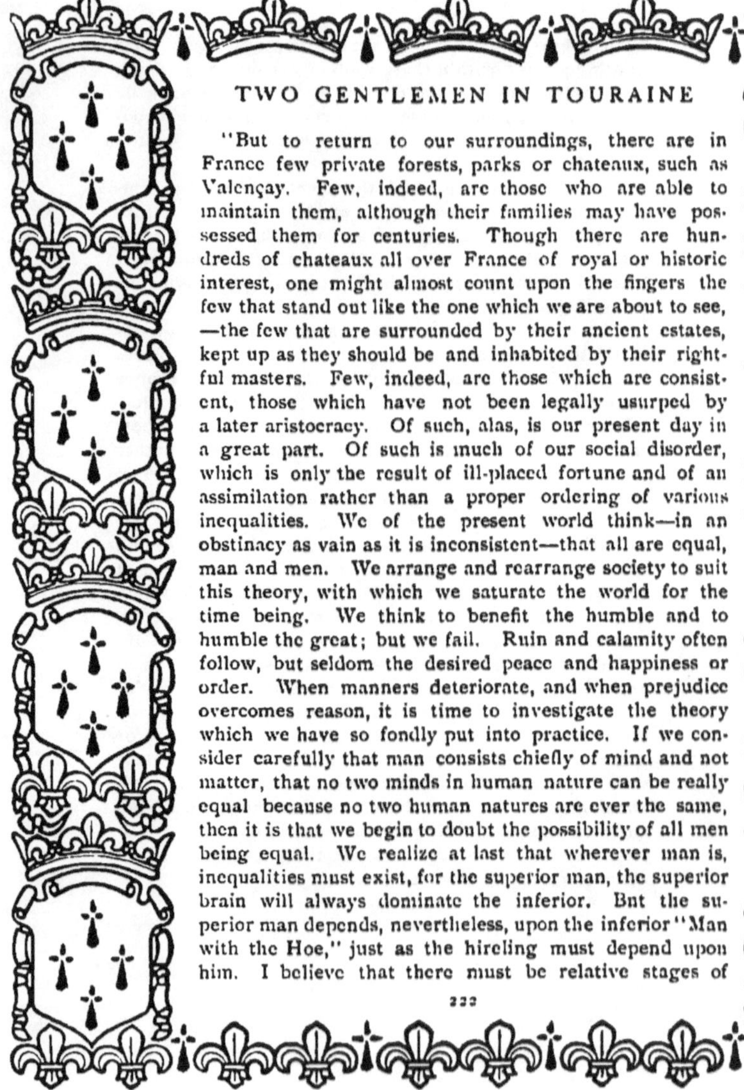

"But to return to our surroundings, there are in France few private forests, parks or chateaux, such as Valençay. Few, indeed, are those who are able to maintain them, although their families may have possessed them for centuries. Though there are hundreds of chateaux all over France of royal or historic interest, one might almost count upon the fingers the few that stand out like the one which we are about to see, —the few that are surrounded by their ancient estates, kept up as they should be and inhabited by their rightful masters. Few, indeed, are those which are consistent, those which have not been legally usurped by a later aristocracy. Of such, alas, is our present day in a great part. Of such is much of our social disorder, which is only the result of ill-placed fortune and of an assimilation rather than a proper ordering of various inequalities. We of the present world think—in an obstinacy as vain as it is inconsistent—that all are equal, man and men. We arrange and rearrange society to suit this theory, with which we saturate the world for the time being. We think to benefit the humble and to humble the great; but we fail. Ruin and calamity often follow, but seldom the desired peace and happiness or order. When manners deteriorate, and when prejudice overcomes reason, it is time to investigate the theory which we have so fondly put into practice. If we consider carefully that man consists chiefly of mind and not matter, that no two minds in human nature can be really equal because no two human natures are ever the same, then it is that we begin to doubt the possibility of all men being equal. We realize at last that wherever man is, inequalities must exist, for the superior man, the superior brain will always dominate the inferior. But the superior man depends, nevertheless, upon the inferior "Man with the Hoe," just as the hireling must depend upon him. I believe that there must be relative stages of

society, so long as society shall exist. There must be, and there will be, one to govern as well as one to be governed, one to serve as well as one to pay for service, one to live in great houses, to hunt in forests, to sit in judgment, as well as one to wait upon his master, to cut down trees or to be judged. For the separate classes of society are far too important, far too necessary one to another, for us to think of destroying their various functions. And those functions are separated far too widely to attempt to combine the whole, to attempt to make the master servant, and the servant master. If we do so we shall find merely that neither knows his business, that each one is in a position which he is neither educated for nor capable of filling. If we continue to make laws and arrangements for such a state of impossible equality, we shall find only that the elements dismember each other more and more. They will no more join together than would certain chemicals, and we obtain only chaos and disorder as a result. Therefore it is but natural to see a changing of great fortunes and places from their rightful owners into the hands of those who are incapable, both by birth and by education, to use them for the benefit of others, whether these be their superiors or their inferiors.

"All men should have a call upon our time, our fortune, our assistance. It is but lent to us, with our own lives, to use for the benefit of mankind; and how is this benefit to reach the poor and the needy if we take away the power of doing so from those that are born and bred to use it? How are good manners and refinement and good taste to reach the poor and vulgar save by object lessons, such as beautiful examples of castles and forests and their incumbent life; how but by the influence of a well-directed aristocracy? If we do away with all these, if we destroy great fortunes by excessive taxation, if we pull down great names by 'popular measures' which look no further into the future than to-day, how are these things

to come to pass? How are men who have spent their lives accumulating a fortune, who have used all their energy and talents in climbing up the ladder of success; how, I ask you, may these men be expected to teach those who need their teaching? How are these men, or those who surround them, qualified to exercise the duties and the functions which are meant to fall upon others who have devoted their lives to the study of the more advanced tastes? Surely, a man may not do everything, nor may even those who go to make this class. By the time a self-made man has gained his fortune, his chateau may-be, his forests or estates, he is too old, too tired, to start afresh the study of the wisest way in which to spend this treasure. The men for whom these things were made were never intended to occupy themselves with money-making, but with money-spending, an important matter to society. Indeed, I think that there is good reason to consider it a more important matter, for money-making concerns but one man, or at most his own family, while the judicious use of a great fortune may affect a whole community.

"How much better would the world be if all places, such as Valençay, were in the hands of their proper masters, and if those masters, controlling the greatest fortunes, were worthy of their names; if they were only true to their trusts and to their great responsibilities to all about them; if the master did but sit in his proper place and honor it; if the servant knew the happiness of being servant, of loving his master, of serving his interests, and of being in his turn protected and maintained! Then would disorder and chaos give place to harmony and prosperity. Then would more things be in their proper conditions, and the world, as well as France, as well as old Touraine, would feel gradually those joys that are to be found only in contentment and in universal order."

VALENCAY

The Comte had finished speaking, and upon his concluding remark ensued a silence more eloquent than the long appeal which he had made against the present state of our society at large.

"I fear that I have tired you," he said at last, "with the expression of so many thoughts inspired by our surroundings. If so, I must apologize; but I fancy that you may have shared with me the feelings that I have referred to, in connection with these beautiful avenues, these ivy-covered paths of the forest of Valençay. Believe me, they are not mere idle thoughts, but conclusions which have been drawn from a far too intimate knowledge—I am forced to own—of the evils, both social and political, of the present day. The chateaux which we have been visiting and the one that we are about to see are conspicuous examples of what there should be in France, but of what is seldom to be met with.

"Here we are, at the large rendezvous de chasse which is at the end of the forest and the beginning of the park. See, there is even a faint view of the castle towers over the distant trees."

PART II

Not unlike Chenonceau, the chateau of Valençay is approached by a long, straight avenue of lime trees. Their overlapping branches cut off the view until we reach the foot of a hollow, succeeded in turn by the rising ground upon which the castle stands. Here the climax of a truly royal approach is reached, and the long miles of forest give place to a scene as beautiful as it is impressive.

The first object which presents itself to view is the great outer court. This is in the form of an octagon, enclosed by a wall of white stones, hidden by linden trees and ivy, and broken upon four sides by iron gates

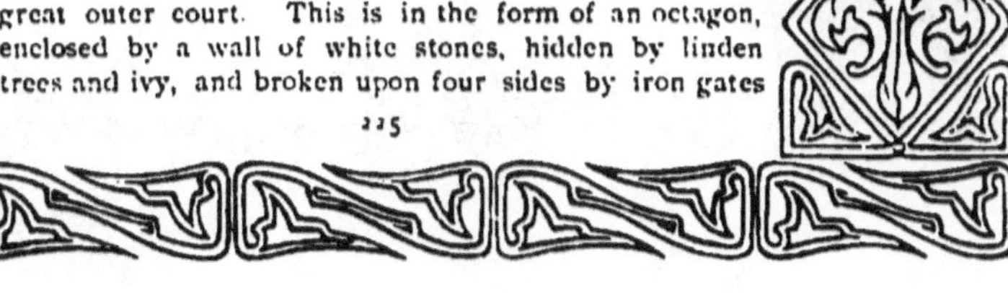

with stone pillars.   Behind it, and upon the right, a small gate leads into the garden, a worthy introduction to so noble a chateau.   Old walls are hung with grape vines, or covered by creeping pears and apples, faintly visible behind the iron gate.   Plums and peaches grow enticingly above the head.   Rose-colored dahlias, asters of every shade and tint, and other flowers grow in profusion behind the lines of boxes upon either side of the alleys. And for the rest you must allow the imagination to picture what may not be seen at a passing glance.   Dreams and fairy-like ideals may hold their fullest sway; they will not often be disappointed in the garden of a French chateau.   In it the most unsightly things assume some picturesque charm, a simple and artistic beauty that must needs satisfy the most fastidious.

Upon the left a gateway with a high stone arch leads to the Bourg which grows up to the very walls.   Close beside it another arch leads to a series of smaller courts which form the stables.   Upon the right a grille, flanked by two massive pillars, opens into an avenue that stretches through the park in a long, straight line.   It looks at least a mile in length, ending in one of those vistas with which the feudal French so loved to fill their parks and forests.   In front and in the centre of the whole the great donjon of Valençay rises out of a moat. Its pointed roof, beetling with round minarets, with ornamented windows and with carved chimneys, is still some distance from us.   An iron grating, supported by nearly a dozen carved stone pillars, culminating in the central gate, guards the entrance to a great terrace in front of the castle.   A long narrow Louis XV building of admirable lines but of unfinished appearance occupies a position on the right.   It is the orangery, while a counterpart to it upon our left is now used as a carriage house.   Beyond this building, which might have been beautiful had its single story been more richly ornamented, are situated the kennels. Here the visitor is enabled to appreciate the value of an iron screen by the savage barks and growls of a pack of hounds looking as if they would gladly make a meal of any one who chanced to fall among them. A grass-grown terrace of several acres divides us from the castle, which rises like a great giant out of the shrubbery and vines adorning the empty moats.

The first view of the castle is indeed imposing. Its noble proportions, its massive towers, its white stone walls, rising like a cloud before one, would alone be enough to draw forth one's admiration; but the beauty and grandeur of the approach, the gates, the courts, the terraces, all add to the effect, and they assist in making the whole scene one of the grandest in France.

Valençay is built around two sides of a hollow square, the open spaces behind being formed into terraces and parterres, such as only the French know how to beautify. The court or terrace within looks out over a fairy-like panorama, the grandeur, the dignity, the beauty of which may be conveyed only to those who have seen it. The walls of both wings are alike in the architecture of the Renaissance, and they show to advantage the talents of Philibert Delorme. Two round towers upon the right rise at each extremity of the building, but they are so different from the central one that the effect of the whole lacks somewhat in unity. The motif of ornamentation is simple but yet effective. It might indeed be called a lattice-work of Ionic pilasters, starting at the foundations, and covering the walls with innumerable squares up to the cornices of the roof The towers, as well, share in this form of decoration, and into many of the squares thus made the windows of the chateau have been inserted. The pilasters, acting as both their support and decoration, are capped by the double lines of stone cornice which divide the different stories.

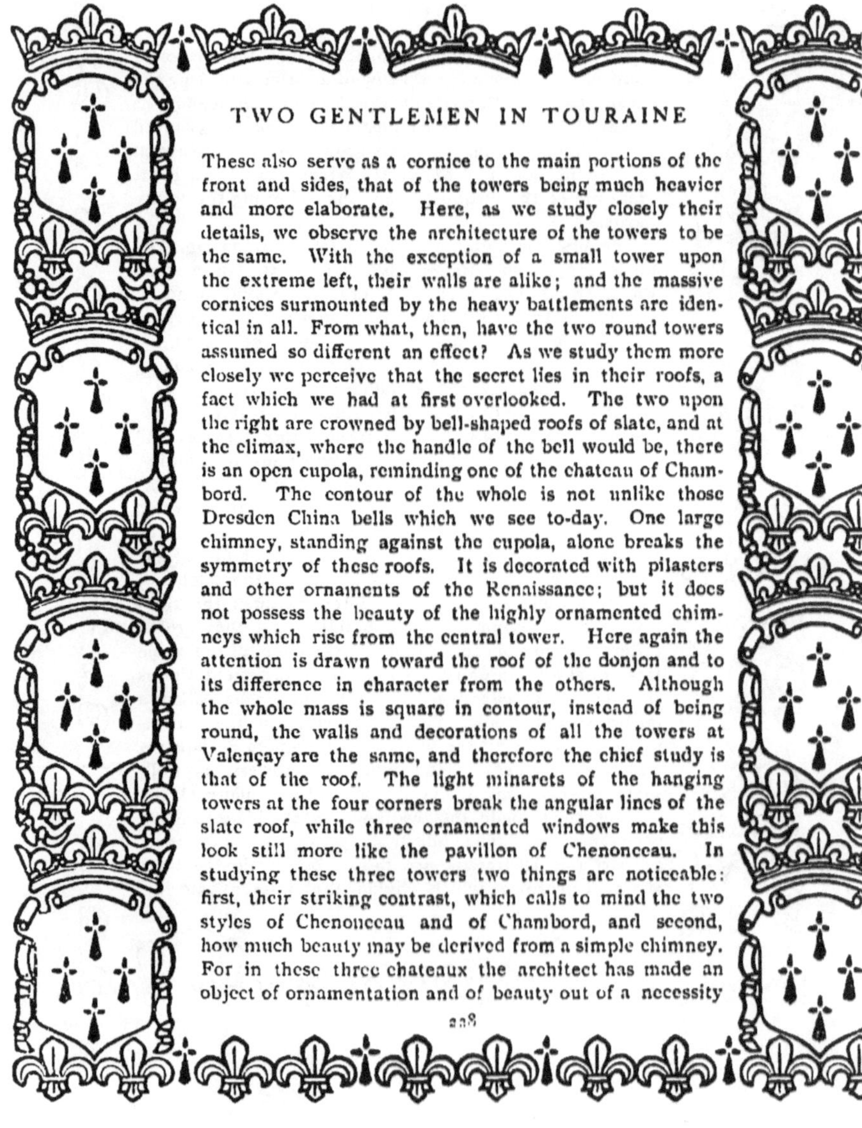

These also serve as a cornice to the main portions of the
front and sides, that of the towers being much heavier
and more elaborate. Here, as we study closely their
details, we observe the architecture of the towers to be
the same. With the exception of a small tower upon
the extreme left, their walls are alike; and the massive
cornices surmounted by the heavy battlements are iden-
tical in all. From what, then, have the two round towers
assumed so different an effect? As we study them more
closely we perceive that the secret lies in their roofs, a
fact which we had at first overlooked. The two upon
the right are crowned by bell-shaped roofs of slate, and at
the climax, where the handle of the bell would be, there
is an open cupola, reminding one of the chateau of Chambord. The contour of the whole is not unlike those
Dresden China bells which we see to-day. One large
chimney, standing against the cupola, alone breaks the
symmetry of these roofs. It is decorated with pilasters
and other ornaments of the Renaissance; but it does
not possess the beauty of the highly ornamented chimneys which rise from the central tower. Here again the
attention is drawn toward the roof of the donjon and to
its difference in character from the others. Although
the whole mass is square in contour, instead of being
round, the walls and decorations of all the towers at
Valençay are the same, and therefore the chief study is
that of the roof. The light minarets of the hanging
towers at the four corners break the angular lines of the
slate roof, while three ornamented windows make this
look still more like the pavillon of Chenonceau. In
studying these three towers two things are noticeable:
first, their striking contrast, which calls to mind the two
styles of Chenonceau and of Chambord, and second,
how much beauty may be derived from a simple chimney.
For in these three chateaux the architect has made an
object of ornamentation and of beauty out of a necessity

which is too frequently considered unworthy of architectural treatment. Indeed, a study of French architecture—we mean among these chateaux—opens the eyes to the possibilities of beautifying chimneys, if nothing else. Those of the chateau of Blois, as well as the ones already mentioned, are well worthy of study and should be an example to modern architects.

But to turn suddenly from one subject to another, and to descend from the roofs to the moats, let us leave these spires and chimneys, to plunge into those mediæval appendages to the French chateau which have remained to add their attraction to so many of the historical monuments of France. The moats of Valençay are very large, and they surround the two sides of the chateau, their empty beds being converted to-day into shrubberies which add not a little to the pleasing effect. A heavy coating of ivy clings to the old foundations, and is relieved by small trees and larger bushes. The yellow-green of the laurel joins with the deeper colors of "fusins" grouped in the corners, while graveled walks wind in and out over velvety grass. Any sad or dreary ideas of the castle moat are overturned completely by the effect of these at Valençay. Here is a mass of mahonias, to blossom in the spring when all else in nature is asleep, as if to warm the atmosphere with golden flowers. They have faded away long since, and now only the deep purple berries remain behind, to relieve the green leaves that remind one of holly. But by this time we are standing upon the stone bridge, with its three great arches over the moat. Before us is the archway through the donjon tower surmounted by the family arms carved in the stone. The three lions of Talleyrand, crowned by a ducal coronet, look down upon us from their place of honor, as we ring the great bell of the castle and pass on to the inner court.

The scene here is indeed fairy-like, and one which

holds the spectator in an almost fascinated trance, making him think that at last the dreams of childhood have become true. The visions of enchanted castles, the pictures which fairy tales and nursery stories have brought to mind, the ideals of an imaginative disposition, are all fully realized. A square terrace, some hundred feet in length and covered with grass, is the first object to attract our notice. Behind us and upon the right the beautifully ornamented walls of Valençay rise two and three stories, with the black domes of their towers above them. An arcade runs the length of the right-hand portion of the court, ending at last in one of the entrances to the chateau. Busts of white marble upon black pedestals stand against the walls of this arcade; and though they are too small they lend dignity to the general effect. A basin of darkened stone occupies the centre of the court, and a fountain rising from it sends silvery sprays over the otherwise unruffled surface of the water. Trees and bushes upon the left hide the view, and beyond us a carved stone railing is broken by a flight of steps leading to the parterres already mentioned. Beyond all this stretches ideal scenery, forests and rows of poplar trees, a portion of the park, the tower of a distant church, all in blue-green haze, mystifying the poetry of it all and delighting the joyous eye.

Inside the chateau the rooms are arranged like those of a palace, opening one into the other through small doors, so that if one should stand in the first room he would look through the entire suite of apartments to the further end. Salons and antechambers, the dining-room, the hall, the royal bed-chamber—all succeed one another in a most effective manner. The salons are furnished principally in the periods of Louis XVI and of the Empire. Beautiful things and beautiful furniture abound on every side. In one room a magnificent clock of the time of Louis XVI strikes the eye and calls forth a word of admiration.

In another room an Empire chandelier tells of the taste and art in the smaller ornaments of that period. In the state bed-room (occupied by the Spanish princes during their confinement at Valençay) there is an Empire desk which is a wonderfully complete and perfect example of its period. This room is one of the most interesting in the chateau, apart from its historic interest. The pictures are very fine, many of them by famous masters. A curious fact to be observed, by the way, in the pictures at Valençay is the varied collection of royal portraits which show—perhaps too plainly—the appreciated devotion of the great diplomat to those sovereigns who were in power during his public life. Conspicuous among them is the portrait of Napoleon, painted in his imperial robes.

On the left of an elaborately decorated bed is a large case containing the various state and diplomatic uniforms of "le Grand Talleyrand"; but perhaps by accident, or possibly for other reasons, the violet robes of the Evêque d'Autun have been omitted from the collection. There they hang, these relics of former power and of glorious achievements—achievements which were sometimes greater than they were glorious, and more remarkable than great. Beneath them are the shapeless shoes which the famous diplomat and statesman wore during his lifetime, a strange round mass of leather, with a sole many inches thick. Such objects as these and the knowledge of how much they represent bring vividly to mind the character and history of him who brought this chateau into the family of Talleyrand. The same air of grandeur, of dignity, of an old régime, pervades the apartments, which is wafted through the trees of the forest leading to them.

We mount the broad staircase of the central hall, turning at every step to admire or to study the pictures which line the walls. For many of them are interesting,

especially some larger ones of Philippe de Champag
representing famous incidents or scenes. Portraits
pictures of a varied character are hung indiscriminat
making the rather gloomy walls alive with cha
ters. But in spite of this art the staircase is not a be
tiful one, and it is somewhat eclipsed in beauty by
galleries above. Of these the largest and perhaps
most interesting is the long gallery overlooking
court. Every corner of it, from the bookcases to
walls, is occupied by some object of interest, eil
historical or artistic. In fact, this remarkable collec
of old pictures, of prints and sketches, of rare bits
china and glass, of statues in bronze or in marble, v
many other things too numerous to mention, form:
this gallery a veritable museum. Although this is c
one of the many collections made by the Prince
Bénévent, days and weeks even might be exhaus
in the study of its details; at the end of this time tl
would yet remain a thousand objects still unnoticed,
unstudied. Perhaps the most valuable things belong
to this remarkable collection are the Raphael sketcl
These hang against the dull and ugly walls of the
lery, looking almost as fresh as when the youthful gei
of Italy first traced their outlines. Their wonderful fine
of detail, as well as their artistic coloring, are as if
famous master had just sent them forth to claim the
plause of an admiring world. As one looks in adm
tion, almost in reverence, at these examples of an
imitable art, it is difficult to realize that the sketches
but a few years of their four hundredth birthday.

The gallery itself, apart from its wealth of treasure:
a very ugly one. Its walls, like many of those
Valençay, are of that hideous dull brown which is
characteristic of the somewhat uneducated perioc
the First Empire. For Napoleon, whatever his r
tary genius, his personality, his statesmanship, or

greatness may have been, could hardly have been expected to bring to the imperial court that refinement of taste or culture which characterized the periods of hereditary kings rather than those of self-created emperors. We refer, however, more to the style of building and of decoration during the period of the First Empire than to the furniture, which many people consider as a type of the beautiful. The Comte is not among this latter class, as we shall see.

"Look at these dusty, old gold, brown or gray colored walls," said he, with evident displeasure at his surroundings. "It depresses me even to move between them. These polished tiles, painted brown also, do but increase the general effect. Were it not for the beautiful collections within this gallery, I think that I should have been upon the other side of the door ere this in search of pleasanter surroundings. Here there is not an atom of color to relieve this dull monotony of browns. The floor is brown, the walls are brown, the ceiling is brown. I feel as if I were about to turn into brown myself, so impossible is it to escape from the incessant color."

"You need not complain of the polished tiles," said I, by way of defending them, though they ill deserved it, "for you were glad enough to admire them at Chaumont, even though I had the pleasure of falling twice and nearly spraining my ankle."

"Ah," replied the Comte, "but there we had those beautiful tapestries of the Salle des Gardes, and the fifteenth century tapestries in the chamber of Catherine de Medici. Those matchless works of art, rich in all the colors of their time, needed just these tiles to relieve them. The carving of the woodwork, the ancient air of everything, the chamber of Ruggieri, all were in perfect harmony. But here," he continued, turning to the gallery in which we still remained, "here I will have nothing to do with them," and shrugging his shoulders,

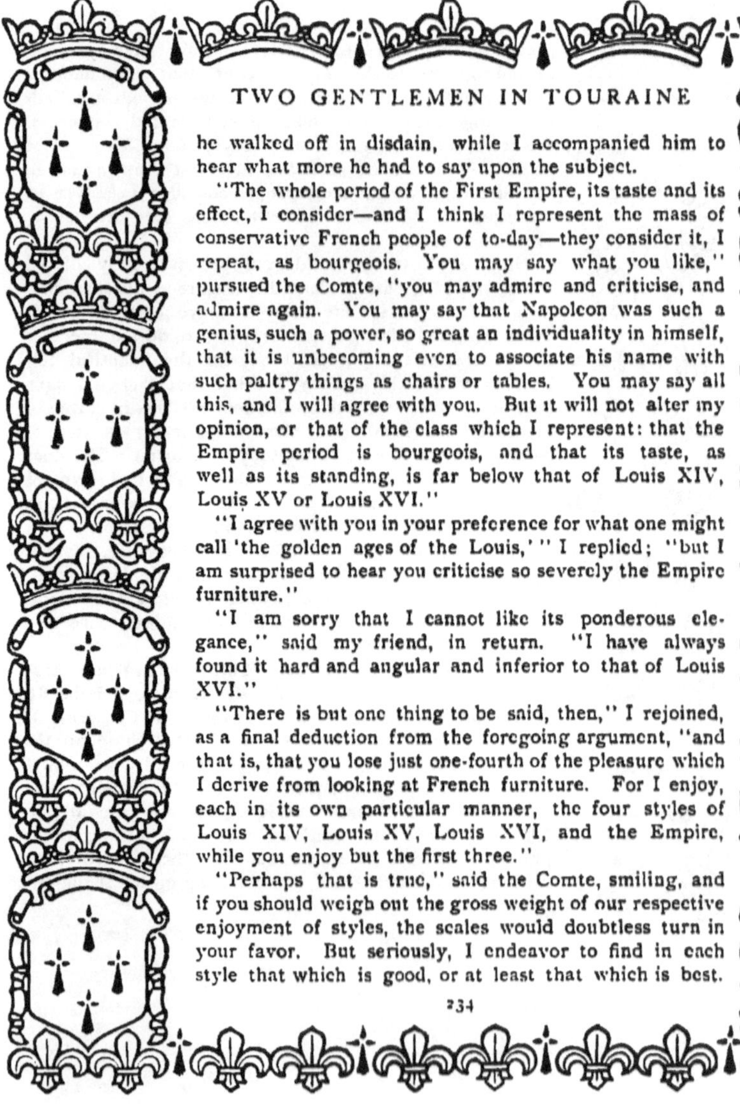

he walked off in disdain, while I accompanied him to
hear what more he had to say upon the subject.

"The whole period of the First Empire, its taste and its
effect, I consider—and I think I represent the mass of
conservative French people of to-day—they consider it, I
repeat, as bourgeois. You may say what you like,"
pursued the Comte, "you may admire and criticise, and
admire again. You may say that Napoleon was such a
genius, such a power, so great an individuality in himself,
that it is unbecoming even to associate his name with
such paltry things as chairs or tables. You may say all
this, and I will agree with you. But it will not alter my
opinion, or that of the class which I represent: that the
Empire period is bourgeois, and that its taste, as
well as its standing, is far below that of Louis XIV,
Louis XV or Louis XVI."

"I agree with you in your preference for what one might
call 'the golden ages of the Louis,'" I replied; "but I
am surprised to hear you criticise so severely the Empire
furniture."

"I am sorry that I cannot like its ponderous elegance," said my friend, in return. "I have always
found it hard and angular and inferior to that of Louis
XVI."

"There is but one thing to be said, then," I rejoined,
as a final deduction from the foregoing argument, "and
that is, that you lose just one-fourth of the pleasure which
I derive from looking at French furniture. For I enjoy,
each in its own particular manner, the four styles of
Louis XIV, Louis XV, Louis XVI, and the Empire,
while you enjoy but the first three."

"Perhaps that is true," said the Comte, smiling, and
if you should weigh out the gross weight of our respective
enjoyment of styles, the scales would doubtless turn in
your favor. But seriously, I endeavor to find in each
style that which is good, or at least that which is best.

VALENCAY

For instance, I may say that the Louis XIV furniture, with its great patterns and lines, was appropriate to the larger rooms and larger conceptions of 'le Grand Monarch.' The more temperate Louis XV period, which does not indulge in so much of the 'rocaille,' is appropriate for a drawing-room with panelling. If I take the Louis XVI period it is the most graceful, and when it is well finished (which is seldom to be found), it is in keeping with the period of Marie Antoinette. It is wonderful to see how much the character and the influence of that ill-fated queen is delineated in the furniture and in the ornaments of her day. In fact, I believe that each style, each period of which we have been speaking, is in a sense the image of its respective reign. This is why the Empire furniture, some parts of which are beautiful, if taken bit by bit portrays in its straight, uncompromising lines the stiff, unfinished manners of a court which certainly lacked that refinement that is the result of long generations of training."

As there was little that could be said in answer to this statement we left the gallery in silence, and entered a second one, leading to a library in the great tower. This gallery is much smaller than the preceding one; but is still rich in collections of busts, of smaller statuary, of medals, of a hundred objects gathered together by him who placed them there. Gifts of all kinds, frequently by royal favor, are interspersed, telling more truly than aught else the varied career of Talleyrand. In fact, the collections at Valençay are by far the most interesting portion of the interior, which is otherwise inconsistent and inferior to everything outside. The internal arrangement as a whole, the rooms, the entrances and the halls, do not seem to possess their natural relative positions. The styles are intermingled, though for the most part of the Empire period, and the visitor is forced to acknowledge that the chief attraction lies in the beau-

tiful things which abound on all sides. As we have already seen, it is impossible to do justice to these, or to describe them in detail. We can but touch, in passing, upon those collections, or special objects which offer themselves for our consideration. Many royal presents are distinguishable from the various sovereigns to which the Prince de Benévent was sent as ambassador, from noted men of church and state, while he held the office of Evêque d'Autun, and from all the representatives of the time in which this wonderful life played so important a rôle. On all sides there are emblems of past accomplishment. On all sides are the evidences of relationships which, whether of a public or private character, affected often whole nations.

In a small private closet leading from the library the most prized of all the collections are enshrined. The walls are hung with hundreds of tiny prints in gilded frames, each representing a famous person, each bearing its history attached, each hanging there through some significance. Several framed bas-reliefs of white marble are interspersed among the prints. The delicacy of their detail, the finesse of their workmanship, we have rarely seen equaled.

Collections of medals fill the cases which line this remarkable little room. Minerals of a rare character, with valuable specimens of different ores, are also to be found in numbers. A royal baton, of gold and ivory, hangs on the left, while other objects, too rare or too precious to be placed elsewhere, are enshrined in this chamber. But the climax of the whole is yet to come. In an inner closet, situated in one of the round corner-towers of the façade, is placed a wonderful collection of snuff boxes, known the world over. These snuff boxes were collected by Talleyrand in the most interesting and original manner. Whenever he was sent upon a mission to a foreign sovereign, he asked, in return for his services, the royal

portrait as a souvenir. And as snuff was used constantly at that period, the royal picture invariably appeared upon the cover of a golden snuff box. The famous diplomat ended by having the most perfect collection of contemporary royal miniatures in the world. They are certainly works of art, and they tell, perhaps better than any of the other collections, of the greatness and the extended power of the man to whom they had been given.

With these the visit is concluded, and the guest is conducted to the court once more, there to think over all that is within the chateau, and to enjoy another hour among the fairy-like alleys of the park.

PART III

The principal façade of Valençay is placed so that it overlooks a high plateau as well as the valley, which is perhaps the prettiest portion of a park well calculated to enclose so great a castle. From the central door a bridge of solid stone, divided by a narrow draw, joins the castle with the terrace. A few steps lead to a broad alley running in a straight line between the lawns. The alley is flanked on either side by giant orange-trees in stiff green tubs, and it disappears at last in a misty group of foliage. On the right a long row of elms projects giant arms over the grass for more than a mile. The shadows of their twisted trunks are thrown upon the ground in long, dark reflections.

Let us plunge into this leafy tunnel upon the left, with moving walls and with high vaults of waving branches. Let us linger upon this avenue, for it is "l'allée des Princes." It runs between rows of beautifully porportioned trees, which grow in such a manner that they suggest a great curtain, lowered that it may hide the view. These noble effigies of time live yet to tell us in a whispering voice of memorable days in the years of

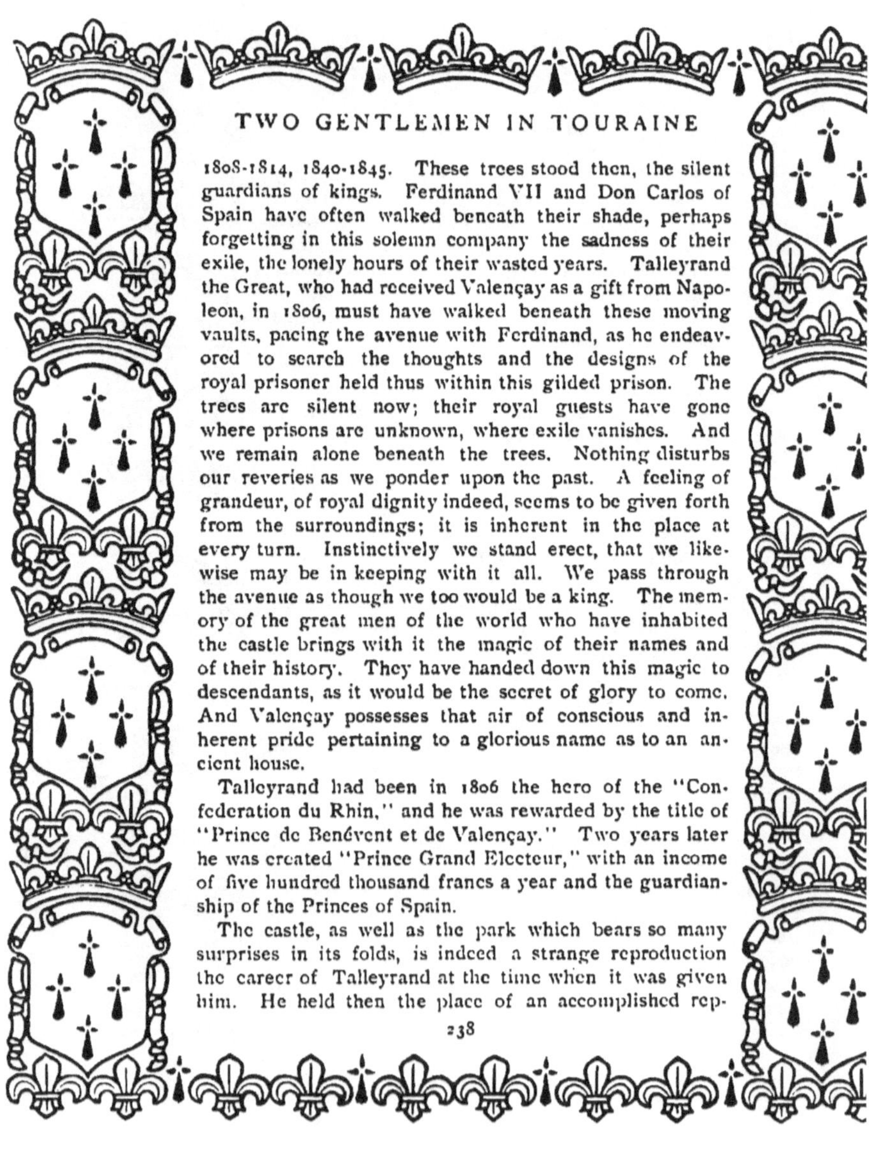

1808-1814, 1840-1845. These trees stood then, the silent guardians of kings. Ferdinand VII and Don Carlos of Spain have often walked beneath their shade, perhaps forgetting in this solemn company the sadness of their exile, the lonely hours of their wasted years. Talleyrand the Great, who had received Valençay as a gift from Napoleon, in 1806, must have walked beneath these moving vaults, pacing the avenue with Ferdinand, as he endeavored to search the thoughts and the designs of the royal prisoner held thus within this gilded prison. The trees are silent now; their royal guests have gone where prisons are unknown, where exile vanishes. And we remain alone beneath the trees. Nothing disturbs our reveries as we ponder upon the past. A feeling of grandeur, of royal dignity indeed, seems to be given forth from the surroundings; it is inherent in the place at every turn. Instinctively we stand erect, that we likewise may be in keeping with it all. We pass through the avenue as though we too would be a king. The memory of the great men of the world who have inhabited the castle brings with it the magic of their names and of their history. They have handed down this magic to descendants, as it would be the secret of glory to come. And Valençay possesses that air of conscious and inherent pride pertaining to a glorious name as to an ancient house.

Talleyrand had been in 1806 the hero of the "Confederation du Rhin," and he was rewarded by the title of "Prince de Benévent et de Valençay." Two years later he was created "Prince Grand Electeur," with an income of five hundred thousand francs a year and the guardianship of the Princes of Spain.

The castle, as well as the park which bears so many surprises in its folds, is indeed a strange reproduction the career of Talleyrand at the time when it was given him. He held then the place of an accomplished rep-

resentative of the old régime before a newly-mannered court. He brought to it the refinement and the captivating charm so characteristic of his whole life, and thus he became by his diplomacy the necessary link between the remaining sovereigns of Europe and the new-made Emperor.

We have crossed the great lawn. The lines of the massive building lose their harshness in the distance, and the towers upon either side are veiled by the branches of trees. We are standing upon the edge of a tableland which overlooks the panorama. Before this only a glimpse of it could be caught from the courtyard of the chateau. The trunks and the lower branches of the trees now lose themselves at our feet in the slope of the hill, while the higher boughs cluster around us, and rise above the head. We endeavor to find an open space between them, that we may take in a landscape whose misty outline has been until now more than half hidden behind the green curtain. Our hopes are more than realized, and the scenery unfolds itself more beautifully on account of the lacework of leaves which frames it. There is first a bed of foliage, so thick that it hides the sloping ground completely. Its graceful undulations, its shadows, here light and transparent, there dark and impenetrable, alone betray the mounds or hollows. The hill on which we stand stretches toward the right, like a long arm, bent gracefully in an endeavor to meet the one which rises upon the opposite side of the vale. This also seems to join it in the same effort; but both these arms are too short and out of reach.

A small bridge stands in relief against the green and makes a hyphen between the two hills. In the meadow below the river Nahon winds through the long grass like a thread of shining silver. Its clear waters, shaded by the lilies which look like stars of white, run amidst bending reeds and purpled flowers. At times they are hidden by a clump of trees, but only to reappear and wander through the meadow. Suddenly, however, as if they wished to escape from the encircling hills, they make a bold rush toward the bridge and lose themselves beneath a single arch. A group of deer frisks about upon the narrow tongue of grass surrounded on three sides by the brook. A doe stands upon the edge of the stream, and the water reflects her graceful form. Further on, an unexpected sound has startled her companions, and from all sides the frightened animals assemble round the oldest buck. All follow him, their anxious eyes wide open, their ears on high, and they disappear behind the trees and woods upon the opposite slope.

Involuntarily I cry: "Make haste, my friend; let us pursue them in their erratic flight; come here that we may run down these many windings toward the meadow, toward the brook, there to sit amid the shade of trees, deep within the vale!" We start, and as we follow a sandy path we meet another, winding towards the place that we have wished to gain. But a strong hand draws us forward, toward the unknown, toward those bowers and avenues which hold for us so many unlooked-for enchantments. Here the branches meet above the head and make a vault so perfect that it must have been chiseled by an artist's hand. An old gardener is bent almost in twain, picking up the dead wood, while others are clipping the branches that grow beyond the borders of the walk. The trees come to an end, and the scene changes into a glade, spread over with a carpet of verdant green, sprinkled with gold and white. Here we may obtain a glimpse, though only a glimpse, of the landscape beyond, for another avenue, with grass beneath the foot, runs in curves through hedges of meadow-sweet and laurels. It twists itself into large bows, the loops of which stretch far toward the right and left. Finally it leads into what seems to be a great natural cathedral formed of trees. The nave is bordered by gigantic firs, whose branches have been cut off many feet above the ground. They stand like so many tall and slender columns, and from their capitals spring up innumerable groins formed of branches. They cross and recross, branching in every direction, only to end at last in the keystone of the top. This is like lacework, and brilliant with diamonds left by the rain, which await the last rays of the sun, that they may sparkle once more, and then fade into air. The chancel is made by nine columns growing in a circle. They have been hung by Time with draperies of a velvet-gray, and they support the leafy dome. A large stone bench or table at the further end looks as if it were an altar. Behind it there runs an apse of misty foliage, and from this many doors lead into silent paths or into natural chapels made for thoughts or for divine love.

How often must Talleyrand have paced this nave, slowly extending toward the chancel and the large stone altar! How often must he have listened to the great organ, as now the storm rages through its pipes, or as a "voix celeste" comes out like a whisper to lull the passions like some angel's voice! These high vaults, these slender columns, might perhaps tell us if Talleyrand had borne his head erect as he faced the altar, or if he had bowed beneath an unseen weight as his eyes wandered about him. The sight of these naves and vaults might, by some chance, have carried his thoughts back to another cathedral, "le Cathédral d'Autun." The organ was playing there upon a certain day in 1788, when, in his pontifical robes, the new bishop entered the church and for the first time ascended the altar steps. But here, above his head, the trills of the nightingale answered to the whistling of other birds. While winged throngs around him joined in the natural choir, he may

241

have thought how different such songs were from the swelling sounds of revolutionary mobs surrounding an altar erected in the centre of "le Champ de Mars," where he had officiated at mass, on the 14th of July, 1790.

This natural cathedral, with its thoughts and visions, fades behind us, as we sink deeply into other bowers where the shadow of Talleyrand seems still to haunt us. Here and everywhere the trees grow high and thick, so that the sunlight is unable to pierce their leafy curtains. We are surrounded by an atmosphere of everlasting twilight, spreading over man and nature its feeling of calm and peace. The wanderings, the sad experiences, the mistakes, the disappointments, the griefs and sorrows of days gone by,—all seem to have remained behind upon the thresholds of these avenues. For as we enter them we live within the present, which in our eyes appears to be everlasting, and it has lost all else material about it. Our thoughts rise high above these earthly surroundings, above the vain ambitions of the world, as in the undisturbed silence it lies forgotten at our feet beneath its shroud of dead or dying leaves.

How could we help wondering idly about many things, as Talleyrand had done while following these selfsame paths so many years before? It was upon the threshold of these avenues that he had left the earliest and the latest recollections of his public life. His priesthood in 1780, his adhesion to the French Revolution, his friendship with Mirabeau in 1790, his unsuccessful mission to London, his flight to the United States in 1794 (to escape the raging Terror), all these episodes in his career must have welled up before him. Could he here forget his early English love, or his devotion to Madame de Stael, who had been the first rays from his star of fortune? Here, in June, 1797, we find him as Minister of Foreign Affairs, and the friend of Bonaparte, who makes him his confidant about the expedition to Egypt. In 1799 he hands

in his resignation, and becomes the mainspring of the
"Concordat." As a reward the Pope releases him from
his vows, and he marries Mrs. Grand, a "divorcée," in
1802. Now at the height of his glory, loaded with titles,
honors, fortune, he sees that his benefactor is losing
ground in the opinions of the people. He sees that the
Empire must soon give way to the Monarchy; and slowly
the great diplomat begins—and having once begun he
finds it wonderfully easy—to forget the kindnesses and
the favors of his Emperor.

In 1814 he is the ally of the Czar Alexander and the
Comte d'Artois, to overthrow Napoleon. He dictates to
the Senat the act by which the Emperor is deposed, and he
becomes, again, the Minister of Foreign Affairs. During
the "Cent jours" he resists the advances of the Emperor
and becomes the Great Chamberlain under Louis XVIII.
He is among the first to acquiesce in the fall of the
Restoration, and in 1830 Louis Philippe sends him as
ambassador to England.

Still we wander on, and we wonder if in the undisturbed silence of these peaceful surroundings a voice
which never shall be hushed did not at times sound harshly
in the ears of Talleyrand. For though the voices of the
world may applaud, and say, "The end is a success, and
so it has been good," the voice of conscience is ever there
in answer that the means were evil. Perhaps, however,
the diplomat had made a compromise between his world
and the voice of conscience, and believed that the services to his country more than counterbalanced the harm
which he had done to many. Perhaps, thus easily satisfied, he rested in the shade of laurels gathered from so
many hapless trees.

Now we linger in the vale, beside the peaceful Nahon,
with the deer. Far above the head the castle stands,
cold and dignified, while trees cluster about its base.
Here and there they hide the white stone of its terraces,

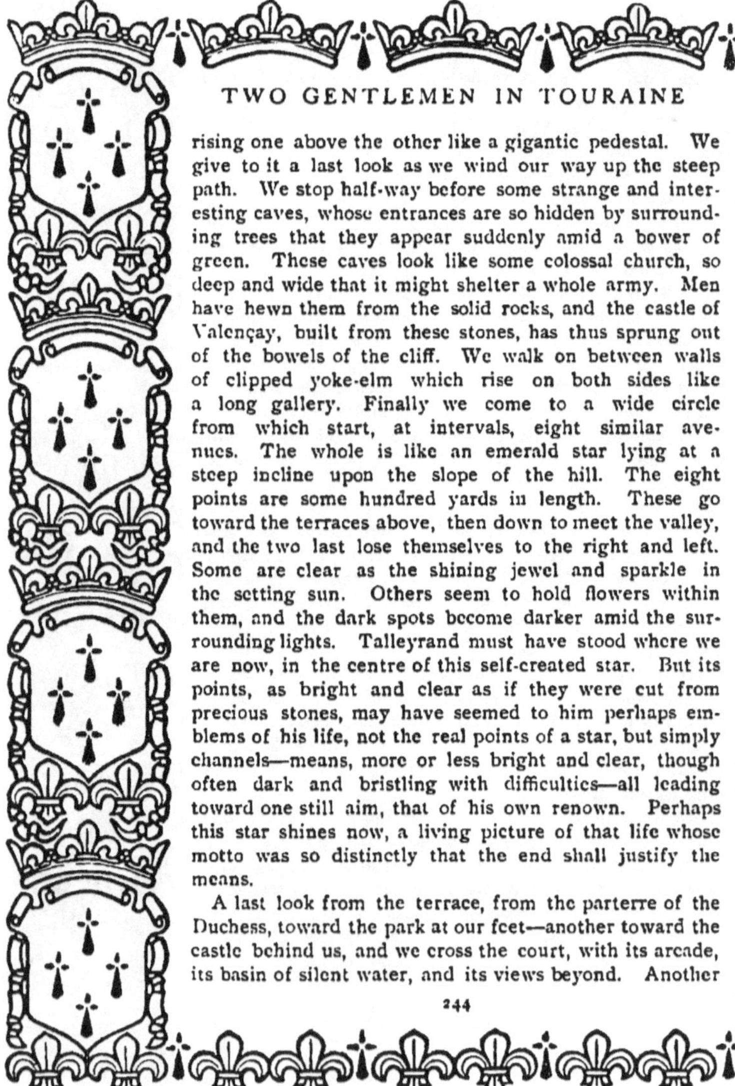

rising one above the other like a gigantic pedestal. We give to it a last look as we wind our way up the steep path. We stop half-way before some strange and interesting caves, whose entrances are so hidden by surrounding trees that they appear suddenly amid a bower of green. These caves look like some colossal church, so deep and wide that it might shelter a whole army. Men have hewn them from the solid rocks, and the castle of Valençay, built from these stones, has thus sprung out of the bowels of the cliff. We walk on between walls of clipped yoke-elm which rise on both sides like a long gallery. Finally we come to a wide circle from which start, at intervals, eight similar avenues. The whole is like an emerald star lying at a steep incline upon the slope of the hill. The eight points are some hundred yards in length. These go toward the terraces above, then down to meet the valley, and the two last lose themselves to the right and left. Some are clear as the shining jewel and sparkle in the setting sun. Others seem to hold flowers within them, and the dark spots become darker amid the surrounding lights. Talleyrand must have stood where we are now, in the centre of this self-created star. But its points, as bright and clear as if they were cut from precious stones, may have seemed to him perhaps emblems of his life, not the real points of a star, but simply channels—means, more or less bright and clear, though often dark and bristling with difficulties—all leading toward one still aim, that of his own renown. Perhaps this star shines now, a living picture of that life whose motto was so distinctly that the end shall justify the means.

A last look from the terrace, from the parterre of the Duchess, toward the park at our feet—another toward the castle behind us, and we cross the court, with its arcade, its basin of silent water, and its views beyond. Another

look behind at the toweres, at the moats, and we are
already beyond the gates and in the forest.   Once more
beneath the leather hood of our victoria we review the
vivid impressions left upon our minds by Valençay.
The rain and hail of a second storm fall in torrents
around us, and drop so heavily from the leather hood
that we are drenched and cold.   But our chestnut
mare plods on faster at every turn, as if she had but
just left the stable.   Villantrois appears against the
sky once more, and vanishes again like a faint flash of
lightning.   Now we are within the valley of the Cher, and
at last our mare, our driver, the victoria, the Comte and
I all stop in front of the hotel at Saint Aignan.   And
here once more the master, the mistress, the servants,
and the men and maids await us.   "Make haste; a drop
of brandy!—'c'est si réconfortant!' "   But we have no
time for omelettes or for imitation coffee this afternoon
—and we start again, this time for the station at Chenonceau, where we are to spend our last night.

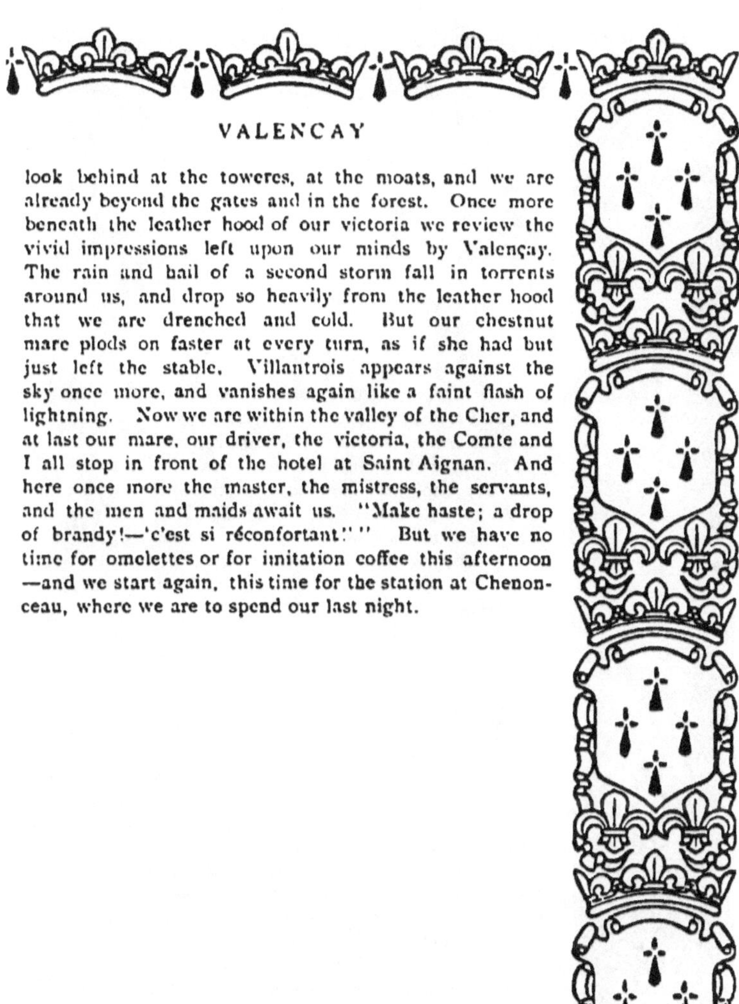

CHAPTER XI

Once more we are to make an early start, for we have twelve French "lieues" to walk during the day. It is the distance from Chenonceau to Montbazon.

The name of the little town sounds familiar to our ears, and our thoughts turn back instinctively to the days of Anne of Austria, and of Louis XIII. It was then that the famous Duchesse de Montbazon engaged in a court intrigue with the Duchesse de Longeville which ended in that singular epoch of French history known as the "Women's War."

As we gaze back over the centuries we may see the Princess Louise de Montpensier, "la Grande Mademoiselle," turning the guns of the Bastille against her cousin, the Regent. The all-powerful Richelieu is conquered at last by the hand of death, and is succeeded by the hated Cardinal Mazarin. Again our thoughts drift back to "Madame la Duchesse"—and to Montbazon itself, twelve "lieues" distant. Madame Dessert stands upon the threshold of her door, wishing us a last farewell in a tone of deep regret. We had become great friends with our quaint old hostess, with her gossip about the chateau and its neighbors, and with her wonderful chignon— forever in the way, and utterly without use. We had all become great friends during the three short days of our stay at Chenonceau, and now we were sad at parting.

"I hope that ces messieurs have been made comfortable," says Madame Dessert, as we are leaving the "Bon

Laboureur." "And I hope that they may return next spring, when my father's collection of peonies is in blossom. The peonies are very well known about here. Au revoir, messieurs. Ces messieurs would not care to purchase a little souvenir of Chenonceau, I suppose, a vase or a cup of faience de Blois?"

The fact that Madame Dessert possessed a father would alone have been enough to entice our steps once more to Chenonceau; but this seductive invitation to carry away some souvenirs with us was not to be refused, and we purchased a tiny saucer of blue china, molded into the shape of a heart. In the centre of it was a little medallion representing a swan in silver, pierced by an arrow. It could scarcely have been called pretty; but that was of no consequence.

"This was the emblem of Queen Claude de France," said the Comte, as we started. "She assumed it as a symbol of her unhappy love. But we will take it as the symbol of our sorrow at leaving this beautiful chateau and its little auberge."

As I looked back, Madame Dessert was still standing at the door waving an old lace handkerchief to us as we disappeared.

"People say that Frenchmen have a love for change," the Comte continued, as we walked along. "But every now and then we take a fancy to a place, although it may often be unworthy of the fancy, and we love to remain there as long as it may last. In my own case I know that I am often apt to associate a place with some interesting parts of my own life, and while I am there I even live through many different lives. For instance, since we have been here I have lived the lives of all the owners of Chenonceau, and I must confess that the lives of the last two have not interested me as much as the others." The Comte looked very wise, as if he were about to announce the solution of a great problem, and then

added: "It is because they lacked the brilliancy and glamour necessary to such a chateau. Chenonceau now is to me cold and bare. Everything is beautiful, and yet all needs more life, more action. I would rather see the park open to all, instead of these closed gates, behind which a gardener or a servant crosses an avenue which should be rutted by the wheels of royal coaches, or lingers in alleys where the ladies of a court should wander." My friend paused for a moment, and then started off again. "I love to see the peasant have a feeling of respect, as well as love, for the chatelains, instead of the fear and defiance one finds so often in our days. The only way to produce and increase these emotions is to see something of the peasants themselves and to make them feel that it is a real pleasure to speak with them or even to meet them. They will both love and respect a man who surrounds himself with that outward form and decorum which his station may call for, and who does not allow those beneath him to forget that he is their superior. They see that he is so sure of himself that he fears nothing, and that nothing can alter his opinions. Familiarity never brings this feeling. It will only breed contempt, the most fatal thing to gain control of the peasant's mind.

"I have seen the strangest things done to win popularity. Chatelains will sometimes force their children to play with those of the village and even give them toys or things to eat." And the Comte fairly shuddered at the thought of such familiarity. He would have died rather than allow it!

"A very odd habit of becoming popular," I put in, with emphasis, "a very odd habit indeed."

"Do you suppose that, once grown up, these children would allow the peasants to call them by their Christian names?" he continued. "Certainly not, my friend, certainly not. And very naturally the day they forbid it

they will be called proud, and will be disliked by the peasant. There is nothing more important to society at large than for the right persons to be in their right places. The very order of things requires it, just as it does in everything else, and I think that the chatelains of chateaux inherit duties which very few understand in our days."

"You are so conservative in all your ideas, my friend," said I, when he had finished, "that you must be struck, continually, by the lack of outward observances in all classes and in all things nowadays. Why, even I notice it greatly; and you know that I come from a country and from surroundings which have had a great influence upon the whole world in such matters."

"Yes, indeed," the Comte broke in, "and it is extraordinary how much it has affected Europe in this direction. I am sorry for it; for what may produce good results in that New World, which is based upon such principles and doctrines, does not succeed always in older countries where the traditions and training of centuries call for other methods and for different institutions. We see it immediately in the very question before us. Familiarity, possibly a good thing among people who consider one another upon an equal footing in society, does not produce the same effect among those who have been irreparably divided for centuries and must always be. It is misunderstood on account of the existing customs, from which Europe will never break away. These are so firmly rooted and so solid in their foundations that to tear them up now would only be to destroy the peace and order which exists, without giving an improvement in return."

"It seems to me a mistake to make changes in the institutions of a country which are of no benefit. This restlessness is far too popular at present. You can see it as well as I. But the reaction is bound to come, as you

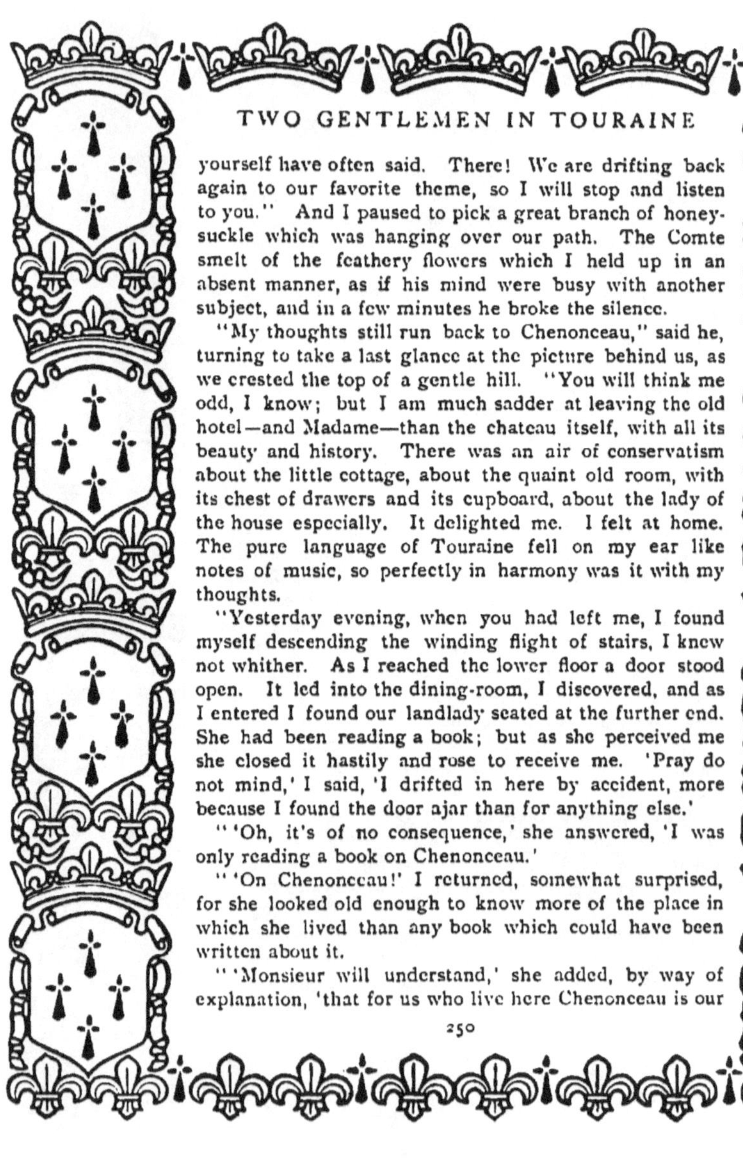

yourself have often said. There! We are drifting back again to our favorite theme, so I will stop and listen to you." And I paused to pick a great branch of honeysuckle which was hanging over our path. The Comte smelt of the feathery flowers which I held up in an absent manner, as if his mind were busy with another subject, and in a few minutes he broke the silence.

"My thoughts still run back to Chenonceau," said he, turning to take a last glance at the picture behind us, as we crested the top of a gentle hill. "You will think me odd, I know; but I am much sadder at leaving the old hotel—and Madame—than the chateau itself, with all its beauty and history. There was an air of conservatism about the little cottage, about the quaint old room, with its chest of drawers and its cupboard, about the lady of the house especially. It delighted me. I felt at home. The pure language of Touraine fell on my ear like notes of music, so perfectly in harmony was it with my thoughts.

"Yesterday evening, when you had left me, I found myself descending the winding flight of stairs, I knew not whither. As I reached the lower floor a door stood open. It led into the dining-room, I discovered, and as I entered I found our landlady seated at the further end. She had been reading a book; but as she perceived me she closed it hastily and rose to receive me. 'Pray do not mind,' I said, 'I drifted in here by accident, more because I found the door ajar than for anything else.'

"'Oh, it's of no consequence,' she answered, 'I was only reading a book on Chenonceau.'

"'On Chenonceau!' I returned, somewhat surprised, for she looked old enough to know more of the place in which she lived than any book which could have been written about it.

"'Monsieur will understand,' she added, by way of explanation, 'that for us who live here Chenonceau is our

all. My father, grandfather and great-grandfather were all born and bred here; and they kept this same hotel before I was born. You know, monsieur, that a change of owners at the chateau may have for us a vital importance. If Chenonceau is beautifully kept up, the park opened to visitors and the castle filled with guests, it means life to the whole village, and to some of us wealth even. But if, on the contrary, the park is closed and strangers are not permitted to visit the chateau, then the travel, the visiting, the tourists, all stop, and it is ruin for us. So you see, monsieur, that this is why every one in Chenonceau is interested in the doings of those who live at the chateau. When it was sold the last time every one asked, "Will the new masters be severe, or will they be chatelains like our dear old ones who are gone?" It was a vital question, monsieur, a vital question.' And the poor old lady seemed lost for a moment, as she shook her head at the thoughts which came into her mind. Then she continued: 'So, monsieur, when you see the whole village running to their doors at the sound of a carriage, of people, you must not take it for curiosity, though it may be that in part, for it is chiefly because each carriage that enters Chenonceau brings visitors who stop. And that means money, and *that* means life and existence for the village.

"'Ah! It is no more as it used to be in olden times, some twenty-five years ago. Not a day passed then without bringing several of those large coaches drawn by four horses, with postilions cracking their short-handled whips. I remember mighty foreigners, known as "lors Anglais," sending their couriers before them to reserve the whole hotel. And what a stir it would make in the village! The news would spread like wildfire, and each of the neighbors would bring something from his garden or larder, something which they thought might please the "lor" and induce him to come back again and bring his

friends. And what tips those "lors" used to give! But now, monsieur, each year brings fewer people, and the "lors" have been replaced by bourgeois, who never pay their bills without discussing each item and losing their temper over ten sous.

"'If you only knew, monsieur, how pleased we are to see some of our old aristocratic French families again, who have a fellow-feeling with us about the olden times. Ah, monsieur, money is no more in the right hands. People have it, but they do not know how to spend it any more. Monsieur will do me the honor, I hope, of inscribing his name in my visitors' book.' And she opened a large leather-bound book, in which I signed my name.

"'Thank you, monsieur, thank you,' said she, and she made me a sweeping courtesy.

"I left her, and as I returned to my room I thought with interest of this family born in the very shades of the chateau, living by it, respecting it and loving it for more than six generations. I thought of how much the walls of my own room might tell, if only they could speak, of fortune, sorrow or adversity. And I thought how much good a chatelain could and, in fact, how much good all can do to-day for a village and for the lives around them. I thought of how, in this way, they might work for society itself. And I thought, too, how few who possess the means to do so know how to distribute the little good that they do.''

"You take a very discouraging view of the present state of affairs," said I. "If things are as you say, what do you consider the cause of them to be?"

"I think it comes first," the Comte replied, "from money changing hands as it has done of late years. You have precisely this same state of affairs with the same results in your own country, only to a greater extent because it is more universally adopted there. I am surprised that you even asked me the question. It may look well with you, like a thousand other things appropriate to a new continent, framed upon a new basis and with new ideas; but it could never do good adopted here." The Comte shook his head sadly. "That is one of the misunderstood principles, one of the disadvantageous effects which the New World has had upon the Old. You remember our conversation yesterday on the road to Valençay. It is the same old story, old in its working and yet ever new in its result, money leaving the hands of an aristocracy which has lost the power of producing it through idleness or prejudice, money leaving the higher class, which has been taught to spend it, to be accumulated by a lower one, which knows not how to spend it, but has been taught to work for it. That is what we spoke of yesterday, and see how even to-day it is brought again to our notice.

"You asked me what the causes were for our present state of affairs. Well, that is the first one, I think, and the second is this: Those members of the aristocracy who still retain the power and the means of exercising a salutary influence upon the community are enveloped in a pall of inactivity, an apathy which seems to prevent them from making a bold stand or asserting their position. Religion and inherited principles, so strong in all of us, are the great checks to the present overflow of vice. In your own country you have a striking example of this in the influence of Puritanism upon the morals of New England. You may think this rather a far-stretched simile. But we realize all this in France; only the effects are not so strong with us because we do not know how, or more correctly, we do not take the trouble of keeping these influences alive by giving the example ourselves. The peasant of France is like the sheep of a flock. He follows the majority, and the majority in turn follows the chatelain of its village, so that if all goes wrong the responsibility as a rule must fall upon the latter.

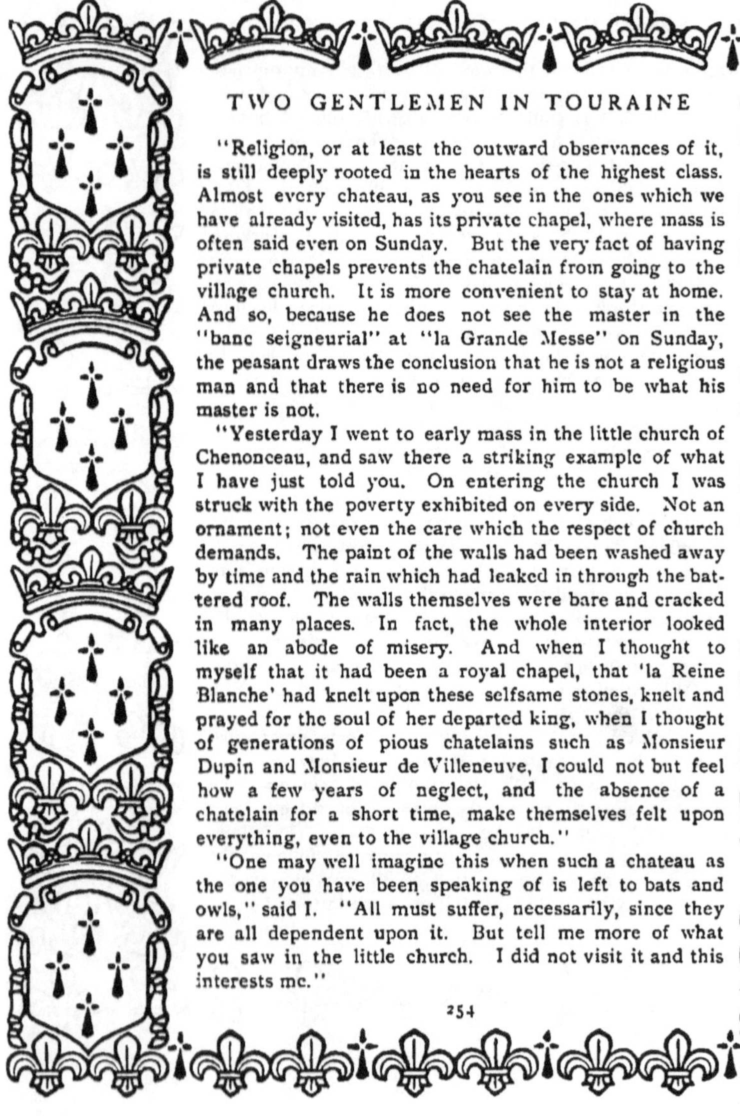

"Religion, or at least the outward observances of it, is still deeply rooted in the hearts of the highest class. Almost every chateau, as you see in the ones which we have already visited, has its private chapel, where mass is often said even on Sunday. But the very fact of having private chapels prevents the chatelain from going to the village church. It is more convenient to stay at home. And so, because he does not see the master in the "banc seigneurial" at "la Grande Messe" on Sunday, the peasant draws the conclusion that he is not a religious man and that there is no need for him to be what his master is not.

"Yesterday I went to early mass in the little church of Chenonceau, and saw there a striking example of what I have just told you. On entering the church I was struck with the poverty exhibited on every side. Not an ornament; not even the care which the respect of church demands. The paint of the walls had been washed away by time and the rain which had leaked in through the battered roof. The walls themselves were bare and cracked in many places. In fact, the whole interior looked like an abode of misery. And when I thought to myself that it had been a royal chapel, that 'la Reine Blanche' had knelt upon these selfsame stones, knelt and prayed for the soul of her departed king, when I thought of generations of pious chatelains such as Monsieur Dupin and Monsieur de Villeneuve, I could not but feel how a few years of neglect, and the absence of a chatelain for a short time, make themselves felt upon everything, even to the village church."

"One may well imagine this when such a chateau as the one you have been speaking of is left to bats and owls," said I. "All must suffer, necessarily, since they are all dependent upon it. But tell me more of what you saw in the little church. I did not visit it and this interests me."

FROM CHENONCEAU TO AZAY

"Do you really care about it?" said my friend inquiringly. "I am so fond of these matters myself that I am inclined to take it for granted that others are also. Yet I feared that it might not interest you. But to go back to the village church. A little girl about fourteen was on her knees in the middle of the centre aisle. Some vases made of blue glass, such as we see at country fairs, were upon the flagstones beside her, and a pile of flowers, some wild, some cultivated, lay near by. She was a very pretty little girl. Her rosy cheeks, her auburn hair hanging down to her shoulders, her bright smile which brought with it two dimples, all made her a picture fair to see. Her sleeves were tucked up to the elbows, and she was picking up the flowers one by one and arranging them in the vases. At last, when they were all in place, she brought an old tin water can and filled the vases with water. As she placed them on the altar of the Blessed Virgin I could see her head move, first on one side, then on another, as she completed her task.

"She turned and called: 'Justin, Justin; bring the candles!' And a little boy of six or seven came from behind the altar bearing them, sad mockeries of what they should have been,—but small remains, half-eaten by the rats. As I looked at them I could picture the care with which these poor, unkempt pieces of wax were put away each Sunday evening to be used the next week.

"'Justin, the tissue paper,' cried the little girl, quickly, 'or it will be time for the mass and all will not be ready.'

"Justin brought the paper, and the candles were made steady by it in the great silver candlesticks ten times as heavy as the taper.

"'Now, Justin, go and ring,' and the little Justin turned once more, this time to drag with all his might the heavy rope which hung from the vaulted roof. The bell

answered in a shrill, almost discordant tone that struck the silence like some sharp stone upon an even surface. The door of the sacristy opened, and an old man in a white surplice entered the church and seated himself in one of the stalls. He was soon followed by the priest in his long robes. The bell stopped ringing; the boy ran to the altar steps; the mass began. I turned my head as the priest began to speak, and saw two women enter the church. One, the elder of the two by some years, was dressed simply in black. The other was a young girl scarcely eighteen. Her golden hair and fair skin made her seem even less. She looked not unlike an angel fallen there from Heaven. There were no other worshippers in the church. We three were the only ones.

"As I stepped out into the sunshine and the day once more after mass, I found my little flower girl standing by the door. I asked her what her name was.

"'Marie L——,' she answered; 'I am the daughter of L——, who was the gardener of the dear masters of Chenonceau who are no more. But we still live here, monsieur; we shall always live here, although my father is no longer employed at the chateau.'

"I found my way back to the hotel, saddened by the thought of all that I had seen and heard. I wondered about the two women who alone out of the whole place had attended the mass. Yes, in this place religion seemed to crumble like the stones and mortar which had needed kings and queens to hold them together. I asked not why, because I knew. The last could be the only answer. But that young girl, with a face so beautiful, so young, so open; who was she? And I answered myself: Perhaps it was the daughter, not of the old servant, put by and forgotten with the departed life of those who were gone, but of the new masters who now replaced them. As she rose up in my mind beside the tiny flower girl, it made a striking contrast, picturesque and yet tinged with

sadness. But if this were true, I thought, then give the
new daughter of the chateau and its life but a little time
and the crumbling stones of the old church would soon
be replaced and the church itself be filled with worshippers. Ah! How much there is in a little influence to
attract our fickle natures!" exclaimed the Comte, as he
concluded.

"There again is an instance of how we may be led by
an example given to us in an appealing way. That little
episode at Chenonceau has impressed me not a little."

"I like your story," said I, when he had finished,
"and I sympathize with the point which you brought out
in it. You made it so interesting that I only now notice
that we are wet through by the mist."

"Oh, that is nothing," said the Comte, lightly. "You
are not made of sugar, I suppose. You will not melt or
dissolve, will you?"

I was uncertain whether or not I should melt or even
dissolve by some unknown chemical process. I certainly
felt as if I might at any moment. But my friend was too
busy with his own thoughts to bother himself much one
way or the other.

We had reached Blère after crossing a stone bridge
over the Cher. The village, once a town, was left behind
us, and we turned at right angles to take the road to
Montbazon by way of Athée. It runs by the river for
a mile or so, and leaves the valley abruptly, to climb
a hill and reach the plateau where the little village first
appears. A Romanesque church rises from among the
houses, and near by the roofs of a little chateau of the
fifteenth century show themselves above the trees of its
park.

"We are to stop here for déjeuner," said the Comte.
"If you will order it I will go as far as the church." And
when he returned we sat down to our beefsteak béarnaise,
our pomme de terres soufflés, our sparkling vin de vour-

ray, and the rest, with tired limbs and a good appetite. It seemed to me that I had never tasted anything so good as this simple déjeuner, perhaps because I had ordered it, as the Comte suggested.

While we were at table a hard wind cleared away the mist, and when we started it was dry again, almost cold, notwithstanding the month of August. We walked along for some miles, ever on this same plateau now swept by the wind. I think that we must have walked for two hours in silence. At last we reached a village, and there my companion broke the long silence.

"What have you been thinking of these last hours?" said he, turning toward me suddenly.

"What have I been thinking of?" I repeated vaguely. The sound of a voice seemed almost strange, so long had we remained silent. "Of—of—I fear it would be difficult for me to say. My mind has been so full of thoughts of many kinds that I find it almost beyond me to put them into words. I have been thinking of the wind, of the pleasure I should feel in reaching the valley and at the same time of the disappointment in leaving the plateau. And then my thoughts wandered off from that into a thousand channels, catching up something long forgotten here and running on ever before me like the ground on which we walked."

"I, too, have been indulging in much the same mood. Let us sit down on this heap of stones, and I will tell you of my thoughts. I feel in a very poetic mood—too vague perhaps for you; but you must tell me if, after all, you have not felt some of the sensations that I endeavor to describe?"

The Comte threw himself down on the grassy bank while I sat upon the heap of stones placed at the side of the road, to scatter in the winter season. He leaned back in a dreamy way. He seemed almost in a trance, as he began to speak more to himself than to me:

"A plateau—so long that its end is lost in the horizon, so wide that its limits are unseen. And this plateau is to be found high up above two of the most fertile valleys of France. The wind wanders over it, beats it, sweeps it, and the sensation which one feels at first is pleasing. The first caress of the wind calls forth a second, one more and again another. But, like a certain love that breathes as many caresses, it is soon fatigued, and finally it dies altogether. Yes, pleasing at first, it seems constant, and we feel sure of it. Ah, it may remain so for a space, for an hour, a day, a month; but seldom for a whole year, seldom even for the day. And this same wind, like the love, ever constant in our mind, ever changing in reality, has passed over the plateau for we know not how many centuries. Now the plain is bare and arid, cut by a single road stoned each year and dried up by the ever-beating wind.

"A few blades of grass, tarnished and of a grayish green, the wild aster, like a blue star made purple by the wind, something yellow, a clover of some kind, a morning glory which is born white at sunrise and dies pink at eve, a poppy which seems to blush because it has blossomed here, these are all that I see. A daisy, without even strength enough to say, 'Love me; love me not,' for it has but one petal left, thyme whose perfume intoxicates the air and those who breathe it, and the vine plants, so scarce, so puny that they seem but scattered leaves, and the pipes which hold them up—these are all which the continuous wind has left upon the plain.

"Oh, yes, I forget,—a bird, that seems afraid of something which we cannot see, cuts the air with its indented wings. The song we might have heard has died away. And the little ones in the nest yonder have stopped their chirping also, for they hear the blowing of the wind. A butterfly has lost its way and flies painfully from one stunted flower to another. It hides itself in the dust as if afraid to be seen. Some trees are scattered here and there, beaten and ragged, but few leaves on their branches, although it is August. In the distance, an old stone wall extends like an arrow over the plateau. The stones have been placed one on another without mortar, and the whole stands challenging the wind to kill those few stray flowers that struggle for existence beneath its sheltering wing. A large ruined tower rises in the west. It is la Tour de Brandon, and it stands on the edge of the plateau, as if to herald the coming of the wind, now here to stay. This is all, all that there is upon the plateau swept by the air.

"We walk—we run over the dry road with its heaps of stones, which look as if they might hide dead bodies and which await the' winter to be scattered abroad. Hush, there is the whistle of the wind in our ears! It tells of death and ruin and waste, and we push on without notic-ing the plants which grow, flower and die beneath our feet. We would leave behind us the wind and its fatal caress, which seems to absorb and kill all that it falls upon. We would depart from this land (it seems a whole country in itself, so desolate is everything around), untouched by sunshine and at the mercy of the wind. We walk on, intoxicated, distracted almost, long-ing only to flee from the blast which seems as if it would do to us what it has done to the flowers and the grass. And always on the right there remains the dismantled tower; always there whistles in our ears the sad moan of the wind. Now it sounds like a harsh note in this dirge of nature; now it is but a cold breath from the grave.

"If we had come alone over the arid plain I wonder if we should have glanced with love or pity at the flowers which die ere they are really born, at the struggle for ex-istence of all that we see about us. I wonder if we should have felt as we do, or if we should have seen only a long waste of stones covered with dust and swept by the

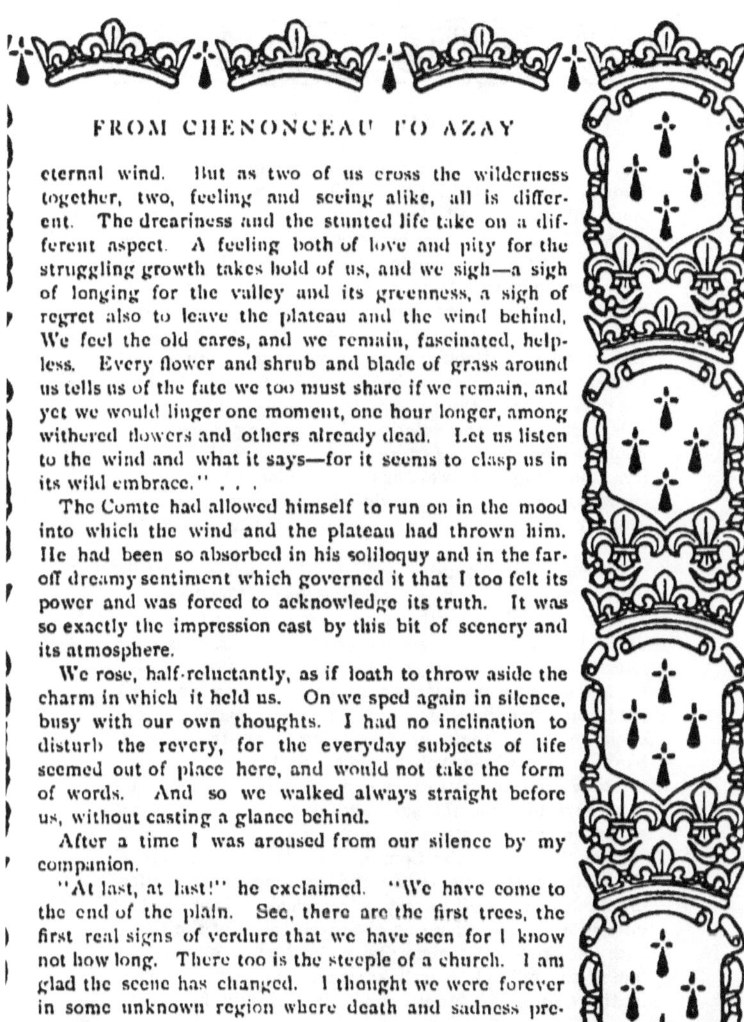

eternal wind. But as two of us cross the wilderness together, two, feeling and seeing alike, all is different. The dreariness and the stunted life take on a different aspect. A feeling both of love and pity for the struggling growth takes hold of us, and we sigh—a sigh of longing for the valley and its greenness, a sigh of regret also to leave the plateau and the wind behind. We feel the old cares, and we remain, fascinated, helpless. Every flower and shrub and blade of grass around us tells us of the fate we too must share if we remain, and yet we would linger one moment, one hour longer, among withered flowers and others already dead. Let us listen to the wind and what it says—for it seems to clasp us in its wild embrace." . . .

The Comte had allowed himself to run on in the mood into which the wind and the plateau had thrown him. He had been so absorbed in his soliloquy and in the far-off dreamy sentiment which governed it that I too felt its power and was forced to acknowledge its truth. It was so exactly the impression cast by this bit of scenery and its atmosphere.

We rose, half-reluctantly, as if loath to throw aside the charm in which it held us. On we sped again in silence, busy with our own thoughts. I had no inclination to disturb the revery, for the everyday subjects of life seemed out of place here, and would not take the form of words. And so we walked always straight before us, without casting a glance behind.

After a time I was aroused from our silence by my companion.

"At last, at last!" he exclaimed. "We have come to the end of the plain. See, there are the first trees, the first real signs of verdure that we have seen for I know not how long. There too is the steeple of a church. I am glad the scene has changed. I thought we were forever in some unknown region where death and sadness pre-

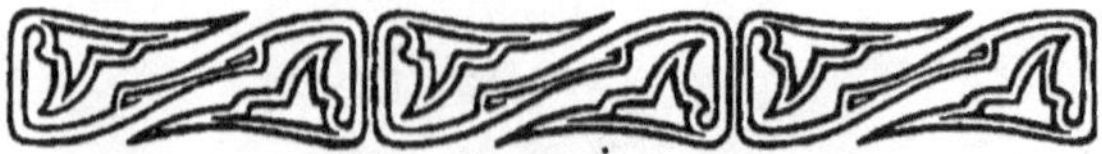

vailed. Let us take this road upon the right. I do not
know where it leads, but possibly it will take us to
some village. At all events, the uncertainty cannot be
worse than that which we leave behind." So we took the
road running at right angles to our own, and soon were
once more in bowers of green with verdant fields and overhanging trees. Before long the road took another turn,
and in a moment we were standing on the edge of a high
embankment overlooking the rich valley of l'Indre. Half
hidden by long grass or bulrushes, by trees or bushes,
the dark waters of the river wonnd in and out through the
vale. The shade and coloring of everything in the valley
made it look more like an enchanted picture than a reality. One longed to wander there amidst the green pastures and trees, where the wind descended to give a soft
kiss only to the leaves and arose again to sweep the
plain.

"What a very beautiful valley!" I exclaimed. "It is
more picturesque than either that of the Cher or the Loire.
It seems to pictnre another world, far different from any,
unless it be that of the golden ages. It wonld seem only
natural to see some satyr dash out from among yonder
foliage, or some mythical creatures play upon pipes and
reeds or gather in a grove where some marble statue
could overlook their merrymaking near the river's
bank. The whole valley seems to live on its own
resources, and to have its own mysterious pleasures hidden there between the surrounding hills. There is an
uncertain mystery about its very attraction and charm."

"Yes," answered the Comte, "look at those hamlets in
the distance, scarcely visible and seeming to be nestled
in the deep folds of a great velvet cloak. There is the
village of Esvres clustering about the banks of the river,
with its well-kept gardens and white houses at the bottom of the hill. It is well known as the richest village
in the Canton of Montbazon. It certainly has every

natural advantage to make it so, for it is placed in one of the most lovable of French valleys."

"What an odd word to use for a valley: lovable!" I remarked.

"You think so?" said the Comte. "It seems to me as if it were the only term one could apply to so beautiful a spot. You must remember that we are no longer in the splendid Touraine of the Loire. I should say here that nature has changed her dress to one of a more delicate tint. These surroundings, to be sure, do not strike that high note of ecstasy, of natural delight, which one feels in looking at the noble chateaux of Vouvray and Roche-carbon. But I think one is moved even more deeply by this quiet, mysterious and finished scenery. It seems to me to call forth love, rather than a feeling of admiration. And then, you know, to love much we should not be too busy admiring and criticising that which we love. Yes, decidedly, I think this valley is lovable."

"I understand what you mean," I replied, "and I do not know but that I agree with you in good part. You seem to be unusually susceptible to the scenery to-day. But we must not linger here too long, for it is already five o'clock, and we have many kilometres before us yet, according to your map."

"Dieu, dieu, dieu, my dear friend," the Comte exclaimed, "how practical you are! You cut short my little dreams and pictures in the most brutal fashion."

"You must not complain," I replied, "for it is not often I who am in a hurry to start."

I had in my mind the day before, and still could see my friend running frantically about with his shaving-brush—a perfectly useless adjunct to our journey, as we were not to pass the night. But so skeptical was he that he would rather have lost the train than leave anything behind which might possibly be ferreted away in his absence. Not even Madame Dessert could be entrusted

with the sacred necessities of his toilet. However, I did not remind him of the scene, and the Comte proceeded to soliloquize in perfect unconcern.

"How can one remain indifferent to such a mixture of life and peace! Both seem to harmonize in the summer evening. Everything seems to bring its share of pleasure to the eye and to give a finish to the picture."

The road now turned again and ran along a railroad track, following with it the thousand curves and twinings of the river. On the right arose far above our heads hills covered with villas and their surrounding parks. The railway crossed our road and was lost in a forest of high trees, and we in our turn followed the banks of the Indre. The soft shades of the evening grew softer as the sun fell toward the western horizon, and cast a myriad of blood-red shafts in all directions, to glimmer for a moment and then fade into nothingness. A quaint old mill appeared, its busy wheel now resting from the labors of the day, and the departing rays fell on it, lighting the old battered walls with golden hue. The valley grew more wide, more fertile and more peaceful still as we pushed on. At last the first houses of the place that we had come so far to reach began to show themselves, surrounded by their neatly-finished gardens. The patches of ground became shallow, the houses more numerous. Soon the road was crowded on either side.

As we proceeded we could see on our left, though yet in the distance, a high, dismantled tower. Beside it stood the remains of what was once an important feudal castle. It rose high above the houses, high above the trees on the hill; and on the very summit of its battlements there stood out against the sky a gigantic statue in bronze which caught the last rays of the sun and flashed them down upon the valley and its village. It was a statue of the Holy Virgin, her arms outstretched as if to bless or to protect the souls gathered at her feet —a fitting climax to imposing walls.

"Show me the man who could remain indifferent to such an evening or to such a scene," the Comte exclaimed, in ecstasy. And I awaited another rhapsody from his reflective nature. "How to describe the effect of this twilight, this strange mauve color on everything, left by the vanishing sun! The stars seem waiting to appear, and, as if impatient, one faint twinkle will show itself and then cease to be, as if called back from whence it came. How to describe the wonderful peace which there is upon everything, the tranquil joy which seems to be the embodiment of this beautiful valley! One black spot only seems to show in relief against the doubtful coloring. It is that statue, colossal, striking, fearful almost, though at the same time it is soothing, and filled with a wonderful peace. She seems to tell the legend of her being to us; telling it in a silence more eloquent than words could be."

"How much longer are you going to rhapsodize over this scene?" I inquired. "Do you not think that a dinner would be more to the point after our long tramp?"

"There is time for poetry as well as food," the Comte replied, laconically. But I feared his ardor was a little dampened, for he followed me in silence over a long stone bridge of the eighteenth century, to the hotel at its further end,—the hotel, that paradise for any one who is not especially fond of long walks and who has just accomplished his twelve lieues with some difficulty!

"Hotel, dinner and bed. Dios gracias'" I exclaimed, as we halted at the door, notwithstanding the stern lack of sympathy in my companion.

A fat gentleman, with a fat wife on one side and a still fatter dog upon the other, was occupying the whole of the doorway. The Comte addressed the former in the most delightful of French manners:

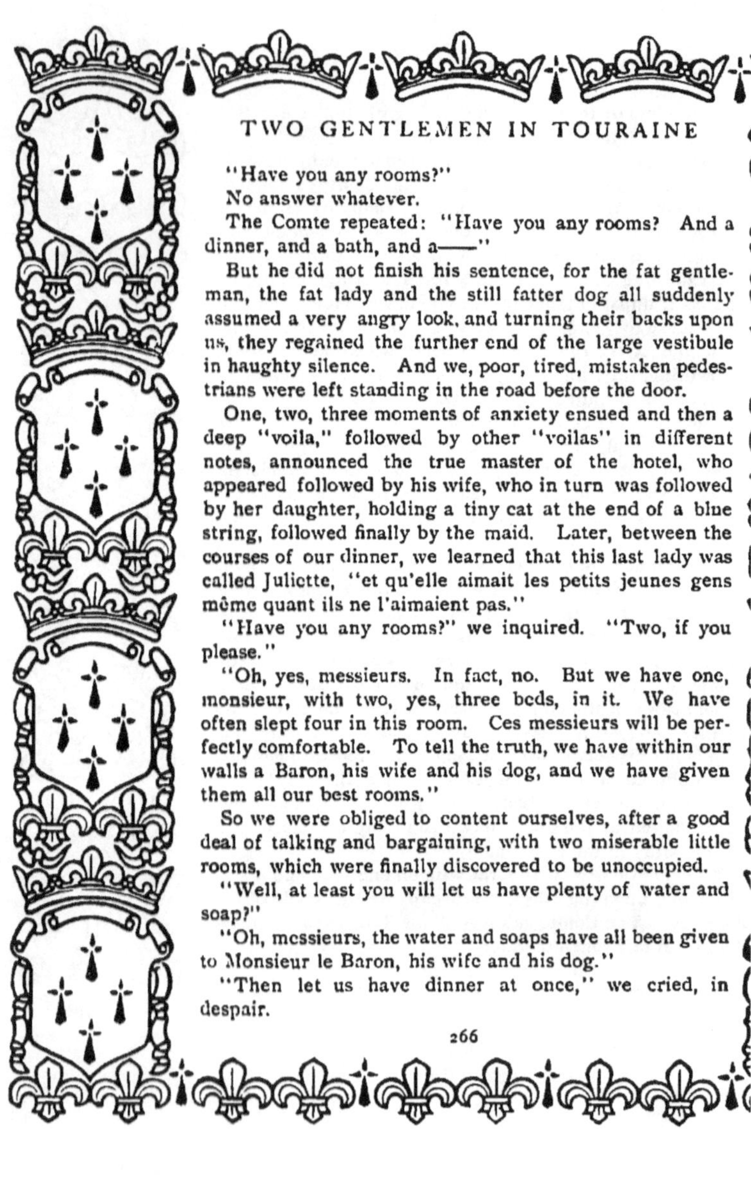

"Have you any rooms?"

No answer whatever.

The Comte repeated: "Have you any rooms? And a dinner, and a bath, and a——"

But he did not finish his sentence, for the fat gentleman, the fat lady and the still fatter dog all suddenly assumed a very angry look, and turning their backs upon us, they regained the further end of the large vestibule in haughty silence. And we, poor, tired, mistaken pedestrians were left standing in the road before the door.

One, two, three moments of anxiety ensued and then a deep "voila," followed by other "voilas" in different notes, announced the true master of the hotel, who appeared followed by his wife, who in turn was followed by her daughter, holding a tiny cat at the end of a blue string, followed finally by the maid. Later, between the courses of our dinner, we learned that this last lady was called Juliette, "et qu'elle aimait les petits jeunes gens même quant ils ne l'aimaient pas."

"Have you any rooms?" we inquired. "Two, if you please."

"Oh, yes, messieurs. In fact, no. But we have one, monsieur, with two, yes, three beds, in it. We have often slept four in this room. Ces messieurs will be perfectly comfortable. To tell the truth, we have within our walls a Baron, his wife and his dog, and we have given them all our best rooms."

So we were obliged to content ourselves, after a good deal of talking and bargaining, with two miserable little rooms, which were finally discovered to be unoccupied.

"Well, at least you will let us have plenty of water and soap?"

"Oh, messieurs, the water and soaps have all been given to Monsieur le Baron, his wife and his dog."

"Then let us have dinner at once," we cried, in despair.

"Very well, messieurs, in half an hour, for Monsieur le Baron—etc., must have theirs first."

"Well, when it is ready, have it served in the garden near the river."

"Bien, messieurs."

We groped our way down a rickety flight of stairs in complete darkness, and at last after many bumps and scratches from unseen obstacles we reached the garden. We were repaid for our trouble, though I must confess we indulged in some rather uncomplimentary reflections upon the Baron, his wife and his dog, who were enjoying their dinner while we were obliged to wait. Our table was laid on the very edge of the river, and as we sat down to wait, everything around seemed to have assumed a pinkish hue in the evening shade, a pink of many tones. The stone bridge in front was the brightest object in the landscape, and its heavy arches were so clearly reflected in the silent water that it seemed as if another bridge were there below. The sky, pink also, was reflected, now showing the first tiny stars appearing in the heavens. The boat, tied by a chain to the willow near us, was pink, and the long arms of the Virginia creepers which stretched from tree to tree and caressed the air in the gentle breeze were more pink than green.

A shadow with the same rose shade upon it passed over the bridge, stopped near the centre and leaned against the parapet. Another shadow appeared, and passing the one upon the bridge it vanished on the other side of the river. Still a third shadow stopped near the first, and leaned over the stone beside it. The two drew closer and closer.

"Oh, what a harmony of pinks!" I was about to exclaim, as the two shadows seemed to be lost in one; but the night had come and the pink had turned to black—to the darkness of night.

"Quick, the coffee of Monsieur le Baron! Fly for the

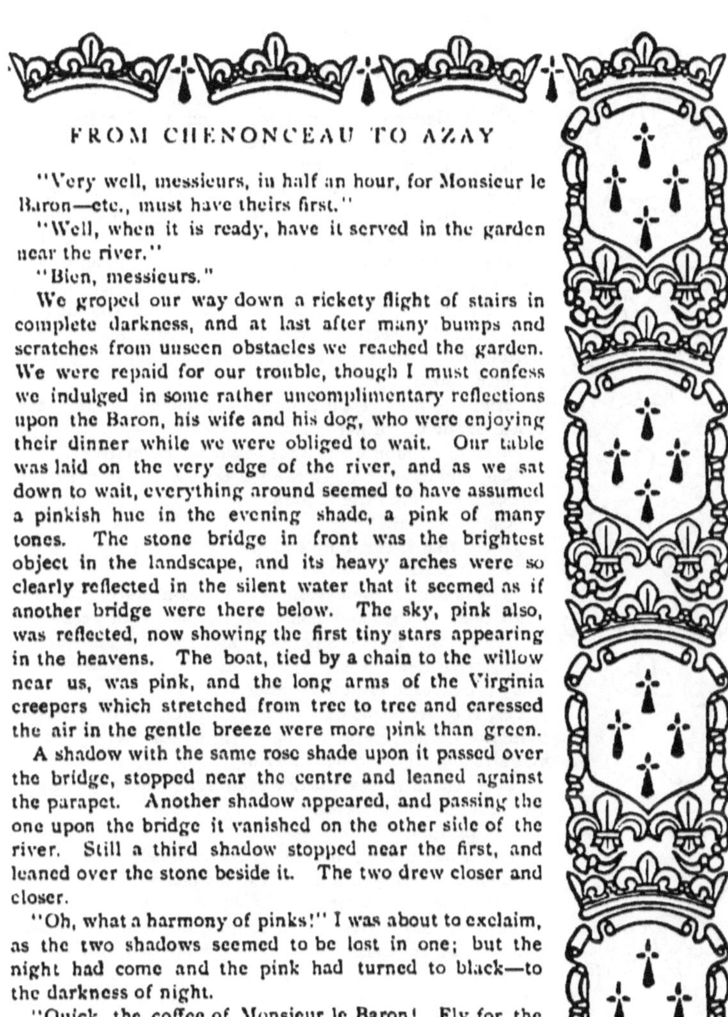

shawl of Madame la Baronne!" cried a voice from the hotel, and our picture was broken by the harsh accents disturbing the calm of our surroundings. The "splash, splash, splash" of the eggs which the cook was beating for an omelette and the faint "mew" of the cat at the end of her blue ribbon were the only other sounds we heard. But between these distractions there was time for thought and enjoyment of a simple kind, but little inclination to talk.

"What softness, what peace!" exclaimed the Comte. "To disturb it seems almost a sin." But the sin came before the words were even out of his mouth, and from Juliette, too.

"Aie, aie, aie! I burn myself! I burn myself!" she cried, at the top of her voice.

"Mon dieu, mon dieu, what could be the matter!"

"Oh, messieurs, the chicken was so hot I burned the tips of my lovely little fingers."

"Oh, is that all?"

"Well, that is certainly enough, isn't it?"

"Ah, indeed!"

"You know, I come from Paris," continued Juliette, unabashed by the cold reception her advances received. "I like Paris. And ces petits jeunes gens? They come from Paris too? I know they do. I know they do. They are pleased with the dinner?"

Yes, they were pleased with the dinner, better pleased with the dinner, perhaps, than with its service. Juliette had already begun to be annoying.

"It is beautiful weather this evening. These messieurs are travelling on bicycles?"

"No, on foot."

"Oh, what a fiby, fiby, fib! I don't believe that. I come from Paris, you know. I don't believe that."

Well, it was immaterial to us whether she believed it or not, and taking the hint at length, our Parisian wiseacre left us in peace, though the echo of her voice from the kitchen brought back to us the words "fiby, fiby, fib," in every note of the scale.

"Such creatures are provoking," I remarked.

"Yes, very," replied my friend, "especially when they are not pretty."

"Juliette, Juliette, Juliette!" we could still hear from the hotel. "Quick, a glass of water for Monsieur le Baron. He wishes to retire."

"And you speak of our love of titles," I exclaimed, turning to the Comte, who was as much amused as I at our little experience. "Really, I do not think it can be compared with yours. Since we arrived at this wretched hotel we have heard nothing but 'Monsieur le Baron,' 'Madame la Baronne,' and that infernal dog of theirs. If I only could see it I should be tempted to drown it in the river."

"I never knew a Baron to create so much excitement in a little place," replied the Comte. "Let us try and find out of what sort of stuff this Baron is made."

We left the table and ascended the rickety flight of stairs once more to reach the vestibule above. The next minute we found ourselves face to face with the very fat gentleman whom we had met at the door on our arrival. And the hotel keeper was actually addressing him as Monsieur le Baron.

"What a strange resemblance!" exclaimed my friend. "If he were not a baron I should say that this was my tailor. The two are identically alike."

"Perhaps he may be both," I suggested.

"Oh, an idea!" returned the Comte. "Wait there, and I will try and see."

And walking up to the fat gentleman, who was airing himself once more in front of the door, he addressed him thus: "How do you do, Monsieur F——?"

The poor fat gentleman was so taken aback that he turned green in the face; Madame la Baronne was

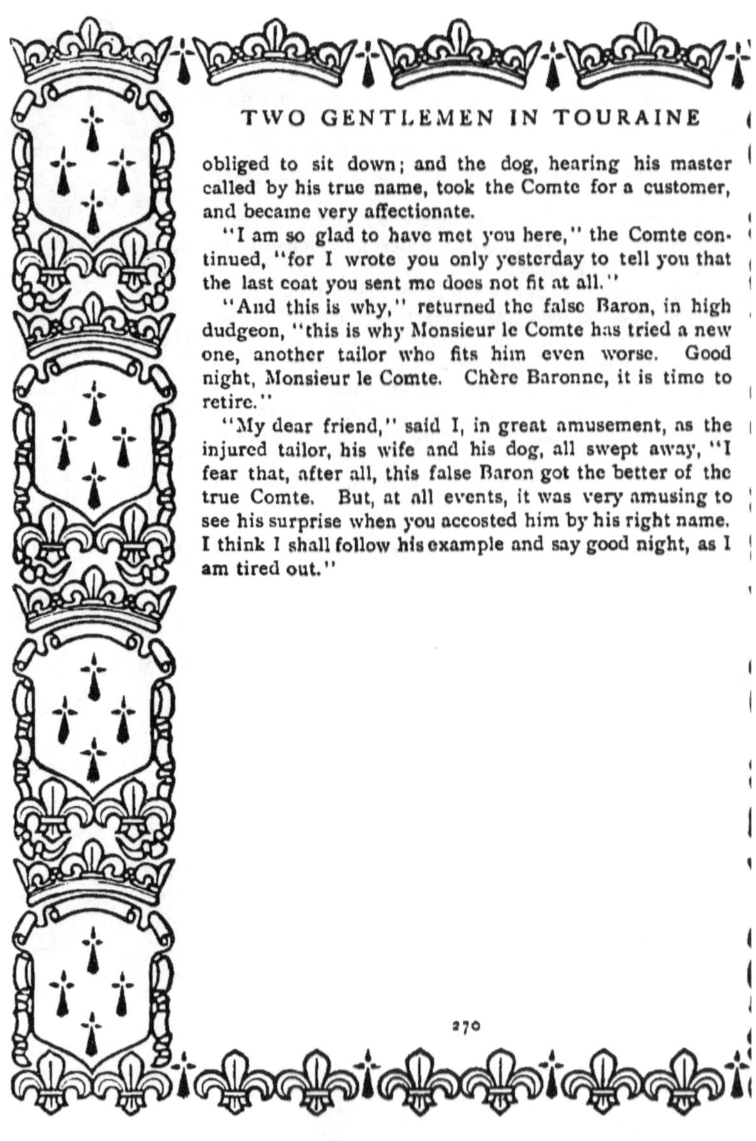

obliged to sit down; and the dog, hearing his master called by his true name, took the Comte for a customer, and became very affectionate.

"I am so glad to have met you here," the Comte continued, "for I wrote you only yesterday to tell you that the last coat you sent me does not fit at all."

"And this is why," returned the false Baron, in high dudgeon, "this is why Monsieur le Comte has tried a new one, another tailor who fits him even worse. Good night, Monsieur le Comte. Chère Baronne, it is time to retire."

"My dear friend," said I, in great amusement, as the injured tailor, his wife and his dog, all swept away, "I fear that, after all, this false Baron got the better of the true Comte. But, at all events, it was very amusing to see his surprise when you accosted him by his right name. I think I shall follow his example and say good night, as I am tired out."

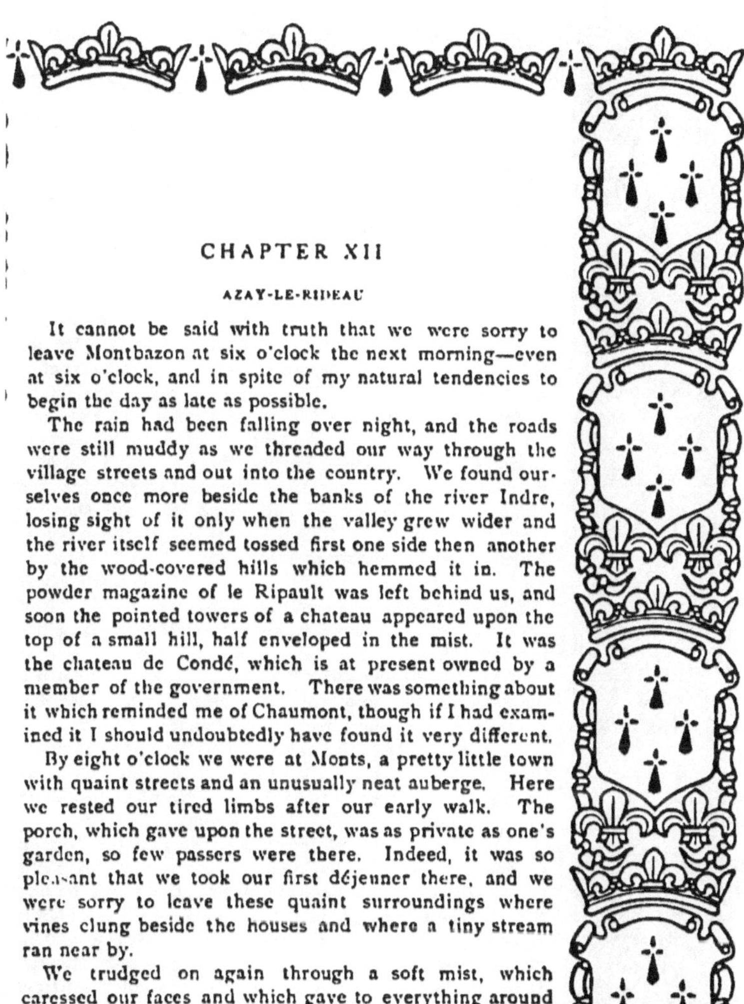

CHAPTER XII

AZAY-LE-RIDEAU

It cannot be said with truth that we were sorry to leave Montbazon at six o'clock the next morning—even at six o'clock, and in spite of my natural tendencies to begin the day as late as possible.

The rain had been falling over night, and the roads were still muddy as we threaded our way through the village streets and out into the country. We found our-selves once more beside the banks of the river Indre, losing sight of it only when the valley grew wider and the river itself seemed tossed first one side then another by the wood-covered hills which hemmed it in. The powder magazine of le Ripault was left behind us, and soon the pointed towers of a chateau appeared upon the top of a small hill, half enveloped in the mist. It was the chateau de Condé, which is at present owned by a member of the government. There was something about it which reminded me of Chaumont, though if I had exam-ined it I should undoubtedly have found it very different.

By eight o'clock we were at Monts, a pretty little town with quaint streets and an unusually neat auberge. Here we rested our tired limbs after our early walk. The porch, which gave upon the street, was as private as one's garden, so few passers were there. Indeed, it was so pleasant that we took our first déjeuner there, and we were sorry to leave these quaint surroundings where vines clung beside the houses and where a tiny stream ran near by.

We trudged on again through a soft mist, which caressed our faces and which gave to everything around

us a silvery tint. The valley widened; and from the summit of another hill we could see the remains of a Renaissance "Gentilhommière," now converted into farm houses, though none the less artistic for the change. The deep waters of the river flow here over a treacherous bed of grasses and weeds that grow to a great length, following the current of the river as if they would run away with it. The river itself looks not unlike a beautiful green serpent stealing its way through a soft carpet of some lighter shade. Little herds of cattle watched by a peasant woman with her white bonnet and her knitting—a pair of woolen stockings for the winter—dotted the meadows in spots. Frequently we would catch a glimpse now of a natural cave dug out of the side of a cliff, now of the towers of some chateau showing through a curtain of foliage, which suggested Azay-le-Rideau and the curtain of green from which it takes its name. Now there would appear only a small tower perched like an eagle's nest upon the top of a cliff. And yet we were ever in the valley where we had been since the day before. All was still calm, sad even.

"Yes, it is all very sad," broke in the Comte. "But if a plateau like the one which we passed over yesterday gives to the traveller a feeling of desolation and of exile, at least it stimulates the physical activity. It awakens in him a desire to hurry his forward course; and he hastens toward the unknown horizon in the hope of finding there the peace and calm which his soul longs for."

"Yes," said I. "But let us suppose that the horizon so much longed for discloses to him even a luxurious valley where waters flow and where the trees, finding their necessary nourishment, spread on all sides their vigorous branches covered with heavy leaves, what will be the result? We have it before us. It is only sadness. If the eye meets naught but harmony in coloring, from the silver gray of the birch to the soft green of the elm

or of the indented leaf of the oak, the result is still sadness. If the only sounds in this symphony of nature
which reach the ear are the footsteps of the cattle, half
drowned in the long grass, or the distant cry of the shepherd, or the monotonous splash of a waterfall near by; if
from far off the echo reaches us of the noise of a wheel,
another wail as it beats the water,—what is the effect of
it all, if it be not sadness?"

"And why should it be so?" asked my friend. "Why
is it that that which we so longed for, and which we
thought would be all sunshine and happiness, has proved
to be but a delusion, sad but none the less beautiful?"

"Because it is the perfection of calm," I answered.
"And because our soul, as it passes through this wonderful place, after the warfare of the plain is not content.
It would have more. It would rise above this, and taste
the delirium of happiness of which it sometimes dreams
and which it feels to be so near yet just beyond its grasp.
The beauty of nature seems to tantalize it. The contented state is just beyond, and it cannot reach it. Thus
a physical weariness, a mental discouragement ensues.
And we call it sadness."

"I feel it also," said I. "It is the effect of this wealth
of nature.

"Look yonder at the river, or rather upon its opposite
bank, and see the two men and the peasant girl with
them. They are dragging a long stick behind them in
the water. They seem to be searching for something
which has fallen into the river. There it is—they have
found it while I was speaking. It is something that is
dead—a dog, a shepherd's dog perhaps—an animal of
some kind. Come, let us go, for everything here seems
so tinged with sadness. I long to shake off this mood
Shall we soon reach the town of Azay?"

"We are almost there," my companion returned, and
some ten minutes later he added: "Let us cast off all

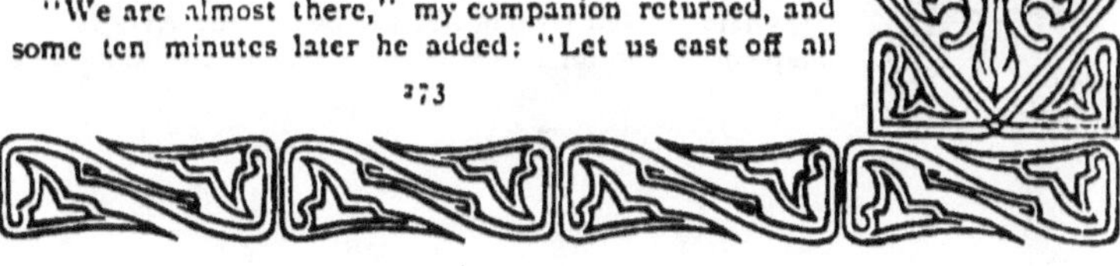

thoughts of sadness or dreariness in the midst of wind-swept plains and valleys, for here they have come to an end. This valley is divided by a curtain of thick trees, behind which some high roofs and pointed spires are to be seen. It is the chateau of Azay-le-Rideau. Here are the first houses of the village."

In another moment we had entered the town, by the high road which runs from one end of it to the other. Azay is built upon the side of a hill, and it slopes down to the gates of the chateau which lies in the very bed of the river Indre. The houses are clean and well cared for. Flowers blossom on the iron balconies, and gray stone gables shade the sidewalks. An ordinary wall of white stone and plaster and a still more ordinary looking gate enclose a straight avenue of rather inferior horse-chestnut trees. But if we turn into this unpretentious entrance and pursue the avenue for one or two hundred yards, we shall see before us at its further end the gem, yes, the diamond, of the French Renaissance. Azay-le-Rideau rises from a setting which at first seems unworthy of such a treasure house. But, imperceptibly, this impression fades away, as we reach the round courtyard and pass through a second gateway with pillars of stone and flanked by two pavilions of the purest Louis XIII architecture. The lines of these pavilions are regular and sober, and half veiled by jasmine and Virginia creepers stretching their long arms in all directions. Their high sharp roofs spring as it were from a bed of verdure and flowers. There is a wonderful charm, as well as an artistic flavor about the whole surroundings. Instinctively our thoughts run back to Valençay, and we are tempted to contrast the two pavilions there with these before us.

As we turn our eyes toward the beautiful pile of stones, the chateau itself rises out of the bed of the river in the shape of the letter L. It is built around two sides of a

RIDEAU

square, each end being flanked by two round towers which arise in graceful proportions; the four spires of their pointed roofs strike the sky in perfect symmetry. The wing on the right, with its two towers, is mirrored in the unruffled waters of a moat, and seems almost to be without a beginning and without an end. We cross a wooden bridge, in order to reach the courtyard, and there study the architecture of the chateau in detail. The bridge is hung with creepers of all kinds, twining around the beams and pillars, and falling toward the river in long garlands. Beneath it still runs the Indre, silent and swift and dark, although here it is but a tiny stream, turned and twisted long since to encircle the chateau and to beautify its park.

In the background the village church half borders upon the park. It is enshrouded in laurel trees and weeping willows, so that we see only a portion of its wall, the corner of a tower, or a chance detail between the leaves. The eyes wander from branch to branch, from flower to flower, like the bird, looking back on what has been left behind, and hesitating before the beauty and the grace of that which stands before them. They rest with delight upon the great wing of the chateau and upon the long terrace to the left, and they wander back with pleasure to the river.

The most striking feature of the principal façade is the motif of the grand staircase, which rises to the high roof and which ends in an architectural performance of such grace in detail and of such beauty of ensemble that it reminds us of Oxford in England.

Unlike the Chateau de Blois, the staircase here is not an exterior one; it is not open, nor is it circular. But though it is flat in appearance and lacking in that wonderful vitality which seems to give to the staircase of Blois its greatest charm, this one at Azay-le-Rideau rivals it in delicacy of carving, in the perfection of its

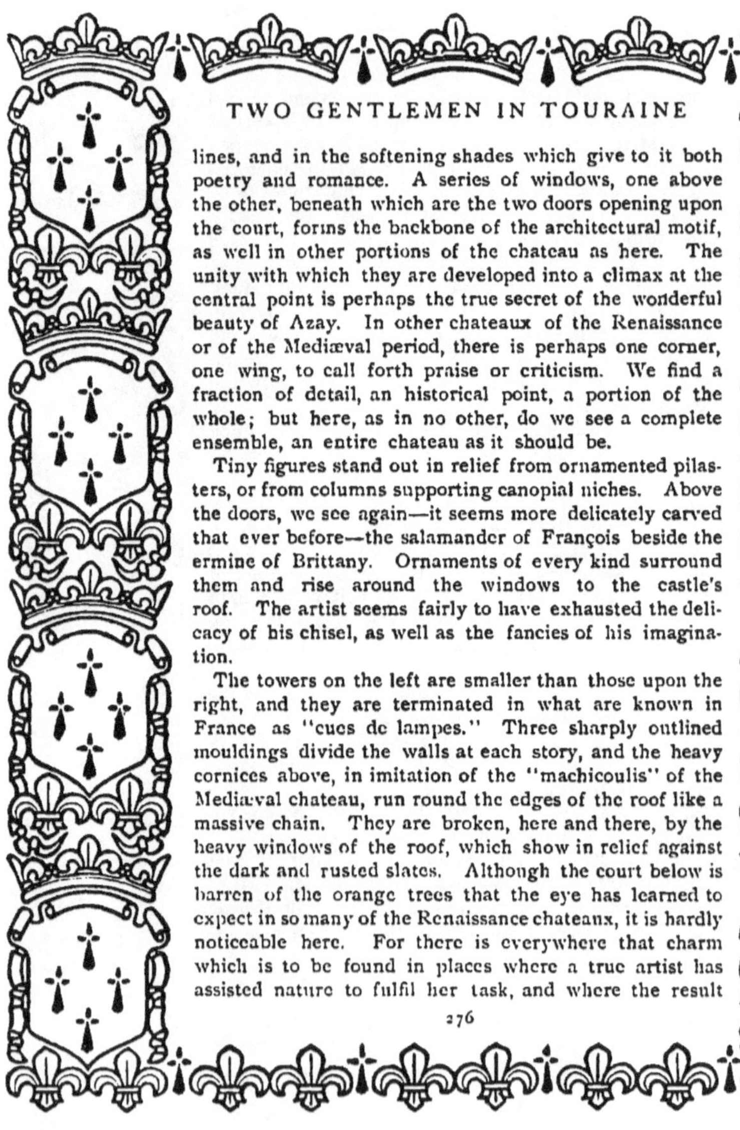

lines, and in the softening shades which give to it both poetry and romance. A series of windows, one above the other, beneath which are the two doors opening upon the court, forms the backbone of the architectural motif, as well in other portions of the chateau as here. The unity with which they are developed into a climax at the central point is perhaps the true secret of the wonderful beauty of Azay. In other chateaux of the Renaissance or of the Mediæval period, there is perhaps one corner, one wing, to call forth praise or criticism. We find a fraction of detail, an historical point, a portion of the whole; but here, as in no other, do we see a complete ensemble, an entire chateau as it should be.

Tiny figures stand out in relief from ornamented pilasters, or from columns supporting canopial niches. Above the doors, we see again—it seems more delicately carved that ever before—the salamander of François beside the ermine of Brittany. Ornaments of every kind surround them and rise around the windows to the castle's roof. The artist seems fairly to have exhausted the delicacy of his chisel, as well as the fancies of his imagination.

The towers on the left are smaller than those upon the right, and they are terminated in what are known in France as "cues de lampes." Three sharply outlined mouldings divide the walls at each story, and the heavy cornices above, in imitation of the "machicoulis" of the Mediæval chateau, run round the edges of the roof like a massive chain. They are broken, here and there, by the heavy windows of the roof, which show in relief against the dark and rusted slates. Although the court below is barren of the orange trees that the eye has learned to expect in so many of the Renaissance chateaux, it is hardly noticeable here. For there is everywhere that charm which is to be found in places where a true artist has assisted nature to fulfil her task, and where the result

would seem to have been fashioned by a fairy's hand. There is nothing to offend the eye. Colors and shades are in harmony one with another. The flowers are of quaint origin, and are those more often to be found in old-fashioned gardens. The parterres and shrubberies are those of a century ago. There is nothing here in tinselled gold, or in a new frame. All is in soft taste. There is neither the overpowering wealth nor the show and the glitter which we find in some places. Here everything is covered with a cloak of mellowness and harmony which time alone has the power to cast over it. There is something which speaks unmistakably of distinction and refinement, something which would never shine too brightly nor be surrounded by too much wealth. Indeed, we might say in conclusion as we gaze at the whole: "Here is something at last which is more than beautiful. Here is something which is almost perfection."

As we cross the threshold of one of the carved oak doors, the staircase appears before us in all its magnificence. It is the "chef d'œuvre" of all the Italian staircases of this epoch. It is better, even, than those of Cour Cheverny and of Chenonceau. These staircases, of which the three mentioned are the best examples, were a novelty in the sixteenth century. They were brought from Italy to take the place of the circular staircases which preceded them. The carving of this at Azay-le-Rideau is especially worthy of our notice. Flowers, fruits, statues, animals, monograms and heraldic emblems are placed everywhere, with a perfect genius of taste in their arrangement.

A butler ushers us into a dining-hall, where the walls are hung with many interesting paintings. These paintings form but a small portion of a large collection. There are in all six hundred and fifty pictures. Two hundred and fifty of these are originals, while the remain-

ing four hundred are good copies. The room is paved in black and white marble, and a great sideboard bearing the name of Jean Goujon almost covers one side of the apartment.

We wander on from one apartment to another, all filled with old furniture of great value—the bed-chambers with their massive four-posted beds, the salons with their pictures and here and there a stone chimney that reminds us of Blois or Chaumont, follow one another in successive interest. We forget, indeed, a faded curtain or a piece of threadbare carpet—the only signs of imperfection in the chateau—in the beauty of their surroundings; the only feeling which survives is one of harmony and refinement.

The Comte soon began to express his satisfaction at what he saw.

"How I enjoy these thick walls and these windows with their lozenges of glass, sometimes beautifully stained in color! They allow only a subdued light to enter or to fall upon these beautiful pictures. It makes one feel at rest after the brilliant restorations of the other chateau. There is something indescribable here, something to be found only in the oldest chateaux. These alone are the embodiment of a true delicacy of taste, and they unconsciously permeate everything about them with its subtle charm, so difficult, so impossible even, to acquire otherwise, and yet so unmistakable when found."

"It seems to me," I replied, still enjoying the details of our surroundings and agreeing with my friend's enthusiasm, "it seems to me that this is true of the conservative element all over the world. Distinction, elegance, breeding, of all of which we are fond and of which historical chateaux and beautiful surroundings are but the offsprings, must be acquired with centuries of blood to add to them. Time and nature must be allowed their hand also. Such things cannot ever be really acquired.

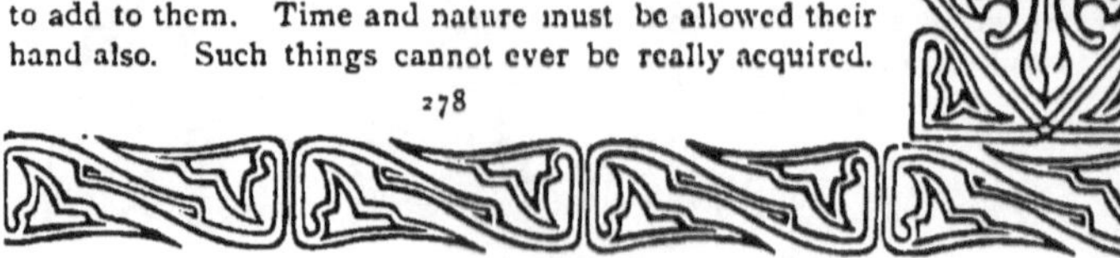

They may be in part, after much labor; but those who strive for them will always find that they lack the very kernel of that of which they would be the whole." And we turned to admire a collection of Clouets in the drawing-room, and to peep out at the view beyond the windows, with their heavy curtains of green velvet, stamped with gold fleurs-de-lis.

To describe the pictures, the enamels, the wood carvings, the library of historical volumes, would alone take up an entire chapter. We may only attempt to enter, and that, even, in a light and somewhat superficial manner, into the atmosphere of this marvelous little chateau of the Renaissance. In brief, let us say that Azay-le-Rideau is one of the very few of the "historical monuments" which, until within a few years, still remained in the hands of its ancient masters. Some chateaux have passed into the hands of the government; others have been bought and restored, in modern taste, by wealthy financiers or foreigners; but a few, like the one before us, have remained as they were originally. They are like reliquaries in which centuries have heaped up their marvels of artistic beauty; and those who have inherited these guard them as the last remains of bygone greatness. And this is why those who love them cling to them also, even as the shipwrecked mariner might to a falling spar. We leave such places with a strange feeling of regret, as if they were to be sold the next year, the next month, as if they might be destroyed and we should never see them again.

Azay-le-Rideau, more, perhaps, than any other of the chateaux of Touraine or its surrounding country, brings to us the life and the atmosphere of bygone days, which still linger through the present century. And with it all there is so much poetry and romance lurking about the architecture, filled with the Italian influence, and its surroundings, less perfect than the chateau itself

but still full of charm, that our fancy is drawn to it irresistibly.

As we leave the chateau behind us and walk out into the park, across stone bridges and by the river that is here smooth as a mirror and there rushing along at head-long pace, I am tempted to tell my companion of the impressions made upon me by Azay-le-Rideau.

"The park would seem to be scarcely in keeping with the chateau and its gardens," I say to the Comte; "it seems almost level, and rather small."

"It is indeed," my friend replies. "But this beautiful little river, which we have accompanied so long and which runs across it like so many winding paths, gives it a freshness that is almost like an eternal spring."

"It seems to be filled with people, as if its master were very hospitable," I add.

"Yes; it is open to all the inhabitants of the village on Sunday afternoon; and they are allowed to wander amongst the flowers, as if they belonged to them. No one would ever touch one. They regard them as almost sacred, so that these privileges are enjoyed by them without abuse. And toward sunset, if one were to pass through the walks and alleys on the way home after a quiet stroll, a single form might be seen walking quietly near the chateau. It is that of an elderly gentle-man of dignified appearance. He wears a martial air, as if he were an officer, a soldier. He seems inter-ested in everything. Often he turns to look back at the chateau. He glances at its lofty towers with their grace-ful finishings in 'cues-de-lampes.' Two of them have been lately repaired and seem especially to attract his attention. Now he pauses to inspect with a lover's eye the beds of flowers and the trees. He seems anxious that all should be in order.

"There is no one with him. He is attended only by a terrier, or bull-dog, which he calls often to his side, as if for company. And as the peasants pass him by they bow respectfully; for it is 'Monsieur le Marquis,' and they are very fond of him.* Living alone in the great chateau, he has bestowed upon it the love and the wealth of an artist and a father. When he inherited it from his own father and great-grandfather, the interior was almost bare. But year after year of taste and care have made it, at last, a perfect museum of artistic and historical ornaments."

How long we remained thus gossiping about the chateau before us, I cannot say. But the garden bench was so comfortable and the babble of the water behind us so musical in its passing notes, that we lingered intoxicated by the beauty of this exquisite picture.

"In the midst of it all, however," I exclaimed, "one cannot but think of the uncertain fate of such a chateau in France. In another generation even, a fortune which now keeps it what it is may be divided, and then, what may become of it we cannot say. It may be sold. The lands may be cut up. And if the estate should be a large one, the chateau, as you say, often goes for little or nothing. It goes, and perhaps into the hands of those who are unworthy of possessing such a jewel or such an heritage."

"Come, let us go," said the Comte, rising. "Let us leave, while the pleasure of looking at anything so beautiful as Azay-le-Rideau is still fresh within us. Let us enjoy it as it is, and not cloud the moment by thinking of what it may be in a few years. There is a little chateau, not far from here, where de Balzac used to live; and we must visit it before we leave the town."

So we wandered out through the court of honor, over the vine-grown bridge, beneath the avenue of horse-chest-

---

nut trees, out again to the road; and the curtain had risen and fallen upon Azay-le-Rideau.

The same afternoon—it was the 15th of August, I remember, the feast of the Assumption, and one of the four great holidays of France—we started out on our walk to the little chateau of Saché. It is situated in a pleasant country about four miles from Azay. This piece of information we received from the master of the hotel, a jolly little man, not unlike a pudding in appearance, whose neck had long since disappeared between an apoplectic-looking pair of shoulders. As we started out, we amused ourselves in speculating how long it would be before his whole head was telescoped by his body. For the process seemed not unlikely.

The little town of Saché is built, like Azay, upon the edge of a hill overlooking the river. Its only street winds up a rather steep incline, and the entrance to the "gentilhommière"—it could scarcely be called a chateau—is perched upon a turning of the road. Opposite to it stands the church, which is a good fragment of Romanesque architecture. As we approached, the bells were ringing merrily, answering one another, whispering, singing and talking; now in solo, now in a duet, as loud as they both could peal. The vespers were but just over, and the last of the procession could be seen marching through the street. White silk banners, embroidered with gold, waved and glittered in the air. At a distance they seemed like swans beating their wings. Four little girls, dressed in white and crowned with roses, held tightly the ribbons of the banners. And as I looked at them their faces were filled with a childish pride and joy; I could not help thinking of the angels about the Virgin of Murillo. Following these came a group of boys holding a red velvet banner, also embroidered in gold. After these came the whole village, two by two, and the

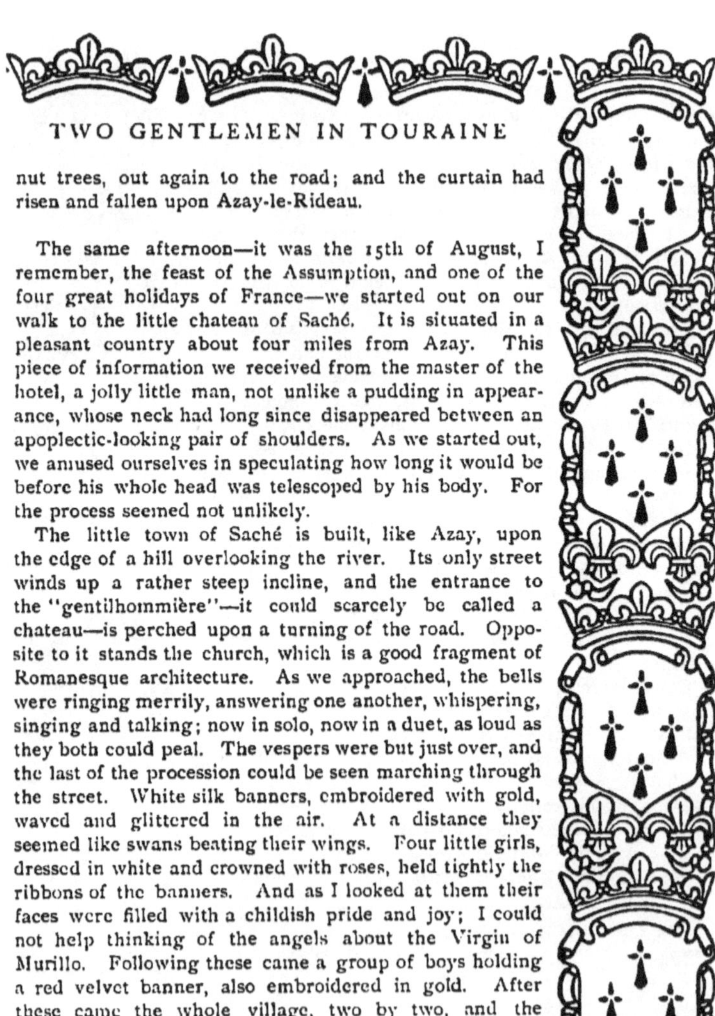

"chantres" in white surplices and the choir boys in red and white, and lastly the Curé, his gray locks flowing down to his robes of white and gold. The litany of the Virgin was being sung, and the bells were joining their voices to those of the village. A long line of devout Catholics wound on, down the hill, like an undulating stream that catches the colors of the rainbow and the sky, singing an unknown song as it rushes over pebbles and stones, or silent as it is lost in groves and gardens.

Saché is of no importance whatever in itself. But its situation is charming, and there is a rustic peace about the building and its park, which attracts the gentler side of one's nature. There is also the interest which the home of Balzac must necessarily gather about itself. In this garden, perhaps where we stand, he has probably reposed and gained inspiration from the view. Within these almost ruined walls, shaded by trees and ivy, he has written some of his most famous works. Yonder in the valley he must have wandered, surely. No one could resist it long. And how often must he have explored the creeks and dells beyond, or strayed by moonlight to a shady nook where a tiny waterfall gushes from a silvery spring down upon some moss-grown stones! We can almost follow the man in his walks, and realize the peaceful life which he must have loved so well after the busy round of Paris.

Far above, in an upper story overlooking all that we have just seen, there is a window. Jasmine grows upon its sash and sends its light perfume to the room within. A winding stair of well-worn stone leads to it. We mount it and discover a little room scarcely nine feet wide. The four-post bed and its yellow curtains are as they were during his life. He himself has passed away; but his brain has left a legacy behind. A small table opposite the window and two chairs were enough for Balzac; for he lived wholly in his dreams.

It is said that once he bought a piece of land near Paris, on a hillside, at an angle of thirty-five degrees. The house upon it could scarcely have been called a pavilion; but Balzac, in his imagination, created of it a chateau. The walls of the dining-room were of simple plaster; but upon them was written in lead-pencil the following inscription: "A superb tapestry from Flanders—a Titian— a Rubens—a beautifully carved side-board." And in the garden the rocks and pebbles were transformed by the same method into cascades, or grottoes. The paths were marked out by small stakes driven into the ground, and the green-houses were drawn upon paper.

His room at Saché was the humble shelter of a great imagination, and the genius of the man has made the place in itself great.

As we left the chamber where so many hours of this great life had been spent in the creation of those characters which were to immortalize it, I turned to the Comte and congratulated him upon the happy suggestion which had brought us here.

"Yes, indeed," said he, "it is a sensation of respect which causes us to linger at the haunts of past poets, or writers of imagery and romance. And we are the more impressed, I think, at every one of these, by the sanctity which time has conferred upon those who have created, as it were, from their own substance a fame which may not be taken from them. Stones and mortar may crumble into dust, trees and flowers die, and nature and her surroundings change. Our physical bodies may even disappear; and nothing really lives after us but the soul, with the mind's expression of its own. The tiny chateau which is now fading behind us in the distance seems to me to bring out this fact more clearly at every step."

"You are doubtless right," said I, and as we turned a corner of the road the home of Balzac disappeared from our view.

CHAPTER XIII

USSÉ

The most convenient way—indeed, the only way, and
not a very comfortable way at that—of going to the
chateau of Rigny-Ussé from Azay is to drive.

If you are stopping at the "Hôtel du Grand Monarch"
the master of the establishment will supply you with a
"charette anglaise," thinking to please you. But
beware of the "charette anglaise." Those who value
comfort and who are not in possession of a lurking desire
—as some unfortunates are—of having their teeth jolted
out of the head, should eschew this means of conveyance.
The horse, indeed, may be a good one; but he will be too
small for the shafts. No horse, however large, could
possibly fill so vast an area. You will start off, however,
in spite of difficulties. And with every movement of the
cart your jovial driver will be jostled against you like a
large bolster, as you sit three on a seat. The whole
affair is innocent of springs, and with every step of the
horse it shakes from side to side, as if to rid itself of a
burden plainly disagreeable to it. Added to this, the
ruts of the road have been cut into deep furrows, so that
their surface is more like that of a plowed field than of a
public thoroughfare. The mud is hardened by the
August sun, and this does not, indeed, add to the pleasure
of your drive.

As we drove along one afternoon in such a manner as I
have described, we discovered the reason for this condition of the roads, a condition so unusual in a country

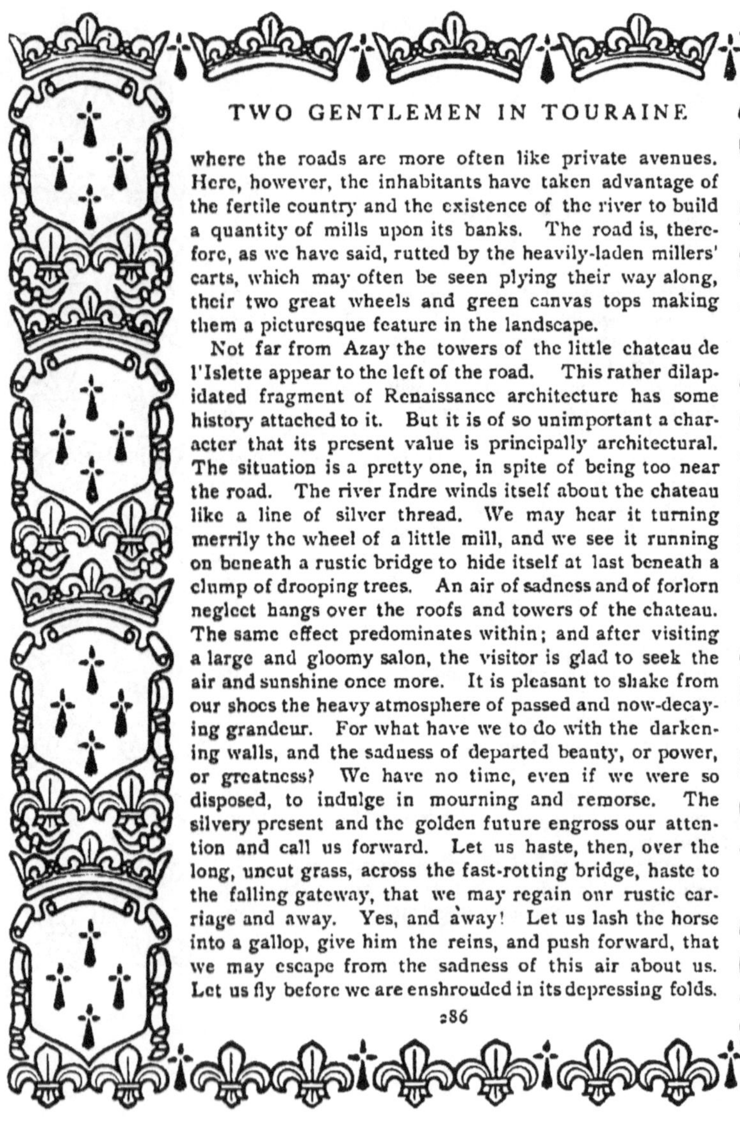

where the roads are more often like private avenues.
Here, however, the inhabitants have taken advantage of
the fertile country and the existence of the river to build
a quantity of mills upon its banks. The road is, therefore, as we have said, rutted by the heavily-laden millers'
carts, which may often be seen plying their way along,
their two great wheels and green canvas tops making
them a picturesque feature in the landscape.

Not far from Azay the towers of the little chateau de
l'Islette appear to the left of the road. This rather dilap-
idated fragment of Renaissance architecture has some
history attached to it. But it is of so unimportant a character that its present value is principally architectural.
The situation is a pretty one, in spite of being too near
the road. The river Indre winds itself about the chateau
like a line of silver thread. We may hear it turning
merrily the wheel of a little mill, and we see it running
on beneath a rustic bridge to hide itself at last beneath a
clump of drooping trees. An air of sadness and of forlorn
neglect hangs over the roofs and towers of the chateau.
The same effect predominates within; and after visiting
a large and gloomy salon, the visitor is glad to seek the
air and sunshine once more. It is pleasant to shake from
our shoes the heavy atmosphere of passed and now-decay-
ing grandeur. For what have we to do with the darken-
ing walls, and the sadness of departed beauty, or power,
or greatness? We have no time, even if we were so
disposed, to indulge in mourning and remorse. The
silvery present and the golden future engross our attention and call us forward. Let us haste, then, over the
long, uncut grass, across the fast-rotting bridge, haste to
the falling gateway, that we may regain our rustic carriage and away. Yes, and away! Let us lash the horse
into a gallop, give him the reins, and push forward, that
we may escape from the sadness of this air about us.
Let us fly before we are enshrouded in its depressing folds.

Cast not a look behind, lest the scene now past should kill the enthusiasm which we yet retain in contemplation of the future!

L'Islette, with its grass-grown walks and weeping trees, fades into the mist behind us, and we ride on, through the long lines of poplars, over the green fields and hills, until at last we see the towers of Ussé in the distant scene. The road runs by the side of a slope. It seems to bound forward, almost, if one may imagine such a thing. As we follow it the motion of our cart is far from pleasing. We pass through a village where the inhabitants are busy threshing the newly-cut wheat, for it is harvest time. Great stacks line the road, and the neighbors have been gathered together in numbers in order to lend their assistance. The machine is puffing vigorously, frightening the horses with its noise, and throwing out the wheat ready to be placed in bags. The peasants tie the straw into bundles for other uses, and as the whole scene passes by, it leaves its own picturesque impression upon the mind. On the right the valley grows wider as it joins that of the Loire, and beyond it the two rivers meet and continue upon their course together. From the surrounding hills a number of chateaux look down upon the wedded waters, and lend to them their dignity. "Rochecotte," a beautiful though modern chateau, rises out of the trees upon the distant hillside. "Villandry," full of majesty and grace, seems to lie against terraces cut into the cliff. In the midst of green vineyards and flower-covered gardens, the little town of Langeais shows its smiling face, crowned by its jeweled castle. In the distance the towers of St. Gatien, the cathedral of Tours, rise against a blue horizon. Even from here we realize the truth of Henry IV's saying, that they needed needle cases, almost, to protect the delicacy of their details. The ruins of Cinq-Mars, upon the left, are speaking

remains of Richelieu's terrible vengeance; and we recall with sad interest the unhappy end of the famous "Monsieur le Grand," with his short reign of glory at the court of Louis XIII. Finally, as we look southward toward the beautiful forest of Chinon, a number of white towers and pointed spires lighted by the sun rise out of their green clusters like a brilliant flower. We look at them again, and as they appear more clearly we see that this is the fairy-like chateau of Ussé.

We draw up at an entrance opening upon the street of the Bourg, and hand our cards to a venerable looking "concierge."

Monsieur le Comte is away, but we are at liberty to visit the whole chateau under the guardianship of an intelligent housekeeper, whose politeness and interest might serve as an example to many above her station. The avenue turns sharply to the right, and mounts the eminence upon which the castle stands overlooking the valley and hills. Like many others, it is built upon three sides of a square; but the symmetry is broken by a long wing extending to the right along the front. The avenue runs over a bridge for the entire length of the façade, opening into the courtyard and ending under a great canopy of trees at the entrance to the park. A balustrade protects the pedestrian from the dangers of a high wall forming part of the ancient fortifications of Ussé, and beneath it is a terrace, laid out in "jardins-à-la-français." Shrubs and orange trees, with flowers and boxes, make this one of the most beautiful parterres to be seen. Another terrace still divides this from the road, upon the other side of which the dark waters of the Indre run like a living avenue of silvery substance.

The donjon tower of Ussé dates back to the fifteenth century. But the rest of the chateau, as it stands to-day, was rebuilt by Vauban, a famous engineer and "Maréchal" under Louis XIV. Perhaps, however, it

would be more correct to say that Ussé was reconstructed
in the sixteenth century, and elaborately ornamented and
improved by Vauban, to whom is due the beautiful
chamber of Louis XIV, overlooking the courtyard.
Vauban did much to improve the chateau and its surroundings, and his daughter lived there for some time
with her husband, Louis II of Valentinay. Certain
details in the façade are worthy of more than our casual
admiration. The whole gallery at the back of the courtyard is a good example of Gothic architecture. Its walls
are flanked by flat buttresses. They reach to the roofs
and end there in beautifully ornamented points of stone,
so common in all Gothic detail, reminding one of the
chapels of that period, both in France and England. The
best portion of the wing upon the left is a lantern or
open cupola, delicately carved in stone, and it would
scarcely be excessive praise to call this little ornament
upon the roof of the great chateau a "chef-d'œuvre." It
stands against the sky, like a great bell, and its graceful
contour is in keeping with the gallery itself.

A great deal of Gothic detail has crept into the architecture at Ussé, so much, indeed, that it plays no small
part in the general effect. The stone windows of the
roof are rich in those points and darkened crevices in
which the Gothic art so delights to clothe itself. Tiny
minarets and jeweled tops surmount the roofs, the towers
and the topmost spires. In its effect the whole chateau
is immense. The two towers of the back rise out of a
forest of spiral roofs, smaller towers, projecting bays and
buttresses. They combine to form a noble pile, too hard
perhaps in its coloring,—like so many other French
buildings,—but yet fair to look upon as a mass, and
interesting to study, if only for its size and shape. One
tower reminds us of "la Tour des Anglais," at Chenonceau. Its massive cornice is carried on around the
exterior walls of the castle, although it is not included

in the façades of the court. Here the cornice is cut off abruptly, and it is continued upon the other side, as if the court had been originally enclosed by a fourth side, now eliminated.

The principal entrance, instead of being placed in the centre of this court, is upon its right-hand side, and it is of unpretentious aspect. It leads into a square central hall, lined with white stone, and chiefly ornamented by a great square staircase. In its decorations, though simple almost to barrenness, this hall with its staircase is nevertheless one of the most beautiful and striking bits of the interior. Its strong contrast to that at Azay-le-Rideau; the exceeding purity of its white stones, enhanced by their only relief—a railing of black iron-work; each plays its share in this excellent example of "beauty unadorned, adorned the most." Guide books and itineraries tell of a beautiful painting hung here and attributed to Michel Angelo. It is invisible, however, to the eye, and the walls remain in maiden purity, undisturbed by any works of art.

Let us ascend this massive staircase that re-echoes our every footstep. It leads to the apartments of a bygone king. A gallery opens upon the left, out of the first landing. It is worth looking into, for it has been well repaired and the Gothic vaultings, ever of white stone, are relieved by family escutcheons, brilliant in their heraldic colors.

Our guide seemed an intelligent woman, and inclined to tell us something of the chateau and its life.

"Monsieur le Comte* spends a great deal of time and money in repairing Ussé," she began, as we were speaking of the condition of the gallery. "He is continually doing something, either to the outside or to the interior. Ces messieurs cannot imagine how much there is to do in so large and so old a chateau. The

* The Chateau of Ussé is owned by the Comte de Blaccas.

stone is so soft everywhere that it must be patched or
repaired constantly. Steps wear out with surprising
rapidity. Window-caps fall down; even towers crack, so
that it is necessary for them to be entirely rebuilt. Ah,
monsieur, it is indeed no joke to keep up a great chateau
in France! At Azay-le-Rideau they have much harder
work, even, than we have; but all is in perfect condition there now. Ces messieurs have been there, of
course?"

"Yes. In fact, we had just come from it this afternoon." My companion sympathized with our guide in
the cares incumbent upon the owner of a chateau. He
doubtless spoke from bitter experience.

As we came out of the gallery our attendant added:
"The next room of interest is the apartment of Louis
XIV."

We waited while she closed doors and opened others.

"The room which we are going to see," said my friend,
"was built by Vauban with this portion of the chateau
to receive Louis XIV. It is naturally the most beautiful
and interesting part."

As he spoke we entered an ante-chamber, decorated
with painted wood, and hung with mirrors. Had it been
well furnished this would have been a beautiful room;
but, unfortunately, it was left barren of such things as
chairs or tables. Two large doors on either side of the
opposite wall led into the royal chamber. It would be
difficult to imagine a more exquisitely appointed, a more
truly appropriate room than this, built that "le Grand
Monarch" might rest but a single night. Its taste
and its correctness in design are striking examples of
the luxury and extravagance during the reign of Louis
XIV. Here was a room, an apartment, indeed the whole
third of a castle, erected expressly to receive a royal
visitor. It took, doubtless, a year or more to prepare it,
and the royal pleasure dismissed it in a single day. But

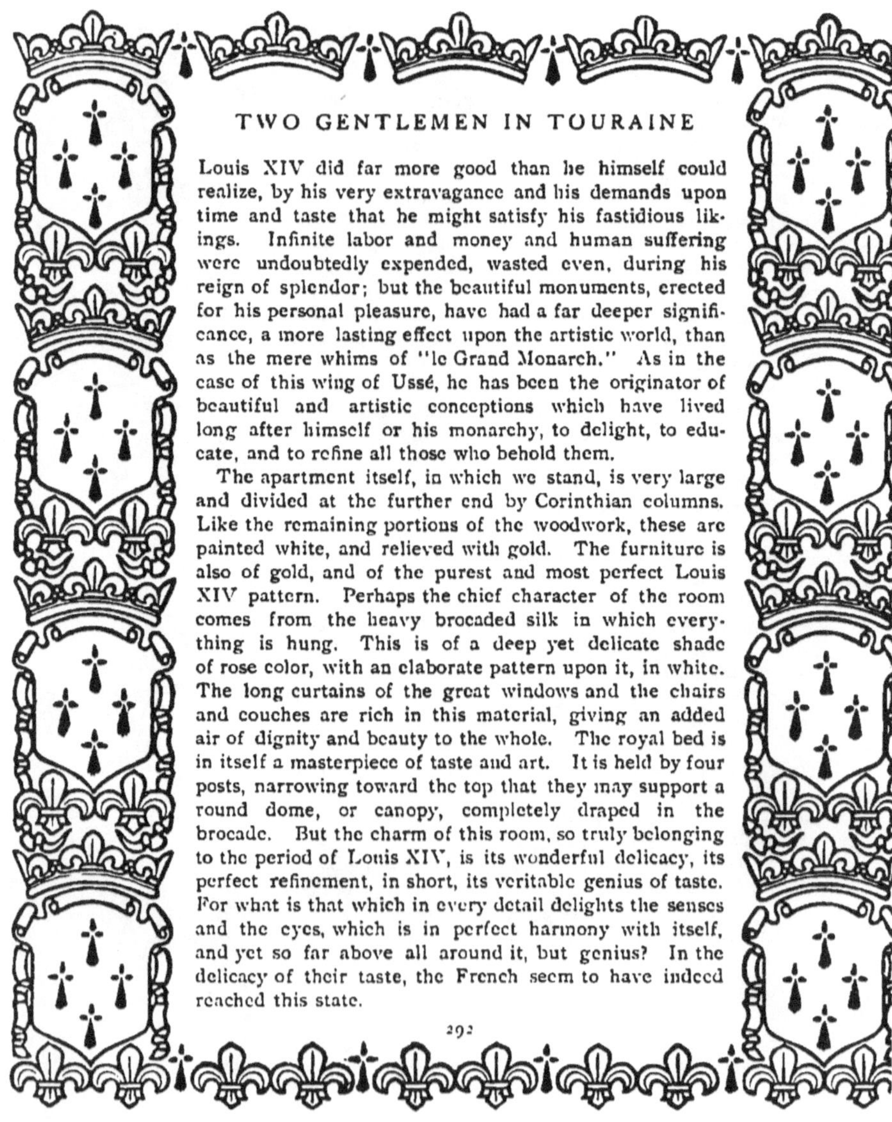

Louis XIV did far more good than he himself could realize, by his very extravagance and his demands upon time and taste that he might satisfy his fastidious likings. Infinite labor and money and human suffering were undoubtedly expended, wasted even, during his reign of splendor; but the beautiful monuments, erected for his personal pleasure, have had a far deeper significance, a more lasting effect upon the artistic world, than as the mere whims of "le Grand Monarch." As in the case of this wing of Ussé, he has been the originator of beautiful and artistic conceptions which have lived long after himself or his monarchy, to delight, to educate, and to refine all those who behold them.

The apartment itself, in which we stand, is very large and divided at the further end by Corinthian columns. Like the remaining portions of the woodwork, these are painted white, and relieved with gold. The furniture is also of gold, and of the purest and most perfect Louis XIV pattern. Perhaps the chief character of the room comes from the heavy brocaded silk in which everything is hung. This is of a deep yet delicate shade of rose color, with an elaborate pattern upon it, in white. The long curtains of the great windows and the chairs and couches are rich in this material, giving an added air of dignity and beauty to the whole. The royal bed is in itself a masterpiece of taste and art. It is held by four posts, narrowing toward the top that they may support a round dome, or canopy, completely draped in the brocade. But the charm of this room, so truly belonging to the period of Louis XIV, is its wonderful delicacy, its perfect refinement, in short, its veritable genius of taste. For what is that which in every detail delights the senses and the eyes, which is in perfect harmony with itself, and yet so far above all around it, but genius? In the delicacy of their taste, the French seem to have indeed reached this state.

USSE

The view from the large window at the end of the room
and its iron balcony is one which, if we saw it in a picture, we would say could not exist, for it would be
too fairy-like.   It is one which exists only in soft dreams,
until we have seen it.   A marble basin filled with water-
lilies lies at our feet, as if waiting for the king to step
upon it.   Flower-covered terraces fall, one below the
other, beneath it.   The river beyond shines like a collection of numberless crystals, as we look down.   For once,
it has ceased to be dark and sad.   The distant scene—
how shall we describe it?   A Greuze, a Poussin could
alone paint it, as it unfolds its faint mysteries to the wondering imagination!

The other windows of the room look out upon the
architecture of the chateau's court.   And as we stand in
these elevating surroundings a thrill of pleasure darts
through the whole frame.   Under such circumstances as
these, life should indeed be pleasant!

The Comte must have been indulging in much the
same opinion as myself.   He was evidently of the latter
class, judging from the sudden remark which he now
made.   He broke in upon my thoughts, taking them up
almost as if I had uttered them aloud.

"And yet I doubt," said he, as we stood admiring the
surrounding picture, "I doubt if the present master of
Ussé is as happy as we are.   The glitter and the first
appearance of such things as we are looking at must ever
be filled with charm, and we are wont to think that all is
a fairy-like reality.   But the moment that we push aside
the surface, and look beneath it, then do we find things
which are far from fairy-like in all life.   This is a sad
truth from which we may not escape, and we find it even
in those who seem to possess the greatest things for
which to live."

It took me some moments to appreciate the mood
into which my friend had thrown himself.   I myself had

hardly felt inclined to analyze or to dissect the actual reality of what I had seen. But finding that he was doing so, I thought a moment, and then said: "If you are determined to moralize in this strain, it seems to me enough to be thankful for to have so beautiful an exterior as Ussé. Few people have even as much as this to boast of. Few are there, gifted with a smiling face to hide an aching heart. Few have the marble staircase even, though it may lead but to an empty chamber.

"If life might once ring true; if we might only find, beneath the beautiful exterior, the longed-for beauty that is so seldom there, then would we know a fairy paradise such as truth only may create. But, alas, all our jewels seem to possess a flaw. All our images are tarnished and imperfect. All beauty seems but skin deep."

"It has often seemed to me," rejoined the Comte, "that since this is so, we should be happier to live a life which many would stamp as shallow. To deal only in the surface matter, to live in a continuous sphere of light-heartedness and gentle glamour, to limit oneself to the charms of polite acquaintances, would be more philosophical than we are sometimes willing to acknowledge."

"Your remark sounds very pessimistic as it falls upon the ear," I replied; "but I cannot deny that there is a certain truth in what you say. If we all lived such a life as you suggest, we would lose many of the joys of intimate friendship, as well as much of our experience of human nature. But on the other hand, we would save ourselves many trials, and often much unnecessary sorrow."

The Comte held to his theory, his "shallow theory," as he called it.

"A man who is wise," said he, "will seldom try to burrow deeper than the surface, for his wisdom will have taught him that every one has something displeasing

underneath, some trouble, some misfortune, some private sorrow which it were better for him not to know. For, if ignorant of it, he may keep a countenance more fit to cheer than if he is loaded down with another's grief, added to his own. A cheerful countenance and a light heart do more good than a thousand mourning friends, however full of sympathy or pity they may be."

By this time we had descended to the drawing-room, and we left our argument behind us in the royal apartments.

"Is the chamber ever used to-day?" I had asked, as the door was closing behind us.

"Not often, monsieur," was the reply, "only when some very great lady comes for a visit."

As we descended the grand staircase the housekeeper continued:

"No, messieurs; the room is not used much nowadays, although it is always open. As you may imagine, ladies are pleased to have it, when they come to stay. . . . Monsieur le Comte's apartments are on the other side of the courtyard. That is his private entrance," said she, pointing to a little door close to the ground. "He must either cross the court, or pass through the long gallery at the back, to reach this drawing-room where we are now standing. Ah, the old chateaux are not always as convenient as the new ones, messieurs."

We lingered for a moment where we were to admire some old portraits hanging upon the walls. We then passed through a gallery similar to the one above, and entered the private library. This apartment was one of the most perfect little rooms of its kind that we had yet seen, and we stopped to examine some Gothic carving over the doors. A long suite of apartments led one into another beyond; but they were of too private a nature to be described here. For some time we wandered through them, seeing many things of interest, and

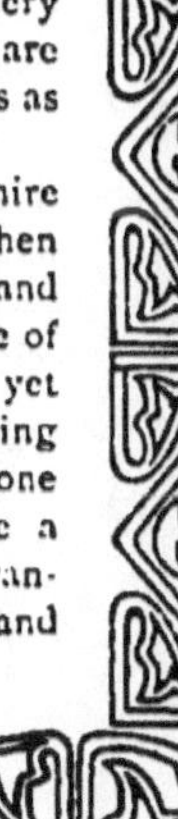

breathing in the atmosphere of Ussé. But in spite of white stones, of flowers, and the sunlight outside, in spite of historical and artistic ornament within, that old air of melancholy and tristesse which we had learned to know so well in many of these ancient monuments of France, thrust itself again upon us here. There was no ignoring its existence, although we endeavored to throw it off by conversation.

We were standing in the dining-room of the chateau at that particular moment, and commenting upon its size. It looked incongruous, we were obliged to own, and out of keeping with the dignity around it. As I expressed surprise at its smallness, my friend remarked that there would be no use for a larger one.

"How strange it seems," said I, "to find a vast chateau such as this, with which so little life is apparently connected! I can never cease to feel the want of this in most of the places that we have visited. It seems to me, with such a place as this, that my first idea would be to fill each room, each corner of it, with guests and brilliancy; to dot each terrace, each parterre with beauty, with birth and breeding; to surround this table here with an intellectual company that would do it honor. And even with this, one would ask for more, for art, for interest, for beauty, noblesse—life, in short."

"Ah," replied my friend, "you paint a most attractive picture; but I fear that you will not find so brilliant a one among all the galleries of the French chateaux to-day. Such pictures were realities in other days. Now they are but food for the imagination.

"That systematic hospitality which is so large a part of English country life you will fail to find in France. The more that you live among French people, the more you will be impressed by their lack of entertaining, their lack, even, of the desire for it when it is possible. There is this, however, to be taken into account, that it is not

often possible to entertain largely in a French chateau. To begin with, the accommodations are frequently limited. Feudal fortifications and towers were constructed more for exterior defense than for their interior convenience. In the largest chateaux there are often but few spare rooms. The French nobility are as a rule comparatively poor, for the expense entailed upon a large estate leaves but a narrow margin to an income. Many people have taken advantage of this fact to retire to their chateaux, where they live almost in seclusion for a large portion of the year. They receive but little, and visit still less. As years go on, they seem to become even less sociable than before. They occupy themselves with the internal management of their estates, living almost entirely in their family circle and playing but a minor part in the national community. It is no wonder, then, that the community shows the effect of such apathy upon the part of those who should be stationed toward the front. There is little wonder that politics fall in their tone and standing, that bourgeois taste and principles predominate, and that half the salons of the Champs Elysées are filled with those who have but little title to their places."

"But, at least," said I, somewhat taken aback by this sudden outburst on the part of the Comte, "there is the Faubourg St. Germain, with the prestige of its ancienne noblesse, that holds its place untouched by outward changes to society, and represents all that is best of the old régime."

"Yes, to be sure," he assented; "but it seems to contract more and more, to retire, as it were, into a shell which may not be penetrated, and to surround itself with a halo of disdain, instead of coming forward and playing the part that it should.

"Indeed, it is scarcely to be wondered at," he continued, "that our aristocracy has lost its relative stand-

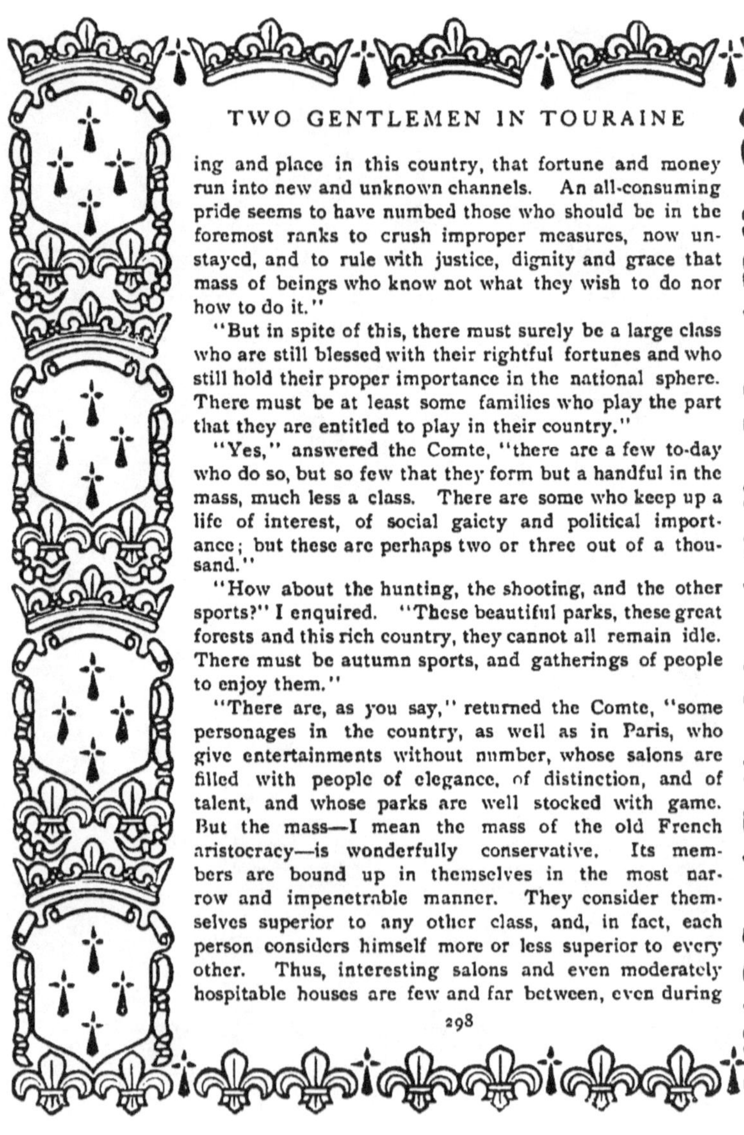

ing and place in this country, that fortune and money run into new and unknown channels. An all-consuming pride seems to have numbed those who should be in the foremost ranks to crush improper measures, now unstayed, and to rule with justice, dignity and grace that mass of beings who know not what they wish to do nor how to do it."

"But in spite of this, there must surely be a large class who are still blessed with their rightful fortunes and who still hold their proper importance in the national sphere. There must be at least some families who play the part that they are entitled to play in their country."

"Yes," answered the Comte, "there are a few to-day who do so, but so few that they form but a handful in the mass, much less a class. There are some who keep up a life of interest, of social gaiety and political importance; but these are perhaps two or three out of a thousand."

"How about the hunting, the shooting, and the other sports?" I enquired. "These beautiful parks, these great forests and this rich country, they cannot all remain idle. There must be autumn sports, and gatherings of people to enjoy them."

"There are, as you say," returned the Comte, "some personages in the country, as well as in Paris, who give entertainments without number, whose salons are filled with people of elegance, of distinction, and of talent, and whose parks are well stocked with game. But the mass—I mean the mass of the old French aristocracy—is wonderfully conservative. Its members are bound up in themselves in the most narrow and impenetrable manner. They consider themselves superior to any other class, and, in fact, each person considers himself more or less superior to every other. Thus, interesting salons and even moderately hospitable houses are few and far between, even during

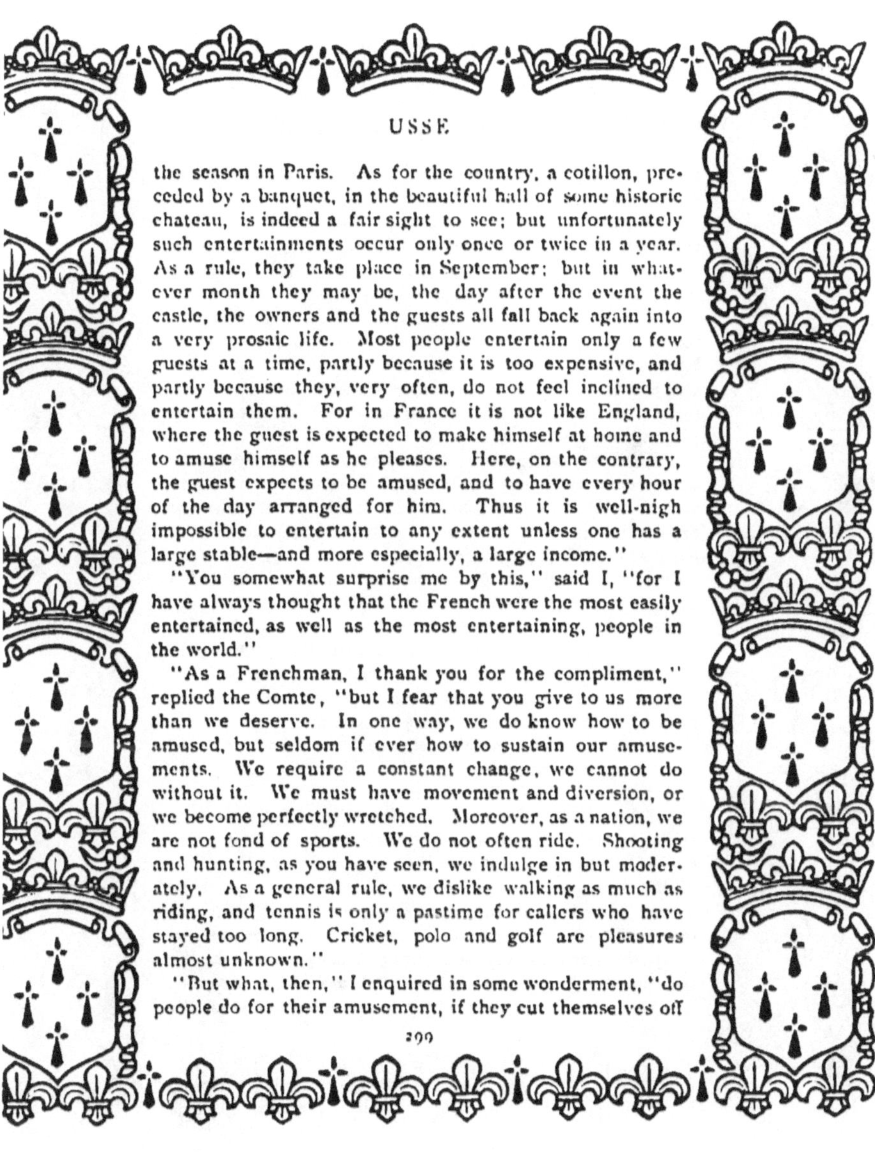

the season in Paris. As for the country, a cotillon, preceded by a banquet, in the beautiful hall of some historic chateau, is indeed a fair sight to see; but unfortunately such entertainments occur only once or twice in a year. As a rule, they take place in September; but in whatever month they may be, the day after the event the castle, the owners and the guests all fall back again into a very prosaic life. Most people entertain only a few guests at a time, partly because it is too expensive, and partly because they, very often, do not feel inclined to entertain them. For in France it is not like England, where the guest is expected to make himself at home and to amuse himself as he pleases. Here, on the contrary, the guest expects to be amused, and to have every hour of the day arranged for him. Thus it is well-nigh impossible to entertain to any extent unless one has a large stable—and more especially, a large income."

"You somewhat surprise me by this," said I, "for I have always thought that the French were the most easily entertained, as well as the most entertaining, people in the world."

"As a Frenchman, I thank you for the compliment," replied the Comte, "but I fear that you give to us more than we deserve. In one way, we do know how to be amused, but seldom if ever how to sustain our amusements. We require a constant change, we cannot do without it. We must have movement and diversion, or we become perfectly wretched. Moreover, as a nation, we are not fond of sports. We do not often ride. Shooting and hunting, as you have seen, we indulge in but moderately. As a general rule, we dislike walking as much as riding, and tennis is only a pastime for callers who have stayed too long. Cricket, polo and golf are pleasures almost unknown."

"But what, then," I enquired in some wonderment, "do people do for their amusement, if they cut themselves off

from all those diversions upon which other nations are so dependent?"

"You will scarcely believe me when I tell you that most of the days are spent within doors, playing at bezique," returned my friend, in amusement. "Indeed, bezique is such an engrossing occupation in the chateau life that it is with the greatest difficulty guests are torn away from it even to attend mass upon Sunday. I have seen many ladies, who after a week's stay at a chateau in the midst of summer weather, had not been once into the park or the garden, so busy were they playing bezique.

"The very suggestion of a picnic is the signal for an internal thunderstorm, which breaks often with some violence upon those concerned. Each guest raises a separate objection. One finds it too damp, another too dry; and a third dislikes déjeuner on the grass. One lady is accustomed to change her knife and fork at every course—a thing almost unheard of! Of course, the hostess has not enough picnic forks to go round under such circumstances, or at least she thinks so. One gentleman is upon crutches, and yet will not remain behind. An old lady is too feeble to go, and yet cannot be left at home. Some shrink at the very idea of meeting a spider, while others dread possible mosquitoes. And, worst of all, the lady of the house has but one idea, that of seeing the whole plan fall through.

"If by chance the picnic—this ill-fated picnic—does take place, the family coach, drawn by an endless number of horses, is needed to carry apparently the whole dining-hall, chairs and tables included, to the appointed place. The gentleman upon crutches inevitably hits his foot against a tree and loses both his balance and his temper. The old lady, who has decided to come at the last moment, has by an unguarded movement dropped her salad on her dress and becomes inconsolable for the

CHAPEL OF THE CHÂTEAU D'USSÉ

rest of the day. She is at last packed into the coach with her fellow-sufferer, the gentleman upon crutches. And so, you see, " the Comte concluded, with a smile, "that chateau life is, after all, not all it is claimed to be."

"Yes," said I, "It is just as well to keep to the outside of life, for your description convinces me that it is often more attractive than the interior."

"Sometimes," rejoined my friend, taking my arm and walking toward the terrace, "sometimes, indeed, we see a golden surface which is not gilded but is really gold beneath. But often, far more often, we find that it is merely superficial."

We continued to walk away from the chateau, and a few steps brought us to a piece of open ground in front of the private chapel of Ussé. This building is certainly not the least of its many beauties. It is supposed to have been built by Jacques d'Espinay, who owned the chateau in 1480. In 1538 Jacques d'Espinay, the second, founded in the chapel a collegiate of eight canons. This probably accounts for its size, which is far greater than that of most private chapels. It leads us to suspect, at once, some historical association, for it assumes almost the importance of a church. As it stands to-day it is a beautiful little church of the Renaissance period, the ensemble of whose construction joins with the delicacy of its detail, to create an example of architecture that is worthy of admiration. The bas-relief over the door representing the Apostles, is an exceptional piece of carving. And the symmetry of the whole chapel is decidedly, remarkable. What a benefit would it be to the western world if, even for one year, it did but stay the overwhelming tide of emigrants and substitute this for an importation of European architecture!

The chapel, within, has been restored—in fact, it has only recently been completed—and the cold and rather barren walls speak of a severe purity more holy perhaps than

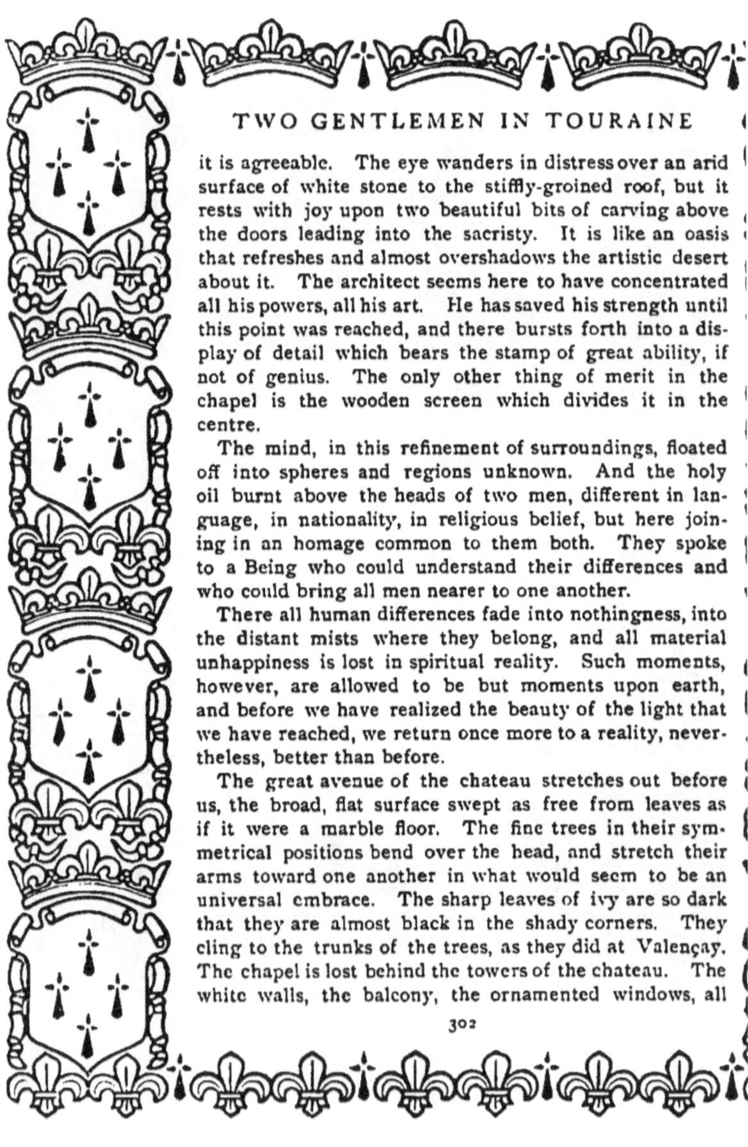

it is agreeable. The eye wanders in distress over an arid surface of white stone to the stiffly-groined roof, but it rests with joy upon two beautiful bits of carving above the doors leading into the sacristy. It is like an oasis that refreshes and almost overshadows the artistic desert about it. The architect seems here to have concentrated all his powers, all his art. He has saved his strength until this point was reached, and there bursts forth into a display of detail which bears the stamp of great ability, if not of genius. The only other thing of merit in the chapel is the wooden screen which divides it in the centre.

The mind, in this refinement of surroundings, floated off into spheres and regions unknown. And the holy oil burnt above the heads of two men, different in language, in nationality, in religious belief, but here joining in an homage common to them both. They spoke to a Being who could understand their differences and who could bring all men nearer to one another.

There all human differences fade into nothingness, into the distant mists where they belong, and all material unhappiness is lost in spiritual reality. Such moments, however, are allowed to be but moments upon earth, and before we have realized the beauty of the light that we have reached, we return once more to a reality, nevertheless, better than before.

The great avenue of the chateau stretches out before us, the broad, flat surface swept as free from leaves as if it were a marble floor. The fine trees in their symmetrical positions bend over the head, and stretch their arms toward one another in what would seem to be an universal embrace. The sharp leaves of ivy are so dark that they are almost black in the shady corners. They cling to the trunks of the trees, as they did at Valençay. The chapel is lost behind the towers of the chateau. The white walls, the balcony, the ornamented windows, all

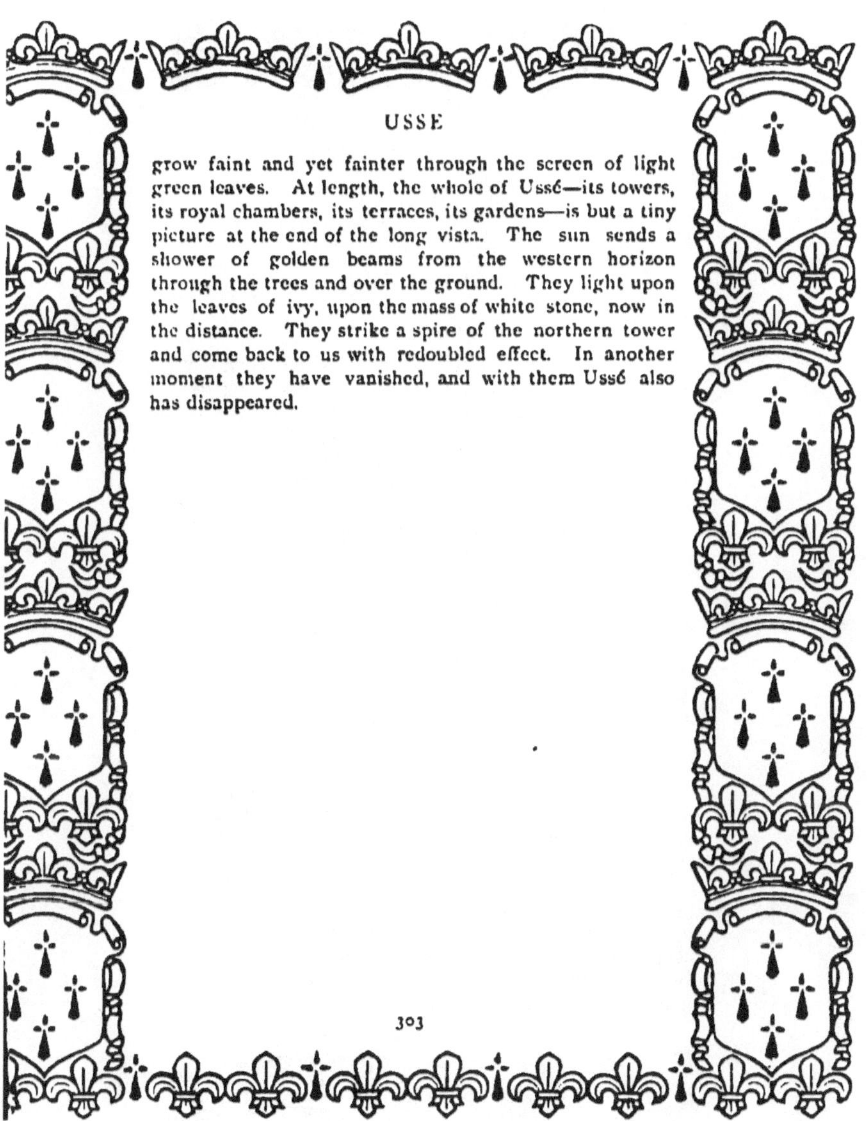

grow faint and yet fainter through the screen of light green leaves. At length, the whole of Ussé—its towers, its royal chambers, its terraces, its gardens—is but a tiny picture at the end of the long vista. The sun sends a shower of golden beams from the western horizon through the trees and over the ground. They light upon the leaves of ivy, upon the mass of white stone, now in the distance. They strike a spire of the northern tower and come back to us with redoubled effect. In another moment they have vanished, and with them Ussé also has disappeared.

CHAPTER XIV

Nothing is more delightful or more invigorating than an autumn morning in France, when the sparkling dew upon every blade of grass catches the rays of the sun and spreads a carpet of crystal drops over the ground.

Let us picture ourselves enjoying just such a day as this, and walking over a beautiful country road from Pontvallain to le Lude. It stretches out before us in a long and whitened line. Now we are winding our way across a newly-plowed field, now cutting the side of a pasture dotted with pink crocuses and surrounded by rough briar hedges. Here and there a pollard rises above the head. We come to a pine forest, fragrant with that peculiar perfume of the needles in the morning air, a perfume, by the way, which makes this country one of the most healthful portions of western France. Some distance further on an open space appears; a field lies to our right, and our road is cut by another at right angles. Near the corner stands a small granite pyramid, surmounted by an iron cross, which is eaten by the rust of centuries and is in keeping with the stone beneath it. From the centre of the cross hangs one of those wreaths, in black and white beads of jet, so common to the French churchyard. No other ornament of any kind adorns this ancient memorial; but at its foot a slate, inserted into the pedestal, bears a long inscription in the French language. My attention was drawn to this rural monument, which looked as if it might possess some interesting story. What the story was it was impossible for

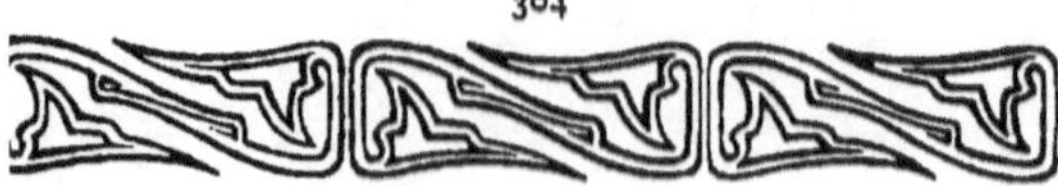

me to say, so I had recourse to the Comte, who never failed in information.

"What," said I, "does this cross mean at the corner of the field? It looks as if it had been forgotten in the midst of the woods."

"Why, that is la Croix Brète," replied the Comte. "I am glad that you asked me, for every one should know about it. It was placed there in 1370 to commemorate the famous battle of Pontvallain, won by the great du Guesclin, and in which the English chief, Thomas Granson, was taken prisoner."

After a last look at the cross and its pedestal, we started to make our way through the forest, while the Comte, forever full of historical facts, and fond of pouring them out, even to the most obtuse, returned to his subject of la Croix Brète.

"Yes, it appears that after the battle (which took place in November and which was a very fierce one), the brave du Guesclin needed a little rest; so he sat down under an old elm tree, and ordered a log cabin to be built near by, where the wounded soldiers could be lodged and properly cared for. In the meantime, his faithful Bretons returned to the battle-field, still stained with the blood of their enemies. They brought back the bodies of the dead, without distinction of nationality, and they buried them in one large grave over which that cross was erected. It has stood there ever since, as you see it to-day, giving to the place the name of Ormeau de la Croix Brète. To-day the field belongs to a family a member of which was one of du Guesclin's companions. Rather an interesting coincidence, is it not?" concluded my friend, as we emerged from the forest on to the summit of a hill which rises far above the valley of the Loire.

The panorama spread before us was certainly worthy of examination. At our feet the road wound down

the hill in many curves, now running between two rustic briar hedges, now along vine-covered slopes, and finally hiding itself beneath us in an avenue of poplar trees. From where we stood they looked like dots of silvery gray in the distant scene, so far below us were they and so persistently did the autumn mist cling to their darkened leaves. Some distance from us, and still in the valley, the slate roofs and the church spire of le Lude, though scarcely visible above the green harmony of trees, denoted the presence of that little town. Close to it and a little to the left, the heavy cornices of four round towers gave evidence of the famous chateau toward which we were directing our steps. The trees of the park behind it sloped down to the river Loire; and there began a scale of many-colored greens which ends in the dark, mysterious forest of the Chateau la Vallière.

There a noisy brook runs at the bottom of a deep vale shrouded by smaller trees. It hurries along, as if anxious to leave its sad surroundings where the ferns and moss grow unmindful of the sun. It runs from one stone to another, skipping over a larger one, or jumping down a tiny rapid on its busy way, talking to itself. It tells of crumbling towers and of time-eaten stones, of the old and beautiful, the ruined and famous chateau of Vaujours. The roofs have fallen in and carried with them the stone entablatures. They have dug large holes here and there, and furrowed the walls with crevices. To-day, upon the shady ground about it, briars and brambles—those rural grave-clothes to the ruined castle—have covered the masses of fast-decaying beams, of broken tiles, of stones and other rubbish with a shroud whose folds of green are filled in with pale pink flowers or black berries. The ivy clings to the remaining walls wherever it may gain a foothold, and this is often all that holds the falling stones together. Between its heavy foliage and the indistinguishable flowers appear the remains of an ornamented window, the carving of a cornice or a gargoyle, grinning at the stranger from above. And when night comes, the death-note of an owl is heard, disputing with the bats and with the midnight wind over the possession of that which long ago was graced by Mademoiselle de la Vallière. For Louis XIV had given this chateau to his first mistress, with the Duché de Vaujours.

Yes, the whole scene is indeed a beautiful one, with its morning lights and evening shades, combined in an artist embrace. The clouds are lighted by the sun, which casts their shadows back upon themselves, and they float swiftly through the sky, giving to all, as they pass in their erratic course over the trees, the rivers and the fields, a darker hue to blend with the surrounding shades. The panorama grows less extended, but more finished, as we descend the hill, to leave behind us, one by one, the windings of the road. We reach the foot at last, and find a hidden avenue beneath the lines of poplar trees, which now escort us up to the very town. Some distance on this avenue discloses a scene, an unexpected scene, making a worthy climax to the whole. A pasture, so large that it is impossible to distinguish its exact proportions, stretches itself suddenly at our feet. The river and the trees behind it cut this enormous pasture upon the right and allow it to extend a mile or so before us. The entire surface is so unbroken that the mossy grass looks to us more than ever like a velvet carpet. At intervals a clump of trees gracefully disturbs the symmetry, and to the left a white wooden fence denotes the paddock of le Lude.

A sharp turn in the road brings one to an old stone bridge whose central arch is well supported by two smaller ones upon the banks of the picturesque Loire. And here again the landscape undergoes a sudden

change. The river flows between two desolate banks
and through a wide and open valley. The hills upon
either side are barren, and the sun pours down its
mid-day rays, untempered even by a tree or house, the
whole effect most unattractive and depressing. Upon
the left, however, the picture which presents itself to
view is very different in its effect. It looks, in fact,
as if the waters, passing beneath the bridge, had under-
gone a metamorphosis in which the scenery had had
its share. The beauties of the park, the high trees growing to the river's edge, the weeping willows that here
stretch their silvery arms, as if to catch a drop or two of
running water, all combine to make this piece of scenery
a gem more beautiful, if possible, by its very contrast.
For nearly a quarter of a mile, and almost upon a level
with the river, there are long lines of flowers like
ribands of a thousand colors. First, a narrow bed of
scarlet geraniums dazzles the eye with its brightness.
Then comes a mass of purple ageratums, grown so
thickly that they present the appearance of one enormous flower. The wax-like surface of the red begonia
looks like a bed of coral over the grass. And added to
this there are large stars of red and white and variegated
flowers, with palm trees in the centre, enhancing, if possible, the beauty of this French parterre. A massive
wall, forming a terrace, rises behind it and creates an
almost ideal background to the jardin a la française.
The soft gray of the stone is relieved by Virginia creepers, already purpled with the cool breath of September.
The vines are clipped and trained into great garlands,
which drape the entire length of the terrace wall, now
wide, now narrow, falling here into a point which ends
in hidden roots, and ending at length in a long, graceful curve. As we look at them the garlands, blown
hither and thither by the wind, seem mysteriously to
play with the rays of the sun.

LE LUDE

We stood some moments upon the bridge, drinking in the beauty of an unrivalled picture. As we leaned over the railing green with moss, the deep waters of the river ran silently beneath us through the long weeds which bent in vain resistance to the current. The trees bowed toward each other from the shaded banks, and upon the left a tiny canal wound through the foliage to a small tannery behind. The romance and the rural poetry of this scene were irresistible. The silent rhapsody was shortly broken by the Comte.

"Have you ever been in a French village when they have had what is called la procession de la Fête de Dieu?" he inquired. "It takes place at noon, on the first Sunday after Trinity. Early on the morning of that day everybody is up and about, to be ready for the 'procession time,' as it is called. Men, women, servants, boys and girls are all hard at work. It is then that along the principal street of almost every village in France a cord is stretched against the wall above the first story of the houses, underneath the roof. The mistress of each house emerges from its narrow doorway, holding in her arms a pile of pure white sheets, used only on that day. She unfolds them carefully, and from their creases there comes that fresh and cleanly perfume of lavender and of old oak, given from the perfumed cupboard in which they have lain from year to year. She stands on a chair or ladder, holding one end of the sheet, while her neighbor keeps the other from the dusty ground. At last a pair of wooden pins holds it firmly to the cord, so that it falls to the very ground and covers the house in a snow-white drapery. The village street soon presents the appearance of a long avenue of white; and then begins the work for boys and girls. On each sheet are fastened wreaths of box, bouquets of roses, irises, lilies, all the flowers that are to be found at that time. Garlands of ivy and evergreens stretch from house to house and

TWO GENTLEMEN IN TOURAINE

across the street from one roof to another, like a giant spider's web.

"The men, with iris leaves, water-lilies and rose leaves in their hands, make designs upon the road over which the Blessed Sacrament is soon to pass. Well," concluded the Comte, "I have always thought that the wreaths upon the terrace of le Lude were exactly like those decorations of a village street on the first Sunday after Trinity."

"Your simile is a pretty one," said I, when he had finished speaking; "but as I have never seen the fête, I must content myself with the simple enjoyment of the present picture, which is, I think, the most perfect example of the French garden that I have yet seen."

The Comte continued, without waiting for me to finish: "Do you see those white marble statues—that of Hercules and Anthé, and the great vases crowned by pointed century plants? The tall heads of while dahlias, and the points of purple salvias arise likewise above the balustrade. They appear to me like so many people, standing in a line and looking down upon the carpet of flowers beneath the terrace. They seem to be waiting for the procession de la Fête de Dieu to pass."

We cross the bridge. The parterre fades behind the shrubberies, and the chateau, though near at hand, is to be distinguished only here and there by a pinnacle, an iron grating, or a pointed roof. The Louis XVI façade, whose rather hardened lines make of it a grayish background, may be seen between the trees, which hide the chateau and the moats around it. A steep incline upon the left brings one suddenly face to face with the north façade, divided from the street by the ivy-covered moat, here so wide and deep that it is almost like a great ravine. The two round towers at each corner sink deeply into the heart of the moat, and their heavy foundations are lost in a cloak of English ivy, growing about

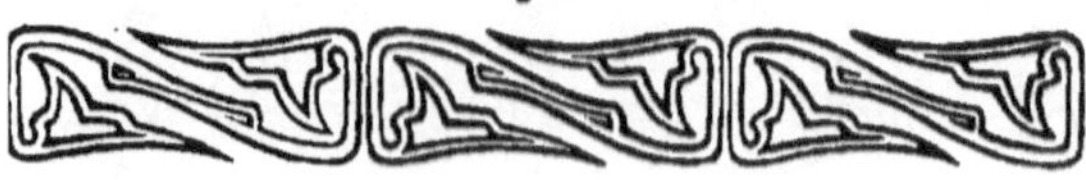

their bases and giving to them height and grace. The
tower on the right is of soft white stone, and was built
under the Renaissance. The carving about the windows, the medallions upon the walls (which represent
the heads of several kings of France) show the strong
link between the present tower and what it must have
been some centuries ago before it was restored. The
beautiful chimneys which crown the roofs of Chenonceau
and Chambord with so much grace are lacking here.
The sculpturing, so delicate and so fine that the finger-
nail might almost injure it, the graceful combinations
which adorn that matchless staircase of Blois and which
look like magic flowers, fruits and birds, have, it must be
said, been more or less reproduced upon the walls of this
tower. But they are found here in larger and much
coarser patterns, losing by this very fact much of their
delicacy and finish. They stand, in short, as an imitation
of that inimitable architecture.

The tower upon the left is built of rough stones covered
with a heavy coat of mortar, the yellow tinge of which
needs softening. This has been lately repaired, and
belongs to the Gothic period. Its walls, however, are too
bare and new. The windows are too few, and their
lines may well be called a little hard. But the porcupine
of Louis XII in the centre of the tower at the second
story gives a striking and unexpected effect, while the
cordon of St. Francis of Assize, taken by Claude de
France as a sign of mourning during her widowhood,
encircles the porcupine and the tower itself effectively.
As for the window which crowns the roof of this
tower, it is impossible to criticise the artistic taste
which has guided an expert chisel through the delicate
lacework of the soft stone. The execution of the pinnacles
which rise high above the entablature is an expression—
and a fine expression—of that Gothic period which is distinguished as the flamboyant. The same might be said

of other windows in the roof.   Their sculpture, as well as
the escutcheons bearing the arms of bygone owners of le
Lude, placed in the centre of their pointed caps, are in
strong relief against the high slate background, and they
bring out plainly the inferiority of the windows beneath
them.   These also are Gothic, or rather, they are meant
to be, for they were repaired, or rather reconstructed,
some forty years ago, at a period when artistic views and
architectural conceptions were both at their lowest ebb.
We mean the period of the Second Empire.   Their proportion, far from being that of those around them, cries
out in harsh, discordant tones "le mauvais gout" in which
le Lude was then restored.

But all these faults, and their resulting criticisms, fade
away beside the beauty of the great moats, which play so
large a part in the effect of this chateau.   These are
about fifty feet deep, and very nearly as broad.   They
surround the castle upon three sides, and are broken,
here by an arched bridge leading to the courtyard, and
upon the other side by another bridge which joins
two separated terraces.   Deep below, a graveled walk
winds between the two high walls, which are thickly
grown with ivy, making the whole seem more like a
natural bower than a cultivated effect.   Bushes and ever-
greens are interspersed with trees, or high clipped elms.
The laurel and other well-known trees abound, and they
lend their air of romance to the whole, an air of deep,
impressive mystery, unequaled even by the chateaux of
Touraine.   Beneath the central bridge a white stone
figure, lying upon a carved sarcophagus and surrounded
by an iron railing, stands out from its shady and retired
spot.   The figure is that of a woman, and the escutcheon
resting upon a costume of the fifteenth century tells us
that she must have been one of the former owners of le
Lude.   One more object strikes the fancy, and adds its
beauty to these moats.   Beyond the bridge, and in the

corner, a round tower, ending in a top not unlike that
of an old stone well, rises to the level of the avenue
and encloses a winding staircase to the walks beneath.

Another turn in the road brings us to a massive oaken
door, framed in an archway of gray stones, in front of
which servants, footmen and stable-boys discuss in high,
shrill tones the news of the town. We ring the bell and
the concierge—a very fat and jovial concierge, who looks
not unlike an Alsatian woman—opens the door and politely
begs us to come in. She takes our cards to the chateau and
returns in a few moments with the news that Mme. la
Marquise will be pleased to have us visit the chateau in
detail.

We are now standing in an outer court formed by
avenues and shrubs into the shape of a half moon. In
front of us the moat lies, as we have described it. Over
it the large white marble bridge, built in a graceful arch,
leads to the most imposing portion of le Lude, the western façade. This is in the shape of a quadrangle, three
sides of which are occupied by the building itself, while
the fourth side, opposite the bridge, is made of three tall
arches surmounted by a carved stone balustrade. The
interior courtyard, which occupies an area of about half
an acre, is thus enclosed in an artistic manner. The
general effect of the three inner façades is much improved by this arcade, which reaches to the second story
and thus cuts the regularity of the lines. The effect of
this façade of the time of François I is softened and
improved by a view in perspective through the arcade—a
happy conception of the architect. This mass of buildings and its details are on the whole imposing, if studied
carefully. We would say that they were strikingly so,
especially to one who has not been spoiled by the stone
lacework, the irreproachable beauty and the purity of
style to be found in the royal chateaux of Touraine.

Our carriage drives over the bridge and through the

central 'rch, stopping before a platform which is paved
with black and white marbles. We are ushered by a foot-
man in green and red livery into a large vestibule or hall,
in which a staircase winds its way up to the top of the
tower. At the foot of the staircase and upon the railing
stands the striking statue of an angel, with folded wings,
holding in its hand a cross like that of St. John the
Baptist. The statue is entirely of bronze, and is one of
those beautiful creations of the fifteenth century. It is
signed: Jehan Barbet. This was indeed a happy idea, to
place it where it stands, in relief against the white rails
and snowy walls of the entrance of the chateau, like the
Guardian Angel of le Lude. The folding doors upon the
right open into what is called la salle des fêtes, which
occupies the entire length of this wing. It is ninety feet
long and moderately high, with very good proportions.
The ceiling is vaulted, and frescoed in rather question-
able taste, and the walls are panelled with light, modern
oak, some feet above the head. Above this the panelling
is replaced by green leather which reaches to the
"chapiteaux" and "nervures" of the vaults. The floor is
inlaid with woods of different kinds, in imitation of
mosaic, and the furniture is rather shabby, the chairs
being of modern Renaissance oak and green leather.
Large palm trees in huge oaken boxes, flowers in every
corner, pianos and harmoniums, other instruments and
children's playthings, make this more of a comfortable
living room than an artistic gallery.

The Comte, who had been looking about him with the
air of one who was reviewing a familiar sight, took my
arm and stood in the centre of the gallery.

"I wish that you might remain at le Lude for some
days," said he, "as a visitor, and attend one of the banquets which are given in this hall. But let me tell you
something of these charming entertainments. It will
give you an idea of the way in which the representative

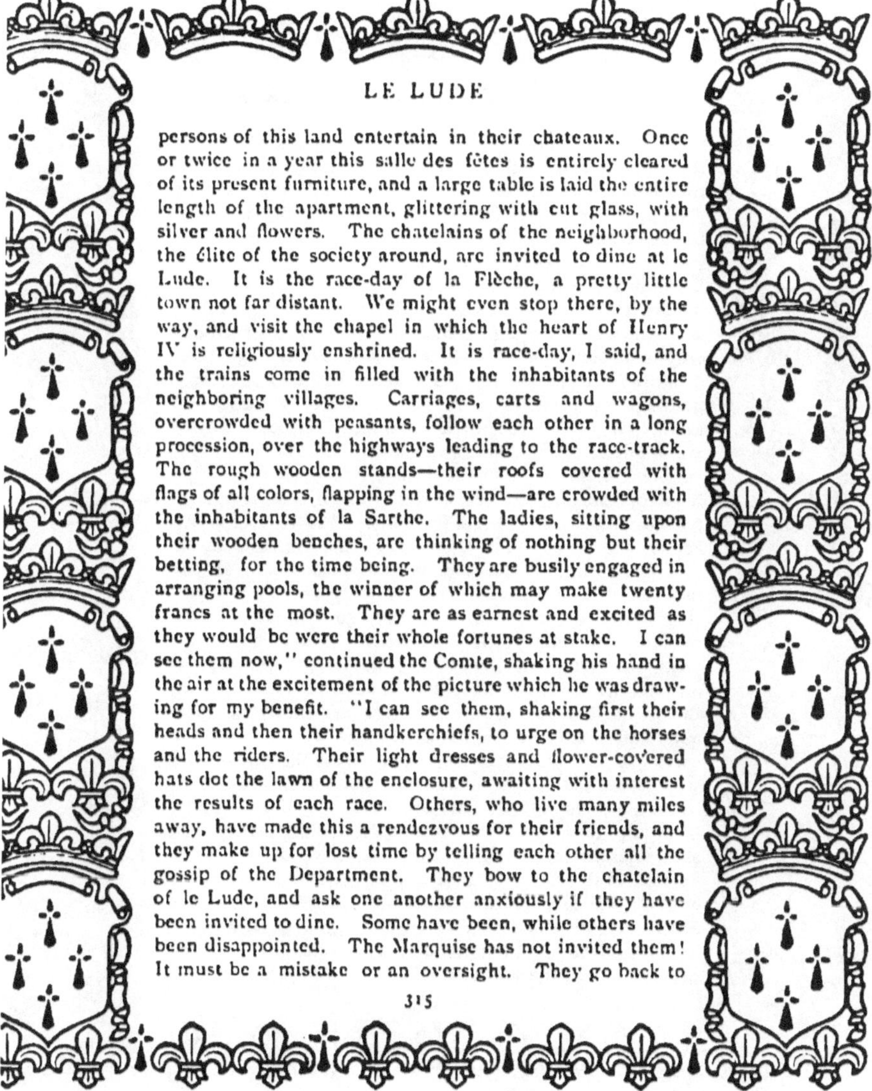

persons of this land entertain in their chateaux. Once or twice in a year this salle des fêtes is entirely cleared of its present furniture, and a large table is laid the entire length of the apartment, glittering with cut glass, with silver and flowers. The chatelains of the neighborhood, the élite of the society around, are invited to dine at le Lude. It is the race-day of la Flèche, a pretty little town not far distant. We might even stop there, by the way, and visit the chapel in which the heart of Henry IV is religiously enshrined. It is race-day, I said, and the trains come in filled with the inhabitants of the neighboring villages. Carriages, carts and wagons, overcrowded with peasants, follow each other in a long procession, over the highways leading to the race-track. The rough wooden stands—their roofs covered with flags of all colors, flapping in the wind—are crowded with the inhabitants of la Sarthe. The ladies, sitting upon their wooden benches, are thinking of nothing but their betting, for the time being. They are busily engaged in arranging pools, the winner of which may make twenty francs at the most. They are as earnest and excited as they would be were their whole fortunes at stake. I can see them now," continued the Comte, shaking his hand in the air at the excitement of the picture which he was drawing for my benefit. "I can see them, shaking first their heads and then their handkerchiefs, to urge on the horses and the riders. Their light dresses and flower-covered hats dot the lawn of the enclosure, awaiting with interest the results of each race. Others, who live many miles away, have made this a rendezvous for their friends, and they make up for lost time by telling each other all the gossip of the Department. They bow to the chatelain of le Lude, and ask one another anxiously if they have been invited to dine. Some have been, while others have been disappointed. The Marquise has not invited them! It must be a mistake or an oversight. They go back to

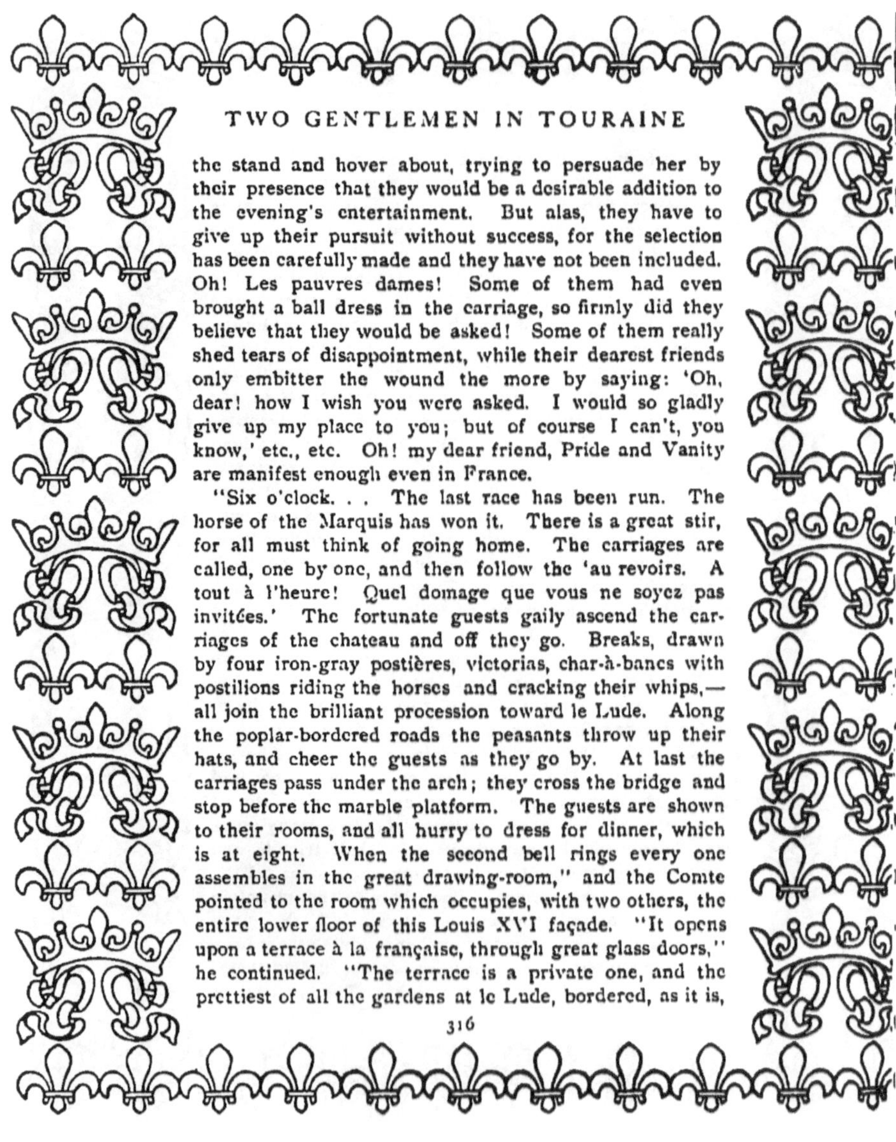

the stand and hover about, trying to persuade her by their presence that they would be a desirable addition to the evening's entertainment. But alas, they have to give up their pursuit without success, for the selection has been carefully made and they have not been included. Oh! Les pauvres dames! Some of them had even brought a ball dress in the carriage, so firmly did they believe that they would be asked! Some of them really shed tears of disappointment, while their dearest friends only embitter the wound the more by saying: 'Oh, dear! how I wish you were asked. I would so gladly give up my place to you; but of course I can't, you know,' etc., etc. Oh! my dear friend, Pride and Vanity are manifest enough even in France.

"Six o'clock. . . The last race has been run. The horse of the Marquis has won it. There is a great stir, for all must think of going home. The carriages are called, one by one, and then follow the 'au revoirs. A tout à l'heure! Quel domage que vous ne soyez pas invitées.' The fortunate guests gaily ascend the carriages of the chateau and off they go. Breaks, drawn by four iron-gray postières, victorias, char-à-bancs with postilions riding the horses and cracking their whips,— all join the brilliant procession toward le Lude. Along the poplar-bordered roads the peasants throw up their hats, and cheer the guests as they go by. At last the carriages pass under the arch; they cross the bridge and stop before the marble platform. The guests are shown to their rooms, and all hurry to dress for dinner, which is at eight. When the second bell rings every one assembles in the great drawing-room," and the Comte pointed to the room which occupies, with two others, the entire lower floor of this Louis XVI façade. "It opens upon a terrace à la française, through great glass doors," he continued. "The terrace is a private one, and the prettiest of all the gardens at le Lude, bordered, as it is,

with its great orange trees. There is no prettier sight
than the grand salon, lighted by colossal chandeliers
of gold and crystal. The hundreds of candles reflect
themselves in crystal prisms hanging from golden arms,
and cluster about the centre like the flowers of an
immense bouquet. Each flower has its peculiar color,
and pours down its full rays upon the beautiful furniture
of the purest Louis XVI. The red brocade, stamped
with graceful patterns of a milky white, adds to the
beauty of the scene, and when the great curtains are
drawn at night they relieve the somewhat deadened walls
of white and gold. The whole—as you will soon see—
together with the beautiful mirrors at each corner,
reminds one strongly of Louis XIV's room at Ussé.
Great palm trees and smaller flowers, screens, and tables
covered with family miniatures of the First Empire,
complete the furnishings of this truly beautiful room.
In one of the windows stands a small table, and upon it is
the 'collier du St. Esprit,' which belonged to the father-
in-law of the late Marquis. The collier, which was the
insignia of the highest order in France under the old
régime, lies in a green leather case, almost in the shape
of a heart. The centre of the case is ornamented by the
royal escutcheon of France, engraved in gold. The
principal ornaments of the collar are its golden fleurs-
de-lis. This famous heraldic emblem, rarely to be
found in coats-of-arms, is said to have been brought from
the East and used first by the kings of France during the
Crusades. Here the "fleurs-de-lis" are linked together
by medallions of enamel, on which is placed the royal H,
thrice crowned, alternating with a helmet, surmounted
by a white flag adorned with fleurs-de-lis, and surrounded
by red tongues of fire. A cross, very much like the
Maltese in design, hangs from the centre of the collar.
In the centre of this golden cross is a white dove, with its
wings extended, emblematic of the Holy Ghost. The

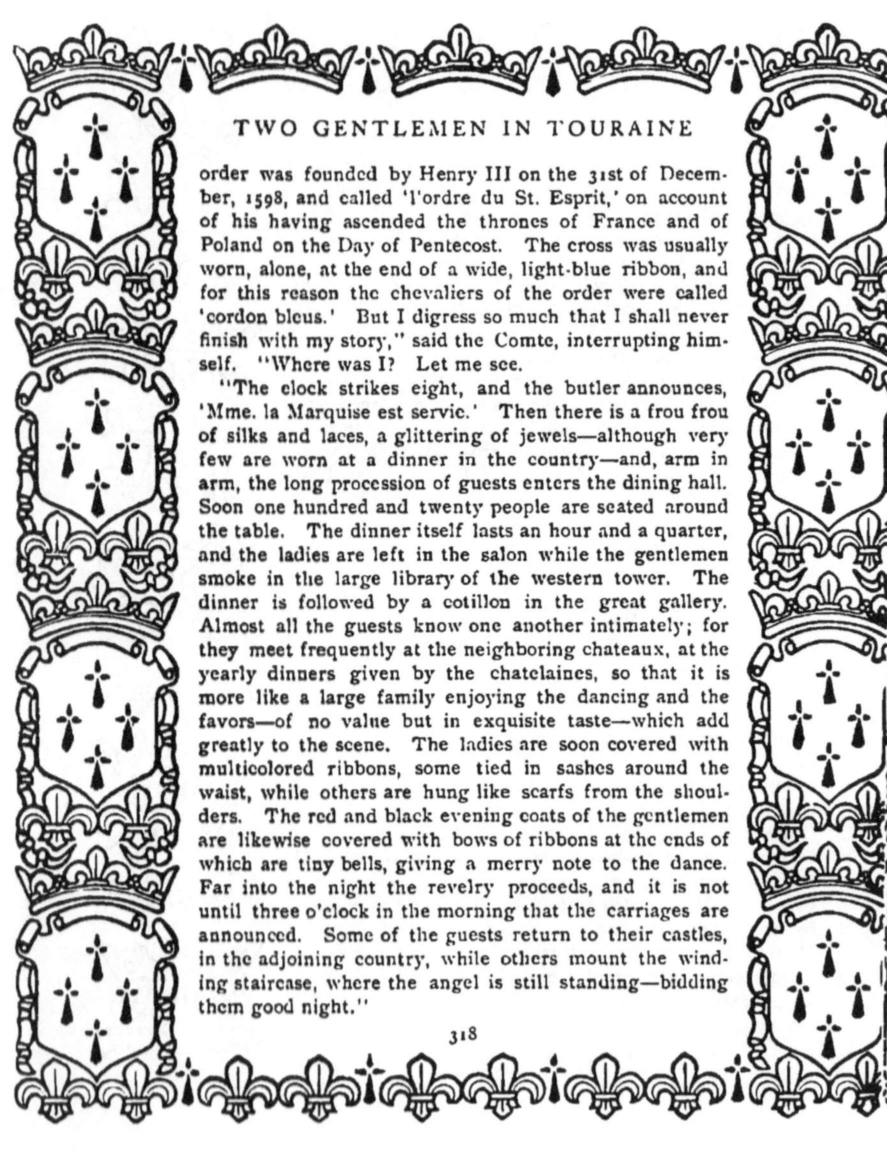

order was founded by Henry III on the 31st of December, 1598, and called 'l'ordre du St. Esprit,' on account of his having ascended the thrones of France and of Poland on the Day of Pentecost. The cross was usually worn, alone, at the end of a wide, light-blue ribbon, and for this reason the chevaliers of the order were called 'cordon bleus.' But I digress so much that I shall never finish with my story," said the Comte, interrupting himself. "Where was I? Let me see.

"The clock strikes eight, and the butler announces, 'Mme. la Marquise est servie.' Then there is a frou frou of silks and laces, a glittering of jewels—although very few are worn at a dinner in the country—and, arm in arm, the long procession of guests enters the dining hall. Soon one hundred and twenty people are seated around the table. The dinner itself lasts an hour and a quarter, and the ladies are left in the salon while the gentlemen smoke in the large library of the western tower. The dinner is followed by a cotillon in the great gallery. Almost all the guests know one another intimately; for they meet frequently at the neighboring chateaux, at the yearly dinners given by the chatelaines, so that it is more like a large family enjoying the dancing and the favors—of no value but in exquisite taste—which add greatly to the scene. The ladies are soon covered with multicolored ribbons, some tied in sashes around the waist, while others are hung like scarfs from the shoulders. The red and black evening coats of the gentlemen are likewise covered with bows of ribbons at the ends of which are tiny bells, giving a merry note to the dance. Far into the night the revelry proceeds, and it is not until three o'clock in the morning that the carriages are announced. Some of the guests return to their castles, in the adjoining country, while others mount the winding staircase, where the angel is still standing—bidding them good night."

LE LUDE

"What a graphic picture you have painted!" said I.
"This is all delightful."

"Yes, of course," answered the Comte; "especially
when the hostess of a chateau is young, beautiful and
attractive, when she knows how to surround herself with
that brilliancy which fascinates as long as it lasts. It is
for this reason, I think, that very few people ought to be
asked to visit a chateau for a long time. Once the glamour
worn out, the interest wears out also. And how very few
hostesses know how to sustain that interest, or, knowing
how, take the trouble to do so! Of course, it needs a
constant care as well as wonderful tact. Were I not
afraid of being trivial, I should say that this care should
go even as far as our clothes. You do not know how
much attraction there is to be found in well dressed
women, in the country. Some believe that because they
are far from town they should put aside their elegance.
Believe me, it never pays to put aside one's elegance.
People have too little to their credit to be able to
afford to put any of it away, especially in the country.
Country elegance, appropriate, is just as important, if not
more so, than elegance in town. What a mistake it is,
this getting out all one's old clothes for the country!
The success of a house party depends largely upon the
care which a hostess takes in making it distinguée, in asking the right persons to meet one another, and in amusing
them, or allowing them to amuse themselves according
to their different tastes. But, unfortunately, in France
—I mean in almost all its chateaux—what is called a
'house party' is simply one or two people who bore
themselves from morning until night. I have learned
by sad experience that chateau life is far more attractive
in books than in reality. But I have already said too
much, I fear, for I do not wish to take from you all the
charm which surrounds a French chateau in the eyes
of a foreigner."

TWO GENTLEMEN IN TOURAINE

From this salon in which we had been standing during the last part of this conversation, we passed on to a boudoir, which had little that was worthy of notice in it, save for some modern miniatures, a great clock and a large bowl. The room, however, is a handsome one, and opens into a second library, which looks more like a morning-room. Finally, the dining-room is reached— "the best for the last"—the gem of the whole chateau. It occupies a large part of the south wing, and it is lighted by four great windows, opening upon a stone terrace which overlooks the moat, the parterres, and the park beyond. The ceiling is of oaken beams, elaborately painted in brown and gold. These were found, some years ago, under a modern ceiling, in as perfect a state of restoration as when François I had caused them to be decorated. They form no small portion of the character of this room to-day. The walls are hung with Flemish tapestries framed in gilded oaken panelling. At the windows the walls are over eight feet thick, and small tables are placed against these massive window-sills, while a large oak table occupies the centre of the room beneath a Dutch chandelier. In the corner, overlooking the court, another table stands, laden with fruits, with silver, and with china cups for five o'clock tea. The great chimney at the further end has been recently placed there, and is a direct copy of the most beautiful specimen at the chateau of Blois.

We leave the dining-room to find ourselves in the tower opposite the one by which we entered. Above, a long and rather narrow corridor runs entirely around the three façades of the courtyard, with rooms overlooking the outer sides of the castle. The principal room of interest is that of Henry IV, which, like most royal apartments, is considered the best of the chateau, if not in size at least in furniture. The only creditable thing here, however, is a large four-posted bed, heavily cano-

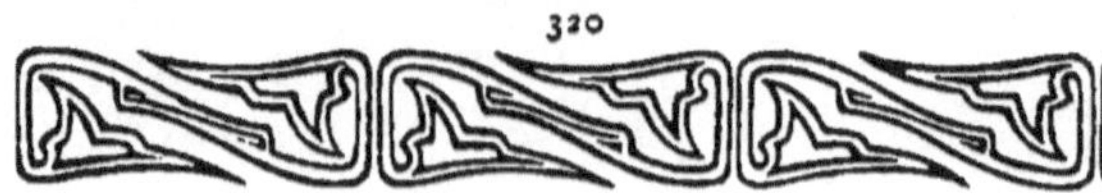

pied and curtained, where Henry IV probably shut himself in and closed his eyes upon the conglomerate mixture
of furniture about him, lacking even the distinction of
being old. The chamber is panelled with wood, on which
are painted some indifferent pictures of flowers. The
king is said to have slept here for a night in 1594, and
the next day to have followed the procession in the
church, for the first time since his conversion to Cathol-
icism. Louis XIII also slept here in 1619.

There is also an Empire room in this wing, which is
worthy of a visit, and which all lovers of the Empire
period could but find beautiful. All is in keeping, the
bed in mahogany and brass, with its heavy canopy and
curtains of stamped, mouse-colored velvet, the arm chairs
of the same, and the tables. A single exception breaks
the symmetry, a small screen, which would have been
more at ease in a Japanese tea-house than in an Empire
chamber. A large family picture of an officer and his
wife in the costumes of that period completes the furnish-
ing of this apartment. With a last look at the interior of
le Lude we are soon outside once more, wandering in the
paths of the parterres, and looking back at the most
pleasing view of the chateau.

"It is really interesting," said I, perhaps in a more
inquiring than decided tone.

"Of course it is," answered the Comte. "It is considered one of the most beautiful places of France. At
least, it is one of those which is most carefully taken
care of, and one of the few places whose owner's fortune
is sufficient for its size and for the life necessary to be led
in it."

"Oh!" I replied. "Though I cannot say why, le Lude
strikes me as lacking something. Is it too bare; is it too
white; or is it a modern coat thrown over an ancient
cuirass? I cannot tell. But it does not entirely satisfy
me. The dining-room, the furniture of the salon and the

completeness of the Empire bedroom, are the only really perfect bits which stand out in my mind after leaving it."

"My dear friend," returned the Comte, laying his hand upon mine, "my dear friend, when I told you that le Lude was beautiful I made a mistake. I should have said that in course of time it will be beautiful. And when you speak of the 'only perfect bits' I can but agree with you. Le Lude was repaired, as you know, about forty years ago, a most unfortunate period for such a work. One sees this at first glance, by looking at the building itself, which lacks unity, harmony and finish. And it has something of the cheaper look to be found in almost every building of that period."

"Where, do you suppose, is the cause for this—this— what shall I call it?—this lack of taste?"

"I think we might answer," my friend returned, "that these results have come as well from past owners as from architects. The latter were not always to blame, though very often. At that time inferior architects took the lead, especially in the western part of France, and these were largely responsible for the fad, the craze, which inflamed everybody, for Gothic art and architecture, appropriated to modern ideas of comfort. This desire became so ungovernable, this longing for Gothic archi- tecture so insatiable, that even the smallest country- house, or farm, aspired to a tower, a pinnacle, a high, pointed roof. And you may well imagine the distressing effect of towers and spires on a one-storied house. The artistic eye has been forced to close itself for very shame at what it sees. One architect especially, named Delarue, prevailed over all the country, and was the father of a style which might be termed the 'Delarue style.' It was, in reality, nothing more than the combi- nation of a good deal of feudal detail for the least possible money. All the chateaux which he designed were upon

the same idea, a high pavilion in the centre, two wings
on either side of it, and a tower at each end. The number of towers was usually in proportion to the money
spent and the scale upon which it was built. But the general effect of the whole was about the same, a chateau
the color of gingerbread, which looked more like a cake
than a building.

"If you are interested enough in the study of this inferior
period I will introduce you to one of these creations.
The distribution is the same in all. First, we shall come
to a very dismal entrance, a vestibule, narrow and dark,
with a door upon either side, leading to the towers and
their steep winding staircases. Open the central door,
and you will find youself in a billiard room which occupies
the central pavilion. If the owner is well off, you will
find leather upon the walls, and consider yourself to be
in luck if you do—if not, it will be a leather paper, or
paper simply; the effect is the same. Come into the
salon, on the right. Very rich owners! White walls,
brass and crystal chandelier; modern Beauvais, or Aubus-
son tapestries representing usually the Fables of la Fontaine on a light-green ground and framed in white and
gold wood—the most expensive product of a very stiff
and tasteless style. If appropriate furniture cannot be
provided, chintz or red velveteen will replace the
tapestry, and a showy paper, with fantastic patterns on
it, will proudly proclaim its lack of taste upon the walls.
Dinner is served. Let us walk into the dining-room. We
must cross the billiard-room to gain it, and when there
we find that it was hardly worth our trouble. Cheap,
light oak panelling, carved in the most modern imitation
of the Renaissance—red curtains to the windows, the
same as those of the billiard-room, so as to be used
indifferently. So much for the lower floor of a 'chateau
Delarue.' As for the rooms above, they are not worth
our climbing the steep and tortuous staircase. On an

average they are about twelve by eight feet, and few have as much as a dressing-room, a very necessary adjunct to so small a bedroom. If this is on the upper floor you may touch the ceiling with your hand, and often with your head, when you do not care to.

"Let us leave the chateau, and take a short walk—all too long—through a park which is in very poor order. The trees are neither well grown nor well arranged. The avenues and alleys have not much to boast of, if they have anything at all. The paths are covered with grass or weeds. There is little to please the eye; still less to strike the fancy. And, indeed, you are glad to leave without delay this representative of three-quarters of the present chateaux of France.

"Le Lude was—shall I say restored?—at all events, repaired by Delarue. Fortunately for the chateau, the walls were far too thick to be torn down and replaced by gingerbread creations, so that the architect was forced to modify his plans and keep them to the surface and the interior. The stone walls nevertheless received their coating of fresh plaster, which carefully hid the lacework and ornaments of the Renaissance. The majestic towers were replaced by imitations, and the gray coating of the François I quadrangle was scraped and scraped, thus ruining the work of centuries! So seldom are the softening shades of Time thrown over the harsh coloring of the French stone that their existence should be guarded as a sacred gift, and not defaced by ever-busy hands. The window-caps of the Gothic façade were but embellished copies of the last Delarue chateau, and they look more like the wish-bone of a chicken than like architectural ornaments."

I had listened to this long discussion by the Comte in a quiet assent (which the sights of the afternoon had somewhat influenced). In the short experience which I had had, this period of architecture had already incurred my

LE LUDE

criticism, and I was glad to hear my friend express himself so strongly on the subject.

"There is little good in it," he continued. "Let us
pass over the Louis XVI façade, which has remained
unfinished, probably unwilling to be massacred by a hand
which did so much to mutilate the rest. As to the
interior, I think that, apart from its real beauties, we
have found in it the whole procession of light modern
oak panellings, white stucco walls, leather paper and
chairs. If you had been there some five years ago, you
would have found also the grand salon crowded with the
tapestry of Beauvais, La Fontaine's Fables, and all the
rest. Monsieur Delarue is gone now, and after him his
style is fortunately disappearing. Money, during the
first period of Delarue's reign, was to be found everywhere, and it was necessary to spend it, so that many
bought castles and places. They repaired them, in
the fashion then prevailing. They knew not how to
do better. Old tapestries of Flandre and Gobelin, old
furniture of the Louis, were mixed in with others, as
of no value; or they were sold for nothing and replaced by new, gaudy creations which have lasted until
now.

"I do not know a better example," the Comte concluded, as we walked off into the beautiful park, and
wound our way down to the river by a long and shady
avenue; "I do not know a better example than le Lude
—at least the chateau in itself, for the park and its surroundings are fairy-like—of the subject that we have
been discussing, the subject, in fact, which it has brought
to our minds. The evils, the bad taste, the ignorance,
the vain attempts at originality, which were so prevalent
half a century ago, have left an important mark to stain
the architecture of to-day These evils have, however,
given place to better taste and to more artistic desires,
which show themselves already at every turn in le Lude,

325

in every chateau, old or new, in every building which boasts refinement or education.

"Let us hope that this 'Indian Summer' to the Renaissance, if I might draw so strong a parallel, may continue and produce a better architecture than we have been accustomed to."

The Comte had finished speaking as the great door of the entrance to the park closed behind us, and le Lude had come and gone.

One word more, we are tempted to add, before leaving the park. It is an unquestionable fact that artistic taste in architecture has made wonderful progress during the last ten years. This comes doubtless from the more careful study of true art, which has been gradually increasing since the arid period of which we have been speaking. Owners of places in France fifty years ago repaired their chateaux all at once, and this may likewise be one cause for the imperfection of the whole. But now, their children have become owners in their stead, and while living in these chateaux they have seen, little by little, how imperfect they were, both in style and in construction. So that to-day, partly because they could afford it more easily, partly because they thought it a better plan, they have been repairing them, bit by bit, outside as well as within.

We have seen the advantages of this system of restoration in the dining-room and library of le Lude, and we are certain that in some years it will be in keeping with the original plans. Of course, it is most difficult, not to say impossible, and it is growing more difficult every day to refurnish an old castle with old furniture which is authentic. Modern stuffs and even modern woods must be used; but we have produced of late such perfect imitations of silks and velvets, of the carving and coloring of woods, that if all is tempered by good taste the old may

thus be replaced by new. There is no place where this is more fully understood than in the newly-repaired portions of le Lude, in the architecture as well as in the furnishings.

But in order to leave the castle and all that it calls to mind, we must beg the reader to accompany us a little further before we part with him for the night. At all events, we will dine together at the Hôtel du Bœuf! The dinner is a good one, and the table d'hôte gay, with plenty of middle class French people for us to study —to speak to in very bad French and to hide our amusement at their diverting conversation in our sleeve. Let us drink to le Lude and a pleasant day in a bottle of Bordeaux! The only drawback to our dinner is an "assaisonnement" from the potage to the café, uncalled for, but, alas, too often found in French hotels—we mean a company of drummers. Oh! If you could but know how much it means to a Frenchman, a "commis voyageur," the sight of one would chill you to the bone! He is vulgarity to his finger tips; the most offensive vulgarity in words and actions,—boasting manners, kicks at the table, eating with his knife, putting his bread into his wine! He has a voice like a trumpet, which blows its blast into your ears, into the room and through the whole neighborhood. And he discusses each course in a manner that reminds us painfully, at least vividly, of Mr. Jos Sedley and Vanity Fair. He knows the scandal of the whole Department, and more too; he speaks intimately to every one with whom he comes in contact, and he rejoices in being everybody's friend. It is needless to say, with such a power of making friends, that he calls the first people of the land by their Christian names.

The Comte shivered at the very sight of four of these aggressive creatures. They occupied the whole half of the dining-room, and the rest of the evening was spoiled by these wretched beings. But here we will let our curtain fall, for it has been up too long already.

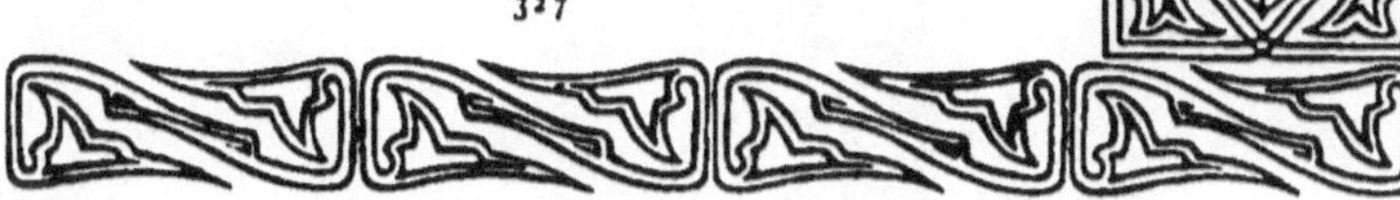

CHAPTER XV

CASTLE-IN-THE-AIR

We had come to our last journey; and as we started
from le Lude, about six in the afternoon, we felt that
the end of our excursion was approaching. So long
had we lived among these chateaux of history and in
the life connected with them that it seemed difficult
to believe the time had come to take up once more
the life of to-day. The beauties and the parterres of le
Lude had caused us to forget this for a time; but now we
could not disguise from ourselves the regret that all was
over.

"However," said I to my companion, "all is not over
for me; the little chateau of yours, to which we are now
directing our steps, has as much interest for me as many
a monument of greater importance."

"Yes," replied the Comte, "I suppose that I too am
glad to see the old place again. I have not been there
for a long time; and I am really very fond of it. But I
must warn you not to expect a chateau. It is only the
simplest little gentilhommière, and I have used it for a
shooting-box, in which to pass a few weeks at a time only,
when I crave quiet and rusticity."

The evening was a beautiful one, and before long the
heavens were sparkling with stars. The moon rose clear
and bright, and it cast its silvery light over the trees and
the road in an almost ghost-like manner. We followed
for a mile or two the same road which we had taken
to come to le Lude, and we then turned to the left,
plunging into a pine forest. A foot-path led through it,

unknown to all save those who were familiar with
this region; but the Comte was one of these. The little
light which was reflected here through the leaves made
the path more ghost-like than if it had been dark. We
walked along, almost holding our breath and fearing to
hear the sound of something unknown. The cracking of a
dead branch beneath the foot made the heart beat faster.
The wings of a startled bird, or a bat which had been lost
among the trees, sounded strange and unnatural in our
ears. Here and there an avenue would cross our path,
showing the white fences of a private park. Further on
a tiny light, like a golden spark, like a shining eye, told
of some small farm where the inhabitants had not yet
retired. We passed near one, and a dog broke out of a
barrel which served him as a kennel, dragging his chain
over the wooden sides, and barking at us until we were
out of sight.

"What are you thinking of?" said I to the Comte.
"You have been silent for so long that you should have
something interesting to say."

"I have been thinking of a strange dream which I had
the other night. I dreamed that I had been living for
some time among castles-in-the-air. The stars that we
see above us between the leaves and branches seemed to
me to grow larger and yet larger. They seemed to have
roofs and balconies and towers, and to have assumed
names familiar to both of us. Do you see the one just
above our heads? That one was Chambord, and it was the
largest of them all. The one further to the left there
was Chaumont. Another, not far off, was Chenonceau.
The brightest of them all was Azay, while Blois,
Valençay, St. Aignan, and others, clustered around
them. They appeared to be human and to speak. One
by one they came down from the sky and told their tales
and helped me to build my own castle-in-the-air.

" 'Oh, if you were mine,' said I to Chambord, 'what

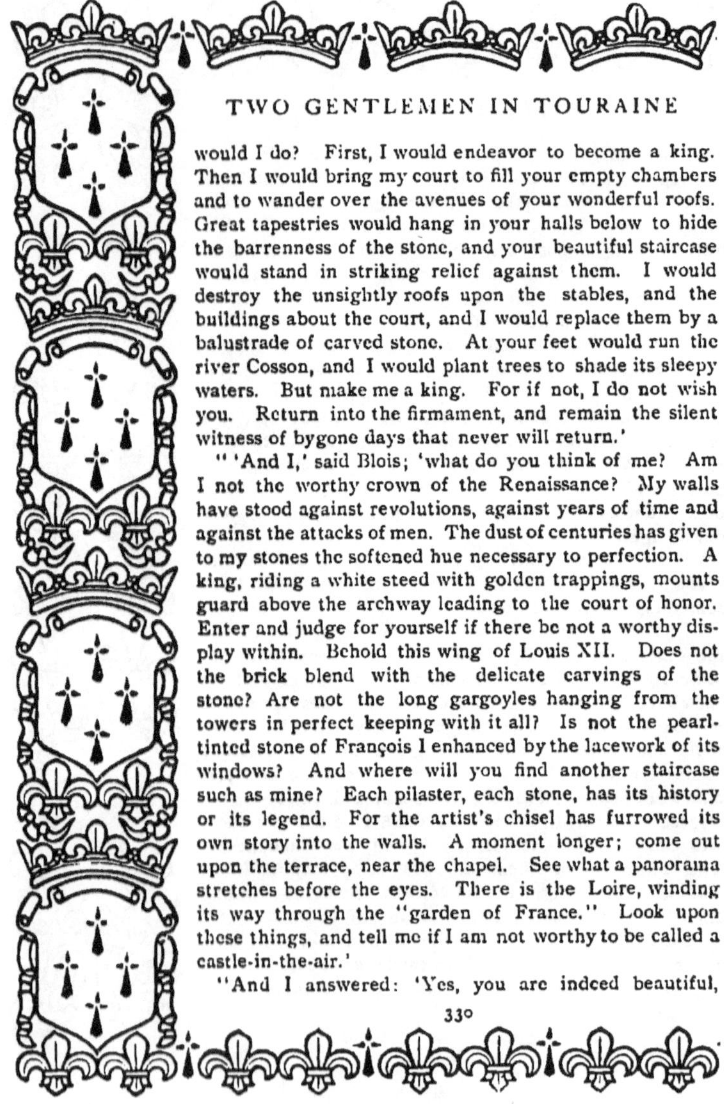

would I do? First, I would endeavor to become a king. Then I would bring my court to fill your empty chambers and to wander over the avenues of your wonderful roofs. Great tapestries would hang in your halls below to hide the barrenness of the stone, and your beautiful staircase would stand in striking relief against them. I would destroy the unsightly roofs upon the stables, and the buildings about the court, and I would replace them by a balustrade of carved stone. At your feet would run the river Cosson, and I would plant trees to shade its sleepy waters. But make me a king. For if not, I do not wish you. Return into the firmament, and remain the silent witness of bygone days that never will return.'

" 'And I,' said Blois; 'what do you think of me? Am I not the worthy crown of the Renaissance? My walls have stood against revolutions, against years of time and against the attacks of men. The dust of centuries has given to my stones the softened hue necessary to perfection. A king, riding a white steed with golden trappings, mounts guard above the archway leading to the court of honor. Enter and judge for yourself if there be not a worthy display within. Behold this wing of Louis XII. Does not the brick blend with the delicate carvings of the stone? Are not the long gargoyles hanging from the towers in perfect keeping with it all? Is not the pearl-tinted stone of François I enhanced by the lacework of its windows? And where will you find another staircase such as mine? Each pilaster, each stone, has its history or its legend. For the artist's chisel has furrowed its own story into the walls. A moment longer; come out upon the terrace, near the chapel. See what a panorama stretches before the eyes. There is the Loire, winding its way through the "garden of France." Look upon these things, and tell me if I am not worthy to be called a castle-in-the-air.'

"And I answered: 'Yes, you are indeed beautiful,

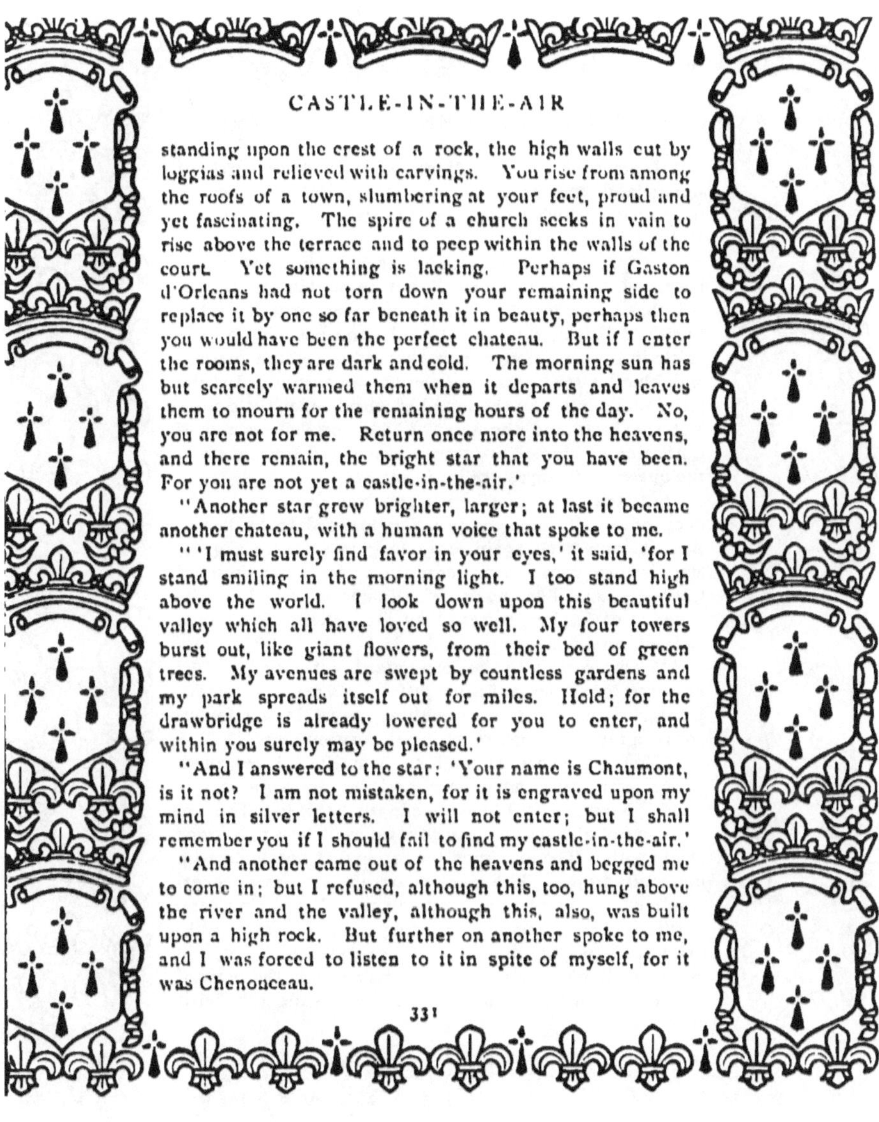

standing upon the crest of a rock, the high walls cut by loggias and relieved with carvings. You rise from among the roofs of a town, slumbering at your feet, proud and yet fascinating. The spire of a church seeks in vain to rise above the terrace and to peep within the walls of the court. Yet something is lacking. Perhaps if Gaston d'Orleans had not torn down your remaining side to replace it by one so far beneath it in beauty, perhaps then you would have been the perfect chateau. But if I enter the rooms, they are dark and cold. The morning sun has but scarcely warmed them when it departs and leaves them to mourn for the remaining hours of the day. No, you are not for me. Return once more into the heavens, and there remain, the bright star that you have been. For you are not yet a castle-in-the-air.'

"Another star grew brighter, larger; at last it became another chateau, with a human voice that spoke to me.

"'I must surely find favor in your eyes,' it said, 'for I stand smiling in the morning light. I too stand high above the world. I look down upon this beautiful valley which all have loved so well. My four towers burst out, like giant flowers, from their bed of green trees. My avenues are swept by countless gardens and my park spreads itself out for miles. Hold; for the drawbridge is already lowered for you to enter, and within you surely may be pleased.'

"And I answered to the star: 'Your name is Chaumont, is it not? I am not mistaken, for it is engraved upon my mind in silver letters. I will not enter; but I shall remember you if I should fail to find my castle-in-the-air.'

"And another came out of the heavens and begged me to come in; but I refused, although this, too, hung above the river and the valley, although this, also, was built upon a high rock. But further on another spoke to me, and I was forced to listen to it in spite of myself, for it was Chenonceau.

331

" 'I am cold,' it said, 'perhaps I am even harsh to some; and my galleries are bare. But the beautiful position which I hold over the river atones for many faults. I have gardens that are worthy of a queen. I have a parterre where many queens have spent happy hours. I have a park, small but unique in its design. All that I now need is life. Give to me once again the breath of Royalty within my walls, and I would be your castle-in-the-air. Let horses that draw a coach of gold and blue be seen once more upon my avenue. Let the trees above but echo the sound of wheels upon the stones. Let the lives and the fêtes of Diane de Poitiers and of Catherine de Medici but return to me, and I would stand the queen of all three castles-in-the-air.'

"But the voice of Chenonceau was drowned by the deep notes of Valençay, pressing forward to be heard. And it sank back again, only to give place to a great star, whose rays were more powerful than those of Chenonceau. The voice of Valençay was like the thunder of Jupiter, softened by the delicacy of Apollo, as it addressed me.

" 'I am worthy to be recognized,' it began. 'An emperor found me a fitting gift to make to a famous prince. I am royal in everything, royal in my forest, royal in my buildings, royal in my surroundings.'

" 'You are great as well as beautiful,' I returned. 'Your park must have been designed by some fairy's hand. No other could have made it what it is. The elm trees meet above the head, as we walk through some shady path. The ivy upon the ground is sparkling with diamond drops. The gentle stream is almost overwhelmed by flowers upon its bank. Birds sing, and nature speaks. The higher Being in our hearts is awakened and is in touch with everything. Yet, in spite of all, oh, castle of stone, rising upon the brow of yonder hill, there is lacking in your walls the spirit

of my castle-in-the-air. Why, indeed, is it that what we have is always so far from our desires, and that what we desire is so far removed from what we have? Let me not ask myself wherein you may fall short of my ideal, lest I lose power to appreciate the beauty of much that I have seen.'

"And I dreamed that many others came and spoke to me, out of the starry sky. Some of them I knew, and some I knew not. But they all lacked something which kept me from finding in them what I sought. At last there came the brightest of all the stars. It was not large. Nay, it seemed one of the smallest of them. But its rays were like a thousand tiny diamonds, shooting out in all directions into the night. There was no such star about it. No one could resist it. And as it came out more distinctly, I saw that its name was Azay-le-Rideau. There was the jasmine, spreading its golden wreaths over the stone pavilions. Flowers grew about them, and all was as I had seen it, a setting worthy of a crown. Every detail of it bore enchantment in its lines; every shadow had its magic touch. And as I looked at it all, I thought: 'Ah! what life might be within its walls! What it would be, even to live near one of these gems of the French Renaissance! This one may be a little small, a little flat. Some other details may be not all that one would have; but this last star, this last castle, comes nearest to my ideal.'

"It was a pretty dream; was it not?" said the Comte, as he concluded. "I have been thinking of it ever since."

"Ah, my dear friend," I returned, "if I could but build upon solid ground my ideal, my castle-in-the-air, my 'chateau en Espagne,' as your countrymen poetically call it, if by taking a bit from each one of these chateaux, a ray from each of these stars that shine in so many different ways; oh, if I could but do this, what a castle

would I build! I would choose the chateau of Azay, for
the central figure, with the situation of Chaumont, and in
the park of Valençay. The river Loire, with its blue
waters, its yellow shafts of sand and its banks of poplar
trees, should flow a hundred feet below. The chapel of
Amboise should be transported there and hidden amid a
bower of trees, showing only through a vista of the park.
But the moment that we opened the deeply-carved door,
the bare stones would be replaced by the soft lights and
the beautiful interior of the chapel at Chaumont. The
great staircase of Blois would rise out of the water upon
the southern façade of this 'chateau en Espagne,' so that a
boat, a gondola, could draw up beside its steps, and the
whole picture would be reflected in the water. The
parterre de Diane, brought from Chenonceau, would be
cut in twain and spread upon either side of the chateau.
And we should approach it from a long, straight avenue.
At its opening would be a massive gate of beautifully
wrought iron, with two stone pillars surmounted by
coats-of-arms. Beyond would be a forest like that of
Chambord or Valençay. Behind the chateau the broad
flight of steps at St. Aignan would lead to the river
below, and to the terrace of le Lude, upon a tiny tributary
of the greater river.

"The great gates of the castle are opened. Coaches,
drawn by percheron postiers and ridden by postilions,
are driving up the avenue and leaving their masters at
the doors of the inner court. Footmen in noble liveries
usher the guests up the great staircase to the salon, where
a brilliant company of people is assembled. It is the
hour for tea. Some are seated at a table where two
ladies of the chateau assist in pouring it into cups, which the
footmen pass upon massive silver trays. A great artist,
who is staying in the chateau, is singing, accompanied by
a harp. Beyond, upon the terrace, young people in the
first blush of youth are playing tennis. Life is before

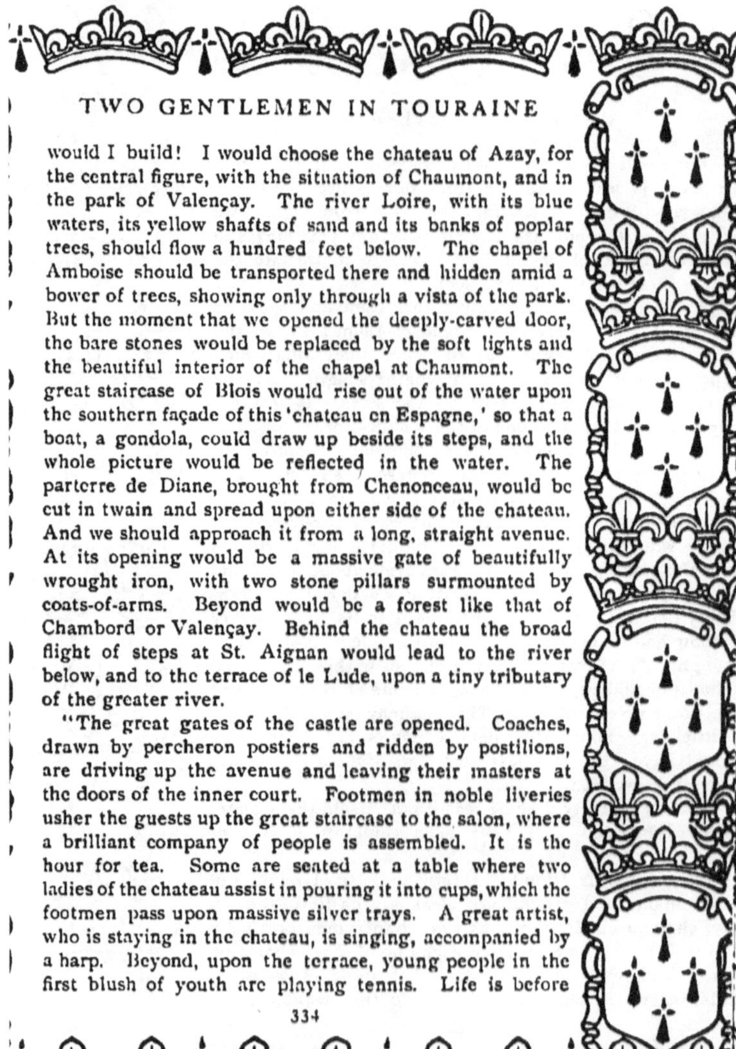

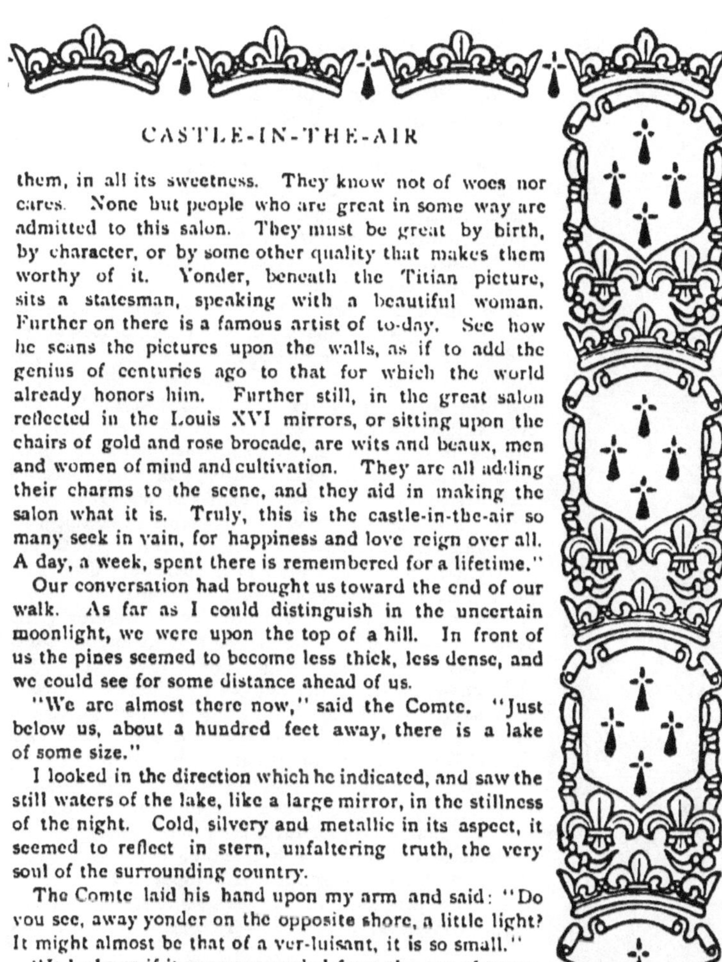

them, in all its sweetness. They know not of woes nor cares. None but people who are great in some way are admitted to this salon. They must be great by birth, by character, or by some other quality that makes them worthy of it. Yonder, beneath the Titian picture, sits a statesman, speaking with a beautiful woman. Further on there is a famous artist of to-day. See how he scans the pictures upon the walls, as if to add the genius of centuries ago to that for which the world already honors him. Further still, in the great salon reflected in the Louis XVI mirrors, or sitting upon the chairs of gold and rose brocade, are wits and beaux, men and women of mind and cultivation. They are all adding their charms to the scene, and they aid in making the salon what it is. Truly, this is the castle-in-the-air so many seek in vain, for happiness and love reign over all. A day, a week, spent there is remembered for a lifetime."

Our conversation had brought us toward the end of our walk. As far as I could distinguish in the uncertain moonlight, we were upon the top of a hill. In front of us the pines seemed to become less thick, less dense, and we could see for some distance ahead of us.

"We are almost there now," said the Comte. "Just below us, about a hundred feet away, there is a lake of some size."

I looked in the direction which he indicated, and saw the still waters of the lake, like a large mirror, in the stillness of the night. Cold, silvery and metallic in its aspect, it seemed to reflect in stern, unfaltering truth, the very soul of the surrounding country.

The Comte laid his hand upon my arm and said: "Do you see, away yonder on the opposite shore, a little light? It might almost be that of a ver-luisant, it is so small."

"It looks as if it were suspended from the top of a tree, to light the woodcutter in a night's work," said I, as my eye fell upon it.

"No, it is not that," my friend replied. "If you look more carefully, you will see that it comes from a window, from the window of a round tower which looks as if it might rise from the water below."

"So it does," said I. "I can see the walls now, with darker patches upon them, looking like other windows, or like clumps of ivy. It is impossible to tell which in the darkness. There I can see the pointed cone of the tower and a corner of the roof."

The Comte drew nearer to me. He seemed almost to whisper in my ear as he said: "You are looking at the end of our walk, at the end of all our walks. The light and the gentilhommière, with its tower and the ivy, is my little place. It is 'le Pléssis.' I feel sadder than ever as I think of the days which we have spent so happily in Touraine and which have joined the past, never to come back again. Perhaps in after years we shall visit Chambord and Chenonceau and Blois once more. But they will never be the same as in this first visit which we have made to them together. Will they?"

"No," I answered, sadly; "the charm of rustic simplicity, the peaceful country life, half buried in history and in antiquity, the atmosphere of old Touraine could never produce the same influences upon us another time. The poetry would be lacking. The imagination and the idealism would be replaced by the practical and the commonplace. I seem to shrink, almost, from going on; each step now cuts us further from the past. I feel as if we had been living in a long dream for the past weeks, and that the moment we arrive at le Pléssis we must wake up once more to work and to reality." But we were obliged to push forward, for it was already late.

We hastened down the hill, feeling our way at every step, and at last the sandy avenue appeared before us, and before we knew it we were standing in a square courtyard that reached to the very edge of the lake. We

could just distinguish a garden to the right, while the pointed roofs and tower rose before us. What tranquillity there was in the sheltering wall, in the soft ripple of the water against the terrace! What a feeling of rest and home in the harmonious and gentle surroundings!

The light which we had seen was still shining from the upper window, which we now discovered to be made of stained glass. The design, the fantastic figure of a knight in full armor, showed clearly from without. Beneath the window was a door—a narrow doorway, surmounted by a carving of the family arms. A faint light was reflected upon it by the moon; but the rest of the building was lost in shade. I had little time to look about me or to take in the whole scene, for immediately my companion touched the great bell hanging from above, the light from the window disappeared, and steps were heard approaching. A key turned and the door opened. An old woman's form appeared in the flood of light which nearly blinded us, and a kindly voice broke through the silence.

"Ah, Monsieur le Comte!" exclaimed the old servant. "It was so late, Joseph and I thought something must have happened. We were getting very anxious about you and monsieur, your friend. Dear me! What would Madame la Comtesse say if she knew you were out without coats this damp September evening?"

"We are very well, Marie. Do not worry," replied the Comte, showing me the way through the vestibule. An old man came hastening down the corridor to meet us, and my friend added: "This is Joseph, an old servant who has been in our family for over fifty years."

"Oui, monsieur," said Joseph. "I can remember well when Monsieur le Comte was born, and what rejoicing there was at the chateau in Sologne over the arrival of a son and heir. And I can remember, too, Monsieur le Comte who is dead now, and what a good master he

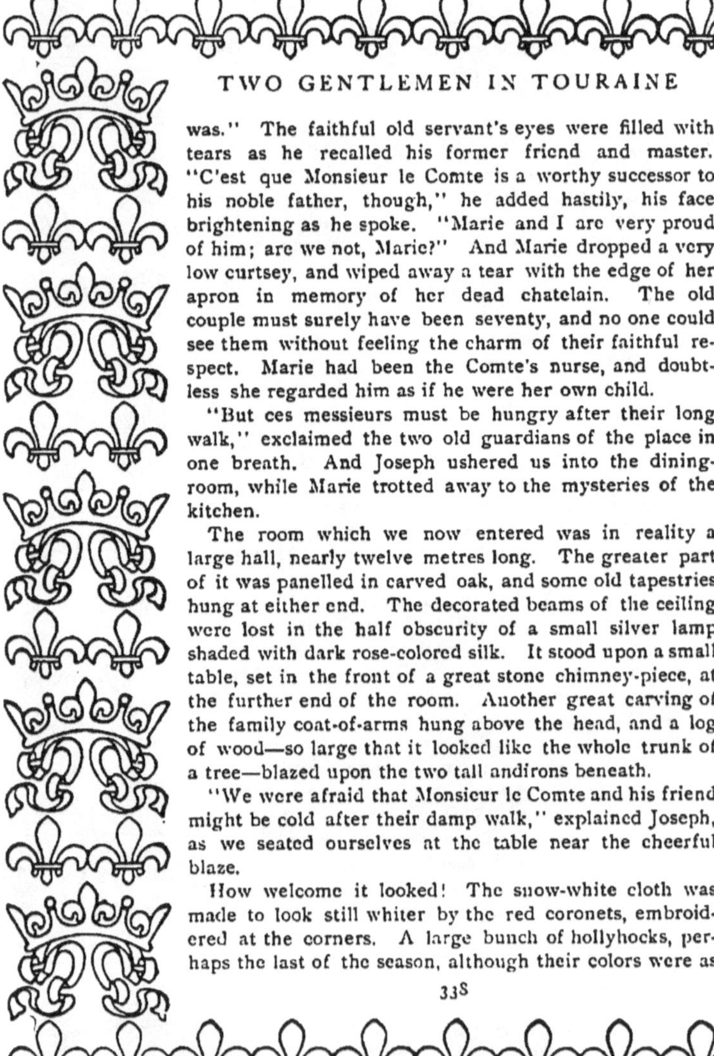

was." The faithful old servant's eyes were filled with tears as he recalled his former friend and master. "C'est que Monsieur le Comte is a worthy successor to his noble father, though," he added hastily, his face brightening as he spoke. "Marie and I are very proud of him; are we not, Marie?" And Marie dropped a very low curtsey, and wiped away a tear with the edge of her apron in memory of her dead chatelain. The old couple must surely have been seventy, and no one could see them without feeling the charm of their faithful respect. Marie had been the Comte's nurse, and doubtless she regarded him as if he were her own child.

"But ces messieurs must be hungry after their long walk," exclaimed the two old guardians of the place in one breath. And Joseph ushered us into the diningroom, while Marie trotted away to the mysteries of the kitchen.

The room which we now entered was in reality a large hall, nearly twelve metres long. The greater part of it was panelled in carved oak, and some old tapestries hung at either end. The decorated beams of the ceiling were lost in the half obscurity of a small silver lamp shaded with dark rose-colored silk. It stood upon a small table, set in the front of a great stone chimney-piece, at the further end of the room. Another great carving of the family coat-of-arms hung above the head, and a log of wood—so large that it looked like the whole trunk of a tree—blazed upon the two tall andirons beneath.

"We were afraid that Monsieur le Comte and his friend might be cold after their damp walk," explained Joseph, as we seated ourselves at the table near the cheerful blaze.

How welcome it looked! The snow-white cloth was made to look still whiter by the red coronets, embroidered at the corners. A large bunch of hollyhocks, perhaps the last of the season, although their colors were as pink as if it had been July, graced the silver bowl in the centre of the table. Four cut-glass decanters, whose quaint patterns belonged to the last century, stood at the corners also. And the vin rouge seemed to be challenging the vin blanc for the best position upon the hospitable board. I was amusing myself in playing with one of the Louis XVI salt cellars, when Joseph brought in the soup in a silver tureen which looked as if it might have been an elder brother to them.

"This is made from the vegetables of the garden," said he, as he served it. "Monsieur must surely take some."

"And monsieur votre ami too," cried Marie from the kitchen. "Oh! Madame la Comtesse would be very angry if she thought that visitors to le Pléssis did not taste everything good here."

"And how is every one since I have been away?" inquired the Comte.

"Oh, every one is very well, thank you, Monsieur le Comte," answered Joseph, delighted to tell the gossip of the village before any one else should have the chance. "Eulalie, the wife of père le Roux, has just lost her last child. That makes four of them that have gone in two years, Monsieur le Comte. Perhaps it's just as well, though, just as well," he added, philosophically. "For, you know, there wasn't much to live upon, and they were never very thrifty. Poor Maitre Briand is to be buried to-morrow. They waited a day for the funeral, so that Monsieur le Comte should be there. Maupetit is almost ill because his pigs do not sell well this year. Two of them were stolen the other night, and the whole village has been upset in consequence. . . . Monsieur le Comte would do well, before leaving, to speak to Jules. He has been tipsy twice of late, in spite of all his promises. And the nose of Eugene, the butcher, is redder than ever. Ah, Monsieur le Comte, there is no curing *him*, I

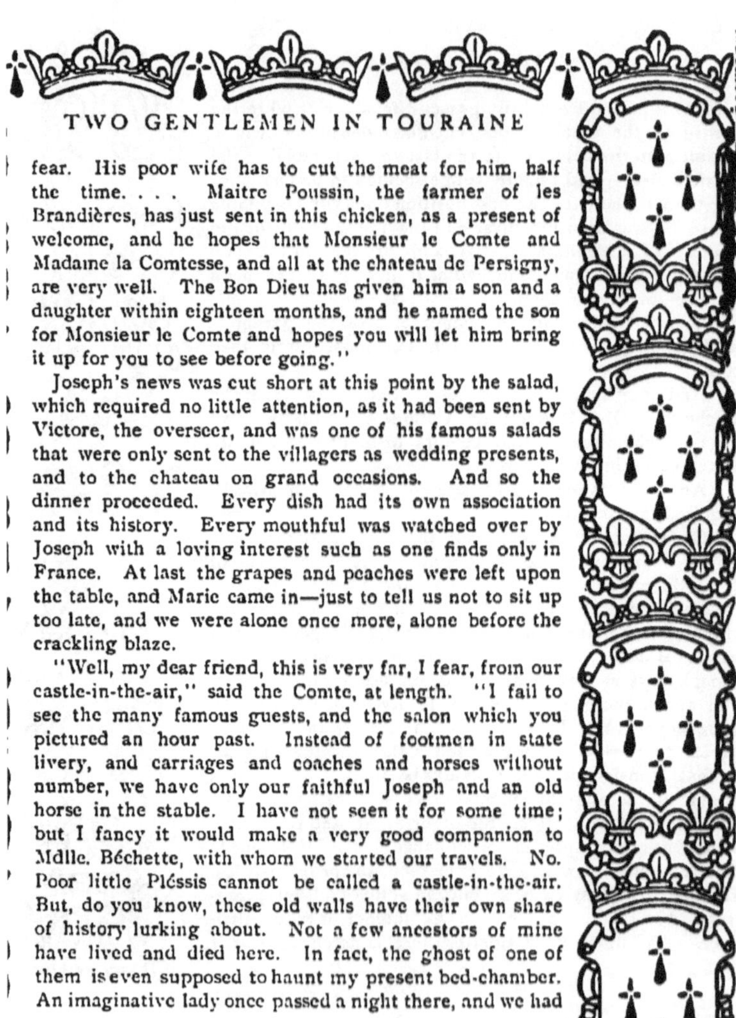

fear. His poor wife has to cut the meat for him, half the time. . . . Maitre Poussin, the farmer of les Brandières, has just sent in this chicken, as a present of welcome, and he hopes that Monsieur le Comte and Madame la Comtesse, and all at the chateau de Persigny, are very well. The Bon Dieu has given him a son and a daughter within eighteen months, and he named the son for Monsieur le Comte and hopes you will let him bring it up for you to see before going."

Joseph's news was cut short at this point by the salad, which required no little attention, as it had been sent by Victore, the overseer, and was one of his famous salads that were only sent to the villagers as wedding presents, and to the chateau on grand occasions. And so the dinner proceeded. Every dish had its own association and its history. Every mouthful was watched over by Joseph with a loving interest such as one finds only in France. At last the grapes and peaches were left upon the table, and Marie came in—just to tell us not to sit up too late, and we were alone once more, alone before the crackling blaze.

"Well, my dear friend, this is very far, I fear, from our castle-in-the-air," said the Comte, at length. "I fail to see the many famous guests, and the salon which you pictured an hour past. Instead of footmen in state livery, and carriages and coaches and horses without number, we have only our faithful Joseph and an old horse in the stable. I have not seen it for some time; but I fancy it would make a very good companion to Mdlle. Béchette, with whom we started our travels. No. Poor little Plessis cannot be called a castle-in-the-air. But, do you know, these old walls have their own share of history lurking about. Not a few ancestors of mine have lived and died here. In fact, the ghost of one of them is even supposed to haunt my present bed-chamber. An imaginative lady once passed a night there, and we had a lively time of it, I can assure you. For about two or three o'clock in the morning the ghost took it into his head—or at least she took it into her own head to think he did—to pay her a visit. We have tried in vain to induce the dear old lady to come within ten leagues of le Pléssis ever since. I fear, though, it is more because she unwarily ran out into the upper hall and showed herself without her wig than because of my great-grandfather's ghost.

"One of my ancestors was taken from this very room to be shot, during the First Revolution. My mother has spent the happiest days of her life here, and all our tenants have been with us for generations and are devoted to the family. Castles-in-the air are very well to build in the air; but if some day they happen to become realities upon this earth they do not always bring with them happiness or joy."

The Comte looked so wise in his own belief that I could not help tempting him with a question.

"Are you very sure that you would change le Pléssis for any castle-in-the-air, even if it were your ideal, your longed-for ideal?" I asked.

But my old friend was not to be caught in any such trap.

"No," he answered, promptly. "I am a Conservative, you see, and the crumbling towers of an old gentilhommière are more in keeping with me than the gilded spires and the white stones of these great chateaux, where the blue-blood of France has had to mix with the new to gild the spires and to whiten the stones."

"Come, my children, it is time to go to bed," broke in Marie, as she appeared in the doorway with two silver candlesticks. "It is very late, and you, Monsieur le Comte, do not forget to say your prayers, just as you used to do to me, I don't know how many years ago. Madame la Comtesse would be very sorry if you forgot them, after all our pains."

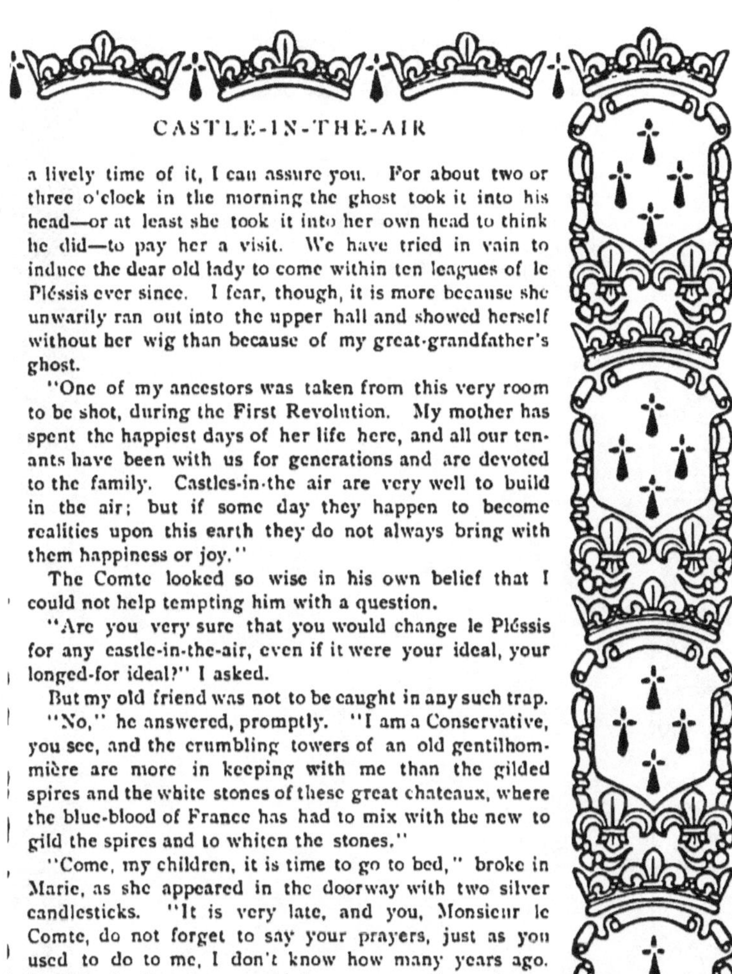

Come, Marie, put out the lamp, and show us up the winding stair, for the day is done, and we have walked already too long among these castles that have been, perhaps, too often in the air.

"Come, Monsieur le Comte, we are all waiting!"

"Good night, my friend."

"Bon soir!"   "Bon soir!"

THE END

PRINTED BY R. R. DONNELLEY
AND SONS COMPANY AT THE
LAKESIDE PRESS, CHICAGO, ILL.